MY CHINA DREAM

by

Douglas W. Bowers

Charlie's Dream Trilogy

My China Dream
My Germany Nightmare
My America Hope

This is a work of fiction. Names, characters, places and incidents are either the product of the author's imagination or are used factiously. Any resemblance to actual persons, living or dead, events, or locales is entirely coincidental.

ISBN 979-8-9857910-0-6 eBook
ISBN 979-8-9857910-1-3 paperback
Library of Congress Control Number: 2022905658

Published by Ink and Paper Press through Kindle Direct Publishing

First United States Paperback Edition

This book is dedicated to my wife and son,
Stephanie and Matthew

Disclaimer

Dear Reader,

While I enjoyed learning about the Chinese military of the Ming Dynasty, life in the Gobi Desert, and NYPD processes during the writing of this book, I've had to bend a couple of rules to tell this story without creating additional arcs and characters that would distract from the plot. For example, a patrol officer would not be given permission to perform any duties outside his or her precinct. Yet I have two characters doing just that to avoid the complexity of having someone follow a lead for them. But for the most part, I try to stick to what I have learned as best as possible.

Thank you,

Doug

Prologue

(Monday, August 6, 2012)

A blue and white cruiser patrolled an industrial grid of streets in east Brooklyn at night, cutting through the steam that rose from grates and sewar lid holes. Officers Charlie Peltman and Mark Robinson were coming to the end of an uneventful shift. The two had become good friends, but Mark always liked to get under Charlie's skin around the end of their watch.

"I hear Lacey's coming back from leave next week," said Mark with a grin.

"I don't care," replied Charlie.

"Yes, you do."

"Okay, sure. She's a good cop and we're lucky to have her."

Robinson smiled and shook his head. "Fine, play coy. But we both know you've been after her since she showed up at the picnic wearing those short-shorts. Why don't you just man up and ask her out?"

"What makes you think I didn't?"

Robinson turned in the passenger seat of the patrol car to give his partner a careful look. Charlie glanced back at him with a smirk before returning his eyes to the road. "No, Peltman. Not buying it. If you asked her...."

"I got a date. Friday. Just a lunch thing, but it's a date."

"You did ask her!"

"No, not Lacey. Samantha Lee from my apartment building."

"Chinese girl on the first floor?"

"That's the one."

"A little young for you, ain't she?"

"No…I mean I hope not. I don't know how old she is, but I'm thinking late 20's."

Robinson chuckled. "Yeah, you can hope!" When Charlie didn't laugh along, he tempered himself. "Seriously, Peltman, it's hard to say how old she is. I mean, if she said yes...she must not think you're too old."

"Thanks."

"That reminds me, you still constipated?"

Charlie grimaced. "Why does my date with Samantha remind you of my constipation?"

"The China connection."

"You're unbelievable, Robinson, you know that?"

"Just bear with me on this. When I was in Beijing a few years back, I noticed some of the toilets there were nothing more than holes in the ground. I mean no seat, no handle bars, not even a wall to lean your back against. Put me off at first. But this one time, I must have eaten a bad mussel or something, 'cause holding it for a better toilet was not an option."

"Is it me, or are our conversations sinking lower and lower…"

"Knock it off, Peltman, I'm trying to help you. So, all I could find was one of them holes. I had no choice. Peltman, let me just say it was one of the best BMs I ever had in my life. Something about the angle..."

"So, what…I should dig a hole somewhere?"

"No, Peltman. Just get a stool or something to raise your feet while you're sittin' down. Hell, jump up on the toilet seat. You ain't dumb; figure it out."

"Well, as it so happens, I had a good crap just yesterday," he lied. "Every three days is..."

The police radio interrupted their banter. "Attention all units in the vicinity of Pitkin and Georgia. Ten-Thirty-One at the Take and Save." Burglary. "Officers Baxter and McAllister are on the scene requesting backup. Suspect fled on foot wearing jeans and a red sweatshirt. Armed."

Robinson picked up the mic. "Bravo-247 responding. Out." He turned back to Charlie. "That's Gina and Fred. Say, you and Gina ever…"

"Shut up, Mark."

Robinson chuckled. "Let's pull around back. Drop me off and drive around Belmont and up Alabama."

"Ten-four."

"Ten-four? You a trucker now, Peltman?"

"Didn't I tell you to shut up?" Charlie dropped off his partner and headed along the route Robinson described. After turning onto Alabama, he saw a man in blue jeans and a red sweatshirt sprinting between two buildings. Charlie radioed to Mark that he was pursuing on foot and parked the car. No light penetrated the alleyway. Charlie pursued quickly but cautiously, mentally persuading his eyes to adjust to the dark. When he arrived at Williams Avenue on the other side, the streetlights struck his pupils, and a brick struck his temple. He immediately lost his balance and fell to the pavement, watching the suspect run through the next set of buildings on the other side of Williams. He could see the brick that hit him resting in the middle of the street. Then he saw a pair of legs in black trousers come into view. Whoever owned those legs bent down to pick up the brick before walking towards Charlie. Charlie heard the man chuckle and say, "So, this is why you asked me if I was hit on the head." Charlie saw the legs walk away before fading into unconsciousness.

Charlie would only remember the rest of the night in flashes. He remembered Mark's voice asking if he was all right. An EMT asked him his name and to say his social security number backwards. He heard Gina Baxter say, "I live near Charlie's building. I'll follow the ambulance to the ER and take him back home." He had a fuzzy memory of Gina holding up a bottle of aspirin and showing it to him at one point. His last thought was of his upcoming date with Samantha. He smiled and remembered nothing else.

Chapter 1

A soft thunder of hooves from behind General Chang Huang told him he had better do something. Though he had no memory of the seconds and minutes before this point in time, he felt as if he had some understanding of where he was and why he was there. He half turned and saw a cloud of dirt rising, though still very far off. In front of him, a two-story structure offered the only protection for miles in any direction. Chang Huang glanced around and squinted at the reflected sunlight. Waves of sand were all he saw. No cacti or rocks broke the plain. The horizon was blurred by haze, or dust, or his own tired eyes. The rumbling grew slightly louder.

Chang Huang did not have to observe Horse's heavy breathing and steaming flanks to understand they had been riding for a long while. He just knew. It was not until he dismounted that he felt the soreness in his own muscles. Though the keratin scales of his armor were baking him, he was grateful for the recent lightening of the military uniform. He hoped that this lightening would continue to include his helmet and the decorations affixed to it.

Nevertheless, it would be unbecoming to show any weariness, even if no one was around to see him. He had learned this from his training. Training of which he had no real memory.

The building in front of him was of some importance. Feelings of anger and a slight sense of caution blended within him when he looked upon it. The frontside was plain with a door, windows, and a roof all painted green with animal characters sculpted onto the frames. He also seemed to know it was recently abandoned. Just as he knew he was in China, just outside a town called Xin in the Gobi Desert, and that he was Chinese without seeing his reflection. "Come on, Horse," he said as he grabbed the reigns and walked to the other side of the—the inn. Yes, he knew it was an inn, somehow. Horse's hooves made a crunching sound in the hardening sand as the general steered him around to the back. "Stop," he said. "Rest here."

The back wall of the inn was plain wood with no paint or carvings typical of the area. Six windows, all on the second floor, peered out from sand-smoothed Chinese red pine. One door in the center allowed access for staff. Chang Huang touched his forehead and felt the salt left behind from his evaporated sweat. The sound of the other horses (pursuers?) was closer. Looking Horse in the eye, he said, "I hope they do not harm you."

(Tuesday – August 7, 2012)

"…and the man didn't stop until the construction workers tackled him!"

"Takes morons of all kinds, Tony. Did he say…" Charlie's big hand slapped down hard on the snooze bar, cutting off The Tony and Bob Show. He squinted to see "6:45" spelled out in red dashes. *Was I just dreaming I was a Chinese general?* His skull felt like it was two sizes too small for his brain. He couldn't resist touching the bruise on his forehead and instantly regretted it. He looked at the clock again. "6:46." Eight more minutes until Tony and Bob or some 70's rock band muscled their way back into Charlie's bedroom and head. After a brief struggle, Charlie's index finger and thumb managed to flip the hard switch, shutting off the alarm altogether. But in doing this, he knew he could not allow himself to fall back to sleep. Forcing his head from the pillow and rotating his legs to the side, he rocked himself into a sitting position and let out a nearly voiceless scream. *Coffee...I hope to God Gina set up the coffee maker last night.* Charlie used the wall for support and caressed the side of his head as he swaggered to the kitchen. The preset timer on his coffee maker had started brewing java the same instant Charlie's clock radio had summoned Tony and Bob. The flow of brown liquid slowed from a stream to a series of fast drips in front of his eyes. *Thanks, G. I owe you two, now.*

He picked up the phone to arrange a cab, then replaced the receiver without dialing. Gina had been a huge help to him, and he had no business calling anyone before her. He brought his nose down to his armpits and took a deep sniff. *I can get by without a shower today. Must have taken one last night.* He hesitated briefly to consider how early it would be for her but figured she would've turned off the phone if she didn't want to be disturbed. She answered on the first ring.

"Hi, Hon. How's the head?"

"Could be worse but could be a hell of a lot better."

"Well lay off the Guns 'n Roses for a while. You'll be back at the pistol range in no time."

"Great, what should I listen to? Manilow?"

"God forbid! Try a little Jimmy Buffet to get you through the next day or so." He ignored this.

"Well, you know, I just wanted to call and say thanks for getting me home...and for setting the coffee maker."

"Didn't do it for you, Charlie," she teased. "My reputation's on the line. I recommend you for this gig and you don't show up, they'll never work with me again."

"Thank you, anyway."

"Need a ride in?"

"Naw, got that covered." It was a small lie. Part of him wanted the company but most of him needed to be alone.

"Okay, then. Break an elbow."

"I'll call you later." Immediately after he disconnected, he started sniffing his shirts until he found one that didn't smell too bad and pulled his only civilian suit out of his closet. Then he dialed Yellow Cab and arranged a pickup in 30 minutes.

His stalky frame gave the appearance of being overweight, though he was stronger and more flexible than most of his peers. He topped off just under six feet and nearly filled the width of a doorway. His forty-year-old hair was raven black and looked good even when it was messy, so he rarely touched a comb. A gut bulged but didn't hang over the band of his black boxers. *Surely Gina didn't undress me.* Charlie's mind didn't dwell on it long enough to remember one way or the other.

As he stepped in front of the mirror for a quick shave, he examined the bump from last night. His head was not bleeding, and he had not been hit hard enough to get a concussion according to the EMT—just enough to give him a headache. Coffee wouldn't really help with the pain, but the flavor would comfort him. He had the day off from the force today but was expected at an appointment in Manhattan by ten o'clock. Companies would often hire off-duty police for security jobs. Gina had recommended Charlie for one such gig. Lextalt, Inc., an importer of Chinese products, was looking for someone to lead a team to protect an expensive delivery in a few weeks. *Chinese importer...between that and my date with Samantha, no wonder I dreamed about China last night.*

Manhattan felt more like home to Charlie than anyplace he'd actually lived. He knew he would never afford to live there, and his beat would always be the outer boroughs. But the pace and attitude of downtown was where he felt the most like himself. He arrived early enough to walk about before the interview. He popped into a convenient store to pick up a bottle of laxatives. The hot dog vendor at the corner near Lextalt was tempting, but it would not be the same without the onions, which are not a good idea before a face-to-face. Across the street was an army surplus store where he could always kill time. But before he started in that direction, movement to his right caught his attention. He turned his head immediately but could see nothing out of the ordinary. Something was wrong. He saw something—something he was presumably not supposed to see. A person. Still in the area—watching him. *Black. Whoever I saw was wearing black. That was a mistake.* Diagonally across the intersection from where he stood was a small park with trees by the sidewalk. *He's behind one of those trees.* Charlie looked at his watch. There was time enough before his appointment to walk to the park, but if he found something worth investigating it would consume all of that time and then some. He looked hard at the trees for another moment, then decided he would have another chance if this wasn't just his imagination.

The interview was conducted on the 44th floor of the Lextalt building just off Park Avenue on 57th St. next to the Four Seasons. Charlie told the receptionist he was here to see Harold but did not know Harold's last name. She brought him back to a large but mostly empty conference room. The north corner was all window, providing a stunning view where Central Park could be seen over the top of a couple of smaller buildings. A red-stained, oaken conference table with ergonomic, black mesh office chairs occupied a small portion of the room. Two men were waiting for him: one in his mid-forties with curly, red-brown hair and a build like a Hercules actor from a 1950's serial. The other man was much older, possibly close to 70 with thick, white hair and a clean-shaven face. Wire-framed bifocals looked natural on his slightly large nose. It was not obvious to Charlie which one was Harold. "Charlie Peltman?" Hercules asked in an Irish accent.

"That's me." He did not feel comfortable in his suit but pushed his discomfort out of his mind as much as possible and smiled, extending his right hand. "One of you Harold?"

"I'm Harold," Hercules said as he took Charlie's hand. "This here's me da, Francis." Charlie offered his hand and said hello. Francis took his hand and nodded but did not say a word. "Gina says you're quite fit. Forgive me if I say you don't look it."

"I have an unusual frame. Gave me trouble in school. I could take your father, here; I'm sure of it." He raised up his fists in a mock fighting stance.

Harold laughed. "Don't count on it. I've seen him handle more than you can imagine. Tell me about yourself."

"Sure thing. But first, did you set up a test for me downstairs?"

"A test?" Harold's confusion seemed genuine. "What do you mean?"

Charlie looked from son to father and back. "Probably nothing. I'm a bit paranoid."

"Paranoia is good. We prefer a little of that in our security captains. How long have you been a policeman?" This sounded more like *How long've ya been a policemun?*

"Nineteen years. Most of it in Brooklyn, but I spent a little time in Seattle and L.A."

"What brought you to the Big Apple?"

"Are you kidding? It's the greatest city in the world."

Harold and Francis exchanged a look which was lost on Charlie. "We're looking for someone to organize and coordinate a detail to protect our investment. It's coming in on ship and will be secured in a container by customs for about four to six days at a nearby warehouse. That's where it will be the most vulnerable. I need to make sure it gets to the warehouse and that nothing happens to it once it's there. Once it is released from customs, I will consider your job complete. Now, what are your thoughts?"

"Honestly? Security for customs is pretty tight. I'm not sure what you need me for. But assuming you really do need me, there's a lot of variables I need to know more about, like the layout of the shipyard, the port docking schedule, and the value of the cargo."

"Why is the value important?"

"I gotta know how much to spend. If I'm guarding a million-dollar diamond, I don't want to spend a million to protect it."

"Suppose I tell you I'd be willing to spend twenty million to protect this item?"

Charlie's mouth froze in the open position. "Twenty?"

"Yes."

His open mouth morphed into an open smile and he glanced back to Francis. *Poker faces. What are these guys up to?* "All right; I'm game. If you're spending that much, you'd arrange a time where the fewest ships are expected, and then pay to push as many ships due in or out that day to another. Maybe you've already arranged that. Then you'd want to keep security beefed up as if it were a busy dock day. We'll want the ship coming in during the day, and a decoy ship as well. Hell, for twenty million, you could have about five ships coming in that day with equal security on each. And each container going to a different, equally guarded warehouse. I'd hire really good lieutenants and the best laser alarm system I could find for the warehouse. We couldn't trust any of the men…not even me. That'd mean redundant coverage and monitors for you and your dad. If I were unethical, I'd want booby traps and the such, but don't expect that from me. Basically, I would treat this cargo as I would a human being." Something stuttered in Harold's eyes at Charlie's last comment. Francis remained unreadable. "Human? The job is protecting a person?"

"Not exactly...no. Let's stop there. I think now we either have to hire you or kill you. Da?" Both Charlie and Harold looked to Francis. He simply nodded at his son and returned his eyes to Charlie. "I will give you a tour of the shipyard next Tuesday. I'll also explain then why I need additional security, beyond what the United States Government has to offer us. I believe you are off duty next Tuesday, just like today?"

I never said I'd take the job. "Where do I meet you?"

"We'll send a car. It will pick you up at nine a.m." *I never gave them my address. Do they know where I live? I'm not sure I like this, but I'm curious.* Charlie thanked them and took his leave. As the elevator brought him back to ground level, he considered the man in black clothes he had seen before his interview. Once outside, he looked around for anyone who might be following him. After ensuring the scene was clear, a thought occurred to him: *Wearing all black wasn't a mistake. He wanted me to see him.*

Martin Killjoy, a forty-year-old transplant from Kentucky, shorter than average and growing soft in the middle, owned and operated Private Storage franchise 32405 in Queens. When he purchased it from the previous owner, he didn't think about what might be kept in those thousands of storage units. At the time, he had been a hard-working, blue collar man bending wrenches in an auto repair shop up in Albany. Frugal was how he described himself, though his ex-wife preferred the word "cheap." Even his son, now fully grown and having little to do with his old man, thought his spending habits, or lack thereof, made him more of a Scrooge than a loving father who provided the essentials. Never mind that Martin paid for his college career, including books, room, food, and spending money.

None of this made him bitter, however. He did love his wife and son and was happy that they had both gone on to better lives than he ever had a chance to live. He also found that he enjoyed the freedom of living alone with little attachments beyond his front door. And his little gamble with Private Storage franchise 32405 certainly paid off. He had bought it at a steal from a man who had lost too much to keep it during the 2008 recession. Martin acquired the man's entire business, fully staffed and adequately managed. His accountant showed that the value of his business in 2012 had tripled in the last three years. *In retrospect, it was worth the divorce*, Martin thought.

Until last year, Martin cared little what people stored in their individual units. He rarely even glanced up from his paperwork to see what trinkets, souvenirs, or objects of obsession people brought into these alcoves. What happened last year to pique his interest in unit 4358 was nothing more than a truck backfiring, causing him to spill his coffee and duck behind the counter (grabbing for the sawed-off shotgun he kept there for protection). After a moment or two, Martin gathered his courage and peeked over the countertop, looking through the glass door of the office. People were milling about as if nothing at all happened. He put his shotgun back in its brackets and stepped outside. It was immediately clear what had happened, as the truck which had backfired was a 50's model Chevy pickup with nearly as much rust on its body as paint. What wasn't rusty was dark green with many scratches. It was backing its load up to one of the larger units with an external, vertical lift door; one item in the pickup's bed was hidden by a sheet of canvas. Martin almost turned to go back inside when an out-of-place gust of wind lifted a corner of the canvas. A wayward sunbeam reflected off the bronze from underneath this flap and caught Martin's eye. He could only see a scaled leg with talons clutching a green gem, and that only for a brief second. It could have been junk antique, or some gaudy decoration from the 70's. But something about that bronze talon touched his heart in a way no other object had before. Some things had to be appraised before you could realize their value. Other things just screamed out that they were special. Martin knew that whatever was under that canvas was something worth more than any single object he had ever seen in his life. He knew he had just seen something that was priceless.

What else has 4358 been hording in there? This question had been haunting Martin for the past year. The lessee of the unit was listed as "The Trustee of Chan Xiang Xiansheng." Martin could not pronounce it, let alone understand what this meant. All signatures on the lease paperwork were made by an attorney: Bob Cain. Since that day of the truck backfire, Martin had tried to pay closer attention to see if any more "treasures" were brought into 4358. None had until this morning, when a tall, Chinese man drove up to the unit in a black Lincoln. The Chinese man exited the vehicle without waiting for the chauffer. A black briefcase was handcuffed to his wrist. He opened the vertical lift door and deposited the briefcase after unfastening it from the handcuffs. It looked to Martin as if the tall man opened the briefcase before closing the door to the storage unit.

Charlie spent the day in Manhattan before coming back to his apartment. As he keyed his lock, the man who lived across the hall came out and started to lock his own door. He was an older man who had the good fortune of signing a rent-controlled lease in 1973. Though in his 80's, he was surprisingly spry. His apartment number was 888, even though he lived on the second floor. Charlie always thought the numbering was a bit strange. Everyone else on his floor was numbered anywhere from 201 through 217. This neighbor was a white American, as far as Charlie could tell, but he often dressed in older Asian garb and wore a white goatee that hung down to his chest. He also celebrated Chinese New Year rather loudly, which didn't bother Charlie. His name was Steve, but most people called him The Egg for reasons Charlie did not understand. Charlie waited before opening his door as if he meant to say something to The Egg, and The Egg held fast before continuing to the stairs. "Yes?" he asked Charlie.

"Um…I'm sorry. I forget what I was going to ask you."

"Quite all right, my boy. Quite all right." The Egg smiled and continued on his way.

Charlie called Gina as promised but kept it short. He told her he was given a chance to tour the site next week. She congratulated him, and they chatted about where he might take Samantha. The next day was Gina's day off, and she mentioned she'd stop by. His head felt better but was glad he had one more day off before returning to duty. Patrol officers work five on, two off, five on, three off. Today and tomorrow were his two off. After hanging up the phone, he grabbed his last cold beer, a portable radio, a bag of Washington cherries and headed for the roof of his apartment building. Night had already fallen. Not much of a view; light pollution outshined the stars if the clouds were not in the way. But the August air felt good six stories off the ground. The webbed lawn chair he set up there was still around and currently unoccupied. Sipping his beer while the Yankees battled the Tigers, he thought about the prospect of providing security for something in a shipping container from China. This something must be precious. Something almost as precious as a person, by the way they looked at him after he compared the cargo to a human.

His thoughts turned to the man in black clothes. Though he could not eliminate it completely, he didn't believe Harold and Francis were behind this. None of his past cases came to mind that would explain the appearance of this man, either. For the most part, his job as a cop was relatively boring. No vendettas had been declared. Somehow, he believed he would see this man again. Until then, he would be careful.

Somewhere during the evening, he placed his empty Coors Light bottle on the rooftop next to him. After the game, he collected his bag of cherries, now a quarter eaten, and the empty Coors Light bottle. A rolled-up piece of paper jutted from the bottle's neck. Charlie dropped to one knee and looked around, realizing as he did so that any defensive action at this point would be much too late. He unrolled the paper, upon which was written:

It begins.

Chapter 2

General Chang's boots clunked on the wooden floor as he entered a kitchen from the back of the abandoned inn. The walls and floors were as plain as its exterior. The exposed wood offered no color or artwork. Support beams disrupted the flow for pedestrian traffic. Exiting the kitchen, Chang Huang saw a wagon wheel of a chandelier with candles in various stages of melt over a large dining area. But the furnishings looked fairly new. Several tables stood sentry. The lack of dust on the tables suggested they had been in service not too long ago. A stairway ascended the wall to Chang Huang's left.

The other horsemen would be at the front of the inn shortly; there was no time to take in the surroundings. He walked around the edge of the bar surrounding the kitchen's entrance, made his way to the front, and opened the shutters of one of the windows just wide enough to see through. The cloud of dust was closer, and he could make out the shapes of riders as well as the horses. He did not have a bow, and his sword would not help him if this small army was set on taking him. He wished he knew something—anything—about who they were and what he meant to them. Something fell past his field of vision between him and the window. He looked up and saw a dark, red stain on the ceiling, flush against the wall. On the floorboards, brown and red splash marks framed his foot. He took a step back but continued to look out the window. The horsemen were close enough to make out some detail. They carried bows and quivers and wore uniform armor. *They are organized...with a leader. These are men on duty. They are*...he glanced down at his own, leather armor and back at the horsemen...*my men.* Chang Huang took a breath and moved to the front door and opened it just as the cavalry came to a halt. The leader looked surprised and alert upon seeing the general come through. Then recognition replaced the alertness, though the surprise remained.

"General Chang. My men are at your service," spoke a rider in the middle of the first row, wearing additional decorations on his leather. *Apparently, I'm in some version of old China where everyone speaks English.*

"Have them create a perimeter around this Inn. My horse is in back. See that no one disturbs her. Wait here. I must check something."

The captain shouted some orders and the men began to circle the building. The general disappeared up the stairs. He paused when he reached the second floor. A corridor divided a dozen rooms, six on the front side of the building, six along the back above the kitchen. He moved to the fourth door on his left—the room directly above the blood stain—and listened to the door. Nothing. He drew his sword and moved the door handle as slow as possible. A small squeak stole his element of surprise, so Chang Huang threw open the door all the way, raising his sword into a fighting position. Four bodies sliced into individual body parts were scattered around the room. Torsos, heads, and limbs were all separated and repositioned so that the head of one person was paired with the torso of another, arms of a second person, and legs of a third. Chang Huang could see that this was likely a family: adult man and woman, child boy and girl. He wanted to vomit but held it back. The smell drove him back out to the hallway. He could not be seen backing away from this horror. Holding his hand over his nose and mouth, he reentered the room just long enough to notice some writing displayed on the side wall, though he could not understand the lines that intersected in seemingly random order. *Chinese. I need to remember what these shapes look like.* The message was written in wide, bloody strokes, as if someone smeared a hand in the blood and wrote with his palm. On the ends of the lines of each character, he could make out finger shapes. He stared at them as long as he could bear the smell.

The stairs were more difficult to negotiate going down, but the general managed to compose himself before emerging from the inn. The cavalry captain was sitting on his horse where Chang Huang last saw him. Sweat dripped into his eyes, but he blinked no more than he would any other time. "Captain, dismount and follow me." The captain obeyed. Back inside, Chang Huang pointed to the ceiling where he had first seen the blood stain. "The room above that spot. I need you to map the room and the bodies, noting which body parts belonged to the man, woman, boy, and girl." He searched the captain's eyes for any fear and found none. "Are you literate?"

"Yes, sir."

"You have paper and ink?"

"Yes, sir."

"There is writing on the wall. Record it as well."

"Yes, sir. Do you know who is responsible?" the captain added. *Careful…I can't reveal that I cannot read the script on the wall.*

"I am holding my own counsel for now. I recommend you do the same until we investigate this a little more thoroughly. Do not trust what you read on the wall. Keep an open mind. What is your name, Captain?"

"Yuan Lin."

"What is your mission in this area?"

"Chasing rumors. The Hei Shui gang is said to be scouting this area. Lots of caravans come through here. Seems like a good opportunity."

"Any sign of them?"

"Not so far. We did not really expect to just yet. From the rumors, there may be a scout in the town nearby, Xin, but he would be hard to identify."

"I will keep that in mind. You knew my name, earlier."

"Everyone knows your name. Your likeness is engraved in our fortress wall."

"I am given too much credit. It should be my captains and lieutenants pictured on your wall." *How do I know that?* "See to the mapping; then have your men wrap the bodies and take them to Xin. Ask to see the mayor and see if you can find out who these bodies belong to. I will meet you there."

"Yes, sir."

(Wednesday – August 8, 2012)

Charlie woke up without the alarm the next morning. He looked about his room trying to reorient himself. *The same dream?* An image of the message flashed into his conscious. He immediately stood up and started searching his desk for a tablet and a pen. The tablet was easy, but his pens seemed to have scampered off. He found one in the back of the bottom drawer, but it would not write. Giving up, he trotted into the kitchen. Another pen was hiding behind the toaster. With little hope, he brought it back to his desk and started making circles over and over at the top left corner of his notepad. At first, all he could get was the impression of his swirling motion. But then ink started to flow.

He tried bringing the image of the wall to his mind again. It seemed to be about half dozen groupings of characters on the first line, one grouping on the second line, then half a dozen on the third line. But he could not conjure up clearer details. He started writing anyway, using large X's for the characters:

XX XX XXX XXXXX XX XXXXX
XXXXXXX
XXXX XX XXXX XX XXXX XXXX

He wasn't exactly sure what he hoped to accomplish but felt better about putting this on paper. If Yuan Lin captures this correctly, he could try to count the characters and get a more exact pattern. *What am I doing? This is a dream, right?*

He pondered what he had just written, then made sure the pen he used was placed into the cup he had bought for the very purpose of not losing his pens. He had just placed the pen when someone knocked on his door. "One minute!" he answered. He grabbed a robe from his bedroom floor and ran his fingers over his face in some sort of imagined cleaning technique. Then he peeked through the peep hole and smiled. "G!" he said as he opened the door. Gina had a longish face and dark, wavy hair. It hung down to her shoulders when she was off duty.

"Nice threads! You planning on getting out at all today?" Only then did it occur to him that he had not looked at a clock.

"What time is it?"

"Going on eleven, sleepy head."

"I'm losing it, G. Plagued by a dream."

"A dream? Was I in it?"

"No, unless you're a 20-year-old man in a Chinese cavalry unit that speaks English."

"In a former life I think I was a man, come to think of it."

"Attractive. What's in the bag?"

"I figured you were out of beer, and today's a good roof day."

"Yeah…the roof." Charlie thought about the note in his beer bottle. "I'm gonna go up there but not to drink."

"Por qua?" Charlie told her about the man in black clothes he saw outside the Lextalt building and the note in his beer bottle. "Serious? He was up on the roof with you? Why didn't you call me?"

"He coulda killed me if he wanted, but he didn't. So, I didn't think I was in danger, and I was dead tired by the end of that game."

"Let's go up and see if he left anything else behind."

"Yep. You know, I completely forgot about the note until you mentioned the roof."

"What's wrong with you, Chuck? Maybe that brick did more to you than you know."

"Maybe."

"Okay, we'll check out the roof together, then I'm taking you to get that looked at again."

"Fine. Let's get upstairs before the wind blows anything away."

Charlie and Gina emerged from the top of the stairs through what looked like a small shack in the middle of the roof. The door made a loud screech upon opening. The temperature up here was mild for this time of year. It would have been an excellent day to beer it up. Charlie walked to his folding chair and tried to determine how his stalker may have snuck up on him. "I was facing this way," he said, pointing to the edge of the building. He sat down in the chair. "Gina, walk to my left." As soon as he could see her, he said to stop. "Mark the spot where you are standing." She did. "Now walk to my right." When he could see her again, he had her stop and mark the spot again. Then he stood up, turned around, and held out his arms in the direction of the two marked spots. "Whoever it was could walk around this area without me seeing him."

Gina walked back to the entry door to the roof and opened it, making that loud squeak. "Any chance you wouldn't have heard that?"

"Unlikely. I was listening to the game but not that loud."

"You thinking he climbed up the side of the building somehow? Maybe a grappling hook?" Although the heat had not yet picked up for the day, the humidity made some of Gina's hair stick to her cheeks, and her bangs started to droop over her eyes. It made Charlie think of the sheep dog in the old Warner Bros. cartoons.

"I don't think so. Unless he preplaced a rope. Throwing a grappling hook would have made more noise than the squeaky door. If he followed me downtown yesterday, then he's probably been surveying me for a while now. He would have known that I come up here to listen to my games on my days off. Probably came up before me. He'd have been nice and comfortable behind the roof access. Would have been in the shade yesterday evening."

Gina walked around to the other side of the roof access. "Yeah, he left you a gift." Charlie expected to see a piece of fabric or a candy bar wrapper. Instead, he saw pieces of different dolls assembled together to form a single grotesque figure, duct taped to the ground. The torso looked like it was from a Ken doll, the head from a Barbie, and the limbs were obviously from some child dolls of some sort. Charlie's head started to hurt.

"I need to talk to the sarge," he said.

"Sure." She saw him rub his head where he had been bricked. "After we get your head checked out again."

The urgent care center ran some tests, including a CT scan but could not find anything seriously wrong with Charlie's head. Charlie didn't think there was, but the doctor's confirmation eased Gina's mind.

"See, I'm as normal as I ever was."

"That supposed to make me feel better?"

"Either way, I'm going to work tomorrow."

"Looks like you're already working today."

"Technically, I'm involved in this, so I shouldn't be doing any police work on it. That's why I want to see the sarge. I want to see how to proceed. Plus, I think I saw some Chinese artwork in his office. I wanna see what he knows about China."

"Just because of your dream?"

"Dreams. The one I had last night was kind of like a continuation of one I had the night I got hit." Gina was silent. "Ever have a recurring dream?"

"Not sure. Maybe." Gina drove Charlie the short distance from the hospital to the police station. Most of the units were out on patrol when Charlie and Gina walked in. The Bullpen always seemed so cold when empty with its concrete floors, army surplus desks, and dirty, white walls. The feel was completely different when it was crowded with other cops discussing cases and making calls.

Sergeant Neo Langmann was a couple inches taller than Charlie but less bulky and more muscular with brown hair. Outside of policing, he was immensely interested in cultures from around the world. Having a diverse background himself, being the son of a German immigrant father and a mother from Kenya, he took to studying any anthropological books he could find whenever he learned of a new people. From a very young age, if he met someone from Lithuania, the next day he would be in the library learning all he could about the country. Yet, this worldly interest did not soften him when commanding his troops.

His office was walled only by glass with venetian blinds always pulled down. He would go out on patrol from time to time, but he was needed mostly at his desk. Most sergeants spent as much time outside the station as their direct reports, but Langmann seemed to get stuck with more desk duty than most. Sergeant Langmann did not look up from his paperwork when Charlie and Gina walked into his office at first. "You both are supposed to be off, so this better be good." Then he looked up at them. "You're not quitting are you?"

"No, boss," Charlie replied. He glanced around the office. There was more Chinese artwork on the walls than he had realized. A palm-sized Buddha statue reclined on Langmann's file cabinet. The smile on this Buddha seemed more like constipation to Charlie than the laughter he'd been accustomed to seeing on the jolly fat men in the Chinatown souvenir shops. A gu-zheng was propped in the corner, though it looked too old and fragile to produce any music. Several glass containers were growing lucky bamboo stalks. "Do you know any Chinese?" Charlie asked.

"Some Mandarin. No Cantonese. Why?"

"I had a dream with some Chinese characters…"

Gina broke in, "Really? You're starting with that instead of the stalker and the Barbie dolls?"

She's right, thought Charlie. *How do I start this… "The term* batshit crazy *is thrown around a lot these days… "?*

"Yeah, I'll come back to that. Boss, I think I got someone stalking me. Might be a joke, but I don't know. They left this note…," Charlie handed the note to Langmann, "…in the neck of my beer bottle when I was listening to the game on the roof of my apartment. Then, this morning, Gina and I went up to the roof to see if there was anything else he might have left behind.

Found this." Charlie held up his phone that had a picture of the piecemeal doll.

Langmann glanced at the phone. "Gruesome!" He looked back at Charlie. "You said 'he.' You don't think it's a woman?"

"Could be, but I saw someone suspicious yesterday morning. Might not be connected, but I'm thinking of them as one and the same."

"Okay. So, I take it you want to look into this yourself?"

"I do. I know that's not the best idea. I'm not a detective, and I'm too close to it."

"Yeah. Let me chew on that. Tell me about the Chinese character dream."

"Just a dream I've had over the past couple nights. I think it took place in China sometime in the past. I saw a massacre with some Chinese writing on the wall in blood."

Langmann looked interested. "Okay."

"Just thinking if I keep having it, maybe there's a way I can learn how to read the characters."

"Dreams don't really work like that, Peltman." Langmann paused, considering options. "Look, if you and Gina want to pursue this guy, I can arrange that. Just keep it informal. You two are patrol officers, not detectives. Who's your partner?" he asked Charlie. "Robinson?"

"Yes."

"He's been wanting to take some time off, so this might work out. Gina, you're with McAllister?"

"Yes, Sarge."

"Might be tricky, but I'll think of something. You two can work on this together. But just for now. Gina, you were supposed to be off today and tomorrow. I'm going to move your days off to align with Charles, here. Any issues with that?"

"None, sir. As long as you square it with Fred."

"McAllister will be all right."

"Thank you, sir."

"Peltman, this dream seems to be bugging you. Somethin' you're not telling me about. That's fine, but why don't you set up some time with Doc Thomason. He's into all this dream stuff." Charlie nodded, and Gina tossed a curious look at him as they left Langmann's office.

"What aren't you telling me, Charlie?" Gina said without removing her eyes from the road. Charlie thought about playing dumb but knew better.

"Something I wish I told you before we found that stupid doll."

"Something that happened in your dream?"

"Yeah. It's about the massacre…a whole family killed. Their body parts were all mixed up. Just like the doll." Gina was silent. The silence unnerved Charlie. "Now you either think I'm crazy or lying."

"Well, I've always known you were crazy, and you're not a liar, so nothing's really changed, right?" Charlie was relieved to see she was smiling, even a little. "I studied dreams a bit myself."

"In college?"

"No, I had rounds with some dreams of my own that I wanted to understand. You know what architypes are?"

"I've heard the term."

"Basically means there are a bunch of symbolic themes that we all share. They're built into our psyche. Might be the two of you share some history, and he either has dreamed something similar, or is trying to send you the same message your dream is sending you. Either way, I don't think you're any crazier than I did this morning."

"Good to know."

"The guy you saw yesterday morning...did you get any look at his features?"

"No. Just a glimpse out of the corner of my eye. I think he wanted me to see him but not clearly. If so, he timed his appearance really well. He either followed me to Manhattan or knew about my interview. That wasn't a secret or anything, but I don't recall telling anyone about it other than you, Robinson, and

Langmann. I might have mentioned something to Samantha." He thought for a moment. "Of course, I didn't tell anyone to keep it secret."

"I can say with ultimate certainty that I did not tell anyone about your interview."

"Most likely he just followed me…or tapped my phone." Charlie reviewed a mental list of people he talked to in the last few weeks. "I don't remember talking about my interview on the phone, but who knows. Let's go back to the apartment to see if my line is tapped. Or if there are any bugs anywhere."

"There's also the question of why."

"Yeah, who'd I piss off recently?"

"Wilkinson was a little upset over the Mets-Yankees game you bet on back in June."

"Wilkinson couldn't stalk his own shadow."

"Old score from another time?"

"Hell, Gina, you know me. I've never been involved in anything big. I'd like to think I'm basically a good guy. It's why I became a cop."

"Old girlfriend?"

Charlie shrugged. "I got exes. I'm sure some of them don't see me in such a good light. Definitely not my ex-wife. I just don't remember doing anything that would lead to this." He paused again.

"You're thinking about it too hard. Let's just check out your apartment and see what we can find in the way of bugs or any other evidence, then let it rest for the evening. I'll give you a ride in tomorrow."

"Na, I'll bus it. I want to get in early to see the shrink before we begin our shift."

They found no bugs or any other signs of Charlie's stalker in his apartment. After Gina left, Charlie called to arrange his appointment with Dr. Thomason, the counselor organic to the unit, and forced all thought of his dream and the stalker out of his head afterwards. He had succeeded, until he happened to glance at the message on his notepad annotated by X's he'd written earlier. He grabbed a couple laxatives from the medicine cabinet he had bought yesterday. *Not sure I can poop with my feet on a stool,* he thought as he downed them.

Magoon's Pub in south Brooklyn was styled after a joint in Scotland Iain Magoon frequented in his younger years. He wanted to use the exact layout, but fire codes required him to make a few adjustments. Every other aspect was the same, however. He imported Sessile Oak from Moray for the furniture and Rock Whitebeam from Isle of Arran. The latter cost him almost enough to reconsider the entire enterprise, but he pushed forward with it nonetheless. And he was glad he had. The market for an authentic Scottish pub was much larger than he imagined. He specialized in fatty appetizers and a large array of Scotch whiskey in various ages. "It's the memories these drinks bring that make them special to each drinker," he would often say when asked what label is best. For him it was twelve-year-old Glenfiddich, a single malt brand that reminded him of the time his son was born.

On Wednesday evening, Iain saw a dark-haired man who looked more Mediterranean than Scot enter his establishment. He wore black khakis and a black, knit sweater. As he walked to the barstool right in front of Iain, he pulled off black gloves and stared at the bottles on the back wall. Iain prepared to repeat his usual comment about memories, figuring this newcomer for a virgin. But to his surprise, the man requested a Kilchoman without hesitation. "Ten-year-old if you got it," he said. "Rocks, please."

"Of course. What turned you on to Kilchoman?"

"I wish I knew. Been with that label as long as I can remember."

"Really? Where else do you find Kilchoman around here?"

"There's a place in Queens." The man in black clothes looked uncomfortable at his own remarks. "You get a lot of cops in here?"

"Scotch is a policeman's best friend."

"Then Charlie Peltman must come here."

"Aye, Charlie's a good customer. You know him?"

For a moment, the man in black clothes did not say anything. "Yeah, I know him." Iain handed the man his drink.

"You from Queens, originally?"

"Depends on who you ask."

"I'm askin' you."

"It still depends on who you ask." He downed his glass, placed a twenty on the counter, and walked out.

Chapter 3

Chang Huang left Yuan Lin and his men to their work and rode Horse east. His instinct told him that the killer or killers had gone that way. From his travels, Chang Huang knew of a watering hole a day's ride ahead. He had water enough to take him there and could refill his water bag before returning to Xin. The responsible party would no longer be there, but Chang Huang guessed they would have stopped there to refill their own water bags. Maybe they left something behind. He rode through the night and arrived at the oasis late morning the following day. At first it appeared to be untouched. He walked around the perimeter of the plant life, careful not to disturb anything while inventorying the area. Once he entered the shade of the palm trees, he memorized each step he took, slowly and thoroughly. After ruling out any trace of evidence on land, he bent down to refill his water pouch and saw a death mask looking up at him from below the water's surface.

(Thursday – August 9, 2012)

The door to the counselor's office looked both forbidding and welcoming at the same time. He'd walked by it several times a day since he started at the 75th Precinct and knew the man who wore the dark-framed glasses within. Michael was his name, but today it would be Dr. Thomason. He wanted a healthy disassociation from this man who had the power to put him on leave or prescribe drugs that he'd be required to take. Charlie expected to see him sitting behind the desk when he opened the door. But he was resting in a recliner by the sun-filled window, reading a newspaper. "Dr. Thomason?" The newspaper dropped so suddenly it startled Charlie. Dr. Thomason's brown buzz cut made him look like a drill sergeant. He was very thin, like a marathon runner hooked on heroine.

"So formal, Charlie?"

"Today, yes."

Dr. Thomason nodded. "I understand. Should I call you Officer Peltman?"

"No, that doesn't seem right. Just Charlie."

Dr. Thomason nodded again. "Okay, Charlie. So, what's this all about?" When he stood, he was nearly the same height as Sergeant Langmann. He walked to his desk and absentmindedly picked up a small, black globe, a little smaller than a baseball, that looked like it was made of glass.

"Sarge didn't tell you?"

"Nope. He told me you could explain it better than him."

Charlie sat in a chair at Thomason's desk, took a deep breath and held it a second before letting it out. "I'm having recurring dreams where I'm someone else."

"Every night?"

"Every. Picks up right where it left off." The counselor's eyebrows furrowed. "But that's not the weird part."

"No such thing as weird in my office. Now before you go on, are you absolutely sure it's the same? Same people, same location, same time of day where it left off?"

"Sure as shit. Sorry, that's my father's saying."

"I don't get offended easily. Say what you want in here. You know, I've read that dreams can pick up where they left off, but it usually requires the subject to fall back asleep shortly after waking up from the dream. How many nights in a row have you had this dream?"

"Just three. But like I said, that's not the weird part."

"What do you consider the weird part?"

"Someone here in the real world made a reference to something that happened in the dream."

Dr. Thomason considered Charlie for a second. "Who?"

"Wish I knew."

"Tell me about the three dreams, Charlie." Charlie told him in as much detail as he could remember. He also mentioned the man in black he saw the morning of his interview and the doll that he and Gina found. When he finished, Dr. Thomason looked up at the ceiling quickly as if something up there grabbed his attention. "But the person who left the doll for you is someone you know."

"Why do you say that?"

"Basic communications logic. The doll was most likely meant as a message for you, unless some weirdo who likes dismembering dolls left it there completely unrelated to you and your dream by coincidence."

"I thought nothing was weird in this office?"

"Touché. Anyway, assuming it was meant to be a message, someone would only make a reference if they knew you would understand the reference. And since we know he can't be witnessing your dream, you two must have something in common that goes back a ways."

"Yeah, Gina said something similar."

"Oh, yeah? She study dreams?"

"Nothing formal. Just good to hear two people confirm the same thing."

"No doubt."

"But these dreams are graphic…violent. Or at least the after effects of violence. I don't recall anything like that in my past."

"Dreams disguise their meanings with symbols."

"Yes, but…"

"But…people don't. Not often, anyway, and not consciously. Look, I'm just theorizing at the moment. I couldn't possibly know enough to tell you what is going on yet. Why don't you write down these dreams, as much as you can remember. Can we meet once a day?"

"Do I get to keep doing my job?"

"Of course!"

"No pills or anything?"

"Not unless you want some. I got some good stuff." Dr. Thomason smiled and winked.

"That's a relief. Sure, I can maybe stop in an hour before my shift. You free at two o'clock each day?"

"I'll make it so."

"We good for today?"

"One more thing: are these dreams lucid?"

"Lucid?"

"Yeah…do you know you are dreaming? From your description, it seems like they are pretty stable…things and people retaining who they are. That's part of lucidity, but the other important part is being aware that you are dreaming."

"I am. Does that mean something?"

"It helps me understand your state of mind. Go forth, Officer Peltman, and protect our streets. I'll see you on the morrow." He might have looked the part, but Dr. Thomason did not sound or act anything like a drill sergeant.

As he departed the counselor's office, Gina's partner was just coming out of the sarge's. Fred McAllister was a little taller than the sarge with handsome features: sandy-blonde hair, chiseled jaw, and dark blue eyes. His good looks were impeded by a gothic mood he carried more often than not. He didn't like being shuffled around. Change was not his friend. He felt more secure with a steady partner. He fought being assigned to Gina from the start, but now that he had gotten used to her, he would not be easily separated from her. He gave Charlie a cold look as he walked by. Charlie braced for an argument but relaxed once McAllister continued on. Still, he felt their collision was only delayed.

Mark Robinson was a different matter. Not only was he looking for vacation time, he could partner with anyone. He was waiting by Charlie's desk before the start of their shift. Another good-looking man, if you ignored the beginnings of a gut he would likely regret in his later years (Mark took the stereotype of policemen and doughnuts as a requirement rather than myth). He made Charlie look short. "Special assignment, eh?"

"Top secret, my man. I could tell you, but then you'd have to kill me."

"As long as I get my vacation. Wife's been on me about getting somewhere away from the city. She's thinking L.A., but I'm thinking upstate." This was Robinson's fourth wife.

"Come on, Mark. Show the lady a good time. Take her to L.A. once. She'll never ask you again. It's not like it looks on TV."

"You payin' for this trip?"

"You'll pay for a long time if you don't take her."

Mark let out a big laugh and patted Charlie on the shoulder as he walked to his desk. "See you at quitting time. Watch out for flying bricks!"

"Hold on a sec. I had an idea earlier. What beat you got tonight?" Charlie filled Mark in on his idea.

Charlie sat at his desk to fill out some HR paperwork before roll call. He did not see Gina walk in but heard the hooting and hollering a second after her hands started massaging his neck.

"Hiya, big boy," she said.

"Mark, your voice has changed," Charlie replied. He glanced at McAllister and saw he was noticeably looking the other way. *There's more than disappointment in changing partners going on with Fred.*

"Come on, silly. We got some patrolling to do before we can start working our 'case'," she said in a quiet voice.

"One moment." He tied up the loose ends on his paperwork as quickly as he could before following Gina out to the drill hall. "Is it me or is Fred taking this harder than…."

"Leave it alone. He'll get over it. Just a little crush."

"Got it." After roll call, the two headed to the motor pool to check out a patrol car for the night. Charlie was usually the driver when he was with Robinson. But Gina hopped in the driver's seat without discussion. He wasn't sure whether it was because she was used to driving with McAllister, or because she was so used to chauffeuring Charlie when they were off duty. "I got a plan for later tonight," said Charlie, "but where to first?"

"I'll decide along the way. Hop in." Charlie obliged. The two cruised the neighborhood for an hour before heading back to Charlie's building, per his request. "So, we already searched the roof and your apartment. What's next?"

"We set a trap. It won't be easy, but we need him to see this trap in order to fall for it."

"I'm not following."

"He knows where I go, and he'll know if someone else is watching me. We need to use that against him. I prearranged something with Mark. He's going to be in the area, but he won't be watching me. See that newsstand across the street from my place? The stalker will see Mark, so he won't do anything suspicious in front of him. So, I've asked the magazine guy to see if anyone is avoiding Mark."

"But…"

"I'm not done. See the two-story building down the block? Henrietta lives in one of the top floor apartments. She's in her 70's but has great eyesight. She also has my binoculars. The opposite way, there's an empty apartment on 21st where I have a camera set up there recording on an eight-hour, digital memory. Here's where it gets tricky. You and I have to split up."

"No, Charlie…."

"Yes, but only for a few minutes. I just need you to drive away and come right back. I will be pretending to be on foot pursuit."

"What do you want to accomplish?"

"Just want to see which direction he's coming from. If any one of my observers sees him, I'll know something."

"But you don't even know if he will be out here."

"No, but he's made an appearance after each dream, and I had another one last night."

"Okay, well, I got nothing better. When do we do this?"

"As soon as we see Mark's patrol car drive by. He's going to make one round and then park around the corner. Right over there, where he can see the front of my building. I'll walk the opposite direction."

The two stayed in the parked patrol car and waited just over ten minutes for Mark to drive by. When he disappeared from sight, Charlie got out of the car. Gina's window rolled down part way. "Good luck."

"Thanks. See you in a few." Gina turned on her flashers and chirped the siren a couple times as she sped off. *Nice touch.* He placed his hand on the butt of his pistol and walked with a slight crouch across the street from his apartment building and disappeared around the corner of the block. Only a few seconds fluttered by before the magazine vendor, Mark, and Henrietta saw something they didn't expect. No less than forty men, all with black clothes and black, wool caps came from different directions, crisscrossing the street and each other, overwhelming the hodgepodge surveillance team. Mark stepped out of his car and stared at the chaos. Henrietta lowered Charlie's binoculars and her jaw. The magazine vendor started laughing and didn't stop until the street was empty again. Later, Charlie would find that his camera had been taken.

Chapter 4

Chang Huang pulled the death mask from the water. More undecipherable characters were painted across the forehead. *This was meant for me. I have to learn how to read Chinese.* He wrapped the mask inside a scarf that he kept in his saddlebag and slid the package into his purse. Most likely it would break, but that could not be helped. He refilled his water pouch and mounted Horse. He felt tired. It would be more than a day's ride back to Xin. *Why do I feel tired in a dream?* He rode until sunset and camped. Chang Huang had stashed enough food rationings for both himself and Horse. Horse ate with greed after having been shunned food for an extended period of time. "You will have to forgive me. I am new to this. I am a city cop, not a Chinese cowboy." Chang Huang looked around and saw the desert horizon in every direction. The chill started chasing away the dry heat as soon as the sun dropped below the sand. His blanket was thick, and he assumed that Horse would be okay.

He fully expected to be back in 21st Century New York when he awoke but found himself still lying in the sand. Horse was still standing, and he felt refreshed. The sun was warming the sand, and he knew he could reach Xin before the day was out.

From a distance, Xin looked like nothing more than a collection of rustic buildings, few of which were taller than one story, set up at various angles with no sense of community planning. As Chang Huang approached from the south, he could see that there was a hint of an opening between the buildings closest to him to what looked like an empty area in the center of town. Yuan Lin and his men had set up their bivouac in this space. Although Chang Huang had seen many towns like this one, the look and feel of this place was vastly different from anything Charlie had ever experienced. The buildings were made of wood and stone. The people walking between the buildings did not stop to chit chat with each other. Their heads were down, and most carried armfuls or sacks of goods. Charlie would have expected to see the conical hats he saw in the movies, but General Chang knew those were not worn in this part of China. Once he was past the perimeter of buildings, he could see the purposes of some of the buildings. To his right was a spice shop, with an inn just past it according to their signs, going counterclockwise around the center of the town. To his left was a furniture maker, followed by a food merchant and then a clothing store going clockwise. On the other side of Yuan Lin's encampment was a tavern. More buildings could be seen to the north peeking between the ones encircling the town center. He had little time to ponder his surroundings before a familiar face approached him.

"General Chang." Captain Yuan was prompt if nothing else.

"What have you learned?"

"I recognized the faces as soon as I entered the room. This family has been close to mine. I have delegated the investigation to my lieutenant. Chai Wen!" he called.

Lieutenant Chai was a smaller man but stalky. He hurried to Yuan Lin's side. "Reporting, sir."

"Explain to the General what you have learned. I will remove myself from listening range." Then turning back to Chang Huang, he said, "When you are hungry, General, please come ask for me. Our cook, Xu Ping, brings many ingredients from his home in Hunan." Chang Huang's stomach started to rumble at the mention of food. *If I'm really lucky, I'll get to try some authentic Chinese meals before these dreams end,* he thought.

"Thank you, Captain. I will stop by later." Yuan Lin returned to his company.

"General Chang," Chai Wen reported, "the murdered family lived in this town. Family name was Bao. Last seen three days ago. They were fabric dyers. Hard working but poor. The father's brother is close friends with Captain Yuan's father. I believe the connection between Captain Yuan and these family members is thin. But I need to learn more. I wish to question Captain Yuan, but I am lower rank."

"I will handle the questioning of Captain Yuan. Continue."

"Thank you, sir. The Bao family had no enemies here in Xin that I can determine so far. Although poor, the family did have an idol, a figure of a Kwan Yin dragon, that looks as though it could be worth more than a year's wage. It must have special meaning, or they would have sold it. If someone killed them for this idol, it would have been removed from the house, and it was not. I cannot understand why the family was killed out at the desert inn, an hour's ride from here."

"What questions do you have for Captain Yuan?"

"How long has he known the Bao family? Has he seen this idol before? Can he account for his location over the last few days? How long has his father known Bao's brother? How did they meet? How often has he been to Xin?"

"I will ask him as soon as I am able. You and I will compare notes later."

"Yes, sir."

"Did someone map the room and record what was written on the wall?"

"Right here, sir." Chai Wen handed over two separate sheets of expensive-looking paper. It must have pained him to use them, but it showed the level of respect General Chang commanded. If only Chang Huang had any recollection as to how he had earned this respect. All he had was a feeling that he had been involved in some sort of battle and had won where he should have failed. Sadness accompanied this feeling, so he assumed the winning involved sacrifices. *Does it matter? This is a dream.* Chang Huang looked at the paper containing the message from the wall. The first grouping contained two characters. He focused intently on the first character. Looked kind of like two identical shapes, one on top of the other. Like two squares, only rounder. He continued to stare at the character as he bit into his tongue, softly at first, then harder. The pain was not enough. He had to will himself—*awake.*

(Friday – August 10, 2012)

As soon as Charlie woke, he ran to his desk and grabbed the pen from his pencil cup and started trying to draw the character at which he had just been staring in his dream. *Two squares but different. One on top of the other. Something like:*  .

He also remembered that the first grouping had two characters, which he had correct in his original scratching of X's on his notepad the previous morning, though he knew that was only coincidence:

XX XX XXX XXXXX XX XXXXX
XXXXXXXXX
XXXX XX XXXX XX XXXX XXXX

He rewrote these lines, replacing the first X with the character he had just drawn. Below these three lines, he wrote seven more X's, as the mask he found at the oasis had seven characters on it. *I need to learn Chinese, or this will be a very long process.* Still, one character was something. It looked right to him but didn't feel right. Something was missing, or wrong, or skewed. It was still dark outside. "3:13" glared at him from his microwave oven. It took him more than an hour to fall back asleep, but he did not dream the remainder the night.

Charlie went back to his apartment to prepare for his lunch date but noticed The Egg returning to his apartment smelling like pipe smoke as he unlocked his door. "Hey Egg," Charlie called to him.

"Yes, good morning, Charlie."

"Good morning. Hey, do you happen to read Chinese?"

"I do. Do you need something translated?"

"Yes! But I only have one character. One second." Charlie disappeared inside his apartment and emerged with the paper with his scrawled attempt at recreating the message, handing it to The Egg. "Ignore the X's. This first character is all I have."

"This accurate?"

"I think so, but I'm not 100%."

"Kind of looks like the sign for the sun, though it's an older version of the character. If this is a part of a sentence, though, it doesn't mean that the word 'sun' is anywhere in it. The Chinese combine characters together to make a word. The word for "Japan," for instance is made up of the character for the 'sun' and the character for 'this.'"

"It's part of a message."

"Are you receiving this message one character at a time?"

"Something like that."

"In that case, you'll need more characters that are next to each other before you can begin to understand it."

"Thanks. I'll come back when I have more."

Between Charlie's dreams and his interview with Lextalt, he didn't have time to get nervous about his date. Now that it was upon him, all the anxiety of a teenager attacked him at once. Mark's comments about her age didn't help. Was he trying to convince himself she was older that she was? He looked at his watch...11:12. He'd knock on her door in 20 minutes and would have to drop her off by 1:30 so he could be at Dr. Thomason's office by two. His thoughts were interrupted by a knock at his own door. "One second," he answered this interruption.

Whoever this is will have to beat it, quick, he thought as he splashed a touch of Old Spice behind his ears.

He opened the door to see the gorgeous set of almond-shaped eyes he was planning on seeing over lunch. "Hi, Charlie. I hope you don't mind me stopping by a bit early. I saw you come in and knew you have to work later, so…."

"No! I mean…no, I don't mind at all. I was going to have to figure out what I was going to do for the next fifteen minutes anyway. Seems all the things I have to do would take too long to squeeze in." *Shut up, Charlie.* Since his conversation with Robinson, he found himself trying to clue in on her age. But it was no use. She was half Irish American but looked nearly completely Asian to Charlie. She had no accent that he could discern, and she seemed to look both twenty and thirty simultaneously.

Samantha chuckled. He tried to tell if it was a sympathy chuckle, but it didn't seem like it. "Good," she said. "Hungry?"

"Starving," he said. "I do have a small adjustment, though. I'll need to bring you back here by about one thirty. I have to be at work by two instead of three."

She raised an eyebrow. "How are you going to bring me back? I'm the one with the car, right?" Charlie blushed. "How about I drop you off at the station at two?"

His blush faded, and he smiled in genuine surprise. "You got it! Sorry to put the driving on you."

"No problem, Charlie. I kind of like the idea of hanging out with a policeman, after the creeps I've met since moving here."

"After you." Samantha took Charlie to a BBQ ribs place she found a few blocks from the apartment building. Charlie was surprised he hadn't seen it before. He also felt guilty that he expected her to take him to an Asian restaurant. "When did you find this place?" he asked as he sat down, glancing around at the western decorations; everything from saddles to replicas of old rifles and spurs hung on the walls. He had a sense of déjà vu when he saw the lights hung from wagon wheels above each table.

"About a day after I moved here. I'm a ribs girl, and was worried I wouldn't find a replacement for my Rib Shack back home."

"Where is home?"

"Louisville." She pronounced it like the natives: *Luah-vuhl.*

"Nice. Been there a few times. Got a cousin who lives in southern Indiana. I made him take me around to the other cities in the area. Cincinnati, Louisville…well I guess it's just Cincinnati and Louisville."

"Been to the rib places there?"

"Can't say that I have. I always love ribs when I eat them, but I don't seem to think of them when I'm looking for a place to eat."

"I won't hold it against you."

"Good to hear. What brought you to New York?"

"Hard to say, really. Part of me just hated being landlocked. But it's more than that. Kind of feel I'm supposed to be here. What about you?"

"Well, I bounced around a bit after my mom died. Was married for a few years in Los Angeles. Some might say I wanted to get as far away from my ex as possible, but I really don't believe that. When you have the whole country to choose from, what better place is there than this city?"

"But don't you see the worst parts of the city being a cop?"

"I see some ugly, but I also see a lot of good that people do for each other. I saw a meter-maid drop a quarter in an expired box the other day. I asked her why she did that. She said the car belonged to Mr. Edwards, who was going in for his follow-up appointment to his MRI. He'd been fighting cancer, and why should he have to pay a fine because the damned fool of a doctor kept him waiting too long. Stuff like that happens more than you'd think. The world really wouldn't keep spinning if it didn't."

She smiled, but it looked like a sad smile. "I didn't think cops had such an optimistic view of human nature. A friend of mine in Louisville was a cop, and he said he saw more of the ugly than the sweet. I guess I have, too. Maybe I'm not looking in the right places?"

"It's hard to. The ugly gets the press. It's more interesting. But hey, we can't control what other people do or don't do. All we can do is avoid adding to the ugly…building on the nice. Do I sound like a narrator for an after school special?"

She laughed. "Yes, and I think it's time to focus on beer and ribs."

"Normally I'd be all over the beer, but I've got patrol tonight."

"Oh…sorry! I wasn't thinking."

"No worries...ribs go great with root beer or ginger ale as well." He winked. He never winks, but that day he did. He'd wonder for the next couple of days whether that wink cost him a second date.

After lunch was served, Samantha surprised him with a question, "Do you like time travel?"

"Excuse me?" Charlie replied.

"In movies, I mean!" She laughed. The comment was innocent enough, but Charlie couldn't help thinking about his dreams. He didn't believe he was really going back in time, but Samantha's phrasing of the question tickled his brain for a moment.

"I like them as long as they don't switch between whether or not you can change things by going back in time," Charlie replied. "I mean, it's fine if they have a solid timeline that can't be changed by someone going back in time, like *Terminator*. Or if they allow a timeline to change, like *Terminator 2*. I just don't like it when the timeline is both changeable and unchangeable, or just don't make any sense, like the rest of the Terminator movies. I take it you like them?"

"I do…all of them. I don't care how cheesy, how illogical or well thought out they are. I honestly can't tell you why. I just do."

"There's a couple coming out in the next month or two. *Looper*, and *Safety Not Guaranteed*."

"I'm not sure that second one is really a time travel movie, but I'd give it a chance."

"So, you've heard of it. It was filmed in some of the places I used to go when I lived in Seattle."

"It also sounds like an interesting concept. You know there really was a classified ad where someone was seeking a time travel companion?"

He smiled. Of course, he knew that. "Really?"

"Yeah…though I think it was more of a joke." Charlie was tempted to mention seeing it together, but that movie wouldn't be out for a bit, and talking too far into the future would be premature.

Charlie paid the bill, and after lunch Samantha took Charlie to his precinct as promised. It had been a while since his last first date. As he left the car, he thanked her and absentmindedly said, "See you back home."

She simply said, "Ciao." He would also play that interchange over in his mind several times over the coming days.

Dr. Thomason was ready for Charlie when he arrived promptly at 2:00. "Afternoon, Doc."

"Hi Charlie. How'd you dream last night?"

Charlie walked in, shutting the door behind him. "Still in China." He sat down on the leather couch.

"Really? I really figured that would be the end of it after you talked so openly about it." Dr. Thomason picked up a notepad and pen that was sitting next to his glass globe.

"I learned something last night: I can go to sleep there and wake up again without returning to New York."

"That is odd behavior for a dream."

"Anyway, I got to see the town of Xin last night. Small place, got a few residential buildings and some commercial. I also got one of the soldiers to write down the message on the wall. This way I could focus on a character and write it down as soon as I wake up."

"You think that will help?"

"Dunno. Do you think it will hurt?"

"Probably not. I guess it depends on what it says. If it tells you to kill your therapist, I'd have some concerns." He laughed at his own witticism.

Charlie moved on to the other part of last night's dream. "I also found a death mask?"

"A 'death' mask?" Dr. Thomason made air quotes when he said this.

"Yeah. I was investigating the path I believed the killer or killers must have ridden after the massacre. I was at an oasis and found a death mask in the water."

"How do you know it was a death mask?"

"Its eyes were shut…but I could be wrong. It had seven other characters on it."

"Death doesn't always mean death in dreams. It could mean change. It could mean loss of some other kind. Or it could be a late-night snack acting up in your stomach."

"There a reason it might have characters on it? And I couldn't read these either."

"Your brain is trying to tell you something but doesn't know how to communicate it in a way you understand. The mask is symbolic, and the cryptic message is also symbolic. Symbols on top of symbols. Maybe there is something you are repressing?"

"Couldn't tell you that."

"Are you writing down these dreams?"

"No, I should really do that."

"Please do. Tonight, or right now if you have time before your shift, write down as much as you can remember from the dreams. Include breaks so that you know when you woke up. Number the dreams, too, so you can reference them."

"I think I have time to do that."

"Each morning, after you try to write down any of the symbols you are trying to remember, keep a running narrative of the dreams. Still thinking someone is stalking you?"

"Undoubtedly. I got witnesses from last night. You wouldn't believe…"

"Keep your narrative locked up. I still don't understand the connection between the massacre in your dream and the doll this person left for you to find, but let's not fuel his imagination."

"Got it. You don't really care about what happened with the stalker last night?"

"Care, but my job is to focus on your dreams. We should spend our time here on what is not in your police reports."

Charlie's laxatives from the night before were finally kicking in right at the end of his session with Dr. Thomason. The urge was overpowering, so he immediately ducked into the men's room. A smile spread across Charlie's face as he sat in one of the stalls. Then…nothing. He waited. After what seemed like a lifetime, Charlie said out loud, "Ah the hell with it." He lifted the waist of his slacks so that he could maneuver his legs enough to climb onto the seat. This was more difficult than he'd imagined, but with some effort, he was able to get into a squatting position. Then he heard the door open and two sets of footsteps walk in at a quick pace.

"It's fucking Peltman. That's what's bothering me." McAllister's voice.

"Wait, man." Jameson's voice. Peter Jameson was assigned to McAllister after Gina had been paired up with Charlie. He was a large, black man with 70's style mutton chops. "Let's make sure we're alone." Charlie remained silent as Jameson glanced below the doors for any sets of legs that might be listening. "All right. We're clear," he said. "Now what's your beef with Charlie? He ain't done nothing to you."

"Something's up with him. First he takes Gina away from me and now he's occupying all Mike Thomason's time."

Peter lowered his voice. "Has it ever occurred to you that he has issues? Just as big as yours?"

"Of course it's occurred to me." Fred's voice lowered to almost a whisper. Charlie had to strain to listen. "Look, my problem with Charlie isn't logical. I know that. But I can't do anything about what is happening to my brother. So just let me be mad at Peltman, okay?"

"No, Fred. I ain't gonna let you do that. I'd rather you be mad at me."

Charlie heard McAllister sigh. "No, Pete. I probably need to let it go. All of it. I just…I miss him so much. And he's over there, in some jail cell in Germany. I still don't get what fantasy he was chasing over there."

"Need a hug?"

McAllister laughed. "Naw, I'm good."

"Good, 'cause if you call me 'Pete' again, I'm gonna knock your fuckin' head off," Jameson said with a soft chuckle. After they left, Charlie waited several minutes before exiting the stall. He gave up on his bowel movement plans, hoping to give it another try later.

Gina was waiting at Charlie's desk when he returned. "Hiya, Hon."

"Hey, Doll. Give me about ten to write something down."

"Sure thing." She disappeared and returned promptly ten minutes later with two coffees in her hands. Charlie hadn't finished but was satisfied that he got the gist of his three dreams for now. "Ready?"

"Almost. Still got some paperwork before roll call." He finally saw the look in her eyes and realized she had something more important than the paperwork. "What are you up to?" She tossed a black, knit cap on top of his shift forms and grinned. "Where did you get this?"

"Your place. I wanted to see if anything was left behind from last night. This was sitting on the grass across the street."

"You think it belongs to…"

"One of the 'stalkers'? Yes. Look inside."

"Property of Southside Theater Troupe." Charlie looked all over the hat for anything that looked important. Feeling inside, he pulled out a couple of black hairs tangled within his fingers. "But who would drop a hat? People don't usually drop hats like this if they're wearing them. They'd notice right away that it was gone."

"Maybe it wasn't dropped accidentally."

"Becky!" Charlie shouted over his shoulder. A thin woman with dark hair and very white skin appeared moments later. She looked no older than a college freshman but had earned her Ph.D. two years ago in forensic science. "Can I get a DNA check on these?" He held up the two hairs.

"Sure. It'll take a couple of days."

"Super." Becky was off. Charlie turned back to Gina. "Used to take months. Even then the results weren't too reliable."

"Doesn't matter. We'll find exactly what the stalker wants us to find. Most likely the DNA of some theater extra he hired. I wonder how much he paid them."

"If he wants us to track this lead back to the theater, let's hit that first."

The theater was just opening by the time Gina and Charlie arrived. The crew was making some changes to the set design, while amateur actors and actresses were arriving from their day jobs and filing into the dressing room area. Charlie casually followed one of the actors and caught an eyeful of a young, attractive red head completely bare from the waist down. He backed out and regrouped with Gina.

"Probably should start with the stage director," she said.

"Yeah." He tried not to look dazed but couldn't get the red head out of his mind. "He'd probably know who'd have access to the costumes." Gina blinked at him.

"Come on, silly, before you start talking crazy talk." The stage manager looked immeasurably busy. "Excuse me," Gina said.

"No, I need four more of those trees. We can't be out!" He turned to Gina and caught her badge shining against the dark blue of her uniform before turning back to the stage crew. "Check back in storage C. If you can't find any there, get creative." He returned his attention to the two cops. "Can I help you? Quickly?"

Charlie held up the hat. "Found this near a crime scene. Looks like it's one of yours."

"I don't know what to tell you. Anyone coulda taken one of them out of here. Maybe even a patron."

"We have reason to believe someone took it from here for the intention of leaving it at the crime scene."

"You accusing me?" Both Gina and Charlie resisted answering. "Look, there was a man here two days ago and asked to speak with the actors. He hired them for a special job. Yesterday the stage was shut down for a special function, so they were all free. The guy paid well. I woulda gone with 'em, but my wife had planned something for me from way back. Hey Mickey! Come here and tell 'em what happened last night."

Mickey was a tall but wiry man going prematurely bald. He answered his hair loss by growing a sandy brown goatee. "Come on, Howie, I gotta get my costume on." Charlie saw Mickey notice the red head coming out of the dressing room with her doctor costume already in place. "Ah, never mind. Too late, anyhow."

Gina opened up questioning with Mickey. "Did you do a job last night over on Avenue L?"

"Oh, yeah. This guy paid us to walk across the street. All of us crisscrossing like a bunch of bugs. Paid us each a hundred bucks!"

"You remember what he looked like?"

"About five-eight, five-nine…something like that. Dark hair. Maybe Italian looking…or Greek. Didn't talk much. He set us all up and told us which way to walk."

"Did you see where he watched you from?"

"He was right there with us. When he gave the signal, we all walked together. Got our money in advance, so after we got to our finish point, we never saw him no more."

"So, he wasn't at the finish point?"

"No ma'am. He went off in the direction that cop was going. The one all bent over like he was following someone. We all got a kick out of it…he was a really bad actor. It was pretty obvious there wasn't no one there to follow." Charlie's face felt warm. "Anyway, that was the last we saw him."

"Thanks. Do you know which one of you dropped this hat?" She held it up for him to see.

"Oh, yeah. That was Charlie's hat."

"Charlie?" Gina asked for confirmation.

"Yeah. See, the guy who hired us—no one knew what his name was—asked if anyone's name was Charlie. When Charlie raised his hand, the guy told him to drop his hat somewhere in the grass. Didn't matter which building."

"Thanks. Could you send Charlie over here?"

"Sure can." Mickey disappeared and another man jogged over.

"I'm Charlie. What's up?"

The cop Charlie stared at him for a moment. The he spoke, "You were on that job on L last night?"

"Yes, sir. Dropped my hat just like the man said. Oh, is your name Charlie, too?" The cop Charlie nodded. "I'm supposed to give you this." He handed cop Charlie a yellowish envelope. Charlie grabbed it by a corner and handed it to Gina without looking at it. The actor Charlie had little else to say. The director confirmed that he had the contact information of everyone in the troupe in case any more questions came up, and the two cops left the building.

"Am I that predictable?" Charlie asked as they entered the car.

"I think we both are, Charlie."

All along the ride back to the station, Charlie was tempted to open the envelope. He knew that the lab needed to give it a once-over, but he was also sure that they would find nothing. When the lab told him that several items of higher priority were ahead of his letter and that it would likely be the next day before he saw it again, he regretted not tearing into it first.

Chapter 5

Chang Huang put the map and the message from the wall in his purse along with the mask, which had yet so far remained unbroken. He looked around at the buildings for the inn, praying that he had some sort of currency on his person and would be able to understand the coin denominations. He thanked Chai Wen for his work and tied Horse at the front of the inn. At the bottom of the purse were indeed coins, and Chang Huang seemed to understand how to use them. They were metallic and round with square holes in the center. The innkeeper told him where the stables were ("around back" he said and indicated with a swing of his right index finger) and gave him his room key. After inquiring of the innkeeper who owned the inn an hour or so south of town, the innkeeper replied that he owned both establishments and was a little concerned that he has not heard from his hired manager from "the annex" in a few days. General Chang figured that the annex manager must have run off around the time of the massacre. He told the innkeeper not to expect to see the man again and let him know what had happened there. The innkeeper looked disappointed but not as distraught as a New Yorker from 2012 might expect. He asked how soon he would be able to restaff and reopen. Chang Huang said he would let him know.

Once in his room on the second floor, he removed his armor and clothes. Chang Huang seemed to have the same skeletal structure as Charlie. Seeing the scars on his body allowed Charlie to access some of Chang Huang's memories. A line from his left nipple to his naval was from a swordfight as a junior officer. A nasty cut on his right shoulder was from a spear that knocked him off his horse. That horse had been named "Horse" as well. *Chang Huang doesn't seem to have much imagination.* There were more markings, but the most concerning was one that stretched across his throat. That one had been from someone close to him. Had the slice from the dagger been any deeper, Chang Huang would never have become general. He would never have grown up for that matter. His father gave him that scar when he was ten years old. From that point on, Chang Huang had never been able to trust another person. His soldiers were always held at a distance. He ate alone and never came close to marrying. *My God...I'm a virgin!* He peeked through battered, yellow curtains to the center of town below. Yuan Lin had the soldiers lined up for inspection. Whether or not Chang Huang would have felt this way, Charlie felt he could trust Yuan Lin. Chai Wen as well. He believed the evil he was hunting was nearby but not in the men he had met so far. Chang Huang dressed and hid the mask behind the dresser. Not the best place to hide something, but it would have to do for the time being. He was very hungry at this point but did not want to make Yuan Lin's man start fixing up meals outside their regular routine. He gobbled on some jerky and dried fruits he brought in from Horse's saddlebag. Then he looked out his window again.

On the street, Yuan Lin was preparing to take the men outside the town's boundaries for training exercises. Chang Huang knew he wished to be on his way but would stay in town as long as requested. "Captain Yuan," Chang Huang called out.

"Here, sir."

"When and where are your men expected next?"

"We return to Peiping in one month's time. I can extend that if needed by sending a messenger."

"That is one week's ride for a company of your size. I want this resolved much sooner than that, so let us try to make this happen. I have some questions for you." Chang Huang noticed a young woman, maybe 20 years old at the most, staring at them from the porch of the tavern. Most others ignored them completely. She was striking in her simplicity. Her face was thin, and her eyes were small. She was not beautiful by Asian standards, but the Western eye would be drawn to her. Chang Huang's persona overruled Charlie's libido, and he avoided eye contact as much as possible. After he finished speaking, he saw Yuan Lin glance in the girl's direction.

"I will answer any questions you have, General. Though I wish not to do so in front of my men."

"Of course not. There is a tavern over there." Chang Huang pointed to where he saw the girl moments ago. She was gone. "And I need a drink."

"Yes, sir. I will also station a guard outside your room."

"Thank you." Chang Huang came down to the street and gave his room number to Yuan Lin, who had Chai Wen set up proper watch. Chang Huang led the way and ordered rice wine for the two at the tavern. Hints of Gobi Desert cuisine—the smells of boiled cabbage, mutton and cumin—were starting to fill the dining area. A crowd gathered, but the noise level was uncomfortably low. One man sat alone at a table near the center. No seat in the tavern seemed to be out of earshot of this man. It could be nothing, but the strategic location would be ideal for a scout who wished to learn all he could about a place. The woman who brought the rice wine to the table was the same woman Chang Huang saw earlier. *Of course my subconscious would do that to me.* Up close she looked even more striking to him. Her hair was dirty and she looked very tired, but that seemed to endear her to Chang Huang, and possibly to Yuan Lin. She did not say a word as she poured the wine and accepted Chang Huang's coin. "Pardon me, miss," said Chang Huang before she could walk away. She turned back to look at the general with an expression of servitude but did not speak. As quietly as he could, Chang Huang asked her, "How long has that man at the center been sitting there?"

"Longer than I would expect, General." Chang Huang looked at the man's place setting quickly, and as much from his peripheral as he could manage. The man had a little bit of bread and a bowl of noodles piled up past the rim in front of him.

"Thank you." The waitress resumed her work. Chang Huang turned back to Yuan Lin.

"Captain Yuan, I have several questions, and could ask them one by one. But you know what I am after. How about you just tell me about your connection with the victims?"

"Yes, sir." Yuan Lin thought for a moment and drank from his glass. "My father ran a farm with the elder Mister Bao, the brother of the man who was killed. They were friends for a long time. I knew the elder Mister Bao's son and daughter. We played together as kids. Elder Mister Bao was much older than the younger brother we found at the inn. He came from a large family where Mister Bao was the oldest, and the man we found was the youngest. Not much older than me. I did see him on occasion or two as a boy, then once as a man, three years ago. That is why I recognized him. But I was not close to him."

"Any bad blood between your families?"

"No."

"How was it you saw the younger Bao three years ago?"

"By chance. Not that unusual, though. I was a lieutenant at the time and had leave to return to my hometown. The Bao's still lived in the same area, and I ran into him at the general store."

"Where is this area where your families live?"

"Lived. My father and mother died about two years ago and the Bao's moved away around the same time. This was in Szechuan."

"That is a long way from here."

"Yes, sir."

"Do you know why the younger Bao and his family were out this way?"

"No, sir. I did not keep up with them." The waitress interrupted them to ask if they wanted more wine. Chang Huang did and bought another round. He glanced back at the man in the center of the tavern. His bread was now gone, but his noodles did not look as though they had been touched.

"There is nothing else I can think of that pertains to this," Yuan Lin said. My connection with the younger Bao is small."

"Chai Wen tells me that the Bao's had an idol. A Kwan Yin. Something that would have been valuable. They had this idol but remained poor."

"Some things are worth more than money. I have seen this idol, but I do not know its significance."

"Can you show me?"

"Of course, sir."

"In a moment." Chang Huang glanced back and saw that the noodles continued to linger in the man's bowl at the center of the tavern. He whispered to Yuan Lin, "Follow my lead." Then, in a louder voice, "Your deal with the Hei Shui, is it finalized?"

Yuan Lin hesitated only slightly before replying, "Almost. The payment has not been settled."

"I am sure you will come to terms. They will give you the name of this scout?"

"That is what they promise. But I think my men will have him before Hei Shui gives me that name."

"You know, I bet it would not be that hard. Why, any one of these locals would be able to point out a stranger who has been hanging around with no companion or no obvious business in town." He made an obvious show of looking around the tavern. "I bet that guy would be able to help us out." He pointed to the man at the center. "Hey, mister!" The man, who had been doing his best to look uninterested, looked up at the general with visible reluctance. "Yes, you. Can you come over here for a minute?" The man stood up and started to put coin to the table. "Do not worry about the bill. I will take care of it." The man put his coin back in his purse and approached. "Have a seat," Chang Huang said as he kicked the chair opposite him out from under the table. The man sat down.

"Am I in some kind of trouble?" The term struck a tone of a kind of reverse nostalgia with Chang Huang.

"No, in fact, we need your help. We are looking for an out-of-towner."

"Lots of people from out of town stop by here to resupply."

"This guy would be different. He would be by himself. And he would stick around longer than someone just passing through."

"I can keep my eyes out for someone who fits that description."

"But you have not seen anyone like that?"

"No, sir."

"Hmm," Chang Huang said, looking at Yuan Lin. "Maybe there is no Hei Shui scout in Xin."

"I do not know," replied Yuan Lin, "I cannot imagine the Hei Shui lying to me about having one here, and Xin is such a prime spot. The rich coming through here are easy targets."

The third man shifted in his seat and repeated, "I can certainly keep an eye out for…"

Chang Huang interrupted him. "You look like a native of this town. I can count on you to know when someone is an outsider?"

The man smiled, "Absolutely. It would be an honor to help you out." Just then the waitress served a couple of drinks to a table behind the third man's seat.

"That is great. Hey, can you grab Chong Mei for me?" Chang Huang asked the third man as he pointed to the waitress.

"Sure," he replied. He turned to the waitress and said, "Chong Mei." She did not respond. "Chong Mei!" he said a bit louder. She started to walk away and he tapped her on the arm. "Chong Mei!" he said again.

She turned to look at the man and said, "I think you have mistaken me for someone else, sir." The man looked back at Chang Huang, then at Yuan Lin with wide eyes, realizing he has been tricked. He stood and drew his sword. Yuan Lin was between him and the door, so he could not run without a fight.

"Do not be foolish," Yuan Lin said. The third man raised his sword and began to drop it down hard onto Yuan Lin's skull when Chang Huang's throwing dagger appeared in his gut, just below his heart. His knees buckled and he dropped to the floor.

"Someone get the town police and a medic," Chang Huang said as he attempted to apply pressure to the man's chest. Both appeared in short order. “See that this man lives. We will have questions for him later.”

As the man was taken away, Yuan Lin asked Chang Huang, “Do you think he had anything to do with the murders?”

“No. Nothing is for certain, but I do not think a scout would bring that much attention to himself by killing a whole family. We do know now that the Hei Shui are on their way for sure. When this scout does not return, they will send another for a shorter recon. Have your men keep their eyes peeled.” His mind wandered back to the idol. “Let us go to the Bao’s apartment.”

“Yes, sir.” The two men left, and Chang Huang noticed Yuan Lin glancing back at the waitress as they passed through the door. Yuan Lin led Chang Huang to the Bao’s home. The men guarding the apartment were not dressed in military armor. Yuan Lin gave Chang Huang a disconcerting look as he walked past them to where the Kwan Yin idol had been. “It is gone!” Chang Huang watched Yuan Lin look around frantically. “Sir, I wish to bring my lieutenants here at once.”

“Go. I will stay here.” Yuan Lin rushed out of the apartment.

(Saturday – August 11, 2012)

Charlie did not go straight to the office but to a Chinese grocer and textile shop on the south side of Brooklyn. Although it was independently owned, it had the appearance of a super Walmart on the inside. A seafood section offered a variety of exotic fish that could not be found in most Western stores. The clothing and appliance sections were separated from the food, and the electronics section almost looked like a different store altogether. Whereas most of the store was well lit with shiny, linoleum floors, the electronic section was purposefully dark, with sound absorbing carpet on the floor and on the walls. The entire mart was so crowded that getting from one end to the other was more of a challenge than Charlie preferred.

But what interested Charlie that morning was a row of rooms along the back wall that were rented out to various, smaller merchants. One of those rooms sold art supplies and decorations. He didn't know what he was looking for until he saw them: a row of Chinese opera masks. Most were classic Peking opera masks, which were the same oval shape painted various colors in symmetrical patterns that flowed away from the center. A few of them were ground masks, which had more elaborate decorations extending upward from the nose and eyes. As Charlie examined them, an elderly Chinese vendor approached him. "Interested in Chinese opera?" he asked. The man was bald with a thin moustache. His ears seemed to stick straight out, and he kept using his middle finger to push his glasses up on his small nose.

"I'm new to it. Do you know much about the symbols here?" Charlie answered as he pointed to the paintings on the porcelain faces.

"The colors have specific meaning. Look at the dominant colors. The reds and purples are the heroes. The greens, yellows, and whites are the bad guys. I can get more specific if you like."

"I'm looking for a death mask."

"Death? I am not aware of any death masks in Chinese opera."

"It might not be an opera mask."

The shopkeeper thought for a moment. "Oh, you might mean 'imagines.' Those are ancestry masks that would watch over the family's rituals. They were made from wax casts of the deceased."

"Do you have one of those?"

"Not here. I do have several in my home back in China. I'm afraid I would not be able to sell them, though."

"That's okay, I don't really need to own one. Just curious."

"You should be able to find them on the Internet, though."

"Thanks…," Charlie looked at the man's nametag, "…Bill."

"I suppose I should no longer be amazed that you continue this dream, but I can't help it." Dr. Thomason stared at Charlie like he was some new alien life form.

"Maybe by next week either you'll be used to it, or this dream will run its course. Then I'll be some Roman serving under Julius Caesar."

"So, in your dream, you are questioning Yuan Lin, but you don't think he is involved."

"No. Not sure if that is cop's hunch, or Chinese intuition. Either way, I just don't want to believe Yuan Lin has anything to do with this murder."

"Any idea who could have taken the idol?"

"Security on the crime scene was questionable. They weren't dressed military." Charlie's eyebrows bunched together.

"Something wrong?"

"Why would they be wearing different uniforms?"

"Different how?"

"Yuan Lin's men were military. But the men guarding Bao's apartment weren't."

"I would say that because the men guarding the idol were wearing different uniforms than yourself and those you are associating with, these guards are a higher level of protection against your conscious mind."

"My brain is messing with me? That sounds about right. First, these stupid messages on the wall and the mask, now it hides this idol that seemed to be so important."

"You can think of it that way, but remember, you and your brain are the same person. The girl waiting tables at the tavern…did you recognize her at all?"

"No. She symbolic as well?"

"Everything in your dream is. Of course, psychologists don't always agree on what those symbols mean. You were attracted to her, right? My thought, and this is only a very early guess mind you, is that she represents something you desire. The fact that your Captain Yuan may also be interested in her means something, too. Whatever the waitress represents…it could be something you feel someone else might take away." Charlie immediately thought of Gina and McAllister, then pushed the thought away. "It might not be a person but something like a promotion or even an auction item on eBay."

"Or my life."

"What's that?"

"This stalker…I don't have time to think about being scared of him. Maybe my dream's giving me an outlet for this?"

Thomason stared at Charlie. "I'd be worried you are after my job if it didn't require an eight-year education."

A note on Charlie's desk told him that the lab was finished with his letter and that Sergeant Langmann already picked it up. He grabbed Gina and went straight to Langmann's office, only to be greeted by an empty chair. "Must have gone out," Charlie muttered, mostly to himself.

"He'll be back. Let's head out and check back later."

"Yeah. I don't know. I'm really afraid that there's something time-sensitive in the note."

"If Sarge read it, he would know if there was something you needed to do."

"Probably right. I'll drive this time."

Although Charlie wanted to check back within the hour, he and Gina had their hands full with "normal" patrol happenings. A false burglar alarm sent them to the south side, a domestic disturbance called in by a neighbor took them to the west border of the precinct, and Gina single-handedly broke up a fight between a teenager and a bus driver. By the time they made it back to the station, it was almost 9:20.

Sarge looked up at the two when they entered his office, then returned his gaze to his computer screen. "Well?" asked Charlie.

"Your boyfriend wanted you to meet him at a warehouse tonight. But you ain't going."

"What? I can't not go, Sarge. You can't know what he'll do if I'm not there."

"Don't tell me what I can and can't know, Peltman. I'm a fairly smart man. You're too close to this. Sending you to meet and/or apprehend your own stalker wouldn't be right. I gave the note to McAllister and sent him and Jameson to the location."

"What location? Where did you send them?"

"Calm, down, Peltman. I don't like the look in your eyes. You don't worry about where they're going. Stick to your patrol, got it?" Charlie turned and walked back to the Bullpen at a near jog. Gina remained looking at Sergeant Langmann. "See to it he stays on his patrol, Baxter."

"I'll do my best." She turned to follow her partner.

In the Bullpen, only a handful of officers were milling about. Charlie was talking to one who happened to be standing near McAllister's desk when Gina arrived. "Are you sure?" Charlie was asking.

"That's what Fred said. Warehouse up on Joralemon. But that was at the beginning of the shift." Charlie looked at Gina.

"Come on, Gina."

"Wait, Charlie. Is it possible the sarge knows what he is talking about?"

"I'm sure he does, but I need to act on what *I* know, and I know this guy is not going to like being stood up." The two pulled out of the station at 9:30. "Joralemon…that's what…about 10 blocks?"

"About."

"Do you recall any warehouses along it?"

"Not offhand. Let's just start at the closest end."

McAllister and Jameson pulled into the edge of a parking lot that overlooked a set of piers. The warehouse sitting at the address on Charlie's note belonged to a restaurant-grade refrigerator supply company. Jameson hated being kept in the dark but knew Fred liked to surprise him. "All right, Fred. What's this all about?"

"Here, Peter. Read this." Jameson took the note and read it. His mouth formed a circle with a flat bottom.

"This man is fucked up."

"Tell me about it!" He chuckled, almost broke into an all-out laugh. "Whatever Charlie and Gina got mixed up in, this guy has it in good for Charlie. But I can't imagine Charlie going to China. Doesn't seem like the world traveler type."

"So why are we here?"

"Sarge wants someone other than Peltman on this. Think's he's too involved."

"Now Charlie's maniac is our problem?"

"Don't worry. The man is bringing a sword. We got guns. What can go wrong? Besides, this guy knows Charlie pretty well. We aren't doing what Charlie would do. He would never…" His words were cut off by a bullet entering his left eye through the windshield of his patrol car. Jameson was able to get off a short yell before the left side of his head splattered across the back seat and rear window.

Charlie cut off his flashers and headlights as soon as he saw McAllister's patrol car in the parking lot. He killed the engine and let his vehicle roll to a stop at the entrance to the lot. He whispered, "Cover me," and opened the door. Gina took position behind the car, and Charlie skirted the perimeter keeping as low a profile as he could. When he reached an angle that allowed him to see the blood from within, he shouted to Gina, "Call it in! Officers down!" and ran to his former brothers. He saw a yellow piece of paper sticking out of McAllister's mouth.

Chapter 6

Yuan Lin returned with Lieutenant Chai and a few other ranking soldiers. He was speaking to Chai Wen as they entered the Baos' apartment. "...and they were standing guard here when you left?"

"Yes, sir," Chai Wen replied.

"Where are they now?" Chai Wen did not answer directly. "Answer me, Lieutenant!"

"Sir, I do not know. Permission to go back to the training area and call roll."

"No, you are with me. Lieutenant Ku, you go and report back with a head count. If Xu Ping and Xian Li are there, bring them here. General Chang, I take full responsibility for the loss of the idol."

"Taking responsibility does not tell me who took it," he said more angrily than he had sounded so far to Yuan Lin. Chang Huang was still reeling from the events Charlie had just experienced. After finding McAllister and Jameson, he spent hours at the police station reviewing everything he had been through with Sergeant Langmann and Gina. The entire force was shaken.

The general looked around the apartment. Nothing else seemed to be disturbed. "Was inventory taken of this room?"

"Yes, sir. Chai Wen, present your inventory to General Chang." Chai Wen complied.

Chang Huang felt annoyed by all this fumbling. "Just review it and tell me if anything else is missing." He could see that the door and its lock were not broken. The dust on the floor had been swept. It was obvious the Kwan Yin idol was the sole target.

"Everything else is still here, General."

"Thank you, lieutenant." Chai Wen looked surprised. He was not accustomed to being thanked for the work that was expected of him. "Captain…." He was interrupted as Lieutenant Ku returned with two other soldiers. "Is this Xu Ping and Xian Li?"

"Yes, sir," said Yuan Lin as he turned to the two newcomers. "Where were you two this afternoon?"

"Sir, Xu Ping and I were relieved by the mayor's men. They had a decree from the mayor."

"Did you report this to your squad leader?"

"Yes."

"Go bring them…."

Chang Huang raised his hand. "Captain, you can discipline your men later. Xian Li, what time did the mayor's men relieve you?"

"Shortly after daybreak."

"Lieutenant Chai, obviously there has been a break in the chain of custody of this apartment. I will report this to the mayor and let him discipline his men. Captain Yuan, has anyone left the city since daybreak today?"

"I will find out, sir."

"Good. Have your men keep watch on anyone who enters or leaves Xin. I will arrange with the mayor to help question anyone leaving town."

"Yes, sir."

"Lieutenant Chai, assume for the time being that the Kwan Yin idol is still here in Xin. This might not be so, but if it is gone, there is little chance of us recovering it. Assign two men to guard this place. I doubt that the mayor will disrupt your security once I explain the misstep in his guards' duties."

Once two new guards were in place, Chang Huang left the apartment intending to go directly to the mayor. Instead, he caught the eye of the waitress from the tavern on his way and diverted his path towards her. He half-expected her to turn away and pretend she had not been looking, but she remained looking at Chang Huang as he approached. The general stopped a respectable distance from the woman. She looked down so as not to stare into his eyes. "What is your name?" asked Chang Huang.

"Hsieh Sun."

"You see a lot from where you stand."

"It is a benefit of this location. Mr. Shen wanted this tavern to be seen from any vantage in town."

"Did you see what happened after the mayor's men took over the guard this morning?" Chang Huang pointed to the Baos' apartment.

"I did see. After the mayor's men arrived, the captain's guards went into the apartment. When they came back out, they bowed to the mayor's guards and left."

"Were you seen?"

"No. Forgive me, but I was spying. Please do not tell the mayor." Chang Huang did not reply to this.

Again, Charlie's desire for the young woman battled with Chang Huang's persona. "Can I ask you to keep an eye and ear out for anything suspicious? That will be dangerous, but I believe someone killed the Bao family for an idol inside."

Hsieh Sun looked visibly upset. "They are dead?" A tear appeared in the corner her right eye. General Chang wanted to slap himself. Of course she would not know that.

"Yes, but please keep that to yourself."

"Please let me know when I am able to discuss this with others. People will need to prepare." Upon hearing this, more of Chang Huang's memories opened up to Charlie. He realized that, although the people of this town looked at the ground when they walked and seemed to mind their own business, the community was very tight. They were very dependent on each other for survival in the harsh environment. When one suffered, neighbors came together to help without being asked.

Chang Huang nodded and replied, “I will let you know.”

“Excuse me.” She turned and half ran into the tavern with her hands in prayer position on either side of her nose. He watched the doors swing closed behind her and fought off an urge to follow her.

Although he was very hungry by this time, Chang Huang did not want to eat until he had spoken with the mayor. He stopped by the inn and asked the innkeeper where he could find the mayor. The innkeeper pointed back and to his right and said, “He lives in a large house at the edge of town. But one of his men told me he left Xin on personal business around midday and will be back in two days’ time.” *Then it’s suppertime.*

Yuan Lin’s men ran to get their captain as soon as they could see the general heading their way. *He must have me on 24-hour watch.* Chang Huang was pleased to find the smells of Xu Ping’s cooking welcoming his approach. *I smell lemon, I think...rice...and something fiery, like chili peppers. I’m gonna like this. And since it’s a dream...zero calories!* Yuan Lin greeted Chang Huang at the perimeter of the bivouac site and brought him to the area dedicated for officer sup. “I hope you were not too hard on Xu Ping,” Chang Huang said. “I would not want him poisoning us.”

“Not to worry, General. He prepared the meal before I beat him.” Chang Huang could almost see a smile emerging on Yuan Lin’s lips. *Could it be that there is a sense of humor somewhere inside this hard captain?* Most of the meal was eaten in silence, though some military stories from some of the officers found their way between bites. General Chang may have simply enjoyed the meal; but for Charlie, it was the best meal he had ever eaten.

After supper, Chang Huang returned to his room and pulled out the characters Chai Wen had copied from the wall at the massacre. He first counted the number of characters in the second grouping. *Three.* Then he focused on the second character and attempted to memorize the shape. After several minutes, he began to will himself awake, this time without wounding his tongue.

(Sunday – August 12, 2012)

Once again, Charlie clicked on the light and ran to his desk upon wakening. He wrote the number three on the paper below his message composed of X's and tried to bring the latest symbol to mind from his dream. But the image would not come. He booted up his laptop and searched Google for Chinese characters. He stared at character after character, until his eyes fell upon a symbol that seemed familiar: 人. *Maybe.* Below it was the word "people."

Slipping back into the chair in front of his desk, he stared at the front page of his tablet. Realizing he couldn't replace Xs with Chinese characters very easily, he ripped the first page off of his tablet and wrote the following:

日人 _ _ _

Feeling pleased with himself, he sat back and started to stretch when he heard a rattling of keys outside his door. Charlie dashed to the door and caught The Egg as he was opening his apartment. "Egg!"

"Hello, Charlie."

"Got a second?"

"I have a bucket full of them. What's up?"

"I got another character." Charlie led him to his desk and showed him the message he was working on. "It's kind of a puzzle. Internet says this one is the sign for people."

"Yes, that looks about right."

"So, I was thinking this might mean Japanese people when its combined with the sun."

"Close. 'Japanese people' has this in between." He took Charlie's pen and wrote the following: 本. "Plus, these two characters are from two different eras. Here is the older version of the symbol for people: ."

"That might be my fault. I'm drawing them from memory."

"I've seen people who haven't studied Chinese attempt to write a Chinese character. It's quite amusing, because to that person, the symbols look the same. But he won't draw the strokes in the correct order, and that alters the meaning of the character. A Chinese person would look at the symbol and not understand it."

"How would the sequence of strokes…?"

"It just does. If you were Chinese, you'd understand." The Egg grimaced and cocked his head. "Aw, hell, what do I know? I'd like to look at it again after you get a few more characters."

"Sure. I'll bring it over."

The mood at the station was still subdued the next day. Charlie was prepared to be the target of the other officers' anger, as he felt he was responsible for McAllister and Jameson being where they were. Instead, his brothers and sisters in uniform were more supportive than he expected. Cops help each other. That's what they do.

Langmann had the dispatch officer send Gina and Charlie to his office as soon as they arrived. Dr. Thomason did not come in that day, so Charlie reported to the sarge much earlier than Gina. When Charlie entered the sarge's office, Langmann looked up at him with red eyes.

"You're early. Oh, yeah…your counseling appointment. Dr. Thomason took was told about this mess last night. He took it hard. He was helping McAllister with something for the past few weeks, so they were kinda close. I was hoping to talk to both you and Gina together, but since you're here, let's go ahead."

"Sarge, I feel terrible…"

"Don't." He held up a crumpled, yellow paper that looked like it had been soaked and then dried. "And don't let this get you." Langmann hesitated.

"Can I see the paper?" The words punched him in the stomach. The note was written in two different colored inks. The first part was in black ink:

> **It's been a long time, Charlie. Longer for me than for you. You bested me, and I died. Now it is your turn. But this isn't China. And I won't hold back.**
>
> **Be at 12 Joralemon St. at 10:00 tonight. I will supply the swords. We will relive our battle, and this time, you will not walk away.**

The second half of the note was in blue ink but was written in the same script:

> **Next time come yourself, coward.**

Charlie could not speak. Sergeant Langmann broke the silence. "You ever been to China?"

"Only in my dreams."

"Then the only conclusion is that this man is delusional. My advice is to disregard anything he tells you about this so-called past he says you share. We'll let Thomason figure out what's wrong with him."

Charlie responded half-heartedly, "Okay."

"You figure out who might be this pissed off at you?"

"No, sir. I've been racking my brain, and I never did anything that would make someone want to track me like this."

"Just like you never went to China. Think about who you might have talked to recently, or what might have occurred in your past that would explain this, even if you think it was small or insignificant. I want to make myself very clear, now. Prior to last night, I wasn't really that concerned about this stalker guy...almost amused. I don't find a goddamned thing amusing about him anymore. As far as I'm concerned, he's Jim Brown,

James Holmes, and Adolf Hitler rolled into one. He's my number one. I'm putting someone else on point for this."

"But, Sarge...."

"You and Gina are still involved, but I can't have you making decisions alone. I need to put the right bodies in the right positions. Detectives. You are in a consulting role, period. I've already talked to Deathrage and Peterson's sergeant, and they've been moved to second shift instead of their normal day for the duration of this case."

Charlie wanted to say something, but any arguments escaped his mind. "Yes, Sarge," was all he could think to utter. He turned towards the door.

"Charlie?" Charlie stopped but did not look back at Langmann. "We will catch this guy, and we need you to make it happen. Keep your mind in this."

"I will, Sarge." Charlie glanced around at the Buddha statue on the sergeant's filing cabinet. "Sarge, you know much about Buddhism?"

"Yes, but if this question has anything to do with your dream, you'd be better off not telling me."

"No sarge, the doll. Is there any religious reason someone might cut up a body in old China?"

"The doll, huh? Some Buddhists believe that a person cannot be reincarnated unless they are whole. Well, that's not really accurate either, but I'm not gonna try to explain the transcendence of the stream of consciousness to you right now."

"Thanks, Sarge."

Charlie filled Gina in prior to roll call. Cards were being passed around to sign for the families of McAllister and Jameson, and a collection hat was placed on Jameson's desk. Every cop in the department wanted the head of the man who killed two of their own. The commanding officer addressed the detectives and patrol officers on the second shift together after roll call. No one needed a cue to quiet down when Captain Reynolds stepped in front of them. "As you all know by now, Fred McAllister and Peter Jameson were taken from us last night. They were killed in a cowardly attack as they staked out a warehouse where a suspect was believed to be holding up. We all owe Fred and Peter our highest respect and honor. Before I go on, please take a moment to remember these officers in silence." The captain bowed his head for just over a minute. "We will hold services for these men on Thursday, the 16th. Details will be distributed as soon as plans are finalized. I know everyone wants on the McAllister/Jameson case, but I can't have that. There are other crimes being committed in this precinct while we sit in this room. Detectives Deathrage and Peterson will be leading the investigation. Officers Baxter and Peltman will assist. The rest of you, stick to your assigned patrols. What happened last night was brutal, quick, and without pause. I want every engagement with this suspect well planned. No renegade antics. Everyone except the four I mentioned is free to begin their nights." The uniforms and plain clothed officers filed out. Deathrage, Peterson, Peltman, and Baxter gathered around Sergeant Langmann.

"Your supervisor already explained the situation to you two?" Sarge said to Deathrage and Peterson. They nodded. "You four are in the most danger tonight. I have no intention of letting Charlie and this nut go at it with swords, but I want him to think I do. Deathrage and Peterson, this is your investigation. What is your next move?"

Nora Peterson had been with the force just long enough to shed her rookie status. Her blue eyes and button nose were cute enough to counterbalance the acne scarring on her upper cheeks. She curled a lock of auburn hair in her finger as she turned to look at Charlie and Gina. "I think Baxter and Peltman will need to get us up to speed on the details." Greg Deathrage, whose mousey looks and pubescent-looking mustache (though he was nearly fifty) juxtaposed his fearsome name, nodded in agreement. Greg was older than Charlie but had been a cop for fewer years.

"I'll let you four work it out, then," said the sergeant. He returned to his office and the others pulled some chairs together. Charlie brought out his notebook and started reviewing the details. He let them know about the security detail he was considering with Lextalt, since he saw the man in black there before his interview.

"Do you think there's a connection between this guy and Lextalt?" Greg asked.

"I can't rule it out. Harold and Francis don't feel connected so far, but I've only met them once." Charlie noticed some hesitation in Greg. He couldn't tell if Greg was nervous or just trying to figure out what the first step should be. "I think the first thing I need to do is to make contact with the stalker. This won't be hard. He knows me, somehow. Maybe someone from high school or a cop where I used to work. Whatever the connection, he will predict what I am about to do next. He may be perplexed that I didn't show up last night. He doesn't know it wasn't my idea not to be there."

"Where will you be?" Peterson asked.

"Same place he wanted me to be last night. His note to me after killing McAllister and Jameson was 'Next time come yourself, coward.' I think this means he expects me to be there again tonight."

"I don't get that from the note." Greg said. His skepticism was emphasized by the way his thin mustache twisted along with his mouth.

"I could certainly be wrong, but if he really knows me well enough to predict my behavior, then he'll know that my instinct is to go back there tonight. He will expect me to have a partner with me; no cop would enter a situation like this alone. So, Gina should be near me. Nora and Greg, I think you should be watching from a distance. He's likely to shoot first if you go in ahead of us. Hang back and wear bulletproof vests and helmets. I don't believe he will mess with you, though, as long as I'm there and you are far enough outside the warehouse that you will not be a threat."

"If we're that far out, what good are we doing?"

"I don't think he's working alone. Part of the point of this rendezvous for us is to catch one of his men. He's used hired hands before—the night Robinson tried to help trail him. Last night, when McAllister and Jameson were tagged, he had to be waiting inside the warehouse for me. He must have paid someone else to watch his back, who spotted Fred and Peter. He'll do that again."

"You're assuming an awful lot." Greg again.

"Not really. Unless he's an idiot, he's not going to face me with a sword and leave himself open to a bullet in the back from another cop. But I'm open to suggestions."

"I got one," said Nora. "Why don't Greg and I arrive in disguise. A homeless pair or something like that that would fit in with the area. That'd be better than bulletproof gear."

"He'd see through that."

"The stalker might, but he won't be the one looking for us, right? His men would be. We could even get closer that way. That'll make it easier to catch one of his men."

"I'm with Nora on this one," said Greg. "But if we're going to do this, let's get to it." Greg's nervousness seemed to linger. *Maybe he's bothered that he's working with a patrol cop on an investigation,* thought Charlie. *We need to come together on this.*

"Thank you both. I'm used to being the one doing the protecting. I look forward to celebrating when we get this guy."

"Yeah, I'll have to have all of you over to my place for dinner," Greg offered. "I'm an amateur chef of sorts."

The warehouse looked angry in the settling fog, the way a hornet nest looks in the shade of a maple tree, even without hornets present. The white building was three stories tall, and the only windows were at the top floor where the white shirts held office. By 10:00, Deathrage and Peterson were in place, wearing clothes they picked up from a thrift shop and dirt smeared on their faces and in their hair. The humidity held the heat close to the surface; Nora was grateful they went for her idea and bypassed the body armor. She watched Baxter's patrol car move into position outside the front entrance to the warehouse. About a football field to her left, she saw Greg walking along the dumpsters. She thought he and one of the other transients were going to come to fists when Greg looked in the third bin. It wasn't until Charlie unlocked the main gate that Nora saw movement from the roof. A man's silhouette was clear against the light from Manhattan. He moved fast, barely revealing the barrel of a high-powered rifle for a split second before flattening himself below her line of site. She pretended to rummage through a trash bin of her own and whispered into a small microphone planted on the lapel of her moth-eaten, wool overcoat.

Gina stayed close to Charlie as they entered the warehouse front door. Charlie felt she was being over-protective for a partner but was glad for it. He expected to have to look around for his foe or negotiate some obstacles like they do in the movies, but a few steps into the makeshift lobby of the warehouse, his flashlight beam fell upon an unsheathed, thin sword with black markings running along the blade. The markings were Chinese characters. After studying the sword for a second, he moved his flashlight up and lit a man looking down on them from a steel walkway that skirted around the tall walls of the lobby. He wore no mask and looked like he could be Greek or Italian in the low light. He also looked about thirty years old, though it was difficult to tell. The walls ended above the man's head but not to a ceiling. The lobby remained open to the rafters far above where the walls ended. Charlie wanted to speak, but now that he was facing the man who had been stalking him, he could not think of a thing to say.

"Pick up the sword, Charlie."

"Who are you?"

The man's solemn expression did not change. "Pick up the sword."

"I'm not going to fight you."

"No, not tonight. Next week we'll finish what we started. I'll contact you before then with the details. You will practice in the interim."

"Practice, I…." But the man on the walkway was no longer there. "Come on," he said to Gina. She thought he was going to move further into the warehouse, but instead he ran out the front of the building. He shouted back to Gina as he ran through the door, "Grab the sword…use a glove!"

Once outside, he turned around and ran backwards, looking up at the roof for the backup man that Nora had reported. "Nora, Greg, give me something!"

Nora's voice barked out of his earpiece, "To your right. He's coming down the wall." Charlie dashed off in that direction and saw a dark-clad man shimmying down a pipe affixed to the warehouse wall. A rifle was slung across his back. As Charlie approached, the figure stopped and reversed his course fifteen feet from the ground. But going up was a much slower trip for the wall walker. Charlie reached for his pistol, then changed his mind. He grabbed a rock about two-thirds the size of a baseball and flung it at the man on the pipe. It hit him in the rib, but the man continued to climb. Charlie grabbed everything he could find—stones, beer bottles, his own shoes—and threw them one at a time, sometimes connecting and sometimes missing wildly, until a brick hit the man in the small of his back, and he let go of the pipe. By the time the man hit the ground, four cops were pointing guns at him, one of them in his socks.

In a gray-walled room with a mirror and door on one side, and another door on the opposite wall, a Caucasian man with straight, brown hair and a thick moustache sat silently at a table with an open Coke can in front of him that remained untouched. Every available officer in the station was on the other side of the mirror. *This is the man who killed McAllister and Jameson*, they all thought.

"I'm going in," Deathrage said.

"No, you're not." Sergeant Langmann had been holding them back. "First, he's going to sweat a little. Then I'm going in. Then we'll see."

"Why you?"

Peterson gave Deathrage a look. True, it should be a detective going in, but she knew Langmann was emotionally invested and wanted to see what happened when he questioned the man. Deathrage caught the look and understood, letting his question hang.

Sergeant Langmann glanced at the thermostat for the room. It was set for 90 degrees, but the temperature had only reached 87 so far. The man in the interrogation room was starting to sweat. He would have found, had he reached for it, that the Coke had been sitting out and opened for a long time.

Charlie watched with mixed feelings. He wanted to hear what the man had to say, but he also wanted to get his hands on the real stalker. "Sarge," I'm outta here," he finally said. "Fill me in on what he says later."

"You're sure he's not the stalker?" the sarge asked.

"Even without the mustache I'd know. If this was the man, he would have known I would be there to pick him up when he came down that pipe. In fact, I'm fairly sure this man was sacrificed. Maybe you can use that to get him to talk." With that, Gina gave him a ride back to his apartment.

Chapter 7

Chang Huang was putting the paper he had been staring at back into his purse when someone knocked at his door. He opened the door to find Yuan Lin standing before him.

"Sir, I request permission to speak freely."

Chang Huang nodded. "Come in, Captain." Yuan Lin entered and the general closed the door. "What is it?"

"I am uncomfortable with the events of today. Ashamed. My men do not leave their posts like that…ever."

"It is not their fault."

"Still, I should have been told. Now, with my connection to the family, and with the Kwan Yin idol missing…."

"Captain, I know you are not stupid. If you wanted the idol, you would have waited until all this was over. You would have wanted this idol for a long time. A little longer would not have been too great a price to pay, now that the idol is no longer in the Bao family's possession."

"I am glad you see it that way. But I fear someone is trying to make me look guilty. I do not understand why."

"If that is the case, you are a scapegoat due to your connection with the family. Do not let that hamper your job."

"No, sir."

"Something else is on your mind?"

"Yes, sir. The men, I as well, have been wondering how it is that you were at the inn alone. Where is your army?"

Although Charlie had no idea why he was there, Chang Huang knew the story down to the last detail. "The victory for which I am well known is not as the story is told. It is true the Xinli army was eradicated, but it came at the cost of too many of my men. I made a mistake that I should not have made. I fell for the leader's feint. If their attack had not been a feint, my actions would have been justified. This town where we currently stand would have been destroyed by Xinli. The women would have been raped and kidnapped; the men and boys would have been killed. I sent three quarters of my army to intercept what turned out to be ten horsemen riding for Xin. The smaller of my group was left to fight the entire Xinli in the middle of the desert.

"By the time the larger portion of my army returned, many of my men had been killed. I believe that the Xinli knew they would not win this battle but wanted to kill as many of my men that they could. To me, this battle represents a great deal of shame and humiliation. I returned to Peiping with the remains of my army expecting to be punished. Instead, I was honored as a hero. My guilt consumed me. For years, I avoided this place. But recently, I was given leave by the emperor. I cannot say for sure why I came back here, but here I came."

"You are too hard on yourself. What brought you to the inn?"

"I had only arrived at the outskirts of Xin when a rider approached. He said that someone was causing a disturbance at the inn. Four men were threatening the patrons as well as the manager. They were looking for someone. The rider fled and said others were doing the same. I did not know where this inn was, but the rider pointed the way." Charlie was learning this as Chang Huang was saying it. *I must keep an eye out for this rider. If he is still in Xin, he can identify the killers.*

"Thank you for sharing this with me. I have one request, General. It has been said that you have many stories from life experience. My men are in need of motivation. They have been following rumors of this Hei Shui gang for a long time. They are used to being more useful to the empire."

"You wish to make a storyteller out of me?"

"Forgive me, General. I should not have asked something so belittling. I was out of my place...."

"Nonsense. I will visit your troops tonight." Charlie wondered what stories he might tell. He could not count on Chang Huang coming forth and taking center stage on command but would worry about that later. Yuan Lin started to leave, then turned back to the general as he reached the door.

"The Hei Shui scout is dead. He did not survive his wounds." Chang Huang nodded back to Yuan Lin.

After Yuan Lin left, Chang Huang went to the tavern. He did want a drink; he mostly wanted to see Hsieh Sun. The place was more crowded now that the sun was starting to set. No music was present to set the mood. Chang Huang did not know whether the lack of music caused the mood, or the mood of the patrons discouraged music. Either way, the Charlie inside really wished someone would start playing some Metallica on a machine that had not yet been invented. Something else was missing from this scene: women. Apparently, only the men came here to drink. Every table was full, but when Chang Huang stepped in, two patrons from one table pulled their drinks and moved to join another twosome, leaving Chang Huang a table for himself. He wondered if the quiet tones of the conversations were for his benefit or if it was always this way.

Hsieh Sun dropped off two drinks at a table and quickly made her way to the general. "Rice wine, General?"

"I am that predictable?"

"It is what all the soldiers have."

"If that is the rule, I must have one, too." She started to turn. "When you have a minute, I want to talk to you about the Bao family."

"Yes, General. However, may I request that we talk in private? Others will talk if they see me sitting at this table with you."

Even better. "Of course." Chang Huang drank his wine and stood up to leave. He wondered how they would meet up but realized all he had to do was be visible. She would make herself known when she was free. Chang Huang could feel free to fulfill his promise and energize the troops with his stories and meet up with Hsieh Sun whenever she found him. He could only hope that words would come about Chang Huang's past once he opened his mouth.

Standard chatter arose from the other tables as Chang Huang walked to the front door. He tried to keep an ear out for key words that pertained to the murder and/or the theft. However, the thing that piqued his interest pertained to neither crime. As a handful of patrons in front of him were leaving, one of them said, "It does not matter. This is all just a dream anyway." He marked the group of men who left and stepped out to follow at a distance.

"You still think this is all a dream, Du Hung?"

"I know it is. The place I come from is a large city with cars and airplanes. You people are mere figments of my imagination." The others laughed. Chang Huang started to approach the men but stopped before getting too close. This would be awkward with all those men around him. But without accepting the reality of these dreams, nothing could be more important than speaking with a man who just said such an outlandish thing. Chang Huang started walking towards the group of men, when he overheard one of Yuan Lin's troops shouting to the others that the general was on his way. General Chang wanted to shout to the man that he was not ready, but that would make him sound week. Plus, in his hesitation, the men he had been following had gotten farther ahead. So instead, he made sure he remembered the face of the man who claimed to be dreaming so that he could question him later, in private.

(Monday – August 13, 2012)

Charlie woke up just before 9am with a raging headache. He gently massaged his temples and went to the coffee maker. There was coffee but no filters. *This is gonna be a lousy day,* he thought as he popped a cherry in his mouth.

But a quick stop by Starbucks picked his mood up a bit. After grabbing a dark roast Venti, no-sugar-no-cream, he stepped into a pawn shop to see if he could find a sword. The sword found from the warehouse was locked away in evidence, and Charlie felt the need to get his hands on one. The shop was small and felt almost overflowing with old band instruments and woodworking tools. A display of cheap looking jewelry took up one entire wall. Charlie figured the real stuff could be brought out upon request. A metal cage protected the seller, and an alarming number of pistols and rifles garnished the wall behind him. It didn't occur to him how convenient his find was, but a long handled, slightly curved, Chinese dao was proudly displayed in a case next to the cash register along with a black, leather sheath—green jewels inlaid along the sheath's length. Charlie made a point to roll his eyes and asked, "How much for the dao replica?"

"It's no replica, sir." The shop manager said. He was at least six-foot-five with dark brown hair tied in a ponytail by a rubber band. His full beard was a little darker than his hair. He wore a plaid, flannel shirt that Charlie assumed covered countless tattoos.

"Don't B.S. me, I've seen my share of Chinese cutlery, and this *is* a replica." Charlie flashed his badge for effect. The man seemed to buy it as his expression changed to one of mild amusement.

"All right, all right. That's what the guy who sold it to me said, too." The man barked a price and Charlie countered. This exchange occurred several times Charlie walked out with something he never, ever thought he'd own. His intention was to take the weapon to his rooftop and see if he had any of Chang Huang's spirit in his sword arm. But a rogue thought changed his mind. *If the city of Xin is a real city, there would be some record of it.*

Before going back into his apartment, he turned and looked at the 888 on The Egg's apartment door. *The number eight is lucky in China, isn't it?* This was not something Charlie picked up in his dream, but spending so much time thinking about China awakened trivial things he learned along the way and stored in the vaults of his mind. Without thinking, Charlie knocked on The Egg's door. The Egg opened the door wide without first checking to see who was on the other side. "Hello, Charlie. Do you have more characters for me?"

"Not yet." *Why did I come here?* He glanced down at his new sword and asked, "You know much about these?"

"Some," he said, glancing at the sheathed sword. "Come in. Would you like some tea?"

"Sure."

"Green or Jasmine?"

"Which has more caffeine?"

"Green." The Egg busied himself with the tea kettle and a package of dried leaves, while Charlie looked for a place to sit where he wouldn't feel like he was about to destroy an antique. The apartment was filled with Chinese art, furniture, and other decorations. In the corner was a mannequin modeling leather armor somewhat similar to those Chang Huang and Yuan Lin wore in Charlie's dream. The sofa and love seat looked as though they were made of solid oak, but the cushions looked like they were silk, designed with beautiful scenes of old China. Unaccustomed to silk, he assumed it was a fragile fabric and thought his weight would at best split the seams. He chose to sit on some cushions on the sill of the window peering out onto L Avenue. "Where did you get all this?"

"Most of it in China. I travel there approximately once a year. You might say I left my heart there instead of in San Francisco. Other pieces I find in rummage sales."

"It's beautiful." *Dreamlike,* he almost added.

The Egg returned with a tray containing a teapot and two small cups. He laughed upon seeing Charlie sit at the window. "Everyone sits there at first. Please come sit on my couch. It's quite sturdy." Charlie obliged but felt ill-at-ease. The Egg set the tray down on a coffee table with a beautiful landscape that looked hand painted. He could see the brush strokes on the wood.

"The tray won't scratch the painting?"

"It might, but it is probably my least valuable item. I painted that myself." Charlie had to look again. He lifted the tray to take in the image. The painted scene was a highly detailed vision of three ladies bathing in a river. Most of the detail, however, was in the trees. Thousands of small branches intertwined, clearing to allow full view of the three bathers. As he continued to look, he began to see shapes in the tree branches: a dragon, a goat, an eagle, and a rabbit. Had he continued to look, he would have found all twelve signs of the Chinese zodiac. Not that Charlie knew all of the signs.

"This is incredible. How long have you been painting?"

"All my life. But you did not come here to talk about that. What have you brought for me?"

"I picked this up at a pawn shop this morning."

"How much did you pay for it?"

"Forty bucks. They guy wanted 80."

"The scabbard alone would have been a bargain at twice that. Can I see it?" Charlie handed it over. The Egg slowly slid the blade from its sheath. "Mother of God, someone gave up a treasure. They couldn't have known what they had here."

"What is it?" Charlie was leaning forward with the eyes of a child who had just seen Santa Claus.

"This sword is about five hundred years old. A little more than that actually. It's a general's sword but not just any general's sword. This is one that would have been given to a general by the emperor himself for acts of extreme heroism. If you are interested in selling this, please let me know."

"I might at that, Egg, but I need it for a little while first." Charlie looked back at the suit of armor and asked, "What timeframe is that uniform?"

"That's one you've probably seen before. They use it in movies a lot. It's Ming Dynasty. That covers about a 300-year period. This one is probably late 16th or early 17th century."

Charlie finished his tea and felt the strong desire to search on the Web for anything related to his dream, and now this sword. But before he left, he had to settle one thing. "Why do they call you 'The Egg'?"

"Oh, that. It's the opposite of a banana." The Egg poured himself another cup of tea.

He started with Google but found nothing helpful. There were plenty of hits on 'xin' but none relating to old Chinese towns. It did not take very long, however, to locate Chinese history sites that included older cities that no longer exist. In the Gansu province of today, a little northeast of the Qilian Mountains, a small town called Xin had once been known as a stopping point for travelers between Peiping and Kumul in the 1500's. The Gobi Desert was a harsh environment, and Xin was dependent on supplies. On a map Charlie found, Xin looked as though it could be several days' ride on horse from Beijing, formerly Peking, formerly Peiping. A company the size of Yuan Lin's should take about a week. A little east of Xin was a blue dot in the desert. *An oasis. This can't be.* But Charlie could not deny what was on his computer screen. He searched on swords as well but was not able to find anything useful. A quick search on "chinese death masks" revealed that the mask he found at the oasis in his dream was, indeed, a death mask.

On the way out of his apartment building, he caught Samantha coming in. She was carrying four plastic bags of groceries and struggled with the door. "Hey, Sam!" he said as he pushed open the door and grabbed the two bags in her left hand. He briefly tried to remember if she had ever said he could call her that, but there wasn't anything he could do about it now that it was out there.

"Hi, Charlie…thank you! Just in the nick of time."

"It's my time machine. I actually was too late the first time but came back in time to give you a hand." *Smooth, idiot.*

"Well, next time, maybe you can pop back to when I left the store and help me carry these all the way back?"

"Duly noted."

"Heading out to save the world?"

"Well, our little corner of it, maybe. Hopefully it doesn't need it." As he walked her back to her apartment, he had a thought. "I know this is short notice, but you free tomorrow night?"

"Well, I'll have to work the next day, but as long as we're not out too late, I think I can spare some time."

"Great! I'll stop by around seven?"

"Seven's good. But Charlie..." Charlie gave her one of those just-got-caught-in-the-cookie-jar looks. "…calling me 'Sam' is not the way to win my heart." She smiled and winked.

"Once again, duly noted," he replied and headed out.

"Are you starting to believe these dreams are real?"

"I don't know, Doc. I'm just saying that the city in my dream seems to match a city by the same name I saw on the Internet. Same general location, same distance to an oasis in the Gobi Desert. It also existed at a time when Beijing was called Peiping."

Thomason pondered this for a moment. "You ever watch magicians?"

"Sure, but…"

"You see them do things that do not have an easy explanation. Once you are given one, the illusion disappears. Is it possible at all that you read about this town of Xin somewhere in your lifetime and filed it away into the recesses of your mind?"

Charlie had been sitting but reclined onto the couch at Dr. Thomason's comments. "I don't know. I really don't think so."

"It doesn't matter whether or not this is the real explanation. The point is, if this explanation were true, it would dissolve the illusion that your dream is real. When the magician levitates the lady, you may consider that strings are holding her up, as it offers a non-supernatural explanation. When the magician waves a large loop around the woman, you know that strings do not explain the illusion. However, you don't just jump to the conclusion that the magic is real. The fact that your mind came up with one explanation means that there is likely another one that you just can't see.

"It is important that you do not give in to the idea that these dreams are real; you are not remembering an old time that really occurred or anything supernatural."

"Why is it so important that I…"

"Because, then I might have to relieve you of duty."

Charlie's face grew red. He sat up and stared hard into the counselor's eyes. "Look, Doc, I'm not trying to hide anything from you or the police force." He leaned closer. "I don't know what I believe about my dreams, but if I am losing it, I'd rather you take me off the force. I don't want to cost anyone else their lives." The redness started to dissipate from his face. He sat back down on the couch and reclined once again.

Whatever Dr. Thomason was feeling did not show on his face. "I'm sorry, Charlie. I should go back through my notes tonight and we'll talk again tomorrow."

"I'm off tomorrow through Thursday. Unless anything new develops in my dreams, I don't plan on coming in."

"Good, maybe every day is a bit much for our sessions anyway. I think my interest in your dream is why I wanted to meet so frequently."

"Sorry I got so lit."

"Don't be. Anything goes in this room."

Ballistics reported that the rounds that killed McAllister and Jameson were from the same gun as expected, but the patterns on them did not match any weapon in their records. Nor did they match a round fired from the rifle taken from the man they caught last night. Trajectory analysis showed that the shot did not come from the warehouse but from an area to the right of it from the victim's point of view. No fingerprints or skin cells were found on the note. Langmann confirmed that the man he interrogated the previous night offered nothing helpful. The little bits of information the sergeant could get out of him were inaccurate. Not lies but rather misinformation that the stalker had likely given him. Becky also reported back that the hairs from the black cap were from a Charles Montgomery, aka Charlie from the theater. His DNA was on file from a prior incarceration from a drug charge several years ago. Deathrage and Peterson were off for two days but had asked Charlie and Gina revisit the refrigerator warehouse and the surrounding area. They found nothing.

After Gina dropped him off at his apartment, Charlie walked two blocks to Magoon's. The pub was nearly empty, but his old friend was manning the bar. "Fit like min," Charlie greeted.

"Aye, fit like min. Glenfiddich?" Not having any Scotch related memories of his own, Charlie took to Iain's brand early on.

"You know it. How's my favorite Scotsman?"

"Missing Aberdeen as usual. But not as much as I used to. The money this place brings in overcomes homesickness quite nicely." He chuckled. "Your version of a weekend just getting started?"

"It's my three-day weekend. I'm off until Friday."

"Doing anything fun?"

"Touring a shipyard." He kept his date with Samantha to himself for the time being.

Iain looked sideways at Charlie. "Is that what charades as fun, these days?"

"It's for a side job. Not sure I want to take it, though. Got a bit of a problem with a stalker."

"I met him," Iain said without diverting his attention from the bottle he was pouring over ice cubes in two glasses. "Dresses darkly."

"He was here?"

"'Bout a week ago."

"I should've come around sooner. What'd he say?"

"Just asked if you come in here. Ordered Kilchoman. Acted as if it was his drink, but I don't think it was. He downed it. Didn't savor the flavor. Lucky the ice didn't crack his teeth the way he did that."

"Why would he pretend…?"

"He wanted me to remember him. He wants me, and presumably you, to think he's from Queens."

"Queens?"

"And he acted weird when I asked if he was native. Said it depended who I asked. That part…I don't think it was for my benefit. Or yours, for that matter. Had kind of a faraway look in his eye."

Charlie stared at his drink then looked up at Iain. "A smarter man than me would understand why he said that."

"Apparently, I'm no smarter than you." Charlie smiled and finished his drink before ordering another one. By the time he left, it was nearly two in the morning.

Chapter 8

Chang Huang tried to call up more memories of previous battles as he walked to the bivouac site but nothing came. *Hopefully something will come to mind when I open my mouth*, he thought. *Maybe looking at my sword will bring back some memories.* He drew his blade and focused on it. *Nothing. Well, this does look familiar.* He brought the handle up to his eyes. It was difficult to make out, but as he focused on the detail carved into the hand guard, he started to remember seeing the emperor in formal dress. *The emperor gave this to me. For my so-called victory.*

The men tried to hide their boredom from the General, but Chang Huang knew these men could not stay in one place much longer without a mission. The latest rumors suggested Hei Shui had altered course and headed west. All Yuan Lin's men must be questioned and cleared within the next couple of days so that they could be on their way. Chai Wen and a few other officers could stay behind to continue the investigation. They could rendezvous with the others at some point.

"General," Yuan Lin called. "Thank you for your presence." In a modern day, American unit, the presence of a General would require soldiers to snap to attention in rank and file. These

Chinese soldiers were already in position ahead of the General's arrival.

"Relax, Captain. Have all the men relax. I am here to tell stories, not inspect. Have them gather round that knoll over there." He pointed to a small bump of sand. "And start a fire to the side, it will get cold soon." Chang Huang was thinking more of the ambience than the temperature, however.

"Yes, sir." Yuan Lin turned and called surprisingly few commands to the men, who moved to a stiff-looking sitting position in concentric, arced lines around the small hill Chang Huang had indicated. After the men were in place and the fire was started, the general ascended the mound.

"You men need to learn how to relax. You look like stiff boards." He meant the comment as a joke but was met with silence and blank expressions. "Your captain has asked that I speak to you of my past battles." *Okay, Chang Huang, this is your cue to take over.* Nothing. He tried to imagine what a battle in old China would look like, but all he could remember was a scene from Kung Fu Theater he watched as a boy where three old men had giant metal claws on the ends of chains that would rip their enemies' heads off. *Fine, I can plagiarize, but that movie won't do at all. I need something a little more believable.* He thought of other movies with battle scenes, but most of them involved machine guns, or hobbits, or lasers. Then an image from earlier in the night came to mind. The last person he spoke with before he fell asleep as Charlie. Iain Magoon. *Braveheart. It doesn't involve advanced technology or magic....* Charlie had seen the movie a dozen times or more. He began telling Mel Gibson's Hollywood version of William Wallace's story, changing the Scottish warriors to Chinese while the British became the Xiongnu. The Xiongnu were too early for General Chang's lifetime, but the warriors he addressed either did not know this or assumed that some lineage to the Xiongnu people were still around.

The men sat with their mouths open through most of the storytelling. He described the violence as graphically as he could. The end became tricky, however. Chang Huang had obviously not been disemboweled, so he had to improvise. In this new version, Wallace (as Chang Huang) had been stalked by an assassin in black clothing. He described being followed near the "Lextalt" Inn and being tracked to his home where a doll had been broken and left by his door.

But he needed an ending, as the General Chang they all knew was not currently being pursued by any assassin. "In the end, he faced me in single combat with swords on an island off the coast of Songjiang. We battled at the base of a giant statue of a woman with spikes on her forehead.

"When he arrived, I raised my sword in front of my face." He lifted his own sword and held it in front of him, much like Obi-Wan-Kenobi did in Star Wars when facing Darth Vader. "The assassin ran towards me, drawing his sword as he kicked sand. The statue loomed over us. It has since been destroyed, but having her there for the battle gave me the encouragement I needed to face my opponent. I barely moved when he struck at my left side. I shifted my weight and twisted my sword only enough to block the blow. He raised his sword in defense, thinking I would attack. But I did not. The look on his face was priceless. He struck again, slicing down toward the top of my head. I lowered myself about a foot and angled my sword, pushing it up to deflect this attack. Strike after strike, the assassin drained himself of energy, while I preserved my own. I waited until his breathing was heaviest and his exhaustion showed true in his eyes before I began my counterattack. I feinted right and then jabbed to his left side, drawing a red line in his exposed bicep. As I brought back the blade, I moved it closer to the assassin's body, slicing lightly into his midsection. He swung at my neck. I ducked and brought my blade up into his midsection again, point first this time.

"The assassin dropped his weapon. Blood flooded through his lips and from his wound. He fell to his knees, crossing his arms in front of him. I threw my weapon aside and tore fabric from my own tunic, but the man refused my help." Chang Huang looked down and closed his eyes. Not knowing whether any of the men believed his story, he slunk away from the mound hoping he looked emotionally drained from the telling.

"General Chang." *That was a woman's voice.*

"Hsieh Sun?"

(Tuesday – August 14, 2012)

Damn it! Charlie's alarm clock did not care what part of any dream Charlie was in, only that it was time for Charlie to hear The Tony and Bob Show. Charlie shut down the radio program and mentally traced his morning routine before opening his eyes. *Coffee…coffee…DAMN IT!* He was supposed to buy more filters before returning home from his shift. He could stop by Starbucks again, though he didn't want to wait until after his shower for his morning cup of sunshine. And this time, he could not skip the shower. But before doing any of this, he sat down at his desk, pulled a yellow legal pad, and continued chronicling his Chinese experience.

An emerald green Lincoln Town Car picked up Charlie and took him to the pier ahead of Harold. He assumed he would be taken somewhere in Brooklyn or Manhattan, but the driver continued up along the Hudson to a remote series of docks in Yonkers. Francis would not be along; he had been told this in a voicemail message that he only listened to that morning. The message also had told him that he would be riding in a limo with Harold to another location after the tour and that he was not to wear a tie or sports coat, so he opted for a newer pair of jeans and a yellow polo. Charlie scouted the docks while waiting for Harold, looking for avenues of approach and places to mount cameras. But not knowing exactly where the container would be stored or for how long, there was little he could do. The window of a control building reflected the image of a stalky, bearded man in a brown, canvas coat sneaking up behind him. "Good morning, Harold," Charlie said without turning around.

"Shit, and I thought I was being quiet." Charlie pointed to the window. "Aw, now that's cheating."

"Surely you don't want me to do this job without cheating."

"I don't care if you use witchcraft as long as you keep my cargo safe."

"Where will the ship dock? And where will the container be kept?"

"The *Skipping Stone* will come in along this pier," he pointed to the left side of Pier 27, "two weeks from today." He saw that Charlie was writing this down in a small notebook. *A little short notice for taking leave, but Sarge is already expecting the request.* "The container will be moved over to that storage building once it's taken off the boat." He pointed to a two-story, white building about 50 yards from the pier with windows that were painted over. "It'll be sealed. Welded shut. Airtight."

"Airtight. Then it isn't a person inside."

"No. But you might say it represents a person. Someone's life depends on it."

"What's your expectation that someone will try something?"

"We've already had two attacks. One before it was loaded onto the ship. One after it had been put to sea."

"Attacks? Not attempts to steal?"

"My adversary does not want to steal this item from me. He wants to destroy it."

Charlie absent mindedly took a step backwards, studying Harold's face. "This changes things a bit."

"You don't want the job?"

"That's not what I mean. It's just a different approach to security. Trying to stop a thief is very different than defending against an attack. Especially if someone is motivated and not afraid of consequences"

"The attacks so far have been bold and resulted in the attackers' demise. We think they are hired hands, but they must be paid an enormous amount for the risk they are asked to take."

"Either that or the risks were understated. I don't know who might want to destroy your item, but two failed attacks so close together makes me think someone is testing your metal. Did your men find any communication devices on the attackers?"

"The bodies of the men attacking us on land had microphones and cameras. No idea about the attack on sea. We blew them up."

"I don't think your 'adversary' expected either of those attacks to be successful. In fact, I would expect another fake attack when the *Skipping Stone* is closer to New York. It will serve to help us feel like we've won and let our guard down. Then, a smaller, more subtle attack will take place at the same time or very shortly afterwards. We won't need to spend twenty million, but what I have in mind is pricey. I think you said the vulnerability would be about four to six days. By the way, how much are you paying me?"

Harold looked at Charlie as if he had never laid eyes on him before. "Gina was right about you. We'll pay you $100,000."

It was Charlie's turn to stare at Harold as if he were a newcomer. "What? A hundred grand for one week's work?"

"Not enough?"

"You haven't done this before, have you?"

"No, and I hope never to do so again."

"I'm still not sure why custom's security isn't sufficient for this. The only thing that sets this apart is that you have been attacked a couple of times. You could give customs a head's up that this boat has been attacked. They will beef up security."

"If I tell them this ship has been attacked, they would never let it dock in the first place. Any other highly secure method of transporting my cargo would require an inspection of what is inside the container offshore, and I simply cannot have this container opened until it is here in New York. It is crucial that the seal is not broken until the ship has arrived. If the ship does make it to port, the attack would occur at the point the cargo container is opened. My adversary might try to open it ahead of time, while it is in customs. You're right, I think it will be a subtle attack…no guns or bombs will be used once the container is in the hands of the government officials." Charlie did not feel he had all of the information he needed, and the money felt too high for what he was being asked to do. *I should walk away from this.* Still, if he accepted the job now, he would have two weeks to check out Lextalt, Inc. He could renegotiate if anything smelled rotten.

"A hundred grand is more than enough. I'll protect your container. Do you have any pictures of it? Or of the boat for that matter?"

"I can get pictures of the boat for you."

"I want to create an illusion for…who is it we are protecting this from?"

"I do not know his name. Let's just call him Mr. X."

"Mr. X. Okay. He's trying to fool us, so I'm going to want to try to fool him first." Harold looked like he was about to ask a question. "No questions now. Mr. X might have spies here for all I know."

"Okay. Thank you for your help, Charlie."

Charlie nodded. "Where're we going in the limo?" Charlie indicated a black, stretch limo just across the street from the pier.

"You'll see. I'd tell you, but, as you say, Mr. X might be listening."

The two rode across Manhattan to Central Park in relative silence. Francis was sitting on a bench wearing a tweed sports coat. He seemed to be concentrating on something further out in the park as Charlie and Harold rounded the bench. Charlie thought the only thing he needed was a bag of birdseed and a folded newspaper next to him to complete the cliché. "Hey, Da," Harold greeted the older man.

"Son," he replied without looking up. It was the first time Charlie heard him speak; no Irish accent. He looked up at Charlie. "Sit down next to me, Charlie." Charlie did as he was asked. "No doubt this all seems unusual to you. Have you ever been to Xin, China?" Charlie felt all of the hairs on his skin at once stand straight up. His legs stiffened and his heart nearly came to a halt for a brief moment. He could not say a word. "You have, even though the city has not been around in a long while. The next time you are there, you need to seek out a monk by the name of Kong Xiao. Tell him you need to preserve your dream self. He will help you."

"How do you know…?"

"No questions for now." Charlie looked up at Harold, who was looking off to his right. "Remember, Kong Xiao." Charlie stood up, started to walk backwards from his two new employers, then turned and jogged to the edge of the park and hailed a taxi.

Paul Goldstein served as an unofficial doorman for the apartment building where Gina lived. At 72, he had been retired for nearly 10 years and claimed he stuck around New York for the food and the fun. He could often be found sitting on the concrete steps in front of the building reading, bird watching, or smoking. He was a small, roundish man with well-manicured, white hair around the edges of a shiny dome. He knew everyone that lived there and most of the people who visited with any sort of regularity. Charlie liked him from their first meeting, probably because he treated Charlie like a long, lost, war buddy. Charlie saw him in his usual place working a crossword puzzle. Today, his short sleeves revealed a series of numbers starting with a "1" after the letter "A" tattooed onto his left forearm. "Hey, Pauley," Charlie greeted him as he approached.

"Charlie! Puttin' them bad guys away?" he said in a slight German accent.

"Most of 'em. Savin' you for last." Paul chuckled. "Gina in?"

"Unless she got up earlier than me."

"Thanks, Buddy. See you on the way out."

"I'll be here."

Gina was half-reading a paperback when Charlie knocked on her door. "Hey, G, it's me." She could tell from his voice that something had shaken him.

"Charlie, what is it?" she said after opening her door.

"I'm scared, G. How much do you know about Lextalt?" She led him inside and they sat down on her couch.

"Just that my friend, Tom, works in the accounting department."

"How long did you know him? And where did you meet him?"

"Known him for years. We met when he did my taxes." She did not like the way Charlie was looking at her. His eyes were too wide. "Charlie..."

He stood up and took a step back. "Why did you need an accountant for your taxes. You don't own stock, or have anything tricky..."

"I had three jobs in two different states the year I moved here. Two of them did not take taxes out of my paycheck." Her look back to him was almost defensive but mixed with something else. Almost forgiving.

"I'm sorry, G. I'm feeling a bit paranoid. I don't think your meeting Tom was happenstance. Or maybe it was, but then him getting a job at Lextalt was arranged." He told her about his morning, skipping the tour at the pier and jumping straight to his conversation with Francis in the park. "You know, the doc said that there was an explanation for all this. I don't think it's just that I learned about Xin somewhere along the line and forgot it. But maybe someone is intentionally messing with my mind...making me dream about China and about the massacre. Now Francis wants me to look for this monk...Kong Xiao. Just mentioning that name might be enough to make my mind invent him."

"What was the last dream you had?" He told her all of it. From Yuan Lin knocking on his door to the rendition of Braveheart he gave and his story of the swordfight at the statue of the lady with spikes on her head. She looked up as if she were calculating. "Your dreams can't be totally controlled by someone else. Maybe they can suggest that you dream about a place, somehow, or an event. But your brain is still in control. You're smart, Charlie. You're gonna start piecing together the mystery of your dream. The people in your dreams, maybe they're talking for your brain. Or maybe one or two of them are. You woke up before Hsieh Sun was able to talk to you. Maybe she's someone you can trust."

"Trust. I can't know who to trust." He stared at the floor. "I've never felt this confused before."

She sat next to him. "Whatever it is, you have your wits about you. You have your gut." Charlie got up and went to the window.

"I don't like what my gut is telling me, G."

"Then let your brain rest. Enjoy this day off. Have a nice date with…Samantha?"

"Yeah, Samantha. Can't call her 'Sam.'"

"Then tomorrow, let's have lunch. I'll pick you up 11:30?"

"Sure, G. Sounds good. See you then."

Charlie's next stop was Magoon's for a drink and a fatty lunch. Both helped slow his mind enough for him to take a nap. Whether it was the scotch, the time of day, or the length of his nap, he did not dream. By the time seven rolled around, he had showered again and picked up some coffee filters. He hadn't felt so awake in a long while. If his dreams were being suggested by someone else, then he was going to do all he could to de-stress and be as unreceptive to suggestions as he could be. He also picked up some sleeping pills but would only take them as a last resort. He didn't like taking medicine, even over-the-counter. Samantha came to his door wearing a stunning red number that made her dark hair seem all the blacker. "You are going to take me somewhere nice, mister." It was not a question. Charlie was in the mood for a distraction, so he changed into a light gray shirt and tie combo with a black vest and slacks. It wasn't the most flattering combination of colors, but he felt good, and his confidence made up for any fashion errs he might have made.

Charlie waved a cab and gave the address of an Italian place in Queens he loved. It was just a small, nondescript building that sat off to the side of *the* Italian place most people were told they must go when visiting this part of NYC. Both restaurants were owned by the same family, but one catered to tourists, while the other catered to people who knew good Italian food. The former subsidized the latter, allowing people on Charlie's salary to get one up on the well-to-do. "Ever been here?" Charlie asked as he pulled Samantha's chair for her.

"No. Is this better than the one next door?"

"Infinitely," said Charlie. Without being asked, the waitress brought Charlie's favorite Friuli in a chiller.

"So, I take it you've been here lots."

"Lots and lots. Thanks Cheryl," he said to the waitress. "Sometimes I even come all by myself. A lot of people go for a Sauvignon Blanc with what I'm about to order, but Cheryl here turned me on to this. Not being much an educated wine guy, I tend to stick with what is recommended."

"Until tonight, I didn't even know there was such thing as a Friuli," Samantha said. "How did you find this place?"

"One of the guys on the force was talking it up. I learned a lot of tricks in this town from other cops."

"Do you like being a cop?"

"I do. Ever think about joining up?" *Did you really just ask her that?*

"No," she chuckled. "I can't say that's ever been one of my career goals."

"How long have you been in the city?"

"Just a couple years. This apartment is the first one I had since I left Louisville."

"Looks like you're getting the hang of the place."

"Honestly, I've only been to Manhattan a few times. I work, then sleep, then get up and do it again for the most part."

Charlie checked his memory. "Where do you work? I don't think I ever heard you say."

"I work at a small gaming company, Digital Strategy. Ever hear of it?"

"I can't say that I have."

"I would be surprised if you have. It's a start up. The owner got backing from an angel investor. Two years and we don't even have a product at market. I code."

"Does that worry you?"

"Not in the slightest. I enjoy what I do, and I get a salary. If the company doesn't work out, I get another job, but I don't lose what I made."

"That's a healthy attitude."

"I can't get too wrapped up in things that are beyond my control. How about you? Worry about things you can't control?"

"On occasion. Not usually for long. I guess my biggest worries are over things that I think should be under my control."

"Like what?"

"Well, I guess it's like when I have a series of bad dreams. Ever have them?" Samantha nodded. "When that happens, I don't sleep well, and I think that I need to do something…that I need to get my head right so that I can sleep better."

"Chamomile tea."

"Tea? I thought tea…."

"No caffeine. It doesn't taste that great, but it helped me sleep when I was fighting a bout of insomnia a couple years back. I slept so well I didn't even dream."

"I'll try it." A loaf of peasant bread arrived with a plate of olive oil and balsamic vinegar. Charlie handed her the menu without looking at it.

"What do you suggest, Charlie?" asked Samantha. Her eyes looked trusting.

"I really like the chicken piccata. They use these little capers that just…well, I never really knew I liked capers until I came here."

"I'm intrigued. You get that, and I'll get the linguini ala scampi. We can share, and I can try them both," she said with a smile.

"Sounds like a plan. Ready for wine?"

"I'm always ready for wine."

They caught a cab back to their apartment building after dinner. They capped off the night with a walk around the neighborhood, including a stop at Magoon's. It was busier than usual. For some reason unknown to Charlie or Iain, whenever the Yankees and Rangers played each other, Magoon's was packed.

"Iain, who's winning?" Charlie had looked at the score on the TV and knew the answer already. Iain shook his head and a round of "Boo!" went up from the patrons in Texas garb. "You see why I love it here?" he said to Samantha. One small table toward the back was unoccupied. Charlie motioned her to grab a seat while he went to the bar for drinks. "Just a couple Coors Lights, Iain."

"Aye, and a note from your secret admirer." The excitement drained from Charlie at once. He was hoping to forget about this whole mess for one fucking night.

"Thanks, Iain."

Once he was seated at the table with Samantha, he opened the yellow envelope and pulled out a single piece of paper, folded once. His face went white as he read the words:

Statue of Liberty. One week from Thursday night. Eleven o'clock.

"What's that?" asked Samantha.

Charlie looked at her, contemplating what he might say. "Samantha, I'm going to be honest with you. There's a guy out there who doesn't like me. He's left notes for me up on the roof where I like to listen to my ball games."

"How'd he know you go there?"

"I'm pretty sure he's been following me."

"You think he was up there while you were?"

"I know he was. Left a note in the beer bottle I was drinking."

"Oh, my God, Charlie." Charlie wasn't sure whether that was a sympathetic exclamation or fear or disbelief. Samantha might have seen this concern in his eyes because she reached out and took his hand.

"None of this started before I asked you out…I swear. I honestly don't think you're in any danger, but he wants to fight me…with swords. This note is telling me when and where."

"With swords?" she asked as she took the note. "The Statue of Liberty?"

"Yeah. Piece o' work, this guy. I'm not sure why…." Charlie recalled his latest dream at that moment. Chang Huang's story of the swordfight at the giant statue of a woman with spikes on her forehead.

"Charlie?"

"Yeah…sorry about that. I just thought of something." That story was something he made up, consciously, on-the-spot. It didn't relate to anything in the past. If the stalker knew about the dream…but he hadn't had time to tell anyone about it. Except…*Gina.*

Chapter 9

Hsieh Sun stood before the General more beautiful than ever in the starlight. "General, the tavern is empty. We can talk if you would like."

"You do not need sleep?"

"I will not collapse anytime soon." She smiled. Chang Huang liked her smile, though he would not show that. The two walked in silence to the tavern. Few candles were lit in any window that Chang Huang could see from the surrounding buildings. Still, he felt that eyes were on him. He thought briefly about having Hsieh Sun go on ahead of him and meeting up a bit later, but she was not the only one who would need sleep soon. *Besides...just a dream.*

"More wine, General?"

"No. Water would be great, though. And none of this General stuff. I am Chang Huang." She disappeared and returned with two clay cups of hot water.

"I only heard part of your story, General. Towards the end. How long ago did your encounter with this assassin happen?"

Chang Huang hesitated. "Can you keep a secret? Not all of that is true." Chang Huang studied her eyes. She did not look disappointed, at least. "Captain Yuan wanted me to motivate the troops." Her eyes lit up with his reveal.

"You are a storyteller?"

"That is a polite way of putting it."

"How much is true?"

"The assassin is real, but that story does not have an ending." Her eyes turned to alarm.

"He might come here looking for you?"

"I do not believe so. He is far from here." She looked relieved.

"I do not know why life is so dangerous. Why men are so willing to kill other men. Or women. Or children. The Bao family were good people. But even if they were not so good, they did not deserve to die. Can you tell me what happened to them?"

Chang Huang's mind flashed on the massacre he stumbled onto in one of his first dreams. "I cannot tell you those details." *Police business, ma'am.* "How well did you know them?"

"I know most people in Xin. But this family paid me for some additional help. I was taught to read when I was young, and I was teaching the Bao children. I also watched over them when the parents were working sometimes. I almost did not want to take their money, as I fell in love with the children." Her eyes were beginning to water.

"Did you know the significance of an idol they owned?"

"Only a little. There was a dispute between the Bao family and another family. The Bao family was given the idol in exchange for work they did, but the other family claimed it was given in error."

"Do you know the name of the other family?"

"No. Only that they had been good friends prior to when this Kwan Yin idol was given."

"The Bao family was poor. Why did they not sell the idol?"

"The father felt it was not right to sell it. He hoped to settle the matter before he could do so, even though it had been many years since the idol had been given to them."

"Do you know why they might have been outside of the city, staying at an inn not far from here?"

"I cannot imagine why they would do that. I saw them three days ago, and was supposed to tutor them the following day.

There is no reason why they would have gone anywhere overnight, unless they fled unexpectedly."

"What is beyond the inn?" Chang Huang pointed in the direction of the massacre.

"A temple. It is at the base of the mountain range."

"A temple?" *What was the name of that monk Francis told me to see?* "Could I find…Kong…?"

"Kong Xiao?"

"Yes! Could I find him there?

"Yes. I am going to see him tomorrow. Would you like me to take you, General?"

"I would be honored. However, I must know what it would take for you to stop calling me General."

She blushed. "Time," she replied.

"Very well. Oh, one more thing." He pulled the paper he had been carrying from his purse and unfolded it. "If you can read, can you tell me what this says?" He handed her the paper.

"I am sorry, General. I do not know this language."

"I understand. I believe it is an older form of Chinese."

She handed the paper back. "I would not know."

Chang Huang memorized that the third grouping contained four characters. Then he stared at the third character in the message for several seconds. *Wake up.*

(Wednesday – August 15, 2012)

Charlie raced once again to his desk in the middle of the night and wrote the character on his notepad as best as he could remember: 十.

He added four placeholders at the end of the first line. Then he added the new symbol above the first line on the second grouping:

日 人 十 _ _   _ _ _ _

He did not wait for The Egg to research the new character. He found a current Chinese character that looked similar, except it had a line that ran horizontally across the bottom. The symbol meant soldier or scholar or gentleman. Then he found one without the extra line, which meant the number "10." He entered all of this into his dream journal. He almost put the journal away but stopped and added, "The stalker's challenge to me is at the Statue of Liberty. Just like the story I told in my dream two nights ago." He shuffled over to his coffee maker and inserted one of his brand-new filters into the filter basket. He retrieved his bag of ground beans from the freezer and watched the remaining contents pour onto his counter next to the filter basket. He brought the bag up to his eyes and saw that the creases had directed the coffee grounds to one corner of the open end, causing him to miss the filter basket altogether. *Damn it!*

Gina arrived a few minutes before 11:30 and took Charlie to an old spaghetti house in west Brooklyn. They spoke little in the car, and Charlie's eyes went straight to his menu upon sitting down. He could feel Gina looking at him and felt satisfied that he set up an uncomfortable vibe. It was similar to an interrogation technique he'd employ to create an uncomfortable atmosphere with a subject. Part of him felt guilty for doing so, but Gina was a cop, too, and supposedly could take it. After ordering, he looked up at Gina and smiled. It was a friendly smile meant to juxtapose the ice he had laid down so far. He would be both the good cop and bad cop. But still did not talk until Gina broke the silence. Which she did, encouraged by his smile. "How was your date?"

"It went well," he said with a slight blush. "At least from my perspective. She could be calling her girlfriends about the weirdo she went out with last night."

"I'd find that hard to believe, Charlie." He let her start to feel comfortable again. "Where'd you take her?"

"Poppy's."

"Nice. Did you suggest the chicken piccata?"

"You know I did. She seemed to really like it. Then we stopped by Magoon's." Charlie allowed himself to show a hint of darkness at the mention of Magoon's. "I'll probably take her into Manhattan next time. She's hardly been there since she moved here. That is, of course, if there's a second date."

"Come on, Charlie, there'll be a second date."

"You think?

"Yeah, I do." After the food came, Gina asked about his latest dream. She asked if Hsieh Sun had given him any insight into the Bao family or the idol. He told her there were no "aha!" moments. Then he changed tracks.

"I think I should turn down the job with Lextalt." Gina was about to put a fork full of spaghetti in her mouth but stopped at Charlie's comment. It was clear she was going to say something but couldn't find the words. "That man Francis knew about my dreams. I can't trust him." Again, Charlie could see Gina's mind desperately searching for the right thing to say. "You think I should still go through with it."

She nodded. "I do, Charlie. It's certainly your decision, but Francis was at least open about knowing your dream. I don't know as I trust him either, but if you separate yourself from him, it will be harder to figure out what he's up to."

"That makes some sense. I haven't made up my mind, yet, but I should by tomorrow. I just get a weird feeling every time I think of that conversation yesterday." He took a bite of his pasta salad. Though it probably had too much Italian sausage to truly be called a salad.

"Then use it." Charlie looked up. "Use that feeling. That's your instincts talking to you."

"Why does that sound so familiar."

"You may recall saying that to a young, female rookie four years ago. You were right back then."

"Okay, I'll use it. There's something else that's giving me an uncomfortable feeling, Gina." He intentionally said "Gina" instead of "G."

"Something happen?"

"Yeah. Last night, at Magoon's." He pulled out the note Iain had given him. "My stalker left this for me with Iain." She read the note.

"Charlie, this is…."

"Just like my dream?"

"Yes…the Statue of Liberty?"

"I'm trying real hard, Gina. The other stuff so far, even that stupid mash-up doll, has some possible explanation. Maybe there is something in my past that made me dream of that massacre, and that something in my past involves someone else who would think to leave that doll on my roof. But the story of the giant lady with spikes on her head…that was a story that I made up to entertain the troops in my dream. I made it up, consciously. There's no way my stalker could have known about that story."

"Then why does he want to meet you at the Statue?"

"He had to have found out. Arranging a sword fight on Liberty Island is way too complicated unless there was meaning behind it. But the only way he could know is if someone told him. But I didn't tell anyone about that dream, Gina. Except…."

"Except…me." She kept her eyes on the table. She wouldn't look up at Charlie. Charlie first took this as a sign of guilt, but then he noticed her eyebrows scrunched together. She was thinking. "Charlie, I can't blame you for thinking it," she looked up into his eyes, "but I didn't tell anyone about your dream."

Now it was Charlie's turn to look down at the table. All his interrogation plans melted. He could no longer remember what his response should be to her denial of guilt. He wished he had never broached the subject. "Gina, I know you didn't…."

"Do you? Do you, really?" She pushed her spaghetti away. "I don't feel like eating anymore. You go up and pay. Get a takeout box if you want." He didn't. "I'm taking you back to your apartment. Think good and hard about who your friends are today and tomorrow, before we go back to work on Friday. You need them now more than ever, and I'm your goddamned partner. The one you trust your life with. If we're going to stay partners, I need to know that trust is there. And remember, this decision isn't completely up to you anymore. I need to decide if I can trust you."

"Gina, I'm…."

"Don't. Don't say you're sorry. Not yet anyway. Think about how you feel. No more talking. Pay for our lunch and meet me in the car."

After the most uncomfortable ride in Charlie's life, he retreated to his apartment. His intention was to hide away the next couple days until facing Gina before their shift on Friday. He'd see her at the funeral but was contemplating skipping that. Then his plan to be a hermit was interrupted by a knock on his door. He was sure Gina would be there when he opened it.

"Samantha?"

"Hi, Charlie. Do you know what today is?"

"Uh…Wednesday?"

"No. Well, yes, but it's also August 15th."

"Ah, the Ides of August."

"Is that right?"

"I don't know. I mean if March 15th is the Ides of March, then…."

"It's India's Independence Day!"

"Oh…." Charlie thought for a moment. He took a hard look at Samantha. "Wait…are you Indian?"

She laughed. "No. But my boss is, and he decided to give everyone the day off. Honestly, I don't think he even knew it was India's Independence Day until he heard it on the radio this morning."

"Nice! What are you going to do with the day?"

"Enjoy it! I've been relaxing so far. Thought about you at lunch but saw you getting into a car." *She's stalking me…awesome!*

"Yeah, had I known you were off, but sounds like you just found out today, yourself."

"Yep. So where are we going?"

Charlie had never been the sought-after type. He decided he liked it. "I can't think of a better place to spend India's independence than Manhattan."

The heat and humidity danced a Tango through the gridlined streets of downtown. Charlie balanced a picnic basket and a folded blanket on his lap as the taxi sped along Park Ave. He had the driver turn left on 34th Street so that he could show Samantha the view of Macy's the broadcasters show during the parade. "Oh my God!" she shouted. "I didn't even realize that this is what I wanted to see. I've seen it so many times on TV, but it's so amazing to see up close!" The driver took a right on 8th Ave. without being instructed.

"Forgive me for taking you to the tourist spots. Sometime when we have more time we'll hang in the East Village and the rest of Lower Manhattan."

"I don't mind the tourist stuff at all. There's a reason the tourists go there, Charlie."

Charlie had a reason for picnicking in Central Park. The south end was near the Lextalt building, and it was in the park where Francis revealed that he knew Charlie's dream. It was also near where he first saw his stalker. Though he had no idea what he expected would happen today. Maybe he was trying to prove something…that he wasn't afraid of them. Of any of them. Whatever the reason, Charlie felt the need to be there.

As the cab circumnavigated Columbus Circle, recognition grew in Samantha's face. "Is this Central Park? I've always wanted to go here!"

"Two years in Brooklyn, and you haven't been to this place you've always wanted to go?"

"It's been a fast two years. You know I have relatives that spent their whole lives in Beijing and have never been to The Great Wall?"

Charlie chuckled. "I'm not judging. Just glad I get to show it to you." To the driver, he said, "Just pull over here."

The heat felt like a brick wall when they stepped out of the air-conditioned cab. They walked far enough into the park where they couldn't see any of the streets easily and spread out the blanket. "I haven't been on a picnic since I was six," said Samantha. "This is nice, Charlie. You had no time to prepare, yet you still show me a good time."

"I usually do better when I have no…." Charlie looked to his right. *You're here, aren't you.* He scanned the trees at the edge of the park.

"Charlie?"

He looked back at Samantha. "Sorry, I thought I saw…." His neck swiveled back to the treeline. *There…that tree.* "Gimme a second. Stay here." He wasn't afraid, but her life was not his to risk. It wasn't the stalker. It wasn't Francis or Harold. He knew this. When he got to the tree and stepped behind it, he didn't see anyone. He felt like he was being watched, but whoever it was hid themselves well. As he turned to head back towards Samantha, he saw two words carved into the tree: "Richard Harris."

He walked slowly back to Samantha with a quizzical look on his face. "Charlie, what is it?"

"I don't know. Maybe nothing. Maybe a message for me. Do you know a Richard Harris?"

She thought for a second. "Just the movie star. Why?"

"What movies was he in?"

"Are you kidding? Well, there's 'Patriot Games,' 'Camelot,' 'Robin and Marion.' Nothing? More recently he was the original Albus Dumbledore, but he died so he was only in a couple of Harry Potter movies. Let me see…'A Man Called Horse….'"

"'A Man Called Horse'?"

"Yeah, I've not seen that one, but I've heard it pop up from time to time. I think mostly playing Trivial Pursuit."

"Hmmm."

"Does that movie mean something to you?"

"It would mean more if it were called 'A Horse called Horse.'" Samantha didn't say anything. "Someone might be trying to say something to me. But why wouldn't they just carve 'Horse' into the tree?"

"Would 'Horse' have meant the same thing to you?"

Charlie thought. "No, I don't think I would have thought anything of the word 'Horse.' But that's where my mind went. So if it isn't meant for me, then I'm just reading into it. But if it was meant for me, then it was written by someone who really knows how I think."

"What does it mean to you?"

"Well…." Charlie was not sure he wanted to discuss this with Samantha just yet. But better now than after they found themselves in the middle of a relationship. "I've been having these recurring dreams. In it, I have a horse...named 'Horse.'" He waited for Samantha to say something, but she didn't. "I've had other people reference things that are happening in my dreams. Most of these things can be explained. My department shrink says I may have had an event in my past that is shared by someone else."

"Your stalker?"

"Yes, my stalker. Say, you're taking this better than I expected."

"Don't read too much into it. I'm listening, that's all. I'll decide later how crazy you are." She smiled. "But remember, I'm the girl who's into time travel movies. I love a good story. So please continue."

"Fair enough. There's other things I've told to a close friend, and I kind of thought maybe she said something about one of those details to the stalker...or to somebody else who told that detail to the stalker."

"That note last night…mentioning the Statue of Liberty. Was that from your dream?"

"It was. But the horse…I don't think I told that to anyone. I also can't imagine that I have some shared event with someone that would cause me to dream of a horse named 'Horse.'"

"Well, that tree carving might have nothing to do with your dream. It sounds like these dreams are really getting to you. You should try the chamomile tea."

"Yeah, it was late last night after we left the bar, but I should pick some up today."

"I'll take you to my tea guy."

"You gotta tea guy?"

"Doesn't everyone?"

After the picnic, Samantha took Charlie to a tea house in Williamsburg. Charlie had been by it before but never stopped in. It actually looked like an antique store from the outside. The gold-painted letters announcing "Joy's Tea Garden" were faded and chipped. Without looking at them intentionally, it wasn't easy to infer what was inside. At night, when the lights were on inside, people could be seen through the windows around small tables sipping from teacups. But Charlie had only been by it during the day when the outside was brighter than the inside. A little bell rang when they stepped inside. An ancient, short, Asian woman looked up from a crossword puzzle spread out upon a counter next to an old-fashioned cash register where the numbers would pop up on little cards. "Sung Mei!" she said as she pushed her reading glasses down on her nose.

"Ni hao, A Yi," Samantha responded.

"Your guy is a gal," Charlie interjected.

"Yes, Charlie. A Yi has been a huge help to me since I moved here." She turned back to A Yi. "I've brought a friend who needs your help."

"My help?" she asked. "You didn't come for more of my Xī Hú Lóng Jǐng?" Her accent was pure Brooklyn.

"Actually, I could use some of that." Turning back to Charlie, "It's West Lake Dragon Well tea. I first tried it in Hangzhou, and A Yi's tea takes me back there." To A Yi, "Charlie here is having bad dreams."

"Then he wants chamomile."

"He might not know he wants it, but he does."

"Chamomile isn't for everyone. I will give him a sample. Should last a couple of nights." She turned her gaze to Charlie.

He suddenly realized that, below her salt and pepper hair, her eyes were a striking shade of blue. "You try this. If it works for you, you come back and buy more. Keep me in business," she smiled.

"Thank you, but I can pay for this."

"No, I have spoken. But if you like, you can pay for Sung Mei's Xī Hú Lóng Jǐng."

"Deal," he replied, "as long as I don't have to pronounce it." He hoped he didn't sound insensitive.

"If you can pronounce it correctly, next time I'll give you a free bag."

He tried.

"Close. Practice. Samantha can teach you."

She handed him a quarter pound bag with a $14 label on it. "This must be good tea," he said.

"It's all in the perspective of the drinker. Taste is a good memory retriever."

"You should meet my friend, Iain. Says the same thing about Scotch."

"Scotch and tea share a common trait."

"They do?"

"Yes…I love them both!" she said.

That evening, Charlie went up to the roof to listen to the Yankees beat the Rangers three to two. Though he barely heard the game. His mind was occupied with thoughts of Samantha and Hsieh Sun. He was talking to her the previous night before waking up, but it seemed like weeks ago. Usually, his insecurities would get in the way when dating women he didn't know very well. But he felt a sort of confidence with Samantha he didn't know he had. He thought that maybe General Chang's interactions with Hsieh Sun gave him this confidence. He smiled when he thought of Hsieh Sun, then shook it off. *I'm not in love with a dream girl.*

Nevertheless, it was difficult to shake off the idea that he was falling in love in two different eras. Both Hsieh Sun and Samantha made him feel the same way. He had not so much as kissed either of them, yet he felt that a bond was growing with each.

At the same time, he realized this was diverting him from a guilt he was feeling about his mistrust of Gina. There was too much he didn't understand about his dreams. Accusing Gina was premature at best…betrayal of a deep friendship at worst.

When he came back down from the roof, he made some chamomile tea and prayed for a dreamless sleep.

Chapter 10

Chang Huang looked up from the message on the paper and saw that Hsieh Sun was more tired than she let on. He remembered instantly where he left off in their conversation, and that they had been discussing travelling to see the monk, Kong Xiao. “When do I meet you tomorrow?” he asked.

“Be here just before midday. Captain Yuan will be joining us.”

Damn. “Good. I will see you then.”

As with the last time Chang Huang slept within Charlie’s dream, he slept and woke without drifting back into modern day New York. It was still early when he rose from his bed, so he knew he would be dragging the rest of the day. The tavern was more populated in the morning. Breakfast was popular, it seemed. He hoped to catch Hsieh Sun, but she obviously had enough sense to sleep later than “the general.” Chang Huang sent a boy who had just finished eating to fetch Lieutenant Chai from the encampment so that he could discuss the investigation. Chai Wen was surprised to see two plates on the general’s table and sat down slowly, almost as if he feared a trick. But at Chang Huang’s insistence, he sat and enjoyed the food in front of him. Once Lt. Chai looked more relaxed, Chang Huang shared what he had learned from Yuan Lin concerning his relationship with the Bao family, as well as Hsieh Sun's connection.

"General, do you suspect either of them as the killer?"

He was tempted to say that he did not feel either of them were involved but did not want to influence his own bias on the lieutenant. "I do not have enough information to form an opinion, yet. What have you found out?"

"Little, sir. The people in the other apartments knew the Bao family, but none seemed to be aware of the idol they kept. I will need more time to question them."

"Do so quickly but do not sacrifice quality for speed. The more time goes by, the less likely we are to find the killer."

"Yes, General."

After breakfast, Chang Huang found he had plenty of time to study the message further before meeting up with Yuan Lin and Hsieh Sun. Memorizing one character was taking too long, so he devised a new plan. His first step was to capture the size of each character grouping. Once he had the number of blanks correct, he would see if he could determine whether or not one of the characters he had copied so far were repeated in the message. He would memorize their placement. Each time after that, when he remembered a new character, he would attempt to remember where else in the message that character appeared. This would still take a while but should be quicker than one at a time.

He already knew the first three groupings were two characters, three characters, and four characters. Looking at the paper back in his room at the inn, he counted the characters in the remaining groupings: three, three, four, two, four, four on the first line; seven on the single grouping on the middle line; and five, two, five, two, five, seven. *Okay, I can do this.* This was too many groupings to remember simply by rote memorization. He had to use a pneumonic method to remember this sequence of numbers.

The middle line was easy. He could remember seven. The last line was not too bad either. Five and two alternating (for a total of five character groupings), followed by seven. If he remembered nothing else, he would remember the last two lines. The first line was the most difficult. But still, it could be managed. *Six groupings after the three I already know: the first two are three and the last two are four. The middle two? Four and two…forty-two. Where have I heard…oh yeah! The answer to the question of life! Thank you, Douglas Adams.*

He wrote this sequence at the bottom of the paper with the message. He would look at it from time to time throughout the day: 334244,7,525257. As much as he wanted to will himself awake, he felt that Charlie had to make a decision about the security contract soon and did not want to do so without first visiting the monk Kong Xiao. It occurred to him that doing this might be playing into Francis' hand, but he had to trust that he could keep his own head straight—that more information was better than less information.

The sun was almost straight above when he approached the tavern. Hsieh Sun and Yuan Lin would wait for him even if he came hours late, but Chang Huang wanted to maintain a reputation of punctuality. Yuan Lin had arranged for Horse to be saddled and ready for the general. "Nice day for a ride in the desert," Chang Huang said.

"I hope you rested well, General," said Yuan Lin.

"Indeed," Chang Huang lied. "How far do we ride?"

Hsieh Sun answered, "Four hours. We will spend an hour there and return."

"The captain and I will follow your lead." Chang Huang said. Then added, "Just a moment." He pet Horse on the nose and dismounted. He had just spied the man from the tavern last night—the one who was talking about his dream. *Du Hung…was that his name?* Chang Huang looked up at Hsieh Sun and said, "I will be right back."

Du Hung was about to enter the tavern when Chang Huang caught up with him. "What part of New York are you from?" Chang Huang asked.

Du Hung pivoted around in an expression of fright followed closely by one of amusement. "Are you the part of my subconscious that can tell me what the fuck is going on here?"

"Something like that." *Interesting, my subconscious is accusing me of being this guy's subconscious.* "Answer my question."

"I am from Queens, but I bet you already knew that."

"Maybe. Tell me your name. The one you use in New York."

"Martin. Martin Killjoy."

"Martin Killjoy." *Martin Killjoy, Martin Killjoy, Martin Killjoy. I hope I can remember that.* "What do you do?"

"You my subconscious or a cop?"

"Both. Please humor me on this. I will make it worth your while."

"I run a Private Storage. Are you going to tell me this dream has to do with unit 4358? Because I already guessed that."

"Maybe."

"How you gonna make this worth my while? The only thing that would do would be to make me stop dreaming of this hideous place."

"I will get back to you on that."

"Whatever," he said and continued into the tavern. Chang Huang walked back to Yuan Lin and Hsieh Sun. *Martin Killjoy of Private Storage in Queens.*

For the first hour, the trio rode in silence. The Charlie part of Chang Huang could only put up with that for so long. Though he was not sure of the protocol on casual conversation in old China among officers and civilians, he had to be true to himself. "Captain Yuan, how long have you served the emperor?"

If the captain was uncomfortable with this question, he did not show it. "Nearly my entire life, sir. As a boy, I was the water bearer on occasion for a general who accepted provisions from my father's farm." Over the low dunes, they could see the roof to the inn becoming visible where the Bao family was killed.

"You were given leadership for your merit?"

"I cannot say. I have accepted the roles that have been assigned to me." *And humble is his middle name.*

"Hsieh Sun, I believe this man has earned his rank through valor. What do you think?"

"I would not dare doubt the word of a general." A smile spread across Captain Yuan's face.

"Permission to speak freely, sir?" Yuan Lin asked.

"You are ordered to speak freely."

"When did you join the military?"

"I was conscripted. I was not a violent man by nature. Previously, I taught arithmetic and writing." *So now Chang Huang speaks through the holes in my "memory." This would have been helpful last night.* "I became a lieutenant when my lieutenant and sergeant had been killed. I was reluctant."

"How long were you a soldier before this happened?" asked Hsieh Sun.

"Four weeks."

"And you remained lieutenant after the battle?" asked Yuan Lin.

"I was lucky. I did not know what I was doing, so I started barking orders…whatever came to mind. What came out of my mouth might have killed us as easily as saved us. But one thing kept me from holding my voice: doing nothing would have certainly doomed us all."

"Then you truly earned your leadership," said Yuan Lin. "Many men in the same circumstance still would not have taken action. I have seen it many times. But I should hold my tongue on that."

"Do not fear discussing other generals in front of me, Yuan Lin. We are off the record."

"I am sure you have seen the same, General."

"Of course."

"Do either of you have a family?" Hsieh Sun broke in.

"No," both Yuan Lin and Chang Huang said simultaneously.

Hsieh Sun smiled. It amused her that some men had no interest in family, that some could be so dedicated to their career or art that they would miss out on something quite important to her. Though at nineteen, she was close to missing her window of opportunity. Chang Huang could see all of this in her smile.

"War does not leave much time for families, I am afraid. And there is plenty of war to fight," Chang Huang replied. Yuan Lin did not add to this. The tone in both men turned to alert in an instant. "Yuan Lin, did you see…?"

"Yes, General. Do you want me to…?"

"We will both go. Hsieh Sun, if we are overtaken, or even look like that might happen, do not hesitate…ride back to Xin as fast as your horse will take you." She nodded. What Chang Huang and Yuan Lin had seen was a shadow of a man stretching out across the sand from the corner of the inn. The man must have seen his own shadow, as he dropped to shorten it and moved back further behind the building. "You go around back. I will face them from the front."

"Yes, sir." Yuan Lin circled wide towards the back of the inn. Chang Huang thought Yuan Lin would stay close to the building in case the men had arrows so that he could engage them up close before they could aim, but he must have decided that he would be the distraction by circling wide, allowing Chang Huang to gain an advantage. Chang Huang moved closer to the inn and approached the corner from which he had seen the shadow. He moved slow and quiet, hoping Horse would not choose this moment to nicker or growl. When he was close to the corner, he waited. He did not have to wait long. From the opposite side of the house, he heard Yuan Lin shout something in a commanding voice. The men hiding on the other side of the building would either be running towards Yuan Lin in combat mode, or away from him. Chang Huang nudged Horse to trot casually around the corner and saw three men running in his direction. Upon seeing the mounted general, all three stopped and moved their hands to grab at their swords. Before any could draw, the middle man fell forward on his face with a feathered stick protruding from his back. The other two stayed their hands. They were dressed poorly compared to the fallen man. "How much was he paying you?" Chang Huang asked.

"Equal portions," said the one on the left. Yuan Lin arrived and hung his bow over his shoulder.

"You are fools. My captain likely saved your lives by taking this one down." He looked to Yuan Lin. "Check to see if there are any more inside."

"Yes, sir." Chang Huang ran through his memory of his last trek through the inn. There was nothing of value left. It was possible these men did not know that, but something felt wrong. This entire encounter was for his benefit. But no one could have known he would be through here in enough time to set something like this up. He only decided last night to make this journey.

"All clear, General," said Yuan Lin. I should not have killed the leader. He was hired by someone else. These two would not know this." Indeed, the two unidentified men, now on their knees, were looking up at Yuan Lin and Chang Huang alternately with confusion glaring from their faces. Yuan Lin dismounted and walked around the two kneeling men and stood beside Chang Huang.

"Do not berate yourself, Captain. How could you know he was the leader?"

"He was the last to turn away from me when I called for them to drop their weapons."

"Please do not kill us!" the one on the right cried. "I just want to feed my children."

"Quiet," Yuan Lin answered. He said this calmly but with such intensity that neither of the kneeling men retorted. "How did you men get here? Where are your horses?"

"We were dropped here," said the man on the left. "Our transportation will return soon."

"These men were left to die here," Yuan Lin said. "Do you want me to go back to get rides to escort these men back to Xin?"

"No. Leave them a water pouch. We have plenty in reserve. If they are still here when we get back, we will take them on the back of our horses." Yuan Lin looked as though he wanted to question this but decided that this event was not covered by Chang Huang's "off the record" decree.

"Yes, sir." Yuan Lin tossed a water bag to the men. "If you want to live, stay inside where it is cooler. If you are not here when we return tonight, and I see you later in Xin, or anywhere for that matter, I will kill you on sight." The kneeling men did not mistake Yuan Lin's promise for an empty threat.

On the way back to Hsieh Sun, Yuan Lin asked, "Who do you suppose hired those men?"

"The same man who killed the Bao family. The same man who took the Kwan Yin idol."

"What purpose did they serve?"

"They are spying on us."

"Do we continue on, or should we go back to Xin?" she asked.

"We continue," Chang Huang replied. "If the man who hired them knew we were coming out this way, he will not learn anything new from these men. They can only confirm his guess. Stay alert, but I do not feel it is his plan to kill us. He could have done that by now.

(Thursday – August 16, 2012)

It had been one of the longest dreams he had so far, but meeting the monk would take an additional night. *Let's see, the middle grouping was seven characters.* At his desk, he grabbed a new sheet of paper added seven blanks where the second line would be. *The last line ended in a seven-character grouping...beginning with...two, five, two, five, two? No, the other way around: five, two, five, two, five.* He wrote down blanks according to this pattern. *The first line is the hardest. I already had the first three groupings. After that, there were two three-character groupings and two four-character groupings. But there was something in between. The meaning of life? No.* Charlie looked at his bookshelf and saw his copy of *The Hitchhiker's Guide to the Galaxy*. Charlie tapped his pencil on his paper. *The answer to the question of life! Forty-two. Three, three, four, two, four, four.* He inserted underscores according to these numbers:

日人十__ ____ ___ ___ ____ __ ____ _____

____

_____ __ _____ __ _____ _______

But there's something else, isn't there? Charlie studied his notepad and reflected on his dream. *Martin. Martin. Martin Killjoy...of Private Storage in Queens!*

Paul was manning his station on the steps of Gina's apartment building when Charlie approached, whittling some large stick into a figure that had yet to be defined. He looked at Charlie through the corner of his eye without saying hi as if he knew something was wrong between him and Gina. Charlie stopped a few feet from him. "She upset, Pauley?"

"You know she is. What did you say to her?"

"The wrong thing. I'm gonna make it up to her."

"Good luck with that," Paul said and scraped his pocketknife across the stick.

Gina sat on her sofa, staring at a blank TV through the steam of her coffee when a knock at the door brought her back to reality. She opened her door as wide as her safety chain would allow and peered through with red, puffy eyes under disheveled hair. Charlie was afraid she would slam the door, but she just stared back at him without saying a word.

"You're far from stupid," he said. She continued to stare without changing her expression. "It would take a real moron to give my stalker information about my dream without knowing he would throw it back at me."

"Maybe I assumed you would think that and used it to my advantage."

"No." She hesitated, then closed the door and unfastened the safety chain. She opened the door a crack and turned to walk back to the sofa.

Charlie opened the door slowly, then followed her further into the apartment. "Coffee?" she offered. He sat down next to her and held onto her hands.

"I'm sorry."

She pulled her hands away. "You have no reason to trust me over anyone else. This situation you're in is weird. But there's an explanation. Until you understand what's really happening, there are a thousand explanations…some of them logical and some of them not so much. Some of them will make your friends look like enemies."

"I understand…."

"No, you don't." She sighed with impatience. "You can't understand. And I think it's dangerous to think that you do."

"I don't know what that means."

"It means, let's focus on this case with an open mind. I'm your partner, and I'm your friend. There will be a time when we all understand what is going on. Until then, you either trust me or you don't. Jumping to conclusions will kill our friendship."

At first, Charlie looked as if he had been wounded. But that quickly melted, and he was able to form a smile. "Okay, he said."

She matched his smile. "Now do you want coffee?"

"Yes."

His cell had been off when he was at Gina's and had forgotten to turn it back on as another cab took him back to his apartment. He only realized it was off after changing into his dress uniform for the ceremony for Fred and Peter. Gina had left a message asking if he wanted a ride. Figuring it was too late, he called her back to let her know he would grab a cab. His call went straight to voicemail. He was half relieved and half disappointed that she didn't answer. But after he left his message and powered down his phone again, he let it slide from his mind.

The service was held in Prospect Park before everyone was moved to the funeral at Green-Wood Cemetery. Being there was more palliative than he imagined. It was uncomfortable seeing Fred's and Peter's families at first and was afraid they might not be as understanding as his fellow officers about how they were killed and why. But he faced them. He was glad he had, too, as they embraced him and told him how grateful they were that their deaths may have saved Charlie's life.

Gina and he said little to each other but embraced and cried together. The emotional coaster Charlie felt he was on with her seemed to be set aside for the moment. Today was not about them.

Chapter 11

Chang Huang took the lead as they continued South. He looked at Hsieh Sun, then at Captain Yuan. *I can't do this now. Not tonight. Wake up.*

(Friday – August 17, 2012)

Charlie woke up shortly after falling asleep. He went back to sleep and slept through the night without another dream. When he woke up, he felt refreshed.

"How was your 'weekend?'"

"I've had better, Doc. But I've had worse. I got some questions, though. Mind if we skip to them? I think just describing my dream to you isn't helping."

"These are your sessions, Charlie. You set the agenda." Charlie had hoped his bad feelings from his previous session would have dissipated before now, but clearly, Thomason was holding at least pieces of a grudge.

"Good. Thanks. I want to know if it's possible to make suggestions to people to influence their dreams."

"I don't believe so. That is, I'm sure it happens unintentionally all the time. Things people say to you manifest, but I get the feeling you are talking about something more direct and intentional." Charlie nodded. "To do something like that, they would have to understand the constructs of the psyche of the 'target' for lack of a better word. Unless you have that machine from that DiCaprio movie a couple of summers ago."

"Then I can't explain what is happening. People I don't know seem to know what is happening in my dreams. How can they know, Doc?"

"I don't have an answer for you. I think you need a dream expert, and I'm afraid the field is as about as concrete as long-range weather forecasting. So much of dream analysis is theory. Plus, finding an expert who is legitimate might be difficult."

"So, what do I do?"

"Have you tried chamomile tea?"

The beginning of his Friday shift was the first time Charlie and Gina had worked together since their uncomfortable conversation. She came to his desk with police station coffee and scones from the bakery outside her apartment. "Fuel for the evening," she said as she set them down on his desk.

"Hi, G." *Still weird. There's an awful lot of tension here for someone I haven't slept with.* "Any thoughts for tonight?"

"I do. Let's meet up with Deathrage and Peterson first though. Still their case."

"Good idea. But I don't want them to know about the stalker's challenge at Liberty Island." Gina nodded her head, though she didn't look as though she fully agreed. After roll call, Gina and Charlie joined Deathrage and Peterson in a small conference room just off the main hall. Deathrage showed no sign of being stumped in the investigation, but Peterson made up for it with her lost puppy-dog eyes. Gina and Charlie sipped coffees as they entered and took their seats at the long, steel table.

Greg started the conversation by saying, "I hope you both enjoyed your weekend. Nora and I interviewed a few people from your neighborhood and from the warehouse while you were out. Your stalker seems to be invisible at night. I don't get the feeling from the people we interviewed that they were hiding anything…like being paid off or anything. I have an idea what we should do next, but I'd like to hear your thoughts first, Charlie."

Charlie started to open his mouth, but Gina was faster. "Actually, I have an idea. Officially, we patrol our sector."

"Off the record?" Greg asked.

"Charlie and I need to visit Francis and Harold. They're the ones that hired Charlie for the security detail."

Charlie cut in, "Woah, what do we expect to accomplish there? And who's going to cover our beat?"

"Sarge's taken care of all that. And as far as what we expect to accomplish, let's just say play it out and see where it goes. I got a hunch."

"So, you do think it's connected?" Nora asked.

"Don't know, but it's the best I got. Either of you got anything better?"

Greg thought for a moment. "Nothing better. Why don't you two do that, and we'll save my thoughts for tomorrow. While you're doing that, maybe Nora and I stop by some of the places this stalker's been. Like the theater and that pub Charlie's always going on about. I'll contact the detectives in Queens and arrange to check out Scottish pubs over there."

"I'd hold off on that last part," Charlie replied. "That sounds like another lead the stalker expects me to follow. And we know what happens when other cops follow up on those trails. But checking out the theater and Magoon's is a good idea."

"Makes sense."

"You might want to have someone run a check on a Martin Killjoy who runs a Private Storage in Queens. There may be a connection between him and the stalker." Gina shot him an inquisitive look. Charlie's eyes told her that he would explain later.

"What kind of connection?"

"Harold mentioned the name." Gina could tell this was a lie. "If there does turn out to be any connection between Harold and my stalker, this guy could be important."

Greg turned to Nora. "You ready to head out?"

"Ready as a teddy." The other three looked at her. "Don't ask," she replied to their unasked question. Greg and Nora left the room while Charlie and Gina stayed behind.

"So, what is this hunch," Charlie asked after they were alone.

"We can theorize all we want about how someone might know your dreams or we can talk to the one person who admits to knowing what is going on in your noggin at night." Charlie felt the tension begin to melt away. Something about Gina's positivity snapped him out of whatever funk he had been feeling.

"I can't believe I didn't think of that. I'm a cop, right? What can a head shrink tell me that Francis couldn't?"

"Don't be hard on yourself. I've said before, you're too close to it to see things clearly. Grab your coffee and let's get on the road. Now who is Martin Killjoy?" He told Gina about the man in his dream who believes Charlie is a part of *his* dream.

Lights were shining through the windows of the 44th floor of the Lextalt building. "How did you know he'd be here?" Charlie asked.

"I arranged it."

"He's expecting us?"

"Yep. I told him that we wanted to discuss his comments about the monk in your dream. He said he would be happy to talk to us, but he said something else, too. He said that talking about it will not do you as much good as following his advice."

"I am following his advice; that's the problem. I'm not 100% sure I should." The two showed their identification to security and took the elevator up to 44. Once the doors slid open, Charlie took Gina to the only place he knew how to find: the conference room where he was first interviewed. The hallway was empty, but soft light dripped through glass doors that lead to various offices.

"Did you see the monk last night, Charlie?" Francis asked as soon as they entered the conference room. Harold, nor anyone else, was anywhere in sight.

"Not yet. We're on our way to see him."

"Good." Charlie made a mental note: *Francis did not seem surprised at the word "we" in his answer*. "He will explain things that I cannot. Sure, I could tell you much of what you need to know. But you would not believe me. I can tell you this much: you are not the only person, or even the first person, to dream of another time and another place."

"Yeah, this is helpful."

"Francis," Gina broke in, "you told Charlie to go to a monk, a specific monk: Kong Xiao. Where did you hear that name?"

"Very well. I have dreamed as you do, Charlie. Not the same dream, mind you, but quite similar. That is how I know the name Kong Xiao." Gina and Francis both looked at Charlie.

"If you dreamed like I do, and you know of Kong Xiao, other people do, too." He looked at Gina. "That's what I should be researching. Xiao is spelled X-I-A-O?" Francis nodded.

At the end of the shift, Charlie saw a note on his desk which read:

Martin Killjoy
Resides at 1300 31st Ave.
Owns Private Storage 32405 on 19th and Broadway.

Before heading up to his second-floor apartment, he stopped by Samantha's door on the off chance she was still up. A light under her door gave him some hope. But as he raised his hand to knock, he heard voices that didn't sound like they came from the television. He started to turn away, then realized that one of the voices was from a man. *It doesn't matter, Charlie. Could be anyone, and she doesn't owe you anything, anyway.* He really believed that. Until he heard Samantha's voice unmistakably say, "I love you, too." *Fuck.*

Charlie started up his computer as soon as he arrived home. Though he was tired and didn't feel like doing research, he decided he needed a little more info on Kong Xiao before meeting the monk in person. Initial searching pulled up many hits. The name was quite common. He had to add "monk" and then "Xin" and "Gobi Desert" to the search before he found anything of interest. What he was expecting was to learn that this was a common dream symbol, something Carl Jung called an archetype of the collective unconscious to which Gina had alluded earlier. There was one hit on the name of a monk called Kong "Shao" of the Shaolin Temple that caught his attention. The temple, of course, was not near the Gobi Desert, but after he was cleansed of the temple…*whatever that means*…by Emperor Yongzheng in 1535, a song was written about him facing a great evil in the desert and banishing it into a dream.
Shao...Xiao...sounds the same to Western ears. What are you doing, Charlie? You're a police officer, not someone who chases rumors and old songs. Get your head back in the game. He shut down his computer, turned off the light, and left modern New York behind.

Chapter 12

I can only take so much more of this, Chang Huang thought. He looked over and saw Hsieh Sun look away. She and Yuan Lin were obviously closer in age, both about twenty years younger than Chang Huang. He had seen Yuan Lin looking her way more than once on the ride through the desert. Yet Yuan Lin was earning Chang Huang's respect with each encounter. *I will not compete with Yuan Lin. Hsieh Sun will do what she will. I will not attempt to influence her path.*

"Why is it you wish to visit Kong Xiao, General?" It was Hsieh Sun asking, but Chang Huang knew Yuan Lin had wanted to ask this from the start of the trip. It was not his place to question a General, however.

"Would you believe I had a vision?"

"You had a vision?" she asked.

"Not so concretely. But I do believe I was meant to take counsel from this monk. Yuan Lin, you are going there to pray?"

"Yes. For my father. And for strength and guidance. Few soldiers are fortunate enough to reach your age, General. I wish to be one of the few."

"May you outlive me, Captain." Chang Huang meant that with all sincerity. As interesting as it was to visit old China, he loved New York that much more, and he was sure that he could not continue living in both worlds for long.

"Hsieh Sun, have you ever seen a desert dragon?" This was the first time Chang Huang heard Yuan Lin speak so casually in front of him.

"Why, no, Captain. I have only seen dragons in the mountains," she said as she tossed him a somewhat mischievous smile.

"Look to the west." Both Chang Huang and Hsieh Sun looked in that direction. A dust devil, large enough to look like a small tornado rose from the sand. All three recognized it as harmless, but it inspired a hushed awe. In their silence, they could make out the whispered roar of the sand crystals sliding against one another as they were pulled skyward.

"It is beautiful!" Hsieh Sun said. Yuan Lin smiled.

The three rode in silence for a bit. Chang Huang pulled out his piece of paper and studied the characters again. He had already identified the first three characters and had written them down on his notepad in New York. So, he looked to see whether or not those characters repeated in the message. They did. The first character was repeated twice, as was the second character. The third character was repeated four additional times. *Two, two, four. I can remember that.* Then he counted the positions of the repeated characters. The first one could be found in positions 17 and 42. The second character in positions 10 and 37. The third in positions 6, 20, 26, and 45. *I'll never remember that. Need to make it simpler.* It would not be possible to use his brush and ink while riding, so he attempted to lightly scratch the numbers onto the bottom of the paper with his dagger. *Good enough for now. I'll need to trace these during the next pit stop.* But as much as he looked at this string of numbers, he could not figure out a pneumonic device to remember them. *Two, two, four is easy. Maybe I focus on remembering 17, 42, 10 first. When I was seventeen, I wrecked my father's Chevette. I can rely on Douglas Adams again for 42. When I was ten, I broke my arm when I was ten falling off the monkey bars at school. Chevette, Adams, broken arm...17, 42, 10.* He repeated this to himself frequently throughout the trip. Before he put the paper away, he looked at the number after 10, and started to draw a correlation between 10 and 37—the next number in the sequence, *ten minus three...,* but was interrupted as Hsieh Sun announced that the temple was approximately one hour ahead.

Shortly after, Chang Huang started to feel a pain in his left knee that Charlie had never experienced before. He tried to ignore it, but it made riding more difficult. This went on for another twenty minutes before Yuan Lin pointed out a growing shadow in the west. "Sandstorm is coming. We may need to stay at the temple tonight," he said.

Great...the general has arthritis or a knee injury or something affected by the weather. "Hsieh Sun, does the temple have adequate protection from dust storms?"

"There are sleeping quarters. Kong Xiao's temple is at the base of the mountain range, so the sand should not be as dangerous there."

"What do you know of Kong Xiao?"

Chang Huang's question was for Hsieh Sun, but Yuan Lin answered, "His past is clouded by rumors. He is reputed to be a master of spiritual thinking. Mind communications, speaking with animals, that sort of thing. If you had a vision telling you to go see him, then you are doing the right thing by following that vision. It is likely Kong Xiao calling to you."

Hsieh Sun added, "Kong Xiao has been in this temple since before I was born. He guided me to Xin when I left home." Chang Huang was tempted to ask questions regarding her past but remained quiet. Hsieh Sun's eyes clearly indicated that this subject was deeply sad for her. *So, if Kong Xiao's been in the temple for twenty-plus years, and he is the same Kong Xiao I read about from the Shaolin Temple cleansing in 1535, then it must be at least 1555 now.* "Hsieh Sun, do you know how long before you were born Kong Xiao moved to the temple?"

"I do not. Why?"

"Just curious." *Why, indeed. Does it really matter at all? Chevette, Adams, broken arm...17, 42, 10.*

The three approached the temple as the wind picked up. Chang Huang felt the first few grains of sand sting against his face. From their vantage, they could only see the front wall, which rose 20 feet and extended about 60 yards in each direction from the center. It was painted a brownish-red color, but the top was trimmed in a brilliant gold. The shadow of the sandstorm seemed to make the trim appear to glow brighter as it caught the sun rays that broke through. An arched entryway contained a double gate that peeled outward. At the corners of the front wall were Western style turrets. Though the gates to the temple were open, two young men with shaved heads and reddish togas emerged, looking as if they meant to close them. One of the men did not look up at the three riders. He looked tired, as if he were at the end of a shift and was looking forward to getting some rest. The other was more alert and motioned the three of them through without saying a word. Charlie's usual knack for banter desired to say something, but Chang Huang knew better. There was a quiet in the temple that deterred voices.

The temple was made up of four main buildings tucked into the inside corners of the walls, with an altar in the center. The walls of the temple grounds were equal in height on three sides, disappearing into the steep slope of a mountain which made up its fourth wall. From inside, Chang Huang could see that the turrets were only for show. No platforms were there to support guards or lookouts. The building to their right as they entered extended all the way from the corner to the gate. The other buildings were of varying sizes but all had the same color and style as the outside walls. The rest of the interior was an open courtyard around the altar. The altar was covered and contained a golden statue of Queen Maya sleeping with her head on a stone.

The boy who looked more alert took the reins of Horse and led them all to the long building to the right of the gate, which turned out to be the stables. It was large enough for Yuan Lin's company but was empty. Chang Huang understood this to mean that hospitality was important to this monk. After settling the horses, the boy led them to the building at the back, right corner of the temple grounds. The boy walked up to the door but did not knock. Within seconds, the door opened, revealing a man who looked both old and young at once. His long, graying hair and his deep wrinkles betrayed extensive wear and tear, but his eyes were bright and alert. "Thank you, Chou Yen," the older man said to the boy. Then to Chang Huang, "Please come in." He looked at the others. "All of you." The three found themselves in a room about twenty feet square containing only a bed, a table with one chair, and a fireplace. Candles on the table and the fireplace mantle cast dancing shadows, as a breeze seemed to penetrate the small quarters from somewhere. "Please sit," he said as he motioned to the floor. A smile appeared on Hsieh Sun's lips. She had obviously experienced this before and was enjoying the expressions on Yuan Lin's and Chang Huang's faces.

"Welcome to this temple. I will speak with each of you individually. Hsieh Sun knows this, but the kitchen is in the building diagonally opposite my quarters. The other building against the mountain…," he pointed in the direction of the remaining building, "…contains cots. Enough to house many men. Seven of my trainees occupy some of the cots, but you may choose any of the others. I do not provide separate quarters for gender. I expect the highest level of respect for each other from my guests. Less will not be tolerated." Again, the Charlie part of Chang Huang wanted to talk, ask questions, speak a courtesy, or something. But nothing would come to his mind that would be appropriate to say. "I will speak with Hsieh Sun first. General Chang and Captain Yuan, please find your way to the kitchen. One of my trainees will serve you. After you are nourished, the two of you can worship at the altar, retire on one of the cots, or meditate in whatever fashion you choose." Chang Huang and Yuan Lin rose in silence, walked to the monk's door, and made their way to the kitchen as requested.

(Saturday – August 18, 2012)

The morning light was almost blinding. *Chevette, Adams, broken arm…17, 42, 10. Two, two, four...this means what?* Charlie looked at the blanks in front of him. *Oh yeah, the first character repeats twice, the second character repeats twice, then the third character repeats four times. Then 17, 42, 10 are the placements of some of these repeated characters.* Charlie sat down at his latest rendering of the message from his dream and started putting the repeating characters in the correct places—at least the three placements he memorized. After putting the second character in the 10th place, he thought he recalled that the number after 10 was 37. *Yeah, ten minus three is seven. That's the connection I was trying to make.* He wasn't completely certain, but he could recheck that in his next dream. When he finished, he had the following:

日 人 十 _ _   _ _ _ _   人 _ _   _ _ _   _ 日 _ _   _ _   _ _ _ _   _ _ _ _

_ _ _ _ _ _ _

人 _ _ _ _   日 _   _ _ _ _ _   _ _   _ _ _ _ _   _ _ _ _ _ _ _

Still a long way to go. And I have a feeling I am missing something important, or misunderstanding. He threw the pencil on the desk and stood up, kicking the chair back hard enough for it to fall over. Charlie didn't know what level of clarity he expected, but his patience was absent more and more. He took a second look at the characters and a thought touched his mind. But it did not seem reasonable, so he shook it away.

Charlie swore to himself he wasn't going to bother Samantha. He again swore this as he stepped down the stairs from the second floor. A third time he swore it as he turned away from the front door and walked towards Samantha's door. He swore it a fourth time as he knocked.

"Charlie? What're you up to this morning?"

"Got some time before my shift and I was struck by a thought." *What are you doing, Charlie? She said the "L" word to a guy just last night. Game over.* "You mentioned Hangzhou the other day. You've been there?"

"Oh, yes. It's one of my favorite places in China. The world for that matter."

"When I first came to New York, I went to Chinatown before going anywhere else. The meal I had wasn't as great as I expected. Later on, Ray…he's a Chinese American who works in my department…took me to a place in Queens that's kind of like a secret Chinatown. It's not as labeled in any map I've seen, but it has the real deal as far as good Chinese food goes. There's a hole-in-the wall place that serves a Westlake fish dish. I can't speak to its authenticity, but I really like it."

"That sounds fantastic, Charlie."

A ruffling sound came from somewhere behind Samantha in her apartment. "Sam, who's that?"

"My friend," she called back to the voice. "The one I told you about. We're going out for lunch. There's lots to eat in the refrigerator, Gary, just help yourself."

"You'll be back later?" Gary called out.

"Yes. Charlie works tonight." She looked at Charlie. "He'll be keeping the city safe tonight."

"Good. See you later," came the voice from the back.

Charlie smiled to hide his confusion. "Are you sure I'm not interrupting…?"

"No, Charlie. I'll explain over lunch."

"Sounds great." Charlie grabbed a taxi and took her to a place with a name he couldn't read and uncovered tables and chairs that looked like they had been swiped from a PTA meeting. The floor was linoleum in big green and white squares in a checkerboard fashion.

"You sure know how to treat a lady!" she said, knowing the meal would far surpass the furnishings.

"Just wait," Charlie said. The waiter brought a menu in English. "Um, sorry," he said handing the menus back to the waiter. "Can you bring the ones in Chinese?"

"You read Chinese?" asked Samantha.

"No, but the item I want isn't in the English menu. Ray showed me what to get." The waiter came back moments later with a different menu. Charlie flipped to a particular page and pointed to a line with two red peppers next to it. "This is the fish?" he asked the waiter.

"Dui. I mean, yes."

"I'll take that and two green teas, please."

"Thank you," the waiter said and left with the menus.

Too bad Chang Huang is not here with me, or he could tell me what the rest of the menu has to offer. Something tickled the back of his mind. Then an image of the message he was trying to decrypt flashed. The answer was there in his head, but he could not piece it together.

"What's happening, Charlie?" He looked up and saw concern on her face.

"Nothing. It's just…I hate it when part of my brain knows something that the rest of it doesn't." The waiter returned with two small cups and a white, ceramic teapot. Charlie checked under the lid to see the color. "Let it sit a little."

"Definitely. I like it strong." She hadn't spoken of the man in her apartment during the ride over, and she paused before continuing. "My brother's in town."

"That was the baritone asking who I was?"

She laughed. "He does have a deep voice. Yes. He's having some marital problems."

"I'm sorry. Serious ones?"

"She kicked him out."

"Ouch. He probably deserves better."

"No, he cheated on her."

"Ah. I honestly don't know what to say. But I am sorry he and his family are going through this."

"Thanks, Charlie."

"I noticed he called you Sam."

"He always has. I think it's because of that I prefer 'Samantha.'" The fish came soon after the tea was ready. It was steamed with very little of anything disguising the fresh taste of the fish. Some chiles gave it a small kick, but neither Charlie not Samantha were strangers to a little fire. Near the end of the meal, Charlie went to the restroom, and Samantha grabbed the waiter's attention and took the liberty of paying the bill without waiting to fight over it. When Charlie came back, he saw Samantha putting the receipt into her purse. "Hey, what gives? Coming here was my idea."

"My turn, Charlie."

"But…."

"Too late," she said with a smile. "What's done is done. You can get me next time." *Next time…yes!*

As they left, Charlie saw someone who looked familiar bobbing in and out of the crowd. "Hold on a second," he said to Samantha. Charlie weaved between the bodies trying to get a good look at the man who stayed just out of sight. Once Charlie caught a good visual of the man, he realized this was the man who had discussed Chinese masks with him in south Brooklyn a week ago. *What was his name? Bob? No…Bill!* "Bill!" he shouted, a little louder than he wanted. The man looked in Charlie's direction. "Hey! Bill! Come over here!" Bill's eyes grew wide and he ran in the opposite direction. Being a small man, he was able to run quickly in between the other pedestrians on the sidewalk. Charlie was not as fortunate. He knocked down more than one person chasing after Bill, one of whom was a woman carrying a child. Charlie looked down at her in horror. "Are you all right?" he asked her. She threw a harsh look back at Charlie but did not say anything. Judging that no one was hurt, he continued in Bill's direction.

Charlie only caught glimpses of Bill and could tell he was getting farther away, when he suddenly stopped. "Bill, wait!" Charlie continued. When he caught up with his target, he saw he was talking to a uniform.

"Officer," Bill said. "That man is chasing me. He's been to my shop and now…."

"It's okay, sir," the police officer said. "Charlie, you wanna explain this?" Bill turned back to face Charlie, glancing every couple of seconds back at Officer Herschal.

"*He's* following *me*. Bill, why did you run when I called to you?"

"You're a cop?" Charlie nodded and produced his badge. "You sounded angry. I thought you were after me."

"Angry? I was just calling to you."

"You did sound a little angry, Charlie," Samantha said as she caught up with him.

"Angry?"

"Yes…a little."

Looking back at Bill, Charlie said, "I'm…I'm sorry, Bill. I just wanted to see what you were doing over here. I thought you might be following me."

"Why on Earth would I do that?"

"Then what were you doing here?"

"I'm Chinese. This area has the best food in the country." Charlie's face turned red.

"Listen, I don't want to keep you," Charlie said.

"You're lucky I don't file charges against you…officer."

"That's your right if you wish to do that."

"Just leave me alone, and we'll call it even," Bill said as he continued in the direction he had been walking before Charlie called to him.

"What was all that about?" Samantha asked.

"That was about me losing my mind."

Although he had resolved not to see Dr. Thomason, Charlie arrived at work about 45 minutes before his shift. Still feeling embarrassed by his behavior in front of Samantha, he couldn't sit around his apartment. As he wandered into the breakroom, Gina was coming in from the other direction. All the awkwardness between them seemed to be gone, at least on his part. He needed at least one person to whom he could talk without feeling weird. He needed a friend.

"Hi, G," he said as he stepped up to her.

"Hi, Charlie." Her smile seemed genuine, but he knew he had some work to do to get back into the friend zone.

"I met Kong Xiao last night." He could see the moment when her smile crossed over from "nearly" genuine to absolutely real.

"That's great, Charlie!" She grabbed his arm and pulled him over to the coffee machine. "What did he say?" She grabbed two of the hard, plastic cups and started to fill them with coffee.

"Nothing useful, yet. But I think I got the timeframe of my dream narrowed down a bit." Charlie described his Internet search and what Hsieh Sun and Yuan Lin had said about the monk. "So, I'm looking at somewhere between 1555 and 1599."

"I get 1555, but why 1599?" She nodded to one of the empty, circle tables and started walking in that direction.

"The article I read said that Xin was a stopping point on routes between Peiping and Kumul in the 1500s." Gina looked at him half amused and half concerned. "What?"

She chuckled. "You should hear yourself. You're not talking about this like it's a dream...narrowing your setting down to a specific time period." She laughed more generously now.

Charlie laughed as well. "Just a little mental breakdown, there. Actually, part of me wants to believe it is real. It's a better thought than thinking someone is messing with my head. But I can't accept it. It's too…"

"Too what?"

"…too…fucked up."

"Is it so hard to believe, really?"

"Well, yeah. I mean, if I really was going back in time and stepping into the shoes of some guy named Chang Huang…for one thing, what happened to the real Chang Huang? He has a history. I know things about his past…that his father abused him…that he can't trust people. He's a hero in his time, but he doesn't think so. But when I'm him, I'm not plagued by his…issues. We're different people. Take Hsieh Sun for example." He paused. What he was about to say could have impacts on his current relationships in the real world. *Ah, fuck it.* "Chang Huang is too reserved to want to have anything to do with love or family. But I, Charlie, am falling for this girl. She's too young for me. Chang Huang thinks she isn't that attractive. I know the Chinese have a different idea on what's beautiful. Ray Chung from the day shift thinks Lucy Liu is unattractive. But most white guys I know think she's a knockout. I think it's like that with Hsieh Sun, except part of me sees her through Chang

Huang's eyes and part of me sees her through mine. Yuan Lin seems to like her, too, though. I don't know.

"But it's just a dream, right?" Charlie said. Both smiled, but neither smile felt real this time. "What time is it?"

"Still got time before shift starts."

"Let's go see if Greg and Nora are in."

Greg Deathrage was waiting for Charlie and asked to talk to him alone as soon as Charlie arrived. They retreated to the same conference room where they and their partners gathered yesterday. "Is this not weird for you?" Greg confessed.

"Which part are you talking about?" Charlie asked with a chuckle.

"Me and Nora being the lead on this case. It's not like we have a lot to go on. Aren't you interested in making detective? You could switch over to the detective bureau and use this case towards promotion."

"I'm not interested in being a detective. You ever read comic books as a kid?"

"Not really."

"I loved them. But I didn't care much for the deeper ones that made you think. I liked to see Spider-Man rescuing someone who needed help. I love the patrol. I love being ready to help. Sure, I may not see much action on a daily basis. But I want to be out there, just in case. Besides, since I'm the target of this stalker, I should be even farther away from this, to be honest."

"But this is not an investigatable case. We're mostly just waiting for him to make the next move."

"Then we wait for it. You're making the right calls, Greg. We can only check out places he's been, talk to anyone who might have been in contact with him, and examine, reexamine any evidence we get. But mostly this is a waiting game since we don't have much of any of those things."

"Really? Okay. We'll just keep doing what we're doing."

"Good. I'll go round up Nora and Gina. Oh, and I'm pretty sure 'investigatable' ain't a word." He left the room. He returned a few minutes later with the other two. After a little non-shop talk, Greg focused them on the plan for the night.

"'Investigable'...that's the word I was looking for." Charlie smiled. "Okay, let's start with last night. Any good come from talking to…," he looked down at his hand-held notebook, "Francis and Harold?"

"Not really. I don't get the impression that there is a relation between that job and the stalker," Charlie lied.

"Nora and I came up blank."

"Not totally," Nora added. "Tell him about the red head at the theater!" Greg blushed. Charlie did, too. "Wait…you saw her, too, didn't you?" she asked Charlie.

"Doctor costume," he replied. The four laughed. It was the first time they seemed to really gel. Greg's confidence was lifted.

"Well, I took the liberty of arranging something with the sarge," Greg said. "Charlie mentioned a possible connection with a Private Storage in Queens. I asked the sarge about it, and he thought he could arrange for you two," he pointed to Charlie and Gina, "to get permission to step into that jurisdiction." Charlie looked impressed. "Sarge wanted you to stop by his office so he could confirm if he was successful or not, but he didn't think it would be an issue."

"Great idea, Greg."

"Nora and I will stake out the area where Charlie lives in case his stalker comes around. Any questions?" There were none.

The sarge was successful in getting permission from the Queens police, and Charlie and Gina cruised to 19th and Broadway. "Are you sure he'll be here?" Gina asked as they approached the intersection. "Owners don't always get involved in the day-to-day operations of something like this."

"In my dream, he said he ran it, not just that he owned it. If he's not here, we'll check up on him at his home address."

The Private Storage was not a hive of activity, but there were a few storage renters milling about when Charlie and Gina arrived. The place looked like a fortress with high walls around the perimeter. A steel-barred gate allowed vehicles to pass through if the proper code was punched in the keypad. The office had two sets of double glass doors which lead both externally to the street and internally to the storage units just to the left of the gate. Large counters displayed many types of packing materials and ropes on spools for purchase. A service counter held three computers, though only one person manned the business at that time. A white, plastic rectangle pinned onto the man's shirt with the Private Storage logo in the corner and the word "Martin" in block print told Charlie he had the right man. He looked nothing like Du Hung from Charlie's dream. As the two walked into the shop in uniform, Martin noticeably stiffened his posture. The shock was apparent on Charlie's face, which alarmed Martin.

"Afternoon, officers. Anything I can help you with?"

"Not sure," Charlie said, looking like he was trying to figure out a puzzle. Charlie wished he could remember the unit number Martin mentioned in his dream, but he had enough trouble trying to remember the characters from his message. "We're looking for some imported goods from China that might be stolen."

"Wish I could help you, officer. The contents of my customers' storage units are their own business. I would be remiss if I were to check on them." Charlie couldn't take his eyes off Martin. Here was proof that someone else exists here in New York who he met also in his dream.

"You never saw anyone unload Oriental looking art or furniture from trucks?"

"You're joking, right? Lots of Asians come to New York and need a place to store their family heirlooms." Charlie struggled to come up with the next question, but Gina cut to the chase.

"Ever been to the Gobi Desert, Mr. Killjoy?" Martin's already pale skin turned two shades lighter.

"Can't say as I have, Officer…," he squinted his eyes at her nameplate and continued, "…Baxter." He then looked at Charlie's nameplate. Making sure they knew he had their names gave him a trifle more confidence.

"Really? Never been to a town called Xin? I hear it's lovely this time of year." Charlie gave her a look of caution, but Gina did not take her eyes off Martin.

Martin's hand dropped casually to the shotgun below his countertop. "Who are you, two? Really?"

Charlie stepped in. "A couple of nights ago, General Chang asked you what part of New York you were from." Martin brought the shotgun up to his shoulder.

"Cop or not, you ain't here for no normal reason. You been in my head. What are you, alien or sump'm?" Charlie wanted to draw his weapon, but the shotgun was aimed at Gina's head.

Gina softened her look and her voice, "Sir, I'm sorry we came across with animosity. We really do not mean you any harm." *Way to not sound like an alien, G.*

"Look," Charlie continued, "I'm going to put my pistol on the floor." He started to reach for his pistol using only his index finger and thumb. "I'm actually here to find out why you were in my dream."

"I wasn't in your dream. 'Twas the other way 'round. Putting your pistols on the ground is a start, but if you're aliens, I bet you got other ways to fuck me up. So, I ain't trusting you." Charlie and Gina both put their pistols on the floor and backed away from them. Martin put the shotgun on the counter but made sure it was clear that he could pick it up again quickly if he needed. "Now how do you know what is happening in my dream?"

"I came here to ask you that," Charlie said. "Until the other night, I thought my dreams were weird, but I hadn't come across any other New Yorkers."

"You 'spect me to believe you were having the same dream as me?"

"I don't expect you to believe anything. I don't care what you believe, really, as long as you don't shoot me. I'm trying to figure out my own mystery. Now, is there anything you can tell me about Chinese artifacts in any of these units that is unusual in some way? Something different than the Chinese stuff you normally see here?" Martin looked as though he were thinking carefully. "In my dream, you mentioned a unit number."

"Yeah…4358. I saw the foot of an idol. Maybe a dragon or something. It had what looked like eagle claws and scales. All in bronze. It was holding a gem of some kind. Only saw it for a split second."

"But something struck you about this idol?"

"Yeah. Can't explain what. That was about a year ago."

"You've been dreaming about China for that long?" Charlie asked.

"No, that's only been going on a week."

"Do you have the keys to that unit?"

"Yeah, but I can't just go showing you what's in there. Got a warrant or anything? At least to cover my ass."

"No." Charlie knew that getting one would not be easy. "Look, this isn't really official police business, to be honest. I'm not even a cop in this precinct. I'm just trying to figure out why I'm having these dreams. Can you help me?"

"Sorry, friend. What kind of steward would I be if I let people look in on my clients' belongings?"

"That's…well, that's quite righteous. Friend." Charlie suspected that this righteousness did not prevent him from taking a peek on his own from time to time. "Here, can you keep my card handy? I'd really appreciate it if you can keep an eye on…what unit did you say that was?"

"4358."

"4358." *4358, 4358, 4358.* "Just if you see something…something that looks out of the ordinary going on with that unit, can you call me or send an email or something?"

"Sure." The man smiled. *I'll never hear from him,* Charlie knew. As he and Gina walked back to the car, Charlie wrote "4358" in the notebook he kept in his shirt pocket. He realized too late that he never asked Martin whether or not his dreams of China followed a bump on the head, by chance.

Chapter 13

Chang Huang studied the message some more during supper. Coincidently, they were served fish that tasted almost identical to the one Charlie had back in Queens. *That takes care of the first two characters. The third is in positions 6, 20, 26, and 45. I was six when I had my tonsils out. I was twenty when I moved to Seattle and 26 when I moved to Los Angeles. After that is 45. Can I relate to that? I'll be 45 in five years. Tonsils, Seattle, L.A., and five years from now. Should I go for the next character?* Chang Huang studied the shape of the character as best as he could. *Let's see...it's in four places. First placing is just the next one available...the fourth position.* He wrote the numbers 27, 31, and 52 onto the paper. He wanted to remember this much at least but would need some connection to the other numbers. *I can remember that 27 is one after 26 (L.A.). And 52 is double 26. 31 is the second character in the second line...the grouping all by itself. Remember to memorize the next character before waking up.* But there was a problem: unless he woke up intentionally, he could wake up at any time. Sometimes his dreams lasted more than a day in this world, and sometimes they would last a very short while. He thought about studying the character and waking himself up right then but did not want to push the next part of his dream out an extra day. Whatever was happening, he felt a strong sense of urgency about talking to Kong Xiao.

"What is that paper you have been looking at?" As far as Chang Huang could remember, this was the first time Yuan Lin spoke to him without saying "sir" or "general."

"The message on the wall where the Bao family was killed."

"You can read that?"

"Not yet."

"Can I take a look?"

Chang Huang handed him the paper. "Be my guest." Yuan Lin examined it as if it were a scientific oddity. Then a thoughtful expression washed over his face.

"What is on your mind?"

"These characters are unusual. They are unlike characters in neighboring countries I have visited. But a few years back, my unit was traveling out west on reconnaissance. We ran into a band of men, white…like ghosts. They were quite lost and seeking a city I never heard of. They showed me their map, and I was able to point out where we were, but I saw that the writing on their map was very different. These markings remind me of the writing on that map."

Chang Huang's lower jaw hung open, unbecoming of a proud, Chinese general in the Emperor's army. "Can I see that again?" Yuan Lin handed it back. Chang Huang looked back at the sequence of numbers and stared at the fourth character on the page. *Wake up.*

(Sunday – August 19, 2012)

Tonsils, Seattle, L.A, my age five years from now. Charlie wrote, "6, 20, 26, and 45" on the notepad on his desk. *L.A. plus 1, L.A. times 2.* He wrote "27" and "52". *Second position in the middle line.* He put a dot above the second space in the middle line. Then he recalled to the front of his mind the symbol he was staring at when he willed himself awake: .

Third character goes in positions 6, 20, 26, and 45. Fourth character goes in positions 27, 52, and one where I put the dot, and of course right after the third character. He drew the characters in the appropriate places:

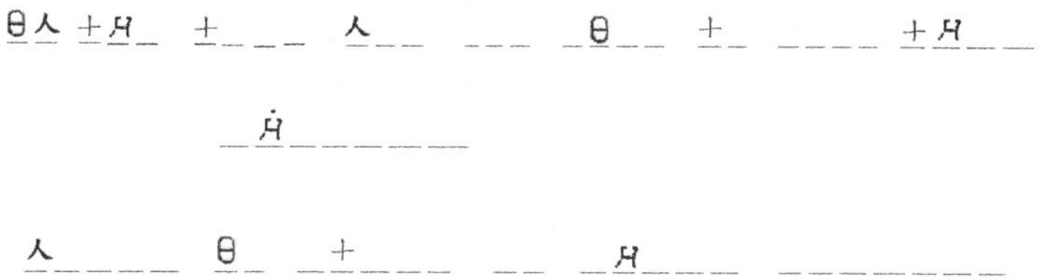

Wait, if I'm right about this, then that must be upside-down, he thought pointing to the second character. Charlie recalled that he had searched legitimate Chinese characters and found one that looked similar to the character in his dream, and that is what he had originally written down. He erased it and drew it inverted. After looking at the results, he did the same for the other two occurrences of that character:

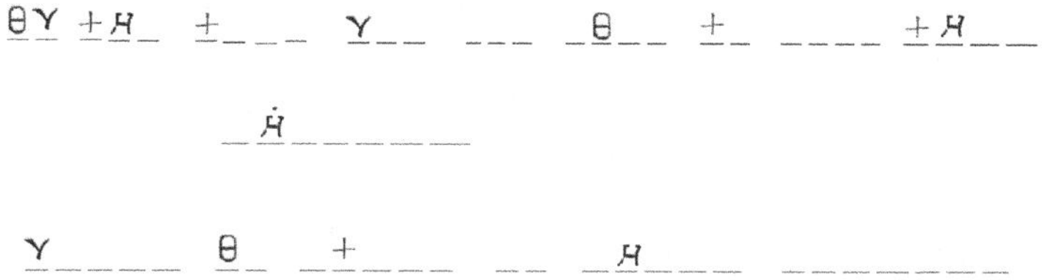

He dropped his pen and kicked his legs out straight, scooting his chair backwards. He picked up his phone and dialed, mindless of what time it was. On the other end of the phone line, a broken voice spoke, "Hello?"

"Gina! It's English!"

"Charlie?"

"The message. It's English!"

"What are you talking about?"

"I guess I haven't brought it up with you since I first talked about it with you and Sarge. The inn where Chang Huang found the Bao family in one of my first dreams…there was a message written in blood. I've been working with The Egg to try to figure it out. But it's in English!"

"Are you sure?" She sounded clearer.

"Positive. In fact, something just occurred to me. In my dream, I can read the signs outside the buildings in Xin. That's how I knew which buildings were for which businesses. How could I read them? They had to be in Chinese. Chang Huang can read Chinese, so I can read the signs when I'm there. But if General Chang can't read the message from the wall at the inn, it can't be in Chinese."

"That's great, but how would you…"

"In the Chinse restaurant today…or yesterday…I couldn't read the menu. That's because I, Charlie, cannot read Chinese. So there's no reason Chang Huang would know how to read English. The characters I'm memorizing, now that I have four of them and am placing them in the right places…assuming I'm doing it correctly…," he stopped for a moment to consider that he could have made mistakes in his transcribing from memory but then shook the thought away. He just needed to get close. Any mistakes would be revealed as he filled in more letters.

"Charlie?"

"Yeah…sorry. Anyway, as I fill out the message on my tablet, the characters look like they are trying to spell words in English. I'll know for sure when I memorize the fifth character. It will be an 'E'."

"So, the man who committed the murders speaks English?"

"Not just speaks it, but writes it, too."

"Run into anyone like that so far?"

He thought for a moment. "No one comes to mind."

"At least you have a lead. Good job, detective."

He laughed. "Thanks. Of course, now I have to wonder why anyone would write a phrase in English on a wall in old China."

"They must have meant it for you, or else there's another person who speaks English that was meant to see it. If that's the case, you shouldn't rush to judgment when you find an English speaker."

"Good point. Either way, it behooves me to find at least one English speaker."

"Martin Killjoy?"

"Could be. But if I can't read English in my dream, why would he be able to?"

"It'd be worth a try to see if he can read that message."

"Yeah, but if he wrote the message, he'll deny understanding it."

"Can you go back to sleep and continue the dream?"

"I doubt it. When I've tried that before, I don't dream again until the next night."

Charlie did not dream the remainder of the night, but he slept long and hard. He woke just after 11:00 in the morning and went up to the roof with the sword he picked up at the pawn shop. He had no intention of actually fighting the stalker but figured he better be familiar with the moves.

He had no idea where to start, so he mostly just familiarized himself with the weight and motion of the blade. Even with a master trainer, a week would not be enough time to learn the art of swordplay, and he had less time than that. But he could go through the motions of blocking imaginary slashes and stabs. *This is nuts*, he thought but kept going. After about an hour, he took the sword back down to his apartment and pulled out his notepad. In the trashcan, he saw the page full of X's he had ripped off the notepad seven days ago. He uncrumpled it and saw that he had written seven X's below the main message at one point. *The mask. I gotta remember to look at the mask next time.*

His thoughts were interrupted by a knock at the door. *Gina or Samantha.* The last time he was with Samantha, he had knocked over a mother and child in front of her in pursuit of an innocent Chinese man. *Please be Gina.* He opened the door. "Hi, Samantha," he said hoping to sound upbeat.

"Hi Charlie. How you doing?"

"Still crazy. Come on in." She came in but seemed a bit stiff.

"Charlie, I make it a point not to judge others. I'm not saying I never do it, but I try really hard not to."

"I wish everyone was like that."

"Whatever's going on with you, I promise you that I give you the benefit of the doubt. But there's a difference between judging and protecting myself." She paused but didn't look away from his eyes. "You know what I'm talking about, right?"

"I do. I made a scene. Scared some people. I could've really hurt that woman and little boy."

"I was impressed that you sought them out after the whole thing was over and made sure they were all right."

"That's just human nature…."

"Don't sell yourself short. Look, Charlie, I didn't come over here to call things off. I like you. I just need to know I'm safe with you. Do you know if I am?"

Charlie had been looking at the ground through most of this conversation, looking up to Samantha's eyes occasionally. But now he looked directly into her eyes. "You are 100% safe from *me*. I have no doubts about that. This stalker…I don't think he would hurt you, but I can't be as sure about that as I am about myself."

"I'm not afraid of people outside our relationship. There's danger everywhere, Charlie. I just need to know you're on my side. I get the feeling there's something you aren't telling me about this stalker."

Charlie hesitated. "There is something I'm not telling you. But it's not because I don't want you to know. I really, really want you to know. It's just that…I don't relish the act of telling you. The whole thing is crazy, and I don't want you to think I'm crazy."

"Charlie…you can trust me. And look, if you have something this important going on in your life, and if I walk away from you for it, then you're better off without me." She stepped closer to Charlie and put her hand on his left bicep. "Do you want to trust me?"

Charlie realized there was nothing really to lose. He needed someone who would accept what he's going through. "Okay, here it goes." He told her about his dreams. He told her about the Lexalt job. He told her about the doll that was left on the roof and how it connected to his dream. He told her about Hsieh

Sun but not how he felt about her during his dreams. He also told her about the meaning behind the challenge at the Statue of Liberty.

"You mean you made up this story about a swordfight at the Statue and then this guy sent you that note?"

"Yeah. The only one I told about me making up that story was Gina, and I nearly ended our friendship over it, thinking she somehow leaked it to the stalker."

"Gina's your friend on the force?"

"Yes."

"She's important to you. This guy is really messing with you."

"Enough to make me chase after that Chinese man yesterday."

"And you did that because…?"

"It's stupid. I had met him in that Asian grocery down on Avenue X. I asked him some questions about death masks because of the one I found in my dream. So, when I see him in Queens, my first thought was that he was following me. Then when I called after him and he ran, it sealed my suspicion."

"Well, he did run. I'll give you a pass on that." She stepped up to Charlie and held him for a second before stepping back. "Charlie, this is messy. But I'm here for you. I meant it when I said I like you. That's not too uncommon…I like a lot of people. But I don't always feel comfortable telling them. Thank you for sharing all of this."

"Thanks for listening."

"I guess you'll be working evenings and I'll be working days for a little while."

"Wednesday is my next evening off."

"That's not so bad. Feel free to stop by. My brother will be heading back to Kentucky tomorrow."

"I will."

Deathrage and Peterson would be off duty this night and the next, so Charlie and Gina were able to follow their own path. It was

Gina's turn to drive, and they continued their regular beat with no particular plan in mind. "Any ideas where to go from here?" Gina asked him.

"Not in the real world. In the other place, I gotta find someone who speaks English, talk to the monk, and try to memorize the next symbol and where it goes. If it is an 'E', it should be in several positions in the message. That's the way it goes on Wheel of Fortune, anyway.

"Sarge is trying to get someone in Queens to pull surveillance on 4358. He's also hoping to get a warrant, but I can't imagine how that will play off. 'You see, Judge, one of my officers had a dream that this guy in another precinct....' So, what do you say we make a stop by Best Buy tonight?"

The sales kid knew less about video cameras than Charlie. Fortunately, this was not Charlie's first, so he had a basic understanding of what he needed. Charlie needed something that would be off most of the time to conserve battery life. A new Royko 380ML model that had just been unveiled caught Charlie's attention. "What does away-store capability mean?" he asked.

The kid, no more than seventeen, scratched his head and said, "You know, that's a new one on me. Let's go look it up." He led them to a computer and began searching various Web sites before trying the Royko home page. After pulling up the model, he said, "Looks like it's a new feature. Check it out." He angled the monitor so that Charlie could see it clearly. The feature allowed the "cinematographer" to set up the camera to send video to a remote server that could be accessed on a smart phone or tablet. *Why don't they just say cloud storage?* Charlie thought. He looked again to make sure it had motion detection auto-recording. It did.

"Yeah, we'll take this one."

"Great! Can I interest you in our Geek Squad Black Tie Protection?"

After figuring out how to set up the camera to connect to the cloud, Gina and Charlie parked three blocks from the Private Storage in an empty alley. By this time, it was a little after 10:30. Gina took a quick glance through the glass door of the office and saw a different manager manning the desk. Even Martin went home at some point. She told this to Charlie and asked, “So what’s the plan?”

“First, let’s sprint down the block and back as fast as we can.”

“Seriously?”

“Yeah, it’ll make it look like we’re a tad out of breath. Then we run into the office. Once we’re in there, I’ll do the talking.”

“K.” The two ran down the block and back, and Gina followed Charlie through the front door. Charlie was talking into the radio mic fastened to the strap on the shoulder of his shirt, but Gina noticed he was not depressing the button.

“Roger…suspect just went over the wall of the Private Storage on 19th and Broadway. No backup required at this time.” Charlie looked at the man behind the counter. *Hopefully this guy’s not a former cop, or he’ll know I’m full of shit.* “You got surveillance on this place?”

“The entryway only.”

“Shit. We’ll be right back.” Charlie and Gina raced through the door leading to the units, hands on their pistols but not drawing them. “Looks like 4015 through 4650 is this way,” Charlie said to Gina. He slowed to a walk as he headed in that direction without waiting for a response. “Here it is: 4358.”

“The best place to secure the camera would be…right here across from the door.”

“Yeah, right where that other camera is.” Underneath the gutter of the roof to the unit opposite 4358 was a small camera almost identical to the one they purchased. It was an older model but was the same basic camera.

“Martin’s got balls,” Gina said.

"Martin's got some kind of fascination with this unit that can't be healthy. I wonder what he's seen in here. Stay out of his camera's view. I don't think I was in the shot. Does his camera pick up sound? I know mine does."

"If it's like yours, a little red light would come on if it woke up," Gina replied. Then looking at the side of the camera, she said loud and clear, "Testing…one, two! Testing…one, two! No light. It doesn't seem like sound wakes it up. Does yours?"

"I'll have to check. No use worrying about it now. Besides, if he does find out we were here, we kind of have him over a barrel knowing that he's spying on one of his customers." Charlie looked to see if he could get a decent shot at 4358 from another unit at a wider angle where he wouldn't get picked up on Martin's camera. He could, but just barely. The angle would make it too easy for someone to block the view. *Beggars and choosers and all that.* He set the camera to kick on only after picking up three seconds of continuous movement and lodged it between the gutter's drainpipe and the corner of the building. "All right, let's get out of here." The two ran back through the front office; Charlie again pretended to talk on his radio. "Suspect has left the Private Storage. We're still in pursuit. Have backup on standby but don't send." They were outside before the night manager could throw any questions at them.

Chapter 14

Yuan looked suddenly concerned. “General, are you all right?”

“Yes, just got caught up in these characters.”

“I do not think you will figure it out without knowing the language.”

“Maybe the monk can help me.” The two men finished their fish and went for a walk in the temple grounds. Some sand from the storm outside had blown over the wall but much less than Chang Huang expected.

“Care to spar, General?” He indicated his sword with his hand, palm up.

Might do me some good. Maybe some practice for Thursday night’s match-up. “I accept your challenge, Captain.” The two drew blades and saluted. This exercise would have to be highly disciplined, as they did not have padded clothing or blunted blades. It occurred to Chang Huang that, if Yuan Lin was the killer, this would be a golden opportunity for him to eliminate the chief inspector of his crime. The two men fought fast and hard as if the fight were real. Each time one would strike, the blow would not be held back or softened. The attacker expected the appropriate defense. Only three times, when a block was avoided by the attacker, did a blade get close to the other man.

When that happened, the attacker would stop the strike within a millimeter of touching the other. The first two times, it was Chang Huang's blade that came close to Yuan Lin's midsection. The final time was when Yuan Lin's blade stopped short of scratching the General's neck. The Charlie inside Chang Huang had never felt so alive as he had crossing swords with Yuan Lin. *Will this skill cross over into my world?* Charlie doubted it, thinking this was the same as trying to read English in China.

As the final "death blow" was being dealt by Yuan Lin, Hsieh Sun was emerging from Kong Xiao's quarters. She waited until she had clear indication that the spar was over before calling out, "General Chang, Kong Xiao will see you next."

"Thank you," he replied. Turning to Yuan Lin, he said, "And thank you for not taking it easy on me."

"Who said I did not?" *Was that trash talk from Yuan Lin?* Yuan Lin walked over to Hsieh Sun and escorted her to the kitchen. The general felt a pang in his gut as the two walked off but then realized he would have his chance to be alone with her afterwards. His eyes had to adjust to the dimness of the monk's quarters. Kong Xiao was sitting on the floor behind a small rock with a flame emerging from the top.

"Have a seat, General." Chang Huang sat on the other side of the burning rock. The monk opened his mouth to speak again, but Chang Huang cut him off.

"If you do not mind, I have some questions for you." Kong Xiao nodded. "How long have you lived in this temple?"

"Forty-seven years."

"Did you come here directly from the Shaolin Temple cleansing?"

The monk smiled. "My journey took a year, but yes, I came here afterwards."

"You volunteered to go."

"You know more about me than you do about yourself, General."

"Then the year is 1582, at least by Charlie's calendar." Kong Xiao did not seem confused by the Gregorian date.

"Is that important?"

"I do not know. Better to know too much than not enough."

"I like the way you think. But you are closed off to possibilities that would allow you to see the true picture."

"I do not think I…."

"I am talking about the reality of this place. If you accept that, you will have additional resources."

"I do not understand…."

"Nor will you. Not until you have proof. Proof more solid that most people would require. You have come here for this proof. Or proof of the opposite. Yes?"

"I have come here because Francis…," *what is Francis' last name?* "…Francis from Lextalt, Inc. told me to come see you."

"And you trust this Francis?"

"No. But he seemed to know about Charlie's dream. Can you tell me anything that would help me figure out why I am here or what I need to do?"

"Unfortunately, nothing." Chang Huang stared back at the monk without expression.

"Then why would Francis send me here?"

"You assume it was for your benefit. Francis sending you here tells me more than you can imagine."

"You mean *I* am here for *your* sake?" Chang Huang might have remained cool, but Charlie felt like he was about to explode.

"Do not be too upset. Your coming here will benefit you in the long run."

"I do not understand."

"Your understanding is not required."

"Francis told me to ask you about preserving my dream self. Do you know what that means?"

"Yes. I will get the process started. You will come back when the time is right."

"Do you want to elaborate on that?"

"Next time."

General Chang took the written message from his purse. "Can you read this language?"

Kong Xiao took the paper. After staring at it, he handed it back. "This is English."

"I learned that just a moment ago."

"Forget this message, General."

"But…"

"You will find no answers in these words. The best thing you can do is to tear this up and forget about it."

The two stared at each other in silence. Chang Huang knew he would not gain any more insight from this conversation. There was no way either Charlie or Chang Huang could just forget about the message, however. He stood up, bowed to Kong Xiao, and left the monk's quarters. When he emerged, he saw Yuan Lin and Hsieh Sun standing face to face. In the modern, Western world, he would have expected them to embrace the way they were looking at one another. But China was more reserved. They had not known each other long enough for that. He walked over to them.

"Captain Yuan, the monk will see you now."

"Thank you, General." He left without exchanging any familials with Hsieh Sun. *Maybe nothing's there.*

"General, you seem sad," Hsieh Sun said to him.

"Frustrated, only," he said.

"Did Kong Xiao not give you any answers?"

"Not exactly. How about you?"

"He provides comfort to me. I see him every week. I am not in Xin on any personal plan of my own. My past is difficult. I may tell you about it sometime."

"I would be honored. Do you plan on leaving Xin?"

"I hope to." She looked like she wanted to say more, but Chang Huang would not push her. "Can you sit with me? We do not have to talk. You can even go back to that piece of paper you keep looking at. In fact, I would prefer it. Just please stay and keep me company."

"Your wish is my command." The sun had begun to set. The mountain range ran from the northwest to the southeast as far as they could see, had they been outside the walls. Inside the walls, the light of the day left long before the sun reached the horizon. A fire had been lit by one of the monk's apprentices atop the altar's shelter, providing enough light for Chang Huang to see the cryptic message on his paper. He glanced at Hsieh Sun as she slipped her arm inside his and leaned against him. *Eat your heart out, Yuan Lin.* He looked back to his paper and studied the fifth character in the message. *Hmm, lots of these.* In addition to its placement in the 5th position, he also found it in the 9th, 15th, 19th, 23rd, 36th, 43rd, 59th, and 61st positions. *Nine times altogether. I don't have to remember the fifth position. But it's usually in the last position of a grouping. Or word...might as well start calling these words. It's in the last position for the 2nd, 3rd, 5th, and 6th word, the middle line, and the 2nd word in the last line. I don't remember much about what happened to me at those ages. But two, three, five, and six is in sequence, except for the "four." I can remember that it's also the last letter in the middle line. And the last letter in the second word on the last line, just like in the first line. It's also in positions 23, 59, and 61. I broke up with Sandy when I was 23. That leaves 59 and 61. One before and one after 60.*

Last letter in two, three, five, six, middle, and two. Then Sandy and either side of 60. He willed himself awake.

(Monday – August 20, 2012)

Last letter in two, three, five, six, middle, and two. Then Sandy and either side of 60. He repeated this phrase until he wrote it down on the notepad on his desk. Then he etched the character he was just staring at: .

Oh yeah, that's an "E" if I ever saw one. But to avoid any technical inaccuracies, he drew the character exactly as he saw if in his dream in each of the correct positions:

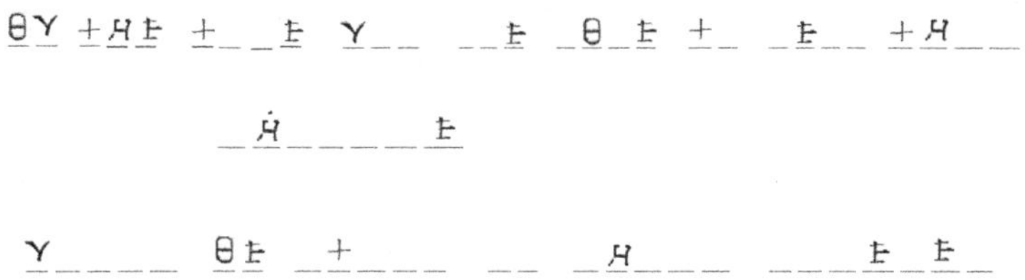

He recalled the mask with the seven characters, but he would have to remember to examine that next dream. The clock broadcasted 5:20am. His head felt like he had been drinking the night before, but he did not want to go back to sleep, so he made his coffee from a fresh bag he had picked up on Wednesday and started to open up the paper left on his door. Before he could do more than glance at the headlines, the glimmer of his pawn shop sword caught his eye. *Wonder if I'm any better after my spar with Yuan Lin.*

The rooftop was cooler in the pastel light of sunrise than it had been the last time he shadow-fenced there. Although he felt more comfortable with the movements, he could not seem to channel the finesse, speed, and confidence Chang Huang seemed to command. He continued practicing but did not feel like it was possible to be ready for mortal combat in the next few days.

Charlie had not visited Dr. Thomason since Friday and had not planned on going back to him at all. But he made the mistake of coming to the station a half hour before his shift. The counselor was propped up against the frame of his office door as Charlie walked by. Charlie slowed as he approached through the hallway to the Bullpen. "Hey, Doc. I'm sorry I ain't been by."

"It's your deal, Charlie. No need to apologize, but let me know if you aren't going to be here, okay?"

"Sure. How about we give it a break for the rest of this week. I'll pop in Friday before my shift if I'm still alive."

"What do you mean by that?" Charlie could not remember whether or not he told Thomason about the latest note or not.

"Well, you know what it's like, people wanting to fight you with swords and all."

"Can't say I do know what that's like. Though I gotta admit, I'm curious about how those dreams are going?"

"I'll bring in my journal tomorrow. You can borrow it, but I'll need it back at the end of my shift."

"I would appreciate that."

"Three days before your swordfight," Gina reminded Charlie as he returned to his desk after roll call.

"Yeah."

"So, what's the plan?"

"Still waiting for one to fall into my lap. I gotta talk to the boss before we take off."

"He's been in that meeting with the CO ever since I got here."

"He's been in there since before I got here, too. If I knew that, I wouldn't have come so early."

"Liable to be in there a while. Why don't we get rolling and you can talk to him afterwards?"

"Sure. Where to first?"

"Your Scottish bartender said that your stalker wants you to think he's from Queens, right?"

"Yeah, but that's out of our jurisdiction."

"I got blanket permission from the sarge to exceed our bounds. We can't make any arrests, but we got the blessing of the city to investigate wherever we want. We just need to pull in the local cops if we want to question anyone or request a search warrant or anything like that. All I gotta do is give Palmers a call to cover our sector. Oh, and we need to shed the uniform. Plain clothes from here on out if we want to step outside the precinct."

"Sure. Queens is a big area. Where would we start?"

"Didn't your bartender say he ordered a particular brand of Scotch?"

"Yeah. I couldn't remember what it was if you asked me now."

"And he downed it, right?"

"That's what he said."

"Do you think he wanted the bartender to think he frequented a Scottish pub in Queens?"

"Anything's possible. Better than anything I got. Let's roll. We taking your car?"

"Affirmative."

The rain steadily increased throughout Charlie's shift, from a light sprinkle at the start to an all-out downpour by the end. By the time Charlie and Gina entered their third Scottish bar in Queens, a pretty steady drizzle began opening up umbrellas. Gina's green Buick found a parking spot a block away and around the corner. Charlie knew as soon as he opened the door to The Edinburgh that his stalker had been there. "You see that?" he asked Gina.

"Sure do." What they had seen was a doll of Groundskeeper Willie from *The Simpsons* tacked to the wall amongst other bizarre keepsakes, such as a plush Loch Ness Monster and a picture of James Doohan before he gained the weight and gray hair. But the Groundskeeper Willie doll had had its limbs replaced by limbs from other dolls. One of its arms was obviously from a Popeye. Other than that, Charlie couldn't tell from where the other limbs came. "Might has well have painted, 'This is the bar, Charlie,' on the wall."

Charlie squeegeed the rainwater off his arms and approached the bar. Gina was better off as she wore a North Face Gortex coat. She found a table and waited. Not wanting to appear conspicuous, Charlie kept his voice low when ordering ginger ales for Gina and himself. This turned out to be an exercise in irony, as his hushed tone caught the attention of more than one patron near the bar area. Charlie felt the eyes on him as he made his way to the table Gina staked and sat down. Her back was to the wall, so his was to the crowd. "How many?" he asked her as he sat down, referring to the number of people who took an interest in them.

"Nearly all of them. One is coming our way now," she said as quiet as she could.

"You here to buy or sell," said a thin voice from behind Charlie.

"Have a seat," he said, turning to see the man. The stranger was as thin as his voice. He styled a retro lambskin vest, tan, with a dark brown shirt underneath. Greg Brady collars protruded from the vest. This clashed horribly with his gray khakis but worked with his red, curly hair and sunglasses. "What should I call you?" Charlie asked.

"Call me Pete." He turned one of the chairs around and sat on it backwards with his arms folded over the back rest. "Now, you buyin' or are you sellin'?"

"Buyin' of course."

"Good answer. What's your medicine?"

"What do you got?"

Pete looked at Charlie with distrust. "Seems to me a man buyin' would know what he wants."

"It's not for me. Let's call it a souvenir for someone else."

"You're looking for something a little more high-class. Something you can't get out in the sticks. You from the Midwest?"

"Kentucky."

"Well I got stuff your someone else ain't likely never had before." He snapped his fingers and a heavy-set gentleman with a dark goatee and no additional hair brought over a briefcase." *Damn it*, Charlie thought. *I need to get rid of this guy.*

"Come on, Mike," Gina said. "We know this place has the stuff, let's catch the show and come back later."

Pete looked Charlie squarely in the eye. "The bitch shuts her mouth now, or the two of you ain't goin' anywhere except feet first." Charlie rolled his eyes to Gina and she looked down at the table. The bald man opened the briefcase to reveal several, well organized packets of white powder. Some of them had a red piece of tape, some had yellow, and the rest had blue. "This," Pete said as he pulled one of the packets with the yellow tape, "is the finest, most pure heroine you'll ever see in the New World."

Charlie would not touch the packet but eyed it as if he were interested. The last thing he wanted was his fingerprints on something that would turn up in someone else's case outside his precinct. "How much?"

Pete tossed the bag back into the briefcase, and the bald man slammed it shut and took it away. "That was the third sign, my friend." Charlie looked at him with incomprehension. "First, you order a nonalcoholic drink all quiet-like. Second, no one comes here looking to buy for someone else. But even a tool like you would reach for the pouch if you were really a buyer. You're too stupid to be a narc, but I'd bet my life you're a cop. Hands on the table and spread your fingers." Pete gave him a second to comply but did not wait for Charlie to make up his mind on what to do next. Raising his voice, he shouted, "I said put your hands on the goddamned table and spread your fingers!" Charlie and Gina did as requested. Pete did not show any weapon, but at least half a dozen men (Charlie was in no mood to count) had revealed an arsenal of guns and knives.

"So, what now?" Charlie asked. He could see that Pete had not expected Charlie to speak so calmly.

"Now, you are going to walk out the back door with Little Tim over there." Unlike the characters Charlie had read about in crime stories named Litte This or Little That, this Tim really was little. He must have stood five-foot-one when he straightened his back, and currently he was not doing so.

"I don't think so." Charlie's calm was beginning to unnerve Pete. A bead of sweat appeared on his forehead. Pete pulled a throwing dagger, seemingly out of the air, and stuck it down on the table between the index and middle fingers of Charlie's right hand. Gina flinched, but Charlie did not. *Why am I not scared shitless right now?* "If it were a good idea to kill us here, you wouldn't want to move us first. The shades would come down and that would be it for the two buyers you seem to think are cops." Charlie saw Pete, ever so slightly, glance at the blinds that were rolled up at the top of the windows. "But you can't close the blinds, can you? Closing the blinds would mean something...a signal to someone else outside somewhere. And you don't want to start that ball rolling, do you? So, if you're going to kill us, do it here, and do it now. Otherwise, let us on our way. Our business is not with you." Pete no longer looked nervous. He looked disappointed.

"You're right, mate. I'm not going to kill you in here. But I can fuck you up before you leave."

"You'll do no such thing," came a cooler voice from the other side of the pub. Charlie thought it was almost comical the way everyone stopped what they were doing and turned to look at the speaker, including Pete. When Pete turned back around to Charlie and Gina, two pistols were aimed at his head. "You don't need those, officers," the voice said. "But feel free to keep them trained on whoever you want if it makes you feel better."

"I didn't think you was gonna be here tonight," said Pete in the general direction of the voice. Charlie stood up and saw a familiar face in black clothes sitting at a table by himself. He was de-shelling peanuts and making a small pile on his table of the beans inside. Charlie had only seen his face at the warehouse, where the lighting was not ideal, but he knew it was his stalker.

"I was not planning to be here. Something changed my mind," Charlie's stalker said. "Charlie…Gina…it took you long enough to find this place. I overestimated you. Forget this place. I already gave you the note about where and when to meet at Magoon's. Best get out of here. You're outgunned, so don't bother trying anything. I'll see you in three days." Charlie and Gina kept their guns raised and backed up towards the front door. They would file a report on what happened, and a local unit would discover the next day that the pub had been abandoned and that the owner vanished from the city. Charlie would think the entire episode had been a dream, except that he only had one dream these days.

They walked in silence until they were around the corner in the steady rain. Then Charlie grabbed Gina with both arms and squeezed. He could feel the warmth of Gina's tears contrasting against the colder rain on his face. Her voice cracked when she spoke, "How on Earth did you keep cool in there?"

"Not sure. I think I channeled General Chang." Gina pulled back as their embrace relaxed. Her eyes obviously had not considered the question answered. "I've been him for quite a few nights. It would be hard not to pick up some of his traits. Anyway, we're out of there now, so let's call this a night."

"What was he talking about? Why was he expecting us sooner?" Gina asked.

"I think he expected us to pick up on his clues quicker and find this pub. That was two weeks ago. Maybe he thinks I'm further along in my dreams? But I guess if I went to his pub a lot sooner, someone would have given me that note about meeting at the Statue of Liberty here instead of at Magoon's."

"Why didn't he just leave the note at Magoon's when he first went there?"

"Probably so he could know when we got his message. He couldn't keep going back to Magoon's and asking Iain."

Later that night, Gina downloaded the video from their Private Storage camera onto her iPhone. Charlie still had a flip phone with no ability to download anything. They viewed approximately four minutes of Martin Killjoy moving in and out of the camera's view as he retrieved his own camera and then brought it back to remount it, presumably after viewing its contents. Other than that, nothing.

Chapter 15

Hsieh Sun's arm was still interlocked with Chang Huang's when Yuan Lin returned. Yuan Lin's expression did not betray any jealousy. *Maybe he's* not *interested in her,* Chang Huang thought. Then he shook the thought away. *That should be the least of my concerns.* "Did the monk provide enlightenment?"

"He did. I need to speak with Hsieh Sun. But first, can I have a word with you General?"

"Certainly." Hsieh Sun released the general's arm and walked toward the sleeping quarters.

"General, I do not know what this means, but Kong Xiao told me that this is not your place. That your home is far from here; that I cannot even imagine how far. I asked him if you have returned from the dead. He laughed at me. He said that I am not far from the truth. Do you understand what he is talking about?"

Chang Huang smiled and looked towards the sky. "I do, Captain Yuan. To be honest, I am not sure why I am here. I suspect it is to find out who killed the Bao family. But I do not know for sure. I believe our fates…yours, Hsieh Sun's and mine…are intertwined."

"He wanted me to tell you that there has to be a beginning. Does that make sense?"

"No. Not in the least. But I am sure it will at some point." Chang Huang felt confident that this was true, though he did not understand from where that confidence came. Somehow, within the walls of this temple campus, his worries were dampened. Not completely removed but tempered. "Have your conversation with Hsieh Sun and we will all meet up afterwards."

"Thank you, General." Yuan Lin retreated to the sleeping quarters and Chang Huang removed the message from his purse. *Next letter: vertical line. Vertical line, vertical line, vertical line. It's so bizarre that I don't know what a vertical line means. Also in positions 28, 35, 49, and 53. The first three are multiples of seven: four, five, and seven, times seven. I do remember a trip to the Grand Canyon when I was four. I started kindergarten at five. Little league at seven. The last one, 53, is reverse of the middle one: 35.* Chang Huang repeated this in his head many times before putting the paper away. Afterwards he walked to the altar and pondered the statue. Queen Maha Maya was the mother of Gautama Buddha. The idol displayed her dreaming of being taken away by the four spirits to Lake Anottatta. There is where she was delivered the news that she would be the mother of the Purest-One. Something about an elephant with many tusks, a flower, and Queen Maya's side, but neither Chang Huang nor Charlie knew all the details. Parallels to Christianity notwithstanding, Chang Huang felt some sort of understanding about this monk without really understanding anything. The Queen's dream was real to billions of people over the years. *Dreams are important to these people. Our host supposedly banished an evil into a dream...whatever that means.* Chang Huang reached down and grabbed a fistful of dirt. He felt its dryness on his skin. He looked up into the night sky. The stars indicated that the dust storm had passed. The stalker in New York knew about the massacre in his dream. Martin Killjoy was a real person he met in this dream. Dr. Thomason said an explanation he might not yet imagine could unfold, but Chang Huang/Charlie faced too many connections between his dream and the "real world." He looked down at the dirt in his hand and let it flow between his fingers. *This dirt is real.* He held his palm up to his face and closed his hand into a fist. *These fingers are real.* He thought about the massacre he saw early in his dream. *The Bao family was real.* He bent over and almost threw up. It was as if he discovered them all over again.

"General, do you feel unwell?" Yuan Lin had returned from his conversation with Hsieh Sun. *How long was I daydreaming?*

Chang Huang composed himself. "I was…praying."

"You think that will help when sparring with me?" *Okay,* that *was trash talk.*

"It might. I prayed that you might offer up more of a challenge next time."

"Ready to see if your prayers are answered, old man?" Yuan Lin drew his sword and waived it in taunting circles.

"I am always ready, young one." Chang Huang drew his as well. The two walked to a clear area between in front of the altar. As the two began their salutes, three of the reddish-robed apprentices gathered around them while a fourth ran back to the sleeping quarters. Yuan Lin raised his sword and swung downward in a feint to draw Chang Huang's sword. At the last minute, he arced his blow to curve around Chang Huang's blade and brought it inward towards Chang Huang's mid-section. Chang Huang easily pivoted his sword without moving his arm much to knock away Yuan Lin's strike. About this time, the fourth apprentice returned, and Chang Huang chanced a glance back to see that several other red robes and Hsieh Sun were coming out to join the original spectators. "You are taking it easy on me. Do not let my age fool you," Chang Huang said.

Yuan Lin answered by increasing his speed and remaining on the attack. For Chang Huang, this battle was different than the last spar. He let his instincts take over as he did last time, but he also concentrated on remembering each technique…how his arm and body felt. He watched himself, almost as if he were an outside spectator, as he blocked Yuan Lin's attacks and shifted his blade to offense the moment afterward. He noted how his feet danced forward and backwards, with little side-to-side movement. He parried, feinted, attacked, and withdrew, all while Yuan Lin was doing the same. He knew that any slips could be just as deadly here in this "safe" environment as it would be in battle. The only difference was the modicum of restraint each used to resist a deadly strike, which only happened after successfully evading a block. Chang Huang could see Hsieh Sun watching with both apprehension and awe. She was enjoying the show. This made Chang Huang fight faster. He had not realized that Yuan Lin's defense was weakening until Yuan Lin stepped back and lowered his sword. Yuan Lin's face was mired in unease until Chang Huang smiled and said, "Sorry, Yuan Lin. This was one of the best spar sessions I ever enjoyed. Forgive my increased enthusiasm."

Yuan Lin's face melted to a smile. "I was beginning to think I had done something wrong, General." Chang Huang looked at Hsieh Sun. She had not noticed any breech of etiquette on his part, if there had been any to notice. He looked back to Yuan Lin.

"Not at all, Captain." For a split second, he had the impulse to reach out to shake Yuan Lin's hand. He bowed instead at the last second. *My Western ways are seeping into Chang Huang's personality. I need to be more careful.* "Come, let us have an ale before we retire. We should leave for Xin early tomorrow."

"Agreed." Hsieh Sun did not join them but instead returned to the sleeping quarters. In the kitchen, an ale barrel was already uncorked. "Your fighting was stronger this time, General," Yuan Lin said after they sat at a wooden table with filled cups. "I would like to learn from you."

"I can share my techniques, but I am not sure I have any additional skills that you do not have. Only by repetition can you improve. To be honest, Yuan Lin, I have been learning from you." *Or, rather, Charlie has been learning from you and Chang Huang.*

"Any additional practice you can give me would be greatly appreciated."

"Anytime, Yuan Lin. We can go a round before we leave here tomorrow morning." Their conversation dwindled and Yuan Lin returned to the sleeping quarters after one cup. Chang Huang stayed after for a bit and studied the message some more. *Vertical line. Vertical line. Multiples of seven...Grand Canyon, kindergarten, and little league. The last position is the reverse of the middle of those. Vertical line. Vertical line. Multiples of seven...four, five, and seven. The last position is the reverse of the middle of those. Wake up.*

(Tuesday – August 21, 2012)

Vertical line. Vertical line. Multiples of seven...Grand Canyon, kindergarten, little league. The last position is the reverse of the middle of those. Charlie wrote these words down. Then he drew the vertical line: | .

Multiples of seven...four, five, and seven. That would be 28, 35, and 49. The last is the reverse of the middle: 53. Charlie inserted his vertical line letter into the appropriate positions in his message:

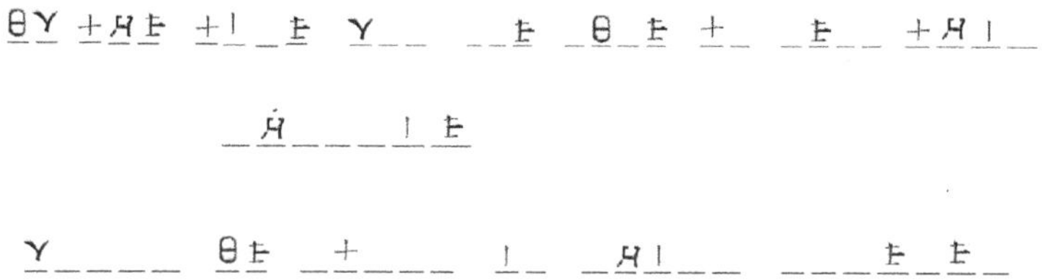

Now we're cooking! That third word has got to be "time," the seventh is "to," and the ninth is "this." Maybe "thin." Probably "this." I'll fix it later if I'm wrong. Charlie filled in the spaces to complete those words on his notepad. Then he placed a dot below them so he could remember which ones are guesses:

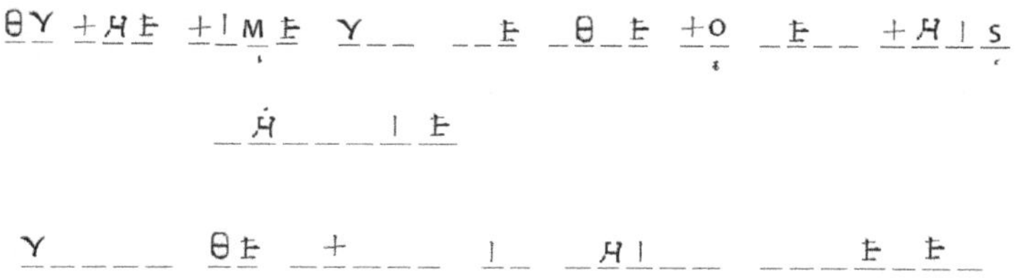

Since I'm guessing, that fourth word is either "yes" or "you" ...or "yet." "By the time you*" makes more sense. The sixth word...with a "B" in the second position, the first position must be a vowel. Abie, able, abre, ebre, ibie, ible, oboe, ubie...I'm sure there's more, but "oboe" and "able" are the only two of those that are real words, and I don't think "oboe" is in that message. "By the time you ___ able...." "By the time you* are *able."*

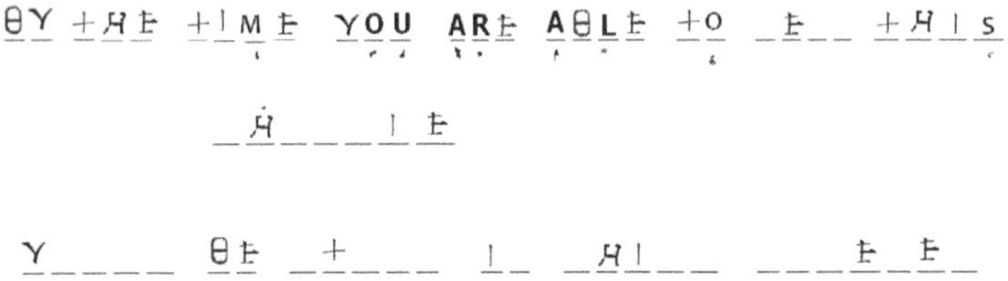

Better. At least in "Wheel" they tell you where all the letters are when you guess one right. Third from the end is either "in," "it," or "is." But this has to be good enough for now.

Charlie was able to sleep a couple more hours without dreaming before getting up and reaching out to his neighbor across the hall. The Egg answered Charlie's knock without surprise or any hesitation in inviting Charlie in. "Tea?" he asked as he moved to the kettle without waiting for an answer.

"Yeah, I completely forgot about coffee this morning." *That is absolutely a first,* Charlie thought.

"I have just the thing. It's a green tea but a little different than what you had the other day. This caffeine will not only wake you up but lower your anxiety and desire for your missing coffee." He poured water into the kettle and turned on the burner.

"I have a favor to ask." He didn't continue until The Egg walked back into the room. "You knew a lot about swords last time we talked. Do you know anything about using them?"

"I've competed in tournaments in my younger years, but it's been a long time."

"Could you teach me? I have some basic moves, but I need some fast instruction."

"Upcoming duel?"

"Something like that." Charlie thought of the theater he and Gina visited recently. "It's for a scene in a play. I opened my big mouth I that used to be a proficient swordsman, and my buddy asked me to come down to give the cast some pointers." He was sure that The Egg didn't buy it, but it didn't matter as long as The Egg would oblige him. And The Egg did. After tea, the two went up to the roof with Charlie's sword. "How long ago has it been since you fenced?" Charlie asked.

"I don't fence. I used to practice Wudang with a qingtong sword. Similar length to your dao, but the handle is shorter and the blade straighter. I've also used this style to compete with European broadswords against opponents using middle-age styles and with Japanese nihonto blades fighting against Kendo styles…all wooden weapons, of course."

"Of course."

"I don't think the Wudang style itself is superior. I'm just that damned good." He laughed out loud at his ego-laced comment, and Charlie could not help but chuckle as well. The two spent the next two hours reviewing techniques and even sparred a little with a couple of wooden qingtongs The Egg had stashed away. But the speed was exponentially slower than Chang Huang's exercises with Yuan Lin. Still, Charlie felt some of Chang Huang's instincts moving his arm. He was remembering. Charlie knew he could not face someone of Yuan Lin's magnitude with his current skill level. He only hoped the stalker lacked Yuan Lin's ability as well.

Charlie brought his notepad with its increasingly clearer message when he met up with Gina for lunch. The outdoor seating at Pedro's Burgers was a favorite of Gina's in the summertime. It was across the street from a group of antique shops that attracted an interesting crowd in the middle of the day. Pedro himself was a black man with a French accent. The burgers really weren't the best in town, and the orders came out slow. But it seemed to Gina that the joint itself was the epitome of the term "melting pot."

Charlie showed her the message. "I could be wrong, but I don't think so. The ones with the dots underneath are my guesses. The rest are memorizations. What I don't get is why I can't understand this in my dream, yet I can bring Chang Huang's understanding of sword fighting to the real world…at least to some degree."

"I don't know, Charlie, it seems like you get the same results with both."

"How do you mean?"

"When you look at that message, you can memorize the shape of the characters. You don't bring meaning from here to there, but you can memorize a shape there and bring it here. Same with the sword fighting. You can memorize the movements and recreate them here. But you're not as good as Chang Huang, right?"

"That makes sense. Any thoughts on the rest of these words?"

"Just a minute. How do you know you can bring Chang Huang's understanding of sword fighting to the real world?"

"I picked up another sword at a pawn shop near my apartment." Gina shook her head as she stared at him. "What? I'm just getting familiar with it. The Egg…you know, that guy across the hall? He's going to show me some moves. It's just to protect myself. I don't plan on fighting the stalker with a sword. But he's determined, and I can imagine a scenario or two where he's able to maneuver me into a situation where it is just me, him, and a couple of swords."

Gina shook her head and rolled her eyes. "Back to this message. Let me have the notepad again." Gina looked at the letters Charlie filled in for several minutes. Charlie noticed her lips were moving while she thought through possibilities. "No. Other than what you already said about that word being 'it', 'in', or 'is'. Except maybe this: have you considered that this message means nothing at all? Or at least nothing that will be helpful to you. I mean, the killer left that message intentionally, and I'm sure he doesn't want to get caught, so what could it say that would lead you to him?"

"That's what Kong Xiao said. I still gotta figure it out, though."

"Of course you do." She smiled and took a sip of her Diet Coke. Pedro sold dogs as well as burgers, which Charlie infinitely preferred, at least here. They had rather large, deep fried hot dogs (fried to the point where they split open) sold two at a time, piled with chili, onions, and mustard and a mess of fries on the tray scattered between them. Charlie dunked a few of the fries, already drenched in grease and malt vinegar, into his paper container full of ketchup before cramming them into his mouth. "Adorable," Gina said.

"General Chang would not be amused at my table manners." He took a swig of his root beer. "We really are different people," he mused. "But only on the surface. It's me when I'm there. I just seem to have a slightly different philosophy or something. It's not like I understand Chinese culture when I'm there…their idioms and manners, but when it comes time to do, say, or react to anything, I seem to do them differently there than here. I mean, to me, it is just like I'm speaking English, even using English slang. But I'm not… the Chinese colloquialisms are just so familiar to me that it seems like English. Here, I don't understand any Chinese culture. Well…actually, I'm starting to. I don't think I'm meant to carry on like this."

"I'm pretty sure it would kill you if you did this for long."

"What's the solution?"

"One will present itself, Charlie. You have to believe that."

"You sound like Chang Huang. I don't know…after all that's happened, I don't feel comfortable believing anything for certain. Chang Huang's pretty much convinced that this is real…that I'm travelling back in time to China when I'm asleep."

"What does Charlie believe?"

"Nearly the same thing. At the very least, me, my stalker, and Martin Killjoy are visiting the same dream. Maybe others. I can't abide by any psychological explanation any longer."

"Good. Then we can forget about caring about whether we are crazy or not and open our minds a bit. Stuff like sanity gets in the way, doesn't it?" Charlie almost thought she was being sarcastic, but her amused expression seemed genuine to him.

"Here's to mental instability!" he said as he raised his paper cup.

"Here, here!"

Mark Robinson, Charlie's partner, returned from his leave that evening. Charlie had been hoping to have his stalker case wrapped up and be ready to celebrate Mark's homecoming by now. Instead, the recent killings shadowed the moment. Still, seeing Mark's face helped him to be normal, like he did before he started dreaming of China. Charlie heard his voice from over his shoulder before he realized Mark was standing behind him. "Never let a man sneak up on you like that, Peltman."

"Couldn't happen…my partner's got my back." He spun around and, after a pretend punch to the gut, the two men embraced. "Great to have you back, Mark. Just wish it were happier times, man."

"Yeah. Bad news." Charlie started shaking his head back and forth, holding back tears of guilt.

"It was my guy, Mark. Whatever I did to piss him off got Fred and Peter killed."

"Shut up, man. Just shut up about that. The chips landed where they did. I would have taken the bullet for either one of them guys. And you would, too. Everyone knows that. Me more than anyone. So, let's not say another word about it whose fault this was. After tonight's shift, you and I are gonna drink to them. Deal?"

"Deal."

"Bring Gina, too. She was McAllister's partner. If I could fly Wilkins back from Pittsburgh, I'd do that, too." Jeremy Wilkins had been Peter Jameson's partner before he moved to Pennsylvania. That move freed up Jameson to partner with McAllister and placed him in the passenger seat of a patrol car overlooking a refrigerator warehouse ten days ago.

"She'll be there. With bells. Who do they got you partnering up with?"

"A rookie. He's been doing desk work since he joined up until I got back. I'm guessing once this stalker thing gets worked out, he'll be Gina's partner and you'll be back with me."

"Shouldn't be much longer."

"You on the back end of this one?"

"Think so. I'll know more in a couple days."

"Aren't you off tomorrow and Thursday?"

"Officially, but when the case is about you, are you ever really off?"

"Are cops ever off, regardless of the case?"

"Why are we talking in questions?"

"Does it matter?" This went on longer than most people would put up with, but Charlie and Mark had a knack for dragging out a bit. As much as Charlie appreciated or liked Gina, Mark Robinson was Charlie's partner, and he would not feel like the world was right until they were partners again.

"So how was L.A.?" Charlie asked.

"Man, that was great advice. She had an awful time! I actually enjoyed it. But I wasn't expecting 90210 like Elizabeth was. I think any thoughts of moving out there are off the table. So how's the constipation?"

"You know, I haven't had that problem in a little while. I actually forgot all about it."

"Doing anything different?"

"I don't know…drinking a few different kinds of tea on occasion." *Plus, I'm infected by dreams of China, practicing sword fighting, and falling in love with my neighbor.*

Charlie and Gina met briefly with Greg and Nora at the beginning of the shift, who agreed that they were still waiting for the stalker to make the next move. Charlie dropped off his journal with Dr. Thomason before he and Gina headed out.

"So, Mark's breaking in my new partner, huh?" Gina asked as she turned left onto Barbey from Arlington.

"He'll show him the ropes. Work out his bumps, so to speak." Charlie was about to say more, but the radio broke in.

"All units in the vicinity of Ashford and Fulton, please respond to a Ten-Thirty-One at Samson Jewelry."

"That's us," Gina said. Charlie picked up the hand mic and reported that they were on their way. When they arrived, they saw three patrol cars parked strategically to simultaneously cut off access to the street and provide cover for the officers who were crouched behind them. "There it is." Charlie pointed to the jewelry store across from the patrol cars. "Looks like the suspect might still be inside."

Charlie did not see officers on the other side. "Isn't there a back door?" Charlie would expect to see all possible exits covered. "Take us back there." As Gina drove, Charlie picked up the hand mic again. "This is Bravo-247. We're heading around the back to cutoff escape route. Out."

"Negative, Bravo-247. Come around to the front. Out." Charlie and Gina looked at each other, shrugged their shoulders, and swung around to the assembly of blue and whites gathering in front of the jewelry store. Gina parked with the right side of the car facing the store and the nose almost touching the tail of another patrol car. They both got out Gina's side and moved with low profile to the front end of the car so they could talk directly with one of the other cops.

"What's the deal?" Charlie asked.

"Look," officer Truman said as he pointed to the store front. Behind a glass window offering the lowest prices on diamond jewelry in NYC stood a man in dark clothes with a sword drawn and resting at the neck of a Chinese man.

"Okay, I see why you want me out front, seeing how this could be my stalker and all, but shouldn't someone cover the back door?"

"McGovern is on the rooftop opposite the back door."

"What's he gonna do, snipe whoever comes out? We wanna catch this guy, not waste him."

"He's a cop killer."

"We don't know that's him. What the hell's wrong with you?" But Charlie knew what the hell was wrong with him. He was pumped up on emotion and not thinking straight. He had seen it before and didn't like it. *We gotta catch this guy, whether he's my stalker or not, before someone does something really stupid.* Charlie pulled the mic off his shoulder and started barking orders. He had one of the cars from the front move around to the back and pulled McGovern off the roof before Truman could think of a response. But eventually, Truman found his voice.

"Now just a minute, Peltman, who the hell do you think you are? This is my scene. And don't forget who McAllister and Jameson took one for."

"Truman, you're not thinking straight. If this *is* my stalker, then it's my call. You and I can talk about this later." Truman slunk back.

After the patrol car had moved around to the back of the store, it was replaced by two more cars and a motorcycle pair. In the ever-increasing swarm of police, the man with the sword (a machete, actually) surrendered. It was not Charlie's stalker. This sprinkled some water on Truman's hypersensitivity, and his anger melted to embarrassment. He would later apologize to Charlie, and Charlie would tell him there was no need.

Robinson had a table all ready for Charlie and Gina with a pitcher of Sam Adams and three empty mugs waiting for them. Charlie usually hated it when Mark did that, as he really didn't venture past Coors Light, but tonight was certainly not about the beer. "'Bout time you all arrived."

"Sorry, one of those nights," Charlie replied. "How long you been here?"

"Not long; just razzin' ya." He stood up and gave Gina a hug before giving Charlie an exaggerated handshake. "I heard Truman gave you a bad time tonight."

"Momentary lapse, that's all. He's just on edge."

"He's a dick, but you didn't hear that from me." Gina giggled but Charlie only smiled back.

"Why don't you fill up our mugs so we can pay our respects."

"You got it." Mark poured the first round and lifted his mug. "To Peter and Fred. May the motherfucker who killed them find a very special place in hell in the very near future." Charlie caught Mark's eye before they said their here-here's and saw a small glimpse of what he had seen in Truman's eyes earlier that night. Mark was not there yet, but the anger was lurking not far away.

"We'll get him, Mark," said Gina. Charlie knew Gina had seen the same in Mark's eyes, and was glad she knew better how to counter it.

"I know you will. Let me know if I can help."

It was late when he arrived home. He turned on his computer, planning on doing a little more research on Kong Xiao. But first, he saw that Gina had emailed him a link to the cloud, where he could check to see if anything interesting happened at the Private Storage that day. It didn't, although he did see Martin standing in front of unit 4358. Martin scratched his chin and looked as though he considered opening the unit. But eventually gave up and walked away.

Chapter 16

Chang Huang continued gazing at the message in his hands. He knew what the first several words meant, but looking at them now, they made no sense whatsoever. *I'll assume my guesses are correct, which means the next character I have to memorize is the first letter of the eighth word. Looks similar to the first letter. The top part is the same, but it's got two legs. It's walking. Maybe I'm wrong about all this and it's some sort of hieroglyph. Either way, I'll remember this one. It's also here, here, and here.* He pointed to positions 33, 58, and the last position. *It's also here.* He pointed to a character in one of the words that he had already translated back in New York. *So, I'll know if I'm right about that letter, too. Thirty-three and 58. Thirty-three and 58. Three plus five is eight. Then remember the last position.*

He repeated this several times and placed the message back into his purse. As he did so, his fingers chanced upon something hard and smooth. The mask he picked up at the oasis had come partly unwrapped. He retrieved the mask and saw that a crack had angled down across the face. He tried to pack it carefully before meeting up with Hsieh Sun and Yuan Lin this morning but apparently not carefully enough. The seven-character word was still intact, however. Charlie retrieved the message to see if any of the characters were the same. All seven characters on the mask were also in the message. They were identical to the seven-letter word in the middle line. *It's the same word.*

He rewrapped the mask and put it back in his purse, then returned to the temple sleeping quarters. He slept for a few hours but woke when the door opened and closed. *Chang Huang, you wouldn't sleep a wink in New York.* Apparently, in addition to sleeping lightly, Chang Huang did not return to sleep easily once awoken. After several minutes, he felt wide awake and decided to see who had been out and about tonight. He heard no shuffling after the door had closed, so he assumed that someone had left rather than entered. *Hsieh Sun.*

She stood in silhouette between the sleeping quarters and the altar. The light atop the altar was still ablaze but had dimmed. She either did not hear the door to the sleeping quarters or chose to ignore it. Either way, she started slightly when Chang Huang put his left hand on her right shoulder. She grabbed the hand and swung it high and forward, keeping it taught, ready to kick or flip whoever dared to touch her. But she stopped when she saw Chang Huang's expression of surprise staring back at her. "Nice one!" he said.

"Sorry…instinct."

"No need to be sorry. It is good to be prepared at all times."

"But you are a general in the emperor's army."

"Not here," Chang Huang said as he waived to indicate the walls of the temple. "Here we are not ranked. Where did you learn your…instinct."

"There is a lot you do not know about me, General."

"Enough time has not passed for you to call me Chang Huang?"

"Close, but not yet."

"I can see that your past is painful to you. I do not mean to pry." Hsieh Sun looked back at the altar's flame. Chang Huang could not track how much time passed but remained quiet until Hsieh Sun spoke.

"Kong Xiao introduced me to Mr. Shen. He owns the tavern. Mr. Shen made a mistake many, many years ago. He regretted this mistake." She turned back Chang Huang but only looked at his chest. Tears started to well in her eyes, but she quickly wiped them away. "Kong Xiao understood that our introduction would benefit both of us."

"What mistake did Mr. Shen make?"

"His daughter had been raped, which brought great shame to the Shen family. A travelling band came through and she ran away with them. He regretted not being there for her, for not being the father he should have been. But he would never be able to find those travelers. For many years, Mr. Shen had to bury his pain deep inside. But when his wife died, he realized he was all alone in the world. He wondered more and more what became of his daughter. He was near to killing himself when Kong Xiao brought me to his home."

"How did your presence help him?" Hsieh Sun looked into Chang Huang's eyes, this time unable to dam the flood. She wiped her eyes and continued.

"When I was raped, my mother had already died. My father could not bear the burden of me, so he sold me. He was heartless. Two years later, I escaped from my captors and took some of their coins. Before coming to Xin, I returned to spy at my father's house to see if he had any remorse. Instead, he had taken a new wife and had two children he could be proud of." Her eyes were no longer wet but dry with anger. "It was soon after that I came to this temple. With my past, there was no where I could go. But Kong Xiao knew that Mr. Shen would take me in and give me work. He lets me have time off to come here every seven days. He is never mad if I stay for an extra day. He is just happy that I am there. He pays me well and always treats me with respect. I could never find anything like that anywhere else. I am…blessed." She did not wait for Chang Huang to embrace her but fell against his chest, wrapping her arms around him. Chang Huang squeezed her back.

"Hsieh Sun, you have been through much." *Come on, Charlie, that the best you got?* "You are blessed. You have Mr. Shen, you have Kong Xiao, and you have me."

She looked up into Chang Huang's eyes. "You will not be here for long."

"That is not yet written. I have to return to Peiping at the end of the summer and may have to return to my command. But this area needs the emperor's protection. The emperor would likely allow me to return here. I will also ask Yuan Lin to join my army. With the two of us around, you will start to feel like you have family again."

Her expression lightened and she once again wiped away her remaining tears. "Thank you, Chang Huang." The two held onto one another for some time before Chang Huang walked her back to the sleeping quarters.

The next day Chang Huang and Yuan Lin battled in the open space for practice for the last time. In addition to the usual spectators, Kong Xiao stood among his pupils. His face was dark, however. It almost seemed disapproving of what he was seeing. Chang Huang saw this, and it cost him ground as Yuan Lin struck in rapid succession, moving towards Chang Huang with power and swiftness. In little time, Chang Huang seceded and the three companions began readying their horses. He thought about confronting the monk about his expression during the spar but decided to let it go. Instead, he simply thanked him for his hospitality and promised to return. "Are you both ready?" he called to Yuan Lin and Hsieh Sun. They were and the three of them caravanned across the sand, aware that they were leaving the temple much closer than when they arrived.

Their trip back to Xin seemed much faster than their journey to the temple. The men they encountered on the first leg of their trip south were long gone by the time the Yuan Lin and Chang Huang revisited the deserted inn. Near the end of their journey, Chang Huang could see what looked like Yuan Lin's troops all standing in rank and file. Yuan Lin and Hsieh Sun were talking about something, possibly a dream that Yuan Lin had, but Chang Huang's concentration was focused on the troop gathering. Their positions did not seem like ordinary drill, and they were not engaged in any training exercise. The closer the three came to Xin, the more details Chang Huang could make out. The most startling was that the front row of men held their bows in their hands with an arrow each resting across the string. Chang Huang had blocked out Yuan Lin's and Hsieh Sun's conversation completely by then, until he heard the last few words of what Yuan Lin was saying, "…it is called New York City."

(Wednesday – August 22, 2012)

Charlie jolted awake. He was covered in sweat and his sheets were bunched up around his ankles. *Yuan Lin is the stalker.* He looked around his room for a moment before realizing how soaked he was. Stumbling to the bathroom, he grabbed a towel and dried himself. *Yuan Lin…no, that's jumping to conclusions.*

His mind searched frantically for something else to think about. It settled on the message he was decrypting. *What was that letter? Just like the first one…no, the top half of the first one…with legs.* He drew an approximation of an "R", except the top half had the round part on top, just like the first character in his message. *Placements…last position, then double number…33. Then what…three plus five is eight…35 and 88! No, that can't be. Oh, yeah,* he smacked himself on the forehead, *33 and 58.* He placed the "R" into the first and last open positions, then in the 33rd, 58th spots:

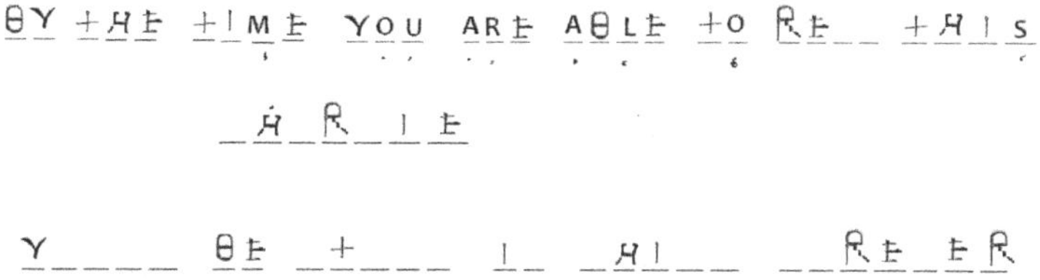

Read this? Charlie tried for a few minutes to see if there were any other words that would fit and make sense, but he could not. He placed an "A" and a "D" in the final open spots of the first line and indicated that they were guesses with a dot:

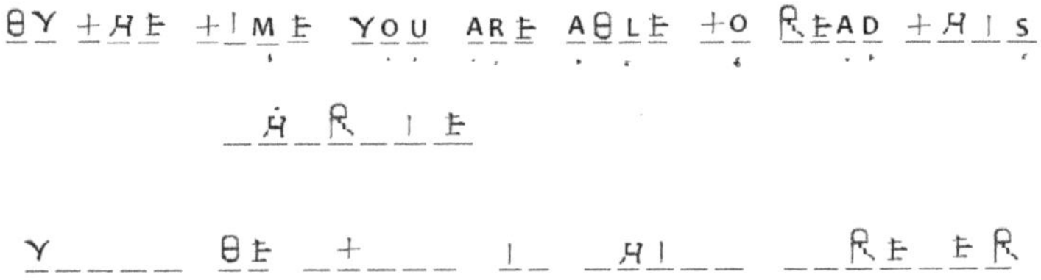

Then the mask is the same as the middle word. But I'm not there yet. He looked at it for a while longer, then put away his note pad and reflected back on Yuan Lin. *It can't be. I'm a cop...I don't misread people. But he did say, 'New York City,' and I'm sure he was talking about a dream.* He shook his head. *Stop it Charlie. Lots of people are dreaming back and forth. Martin Killjoy is, too. And Francis. And Yuan Lin is at least twenty years younger than Chang Huang. The man I saw at the warehouse and The Edinburgh looked a lot closer to my own age. But he did know about the massacre. It would take someone who knew about the massacre to leave that doll on my roof. I need to keep an open mind until I know more.*

"How was your lesson this morning?" Gina asked. Several mushrooms spilled from the bun of her mushroom-Swiss melt.

"It was all right. I learned how to dance today…adding a little footwork to my moves."

"Dancing lessons from a white Chinese sword master…sounds cheeky!"

"It's interesting. I'm really getting instruction from three men: The Egg, Yuan Lin, and Chang Huang. They're all training me for my upcoming bout with my stalker."

"But you're not really going through with it, though, right?" Charlie did not answer for a moment. His hesitation was all the answer Gina needed. "No, Charlie…this is stupid! You can't fight this guy with a sword…I won't allow it."

"Gina, I'm hoping it won't come to that. I'm thinking if I show up with a sword in my hand, I'll have a chance to talk to him. I *know* I haven't done anything to make someone want to kill me. I think if I talk to him, I can…hell, I don't know."

"I can always just shoot him if it looks like he's going to beat you." She attempted a smile but fell short.

"Got plans this afternoon?"

"Washing my hair," Gina replied.

"Good, come with me to Lextalt. It's been five days since I spoke with Francis, and I think I need to touch base. If nothing else, I need to make sure he doesn't give my job away to someone else. The ship will be in dock in less than a week, and I don't even have my plan finalized."

"You're going there just to talk about the job?"

"No, I want to find out how Francis knows the monk in my dream. I know he says he has dreamed like me, but if he met the monk, he must be another Chinese man in *my* dream. Or maybe his *is* the monk. I need to connect all the players there to the players here. I want to eliminate…." Charlie broke off as he realized he did not want to get into the whole possibility of Yuan Lin being his stalker.

"You want to eliminate what?"

"Just eliminate shadows."

"There's something you're not telling me."

"It's Yuan Lin. I'm starting to really like the guy. But I think he's dreaming of New York, too."

"What makes you say that?"

"I think I heard him talking about it to Hsieh Sun."

"Then you gotta confront him. I mean in Xin. He should respect that."

"May not have much of a chance. His whole army is waiting for us to return from the temple, and their weapons are at the ready." Charlie studied Gina, trying to gauge her mood but not feeling like he was doing that great of a job at it. "Do you know what it's like? Knowing that as soon as I'm go to sleep I will be riding with Hsieh Sun and Yuan Lin again, facing an army with their weapons drawn? I'd give anything for just a regular, normal dream. I'd even go for one of those where I'm late for an exam that I never studied for…or where I suddenly find I'm walking around naked in a church."

"In a church?"

"Or school…or a sporting event. The point is: I feel like I am missing out by not having my own dreams. Real dreams. I really would give just about anything for that." He shoved a handful of French fries dripping with ketchup into his mouth. Gina set her sandwich down and stared at it. "You not hungry?"

"This is all just very unsettling to me. I don't want to see my best friend cut up in front of my eyes."

"That won't happen."

"Then why are you learning to fight with a sword?"

"Precaution…I don't know. I'm just…I'm not gonna get pierced." His eyes darted around the table a bit and settled on the dark red cherry on top of his milk shake. Without hesitation, he plucked it from the whipped cream and set it on her plate. Her eyes questioned him, but she picked the cherry from her plate and popped it in her mouth.

"But you love these."

"Not as much as I hate seeing you sad. Come on, let's get outta here."

Manhattan was particularly crowded in the afternoon so close to rush hour. Charlie could tell that Gina had not shaken the mood she was in from lunch. The Lextalt tower would look massive in any other city, but New York had many monster buildings, so its impressiveness was dwarfed to some degree. Still, there was something ominous about it now that he knew the connection between Francis and his dreams was so tight. He had been dreading meeting Francis again, though he wasn't exactly sure why. He let his feet take charge and let them take him into the building and up the elevator to the 44th floor. When he and Gina arrived, a different receptionist than Charlie had seen last time was just gathering her things and was visibly annoyed by the fact that one more person was walking in before she could leave. "Hello," she said. "Do you have an appointment?"

"No, but Francis will want to see me," Charlie said.

"Names?" Charlie told her. "Just a second." She pressed a button on a small box next to her phone, hoping that this man was correct about Francis wanting to see him. Otherwise, she'd need to schedule an appointment, which meant she would have to turn on her computer and wait for it to boot up. "Mr. Bremmer, a Charlie Peltman and a Gina Baxter here to see you."

Francis' voice came back through the black box, and the receptionist was relieved that he requested her to send them back. She told them how to find Mr. Bremmer's office and continued gathering her things. Francis looked up without expression as Gina and Charlie entered. "So, do I need to find another security detail for my shipment?" Harold was nowhere to be seen.

"What? No, I'm still on board. Part of my reason for being here is to review what I have in mind."

"Only part…you must have met Kong Xiao."

"Yes. How do you know him, exactly?"

"I'll tell you another time. Was he helpful?"

"Honestly, no. He took my being there as a message from you to him." Francis laughed. "What's so funny?"

"Your perception of things. Did he say anything at all that sounded like advice or words of wisdom?"

"He said something about a beginning. Everything has a beginning…or that there has to be a beginning. Look, Mr. Bremmer, this seems to be a joke to you…."

"It's no joke, and you have no idea how much I am helping you." Francis' mood turned from jovial to deadly serious but not angry. Charlie could tell he was frustrated, but there was something else tempering him. "You just learned my last name moments ago, and now you're calling me 'Mr. Bremmer.' This tells me you are irritated with me, and that is fine. It really doesn't matter whether or not you like me, and I can't expect you to trust me fully. But you must sense that you are in some kind of danger. Take what I say with a grain of salt, but every piece of information you receive, true or false, is important to you. It's up to you to determine the honesty or deception behind anything anyone says. Call me Francis or call me Mr. Bremmer; I don't care. My ship comes in six days, and what is on board that ship is of vital importance to your existence. Consider it your doom or your salvation. Either way, you can't ignore it."

Charlie did not respond right away. He looked at Gina, who was now looking at her hands. She seemed unusually uncomfortable. *Does she know something she's not telling me?* "Can you tell me what 'everything has a beginning' means?"

Francis looked him over; deciding how much to tell him, Charlie thought. "I can't, but don't spend too much time thinking about it. Just remember it. When the time comes that you need to remember this, it will make sense. If that time comes."

"You're a load of help." Charlie looked back to Gina again and decided to change the topic. "Let's talk security for a minute. I told Harold that I wanted to fool the bad guy before he fools us. His attack on the boat, which will happen before the boat docks, will be a feint. He will want us to feel victorious so that we'll let our guard down. Mr. X…Harold told you we're calling the bad guy Mr. X, right? Good. Mr. X will probably pull the actual theft of, or attack on, the container, or what's in the container, after the feint is over and the ship is in dock. I asked Harold for pictures of the boat. Did he get them?"

"Yes, I've been holding them until we met again." He got up out of his chair and moved slowly with a cane to a file cabinet against the back wall. It was the first time Charlie had seen him move and was surprised to see him so vulnerable. He returned to his chair with a manila envelope and tossed it to the edge of the desk closest to Charlie. Charlie removed the photographs from inside and looked at each one briefly before returning them to the envelope and tossing the lot back onto the desk.

"I want a replica of this boat. I want it waiting at a rendezvous place off the coast, far enough that it won't grab much attention. It will be controlled remotely and will be packed with explosives."

"In six days?"

"Less, actually. I need it in place a few days before the boat will dock." Francis appeared for a moment that this would not be possible, but Charlie wasn't in the mood for dramatics. Francis nodded as he pulled a notepad from one of his desk drawers and made a note.

"You think that will fool Mr. X?"

"Doesn't matter whether we fool him or not. For his feint, he will hire more expendable people. He doesn't think the attack will be successful, and he will expect his hired men to be killed in the process. So when they attack the decoy, two things will happen. First, the hired men will think they are successful, and we will have saved their lives. Second, they will report back to Mr. X that the ship is destroyed. Maybe he will fall for it, or maybe he won't. Either way, I'm hoping to trip him up a bit. Cause him to second-guess himself. Make a mistake. Even if not, it's worth it to save those men he plans to sacrifice."

"Will that be legal…blowing up the decoy?"

"Sure," Charlie said, knowing it would not be that easy. "If my boss can't pull enough strings to keep us in the clear, then I'll figure out a way to do this without the explosion. Either way, I need the decoy boat. Can you get me that?"

Francis smiled. "I can and will, Charlie."

"Good. Once the real boat pulls into customs, I'll have eyes on it. The Port Authority won't allow me to mount my own cameras on their grounds, but I've arranged for them to let me and a couple other off-duty cops into the warehouse where the container will be stored. I also arranged to get priority on the inspection roster, so our window of vulnerability might be less than four days. I know a few cops who will help me out. You won't need to pay them as much as you're paying me. We will all have cameras on our persons, and you will be able to monitor what is happening real-time. As Harold said, we can't let the feds know that this ship has been targeted for attack, but we can tell them the cargo is highly valuable. I'll send you a more detailed plan by email." He bent over Francis' desk and plucked one of his business cards from a gold-colored stand. Francis nodded at him.

By the time Charlie got back to his apartment, it was too late for dinner with Samantha. But he was not going to let the evening go by without seeing her. He grabbed a CD from his shelf and a bottle of wine from his cupboard before heading downstairs to her apartment. He felt the anticipation after he knocked as the light behind the peep hole in her door briefly went dark, then light again before Samantha opened it up. "Hi, Charlie! I was beginning to think you weren't coming." She was wearing jeans and a tight-fitting AC/DC concert tee.

"I was beginning to worry myself. I had to go see Francis up in Manhattan today about the Lextalt job. Got caught up in rush hour on the way back. You got a CD player, or are you all digital?" He flashed a jewel case within illustration of a stone building in the snow on the cover, not long enough for her to make out the title.

"I'm far from digital, Charlie. I still have a turntable," She said with a certain amount of pride. "But yes, I have a CD player, too. Come on in." Charlie had never seen her wearing tight clothes. She wasn't as thin as a lot of the Asian women he knew. She was perfect.

"Thanks," he said as he stepped inside.

"Whatcha got there?"

"I'll tell you after you hear them." Her apartment layout was the mirror image of his own. From the living room, he could see into the kitchen over a breakfast bar. She grew various plants that Charlie could not name in every corner, plus on a bookshelf that hung over a plush, blue sofa. His apartment did not have a similar bookshelf, and he wondered if she secured it there herself. A few art pieces hung on the wall, and a wooden cross hung above her television. A hand-painted, framed script of The Lord's Prayer hung next to the entryway of the kitchen. He noticed a half-empty wine glass next to a bottle on an oak coffee table. "I see you got a head start," he said and showed her the bottle he brought.

"We can save that one for later," she said as she took his bottle into the kitchen.

"This looks like your player. Mind if I pop this in?"

"Help yourself," she replied. She returned from the kitchen with another glass and filled it from the bottle on the coffee table. Charlie hit play on the CD player. A soft drum ushered a folksy beat that was joined by a somewhat bluesy guitar riff. The effect was both mellow and uplifting. Samantha cocked her head trying to place the sound but couldn't quite make it. "Who is this?" she finally asked.

"An old band from Indiana…The Why Store."

"Where your cousin lives?"

"Yep. There's this place called The Vogue where The Why Store would play 'til closing time. Just a five-dollar cover. Brian and I'd drink and smoke in the balcony level until our ears would bleed. Probably shouldn't have sat so close to the speaker. This, my dear, is them." He waved his hand towards the speaker.

"Little bit of buzz," sang the raspy voice of Chris Shaffer, "goin' round in circles. I'm a little bit buzzed, oh yeah, that's what's happenin' here." Samantha moved closer to him held onto each of his hands, swaying to the rhythm of Charlie Bushor's drum.

They moved closer together as they lightly shifted from side to side. His cheek rested against the temple next to her right eye; stubble from his face lightly scratched her, but she didn't mind—was almost comforted by it. "No more talking tonight, Charlie." The pressure of her breasts against his chest aroused Charlie. Samantha noticed. Charlie pulled his head back so that he could see into her upturned eyes, then placed his lips to hers.

Charlie lay awake for a while after Samantha fell asleep. He was not thinking about whether what happened was wrong or safe or dangerous. Instead, he was thinking about Hsieh Sun and Yuan Lin, about a line of arrows draped across bowstrings, and about a sword fight he may be engaged in the following night. But most of all, he thought about reality and fiction, wondering which of those he was in now. His mind flashed briefly on the Private

Storage camera that he failed to check tonight just before fading to sleep.

Chapter 17

Yuan Lin and Hsieh Sun had not seen the bows and arrows readied in the arms of the men awaiting their return from the temple. They were vaguely aware that an unexpected reception was up ahead. Chang Huang halted Horse and raised his hand. The other two stopped a couple steps after Chang Huang. Yuan Lin noticed that the bowmen were armed before Hsieh Sun saw. "Do you know what they want, General?" Yuan Lin asked.

"No. Something must have happened while we were away." He turned to look at Yuan Lin. "Before we go find out what they want, tell me what you said about New York City."

"That? Oh, just a place I have been dreaming about. I have dreamed about it a few times."

"Were you hit on the head before this started?"

"What? No. What are you talking about…sir?"

"Before you started dreaming about New York City…you were not hit over the head first?"

"No, sir. Why?"

Chang Huang looked at the ground and furrowed his eyebrows. "No reason." He looked back up at Yuan Lin. "What do you look like there? Have you seen a mirror?"

"Interesting question. Have you had such dreams?"

"No, but I am familiar with this kind of dream. A captain of mine had a similar dream once."

"What was his name?"

"You have not answered my question, Captain."

"I apologize, sir. I have dark hair, cut short. I am slightly taller in my dream. A teammate of mine calls me 'Guido,' but he means it as a joke. I guess we are both the same race. Why?"

"Just curious." Yuan Lin suddenly remembered that he was speaking to a superior and was being too familiar. There would have been little time, anyway, as Yuan Lin's men had approached while Chang Huang and he spoke.

"Captain Yuan! Surrender for the murder of the Bao family and the theft of the Bao family idol," announced Chai Wen.

Yuan Lin froze but did not speak. General Chang answered instead. "Lieutenant, what evidence do you have against Captain Yuan?"

"The Bao family idol was among his possessions."

"You went through his belongings?"

"Not intentionally. A group of jerboa were milling about his gear, going in and out. We only wanted to chase them away, but we found this." One of the men from the second row advanced and handed an idol to Lieutenant Chai Wen. It was about a foot high and two feet long. It was a Kwan Yin, the Goddess of Mercy, riding a bronze dragon. The front, right talon of the dragon clutched an emerald that seemed to shine of its own light, though that was likely an illusion. Chang Huang's thoughts drifted back to the stalker. *Italian,* he thought. *That man was Greek or Italian. Could have been a little taller than Yuan Lin. But he was older. About ten years at least.*

"Yuan Lin, in New York City, what is happening now?"

"Sir?"

"Events of the day."

"It is a sad time. The city had been attacked two months prior. Two large buildings collapsed, and thousands died." *That's 2001...almost 11 years ago. It would explain the difference in age.* Chang Huang's thoughts turned back to the three men they ran into at the deserted inn the previous day. *As far as I know, no one outside our party knew we were going past that inn.* A look of understanding materialized on his face.

"Step down from your horse, Yuan Lin," Chang Huang said as he dismounted his own stallion. He glanced at Hsieh Sun who was slowly shaking a concerned look on her face back and forth. Flashes of the massacre he stumbled upon when he first started dreaming of China invaded his mind. He thought about McAllister and Jameson. His anger peaked. "You killed them, Yuan Lin? Did the idol mean that much to you?" He waited for Yuan Lin to respond—hoped for a response—a denial or an explanation. Instead, Yuan Lin drew his sword and held it straight up in front of him. His face was a frown. His cheeks reddened. "This is how you answer?" Yuan Lin made a quick nod and began moving to his right. General Chang drew his own sword. The two men began to circle counterclockwise. Chang Huang wanted Yuan Lin to attack first, but Yuan Lin remained at the ready. He stepped inward as he circled and swung from right to left, intentionally striking Yuan Lin's blade instead of aiming for Yuan Lin himself. Yuan Lin beat the blade away to Chang Huang's right with a strength Chang Huang hadn't witnessed in practice. *He was holding back. Did he foresee a fight between us?* Yuan Lin's block was followed by three swipes, all from Yuan Lin's left to his right in rapid succession: the first to Chang Huang's midsection, the second to his head, the third to his feet. Chang Huang blocked each blow, the first by holding the blade pointing down with the hilt at eye level, the second by twisting the blade so that it pointed up and dropping his hands slightly, the third by swinging his blade in a wide arc down to protect his legs.

He didn't wait for another attack but lifted the point and jabbed it at Yuan Lin's midsection. Yuan Lin hopped back beyond Chang Huang's reach, then batted Chang Huang's blade away and returned a thrust of his own. Chang Huang stepped to his right but took a cut to his left arm. Then he attempted to slash at the middle of Yuan Lin's arm, but Yuan Lin pulled back so that Chang Huang's blade only rang against his own. The two men began circling again.

Yuan Lin moved in and slashed downward towards Chang Huang's head, knowing that his attack would be blocked. Anticipating Chang Huang's answering downward slash of his own across Yuan Lin's chest, he spun clockwise and put all his force into a horizontal strike to Chang Huang's right side. He expected Chang Huang to move backwards or block, hoping for the latter. Instead, Chang Huang moved in and thrusted his blade towards Yuan Lin. Yuan Lin moved right but not fast enough to avoid a medium-deep cut into his left side. Chang Huang was remembering some of the instruction that The Egg taught Charlie just that morning. He had taught Charlie to dance. He was not as quick as The Egg—not by a long shot—but he was able to bring a new dimension to the sparring he and Yuan Lin had done. Yuan Lin continued to back away, and Chang Huang pursued. As Yuan Lin tried to make short swings at Chang Huang's midsection and head, Chang Huang stepped sideways away from the swings to minimize Yuan Lin's power, skipping backwards and forwards to draw Yuan Lin off balance. This succeeded in confusing Yuan Lin, and Chang Huang heard a grunt of frustration escape his throat. Finally, Yuan Lin spun clockwise again, this time bringing his blade low. Chang Huang jumped high over the blade, seeing a surprised expression in Yuan Lin's face. He brought his sword up so that it crossed his body in order to block Yuan Lin's next move and place him in a position to strike. But as his feet hit the ground and his knees bent to absorb the shock, he felt a sharp pain in his left knee that continued to throb for the rest of the fight. He lost his balance and fell to the sand on his left side. *Shit! The general has arthritis…I was supposed to remember that.* The pain could not be ignored. Yet neither could the flash of sunlight off the steel in Yuan Lin's hand coming down fast towards his ribcage. He rolled to his right, putting as much strength into knocking the tip of Yuan Lin's sword off target as possible with his own sword. Yuan Lin's jab was so close that when it stuck into the sand, several of Chai Wen's men thought that he had killed the general. Yuan Lin pulled up his sword but felt a sharp pain in his left kneecap. One that would have made Chang Huang's arthritis feel like a mosquito bite. He looked down and saw Chang Huang's blade protruding from his left leg. He bent his unharmed knee and his own sword fell from his hand as he reached to remove Chang Huang's weapon from his wound. Chang Huang did not wait for Yuan Lin to realize what he had done. While still on the ground, he grabbed Yuan Lin's sword and used both hands to jam the point into Yuan Lin's Adam's apple. Yuan Lin made a series of gurgling sounds as red liquid pulsed in large gushes from the new hole in his neck. He stayed upright for several seconds before falling forward. Chang Huang's sword, still stuck into Yuan Lin's kneecap, prevented his fall from having any semblance of grace or dignity, making his body to twist into a contorted position. Hsieh Sun had buried her face in both of her hands. Chang Huang went to her and reached up to touch her elbow. She jolted at his attempt at comfort, and her horse took a couple steps back. When she removed her hands from her face, she looked down at Chang Huang and slid from her saddle into his arms.

"How did you know? How did you know for sure he did it?" she asked.

"I was mostly sure, but he did not deny it when I asked him. His answer was his sword." Her eyes were flooding, but she did not sob or say anything else. Chang Huang let her go and turned to Lieutenant Chai Wen. "Get him to the bivouac site. No one touch his gear until I get there." Chai Wen could not suppress the pride he felt in solving the murder, and of becoming commander of Yuan Lin's company, even if his command would only be temporary. Something about Chai Wen's demeanor made Chang Huang uneasy and just a little bit angry. He did not sense deception in Chai Wen, but there was something wrong about chasing one's own desire in the midst of what was clearly a tragedy.

Chang Huang and Hsieh Sun rode on ahead of Chai Wen's company. Although Chang Huang wanted to investigate Yuan Lin's personal belongings, he needed to make sure Hsieh Sun made it back to the tavern before he left her. Mr. Shen greeted them with good cheer at first when they walked through the door, but his smile left him as he saw the expressions on their faces. "Hsieh Sun," he said, rushing to her, "what happened?" He threw a concerned, yet suspicious look at Chang Huang and then scooped Hsieh Sun up in his arms.

"I need tea," she said. Mr. Shen glanced again at Chang Huang, who nodded once, then he sat Hsieh Sun into a chair and disappeared into the kitchen.

"How do you feel?" Chang Huang asked.

"I do not know," Hsieh Sun responded.

"I have to ask you, you saw Yuan Lin's reaction to my question, did you not? How did you take his silence?"

"I am not sure. I expected him to deny the accusation. But he did not. It is just too hard to believe that he killed the Bao family."

"I know. I feel wrong, somehow. But I am not sure what I could have done differently. He drew his sword."

"I wish I said something to him. Maybe I could have convinced him to put his sword away."

"He would not have listened to you. I saw the anger in his face. He did not seem like the same man I sparred with at the temple."

Mr. Shen returned with a pot of tea and three cups. "I am sorry, Mr. Shen, but I cannot stay," said the general.

"Thank you for bringing her home." Chang Huang left the tavern, intent on going directly to the bivouac site. He changed his mind when he saw Martin Killjoy (as Du Hung) entering the spice shop at the south end of town. Chang Huang stood under the awning of the tavern, glanced in the direction of Chai Wen's men, then to the spice mercantile and headed in that direction.

The scents in the shop were overpowering. *Reminds me of a Yankee Candle shop back in the real world but with a more grown-up smell.* At first, he thought Du Hung had slipped out another exit. But then he saw the man amble around the end of a display, completely unaware that he was being followed. "How is the Private Storage business?" Chang Huang asked.

"You! I have been looking for you."

"Here I am."

"Are you the same guy that visited me at my business in Queens?"

"I am."

"Is the lady cop here, too?"

"No, she does not suffer from our affliction."

"You have to tell me how to stop dreaming of this place. I am sure this is all fun for you…dressing up like a warrior and waging battles. But I am just here. I have no purpose, I run this spice store, but it is so boring."

"I am working on that."

"Figures. So, you are here to buy spice?"

"No, I wanted to talk to you. How long did you say you have been dreaming of this place?"

"About two weeks. Well, two weeks in our time…back home. Only a few days here, I think."

"Did you…," Chang Huang gestured by lightly bumping his fist against his head like a hammer, "bump your head around that time by any chance?"

Du Hung scratched his ear. "Hmm. Not that I can recall."

Chang Huang looked down and let his eyes dart back and forth. He refocused on Du Hung and asked, "Did anything unusual happen that night before your first dream? Anything at all?"

Du Hung looked around the shop, then back at Chang Huang. "No. Nothing." *He's lying. Something happened, but he doesn't want to tell me. Why is that?*

"All right. It looks like I know where to find you. I will let you know as soon as I figure out how to stop dreaming this dream."

"Do you think I would end this dream if I killed myself? I mean here, not in Queens."

"Interesting, but I would not try it." He left without giving Du Hung a chance to ask any other questions. By the time he reached the encampment, Chai Wen's men had already returned with Yuan Lin's body and had begun wrapping it for burial. He found Yuan Lin's belongings well-guarded, for which he was grateful. The guards stepped aside for General Chang. Yuan Lin's items were neatly organized in his tent. His clothing was folded and stacked; his writing materials and other personal effects were arranged for ease of use, taking up the minimal space necessary. His bedding was rolled and tied. *Proper military bearing.* It did not surprise him that Yuan Lin had a high degree of discipline and professionalism. One item that looked like an oversized messenger bag was out of place and looked as though it had been opened.

"General Chang, my sergeant told me you were here," Chai Wen said from behind Chang Huang.

"Where in here was the idol found?" asked Chang Huang.

"It was laying down with a blanket overtop of it, against the side of the tent. A foot was exposed…the one holding the emerald." Again, he thought of Martin Killjoy's description of the idol he had seen.

"I do not see a blanket here."

"We used it to wrap the captain for burial."

The Charlie inside of Chang Huang wanted to put on rubber gloves or use a pencil to lift the flap of the messenger bag until he realized that fingerprints would not be a concern here. Chang Huang opened the bag and carefully removed a metal tea pot, some tightly wrapped and sealed packages of dried tea leaves, and a small ceramic cup that was padded by several layers of silk. He pulled the package of tea leaves to his nose and inhaled deeply. *Nothing. Yuan Lin knew better than to let a smell attract wildlife.* Once the messenger bag was empty, he lowered his face to its open mouth and took another whiff.

"I need a white cloth. Quickly, Lieutenant."

"Yes, sir." He returned in mere minutes with a blanket that was almost white. "Will this work?"

"Close enough. Hand it over." Chang Huang laid the blanket on the ground and upended the messenger bag, shaking it until several pieces of wet dirt were revealed on the towel. "This dirt, it is still wet. Is there a reason Yuan Lin might have had dirty objects in his bag?"

"None that I can think of, sir." Chang Huang shook the bag again and a small piece of a green leaf came floating down to the towel. Chang Huang picked it up and held it close to his eyes. *Smooth, like grass. But soft…like spinach?* "Lieutenant, have the men fall in formation. I will have a word with them. Wait!" Chang Huang looked into Chai Wen's eyes. "When I questioned Yuan Lin, he did not respond. Imagine you are Yuan Lin for a minute and that you were innocent. Why would you not deny your guilt?"

"Sir, you are a general. Your word is to be taken as fact. When you accused Yuan Lin, I knew that my investigation was successful."

"But I did not accuse him. I only asked."

"Sir, that is the same thing." Chang Huang felt sick to his stomach.

"Assemble the men."

"Yes, sir."

Wake up.

(Thursday – August 23, 2012)

Samantha was still asleep when Charlie's eyes flew open. He slid on his boxers and went out to the living room. The sun was still over an hour from its grand entrance. He opened the window and let in some of the cool morning air. It felt good against Charlie's sweaty chest. Something about Yuan Lin's tent bothered Charlie. In his mind, he searched his memory of the tent. Clothing, folded and stacked. Writing materials, personal effects, bedding rolled and tied. *Bedding rolled and tied?* He remembered Chai Wen said that the idol was covered by a blanket. *How could he have covered the idol with a blanket if his bedding was rolled and tied? Yuan Lin…I was wrong. I'm sorry.* This thought repeated itself in Charlie's mind until the first rays of sun broke from the horizon. When he turned to go back to the bedroom, he saw Samantha standing behind him wearing a thin robe.

"How are you feeling?" she asked.

"Terrible. I just killed an innocent man in my dream."

"You…you what?"

"I fought Yuan Lin and had to kill him. He was set up. I can't explain it all now." She took a few steps toward Charlie.

They held onto each other for a moment before Charlie walked her back to her room.

"I need to log onto my laptop," he said. "If you don't mind me using your Internet connection, I can bring it down, along with some breakfast stuff."

"Charlie, I think after last night, you don't need to ask to use my Internet connection. And I will make you breakfast. I have some stuff that I think you'll like, though it may be a bit different than what you are used to." He kissed her and quickly dressed and headed up to retrieve his computer.

When he returned, Samantha was working with a steamer, a wok, and the microwave. Charlie plugged in and asked for Samantha's wifi password. He could not remember the name of the rodent that had led Chai Wen's men to search Yuan Lin's messenger bag, but he didn't think it would be hard to find. A quick Google search on "animals of gobi desert" led to a site that mentioned the jerboa. He then searched on "jerboa" to find a site that discussed them in a little more detail. *What do you eat, rodent?* They eat plants and insects. *Probably need lot of protein and iron for all that jumping they do with those long legs.* Charlie read on to learn that they dig up the roots of plants during the dry season to get to vegetation with moisture. *Something like green spinach would be enough to attract the lot of you, wouldn't it?* Charlie powered down his laptop and slapped it shut. *But you were too disciplined to leave unwrapped spinach in your messenger bag. Someone put it there...but why? So it would attract the jerboa...and then someone else would have reason to look in your tent.*

"Here's your coffee."

"Coffee? I love coffee, so don't get me wrong, but I thought you were more into tea."

"I am, but my brother is a coffee man, and most white guys I know would prefer a cup of joe."

"Thank you, Samantha." He took a sip and began to really appreciate Samantha's brother. "Did I tell you about Martin Killjoy?"

"Killjoy…no, I think I'd remember that name. Friend of yours?" she asked as she fiercely attacked something in her wok.

"No, he's a guy who owns a Private Storage in Queens. He's dreaming. Like me."

"Recurring dream?"

"In China."

"Seriously?"

"There's more. When I met him, he was a guy named Du Hung in my dream." Charlie waited for the boom to drop. Samantha stopped stirring and turned the heat down on the wok.

"You mean he's in your dream, and he's a real man in New York?"

"Yes."

"Charlie, that's…that's unbelievable." She walked over to him and set next to him on her couch. He looked into her eyes.

"I almost didn't want to tell you, but it's only because of Martin that I can believe the next thing I'm about to tell you." He waited for her to say something, but she remained silent. "I know I told you about Yuan Lin. Last night, in my dream, Yuan Lin was set up by someone as the killer. But I, as Chang Huang, believed the lie. I fought and killed Yuan Lin. Dream or not, it feels like I've been punched in the gut." She reached out and took his hand but still did not say anything. "Before I fought him, Yuan Lin revealed that he was dreaming of a place called New York City. But he was dreaming of a time nearly 11 years ago. He described the way he looked, and base on his looks and age, I think that my stalker is Yuan Lin. I mean, no wonder he hates me."

Samantha held him. Charlie stared at a random spot on the coffee table. She studied him carefully before speaking. "Charlie, I don't know what's happening, but unless you are a great actor, I don't believe you are lying to me. I also don't think you are capable of hurting me." Charlie looked up into her eyes. "Don't speak. Let's enjoy breakfast and then we'll talk this thing through. If it is God's path that led me to you, then I am meant to be here to help you." She smiled and walked back into the kitchen. Before turning her attention to the food, Charlie heard her make a call and say that she was not coming in today. When she returned, she carried several dishes on a large tray. Charlie would not have believed she could carry this by herself. She placed each dish on the coffee table and explained what each are in turn.

"First, we will start with my congee. Forgive me, but I had made this yesterday, and it is only warmed up in the microwave." Charlie saw what looked like a rice soup with some translucent vegetables on top that seemed to have a reddish-orange sauce that bled into the congee. "Those are preserved radishes in a tangy pepper sauce." Charlie also smelled seafood coming from the dish. "There are dried scallops inside. Sometimes I eat the congee with no flavors added at all. But most people prefer some additions." She ladled some into two empty bowls.

"After this, I have some stir-fried baby bok choy with some onions and mushrooms, then we'll have some pork and cabbage buns. Those are not homemade…I buy them frozen and steam them to life." There was something familiar about the way he was being served. Perhaps because she was Asian, and Hsieh Sun had served him in his dream.

"This congee is incredible!" said Charlie.

"You like it? A lot of white men I've made this for aren't crazy about it. They eat it, but it doesn't really suit them."

"Seriously? I feel like I was made for this. It really hits the spot."

"Maybe because you've been eating Chinese food in your dreams?"

"Hard to say." A thought occurred to Charlie. He brushed it away at first, but it refused to be forgotten. *Why did Yuan Lin talk specifically to Hsieh Sun about his dream? It was hard for me to say anything of my dreams to Samantha. I didn't want her to think I'm crazy.* He looked at Samantha as she ate from her congee. *He wouldn't have said anything, unless….* He recalled that Yuan Lin needed to speak with Hsieh Sun alone after he had met with Kong Xiao. *He wouldn't talk about such a crazy dream unless they had this in common. If Hsieh Sun is also dreaming of New York, then she is here, too.* Again, he looked at Samantha.

"What?" she asked with a smile.

"I'm just glad I met you." She reached up to his face and he kissed her gently before returning to his congee.

After breakfast, Samantha recommended a walk to clear Charlie's head. "If you feel that Yuan Lin is the same person as your stalker, how do you want to handle the situation?"

"I don't know. But I better figure something out. Tonight is when I'm supposed to meet him."

"Tonight?" Samantha looked surprised.

"Yes, the note said tonight." Now she looked alarmed.

"Charlie, do you have to go? I mean, do you *really* have to?"

"The last time I didn't, two police officers were killed. I don't know what he would do if I didn't show."

"From what you've told me about Yuan Lin, I can't imagine he would kill someone who was innocent."

"I can't take the chance. But I can't kill him again. I need to show him honor by coming prepared, but I should talk to him. Yes, I need to talk him out of his rage."

"That will be difficult, won't it? If he's been here for more than ten years after you killed Yuan Lin and hasn't given up his anger.... Listen to me, I'm talking as if it is absolute fact that all of this is real. Never mind. Real or not, your stalker is real, and you need to be prepared. I don't guess there's any chance you'd let me come with you?"

"Oh, no. No way, Samantha. Whatever is going on, I won't be able to focus if I'm worried about something happening to you."

"I understand. Once it is all over, please call me. I will call in to let my boss know I need tomorrow off, too. When we get back to the apartment, why don't you bring some stuff down, and you plan on staying at my place again tonight?"

Charlie stopped and turned to her and kissed her deeply.

When Charlie arrived back at his apartment, there were three messages from Gina. He picked up the phone and dialed without listening to them.

"Hey, G."

"Charlie! You're alive."

"For now, I am."

"Don't talk like that. You promised me you weren't going to get pierced, remember?"

"I'm not sure I promised, but…."

"Charlie, stop it. Are you still going through with it?"

"Yes, but there's a new wrinkle. I think my stalker is Yuan Lin."

"What? How can that be?"

"I killed him, G. And I did that after I has accused him of being the Bao family killer. What's worse is that I was wrong, G. Dead wrong."

"But why would that make him the stalker? Even if he's dreaming of New York, how could he find you after all this time?"

"I don't know how, but I asked Yuan Lin to describe himself, and his description matches. It just fits. Only one thing doesn't fit." Charlie realized this only as he was saying it. "The reason I thought Yuan Lin was the killer is that when I asked him about it, he didn't deny it. But the reason he didn't deny it was because I was his superior. Why didn't Chang Huang know that his question would have been perceived as an accusation?"

"What?"

"It's like we talked about the other day. In my dreams, Chang Huang's instincts have kept me speaking the way people would expect me to."

Gina thought for a moment. "You also said that maybe you weren't meant to do this long term. That you were starting to understand Chinese culture and idioms while you were here in this world. Kind of like Chang Huang's instincts are spilling over. Maybe it's also the other way around. Your instincts…your cop instincts…are to question a suspect. You question them hard to keep the stress level up, hoping that they slip. You don't comfort them by saying you don't think they are guilty."

"Makes sense. I gotta stop these dreams before I get someone else killed."

"Maybe Chang Huang will start understanding English, and you can read that message."

"Even the message doesn't seem that important to me anymore."

Neither spoke for a moment. Gina broke the silence by asking, "You gonna practice with The Egg this morning?"

"Not sure. I can't kill Yuan Lin again."

"Good, we can call this off and set a trap for him."

"No, I do have to face him. I just can't kill him. No traps. Just me and him."

"He's not completely innocent you know. What about McAllister and Jameson. He did kill them, didn't he?"

"I guess. But I created the monster, which makes me responsible."

"Stop it. That's ridiculous and you know it. There's absolutely no way you could have seen that. Killing them was his choice."

"Okay."

"So, we're going to set a trap?"

"No. I'll face him, with a sword. I still want to talk him down, but I need to look ready to fight him. And then, I guess I need to be able to defend against him, at least until he gets tired of trying to kill me."

"That's not what I was hoping to hear." He wanted to retort that this was not about what Gina wanted. He wanted to yell but realized Gina was not who he wanted to yell at.

"I probably should go to The Egg and see what he has to teach me today."

"Why is he called The Egg, by the way?"

"It's the opposite of a banana."

After dropping off the sword in his apartment from his final lesson from The Egg, he went back to Samantha's apartment. He found her sitting on the far end of the couch with her legs bent beneath her and an untouched tea sitting on the coffee table. She wore her t-shirt, which hemmed just above a pair of white, see-through panties. "You are truly a sight for tired eyes," Charlie said.

"I'd take you to lunch, but I'm not very hungry today," said Samantha.

"You're not the one facing a sword-wielding maniac tonight."

She shook her head. "I am. He is the enemy of my happiness." Charlie frowned. "I feel like I'm just getting to know you, yet at the same time I feel like I've known you a lot longer than a few weeks. I don't want to lose you. Take me again, Charlie. I don't want to sound fatalist, but I'm worried this might be our last chance." He smiled again and wrapped his right arm around her shoulders and kissed her on the mouth hard, lightly cupping her left breast with his other hand.

"It won't be. I'm not going to die tonight. But yes, I'll take you again…right now." He carried her back to the bedroom and kicked the door closed.

Charlie logged onto his laptop to check the Private Storage feed while Samantha showered. He wasn't really in the mood to do so but wasn't sure if he would have a chance after facing Yuan Lin tonight, and he had failed to check it the previous day. He was glad he did, though. He found a video segment of Martin hanging around storage unit 4358, attempting to be inconspicuous. After pacing about for a few minutes, Martin looked to both sides and slid a key into the manual lock for the unit. He lifted the vertical door and revealed a plethora of Chinese treasures. But Martin ignored nearly all of it. He focused instead on a small, stone figurine, about the size of a salt shaker, resting on top of an unmarked crate. Martin brought his face within an inch of it and gently rubbed his finger across its top. Charlie could not make out the details of the figurine. It was partially covered in shadows. He froze the picture and tried to increase the size, but the pixilation hid any defining features. *What have you got there, Martin?*

Charlie and Gina's credentials allowed them past the gates at Liberty Island, though he hid the sword in a guitar case he had from one of his many attempts to learn how to play. He assumed that Yuan Lin was hiding somewhere on the island since before closing. They reached the base of the statue on the front-facing side when a shadow stepped out on the roof of the museum below Lady Liberty's feet and called down to them. "General Chang," he said, then spit. "That phrase tastes like acid to me."

"Then call me Charlie."

"I assume both of you are armed," the stalker said indicating Gina. "That's okay. I have two snipers nearby, one trained on each of you. Have you brought the sword I gave you?"

"I brought a different one." He opened his guitar case but left it and the sword on the ground.

"Your choice." He jumped off the roof and spun around, revealing that he was clipped onto a rope for a short repel. "She needs to get back," he said as he pointed to Gina. "Do you know the truth?" he said, still looking at her. But it was Charlie who answered.

"We both know the truth, Yuan Lin. You should have spoken up."

"If I knew what a fake you were, I would have. I've been trapped in this mechanical world of yours a long time. You trapped me here, and I'll never get back to my own time."

"Do you understand how this works? These dreams?"

"I'm not here to answer your questions, Charlie. I had purpose and men who followed me. I was in love with Hsieh Sun, but you wanted her."

"That's not fair. I would never have killed you for her, if that's what you're thinking."

"It doesn't matter. Draw, Charlie!" He pulled a sword very similar to the one Charlie had and held it vertically in front of him.

"No. I didn't come here to fight you."

"What is this?" he said with disgust. "Pick up the damned sword, coward."

"Our fight might have been eleven years ago for you, but it was just last night for me. I realized shortly afterwards that you had been set up. I feel too guilty to kill you again."

"You don't have to worry about that, Charlie." He laughed. "I could just run you through. But I really prefer you to at least try to defend yourself."

Gina was watching all of this through a thick layer of saline. Her hand kept wanting to reach for the Sig p238 she kept at her ankle.

Yuan Lin took a step towards Charlie, and Charlie's reflex kicked in. He dropped to a knee and grabbed the handle of his sword but did not pick it up. Yuan Lin laughed again. "You don't want to kill me, but you don't want to die, either. If you don't want to fight, why are you here at all?"

"McAllister and Jameson."

"Come again?"

"The cops you killed when I didn't show up at your first rendezvous."

"I don't know what you're talking about."

"You left me a note in Fred's mouth saying that I should come myself next time. You called me a coward then, too."

"I never killed anyone outside of battle in China. And I certainly never put a note in anyone's mouth." Gina's hand, which had been creeping towards her ankle, relaxed and rose to her bottom lip.

"But why would someone else do that?" Charlie asked. Yuan Lin's face changed. "Have you ever stopped to think about who might have set you up back in China?"

"I assumed it was Chai Wen. He wanted command."

"He was happy to take charge, but I don't think he had it in him to set you up." Yuan Lin did not say anything. "Yuan Lin, someone's played us. And they're still doing it. I don't think we're on opposite sides."

Yuan Lin wasn't ready to give up this moment of revenge for which he waited so long. "Let's say that's so. You still killed me without hesitation. All on the word of Chai Wen."

"You think that? How long have you lived here? Eleven years? Here in New York, people can get a little heated. It doesn't mean we're ready to fight. I'm sure you've seen this or even been in such a heated argument here, yourself." Yuan Lin did not respond. "I was not a real general, Yuan Lin. You know this. So, when I asked you if you killed the Baos, I really hoped you would be able to tell me some rationale that would explain what I was hearing." He waited while Yuan Lin processed what he was saying. "Look, can you at least call off your sniper pals?" Yuan Lin looked to Gina and then back to Charlie.

"There are no snipers."

Charlie smiled. "A bluff?"

"Kept you from shooting me. I've spent the last eleven years hating you." Yuan Lin started to reply as he walked forward, when the crack of a rifle cut through the stillness of the night air and ripped away the top of the stalker's head. "Yuan Lin!" Charlie screamed. Gina screamed without words at the same time. Charlie drew his pistol and turned towards the direction of the gunshot. "Who's out there!"

"Relax, Charlie. You knew I'd have your back." Mark Robinson stepped out of the darkness. "I was a little worried until I heard him say there were no snipers."

"Mark, what did you do?!" Charlie yelled.

"Saved your ass, Charlie. Now what's all this 'general' crap?"

Charlie didn't reply. He turned to Yuan Lin, who was unrecognizable. He didn't know when Gina had stepped up, but she was standing at Yuan Lin's feet with both hands covering the lower half of her face, the middle fingers resting in the inside corners of her eyes. Charlie stood up and grabbed her with both arms, moving her back and away. "What is wrong with you two?" Robinson continued. "This man killed Fred and Peter."

Charlie kept his back to Robinson, not letting go of Gina. "No, Mark. No, he didn't."

"What do you mean?"

"Later. Call for the CSU, will you?"

"They're on their way, partner."

"Thanks, Mark."

"Look, if I fucked anything up…."

"I don't think so, Mark. Someone else is fucking things up." He let go of Gina. "How did you know I'd be here?"

"Anonymous email waiting for me when I logged in this morning. Gmail account with a bogus name. They said not to call you or you'd talk me out of it."

"They would have been right." The three cops left for the station as soon as the CSU team arrived. On the way back, Charlie texted Samantha that it was over, and he was all right and would be home later. They spent hours answering questions in separate rooms. Fortunately for Charlie, his questioning was being done by Sergeant Langmann with Dr. Thomason in tow. He was able to be truthful with them, as they already knew about his China dreams. He revealed all the facts he could and took heat for not telling his boss about Yuan Lin's Statue of Liberty challenge. By the end of the questioning, he was emotionally and physically drained and was given a ride back to his apartment. He asked to see Gina, but she had already been escorted to her place.

Samantha was sitting on the front steps of the apartment building when Charlie was dropped off. She stood up and ran to him with chirps of emotion breaking the silence of the night. Charlie picked her up in crossing-the-threshold fashion and carried her back to her apartment.

Chapter 18

Chang Huang sat in Yuan Lin's tent a few minutes before going out to question Chai Wen's troops. He carefully put away each of Yuan Lin's possessions and looked on them for a moment. They were the belongings of a good man who had been set up, conned, and then murdered—twice. Whoever arranged all of this was still free. He was succeeding in whatever plan he constructed. And Chang Huang was unwittingly helping him. *Not anymore.*

Chang Huang pulled the message from his purse. *Gotta focus on this. First line is solved. The next letter I haven't figured out is this one.* He pointed to the first letter in the middle line. *Looks like a fingernail. Or a crescent moon. Like a stick figure drawing of a crescent moon anyway. It's waning. It's also in positions 77...and 81. I can remember 77. Lucky number in the Western world. Reagan was shot in '81. The crescent moon goes next to this funny looking letter in two places...,* he pointed to the "H" in the middle word, *...both here and here.* He pointed to the second to the last word, put away the message, and left the tent to face the men.

Chang Huang questioned them for nearly an hour. No one had seen anyone put anything in Yuan Lin's messenger bag.

There has to be an inside accomplice. Feeling frustrated, Chang Huang headed back to his room for a rest.

He awoke after dark by a knock on his door. It was a soft knock. *Hsieh Sun.* "Enter," he said. She entered and closed the door. She looked nervous. She carried in her hand a rolled-up silk of some kind. It might have been multicolored, but the moonlight muted its chromo variance. "Were you seen?"

"No, General."

"Good." The same moonlight that dulled the colors of the silk had also softened Hsieh Sun's features to a near angelic appearance. He was tempted to leave the lighting alone but decided to light some candles instead. The candles did little to tone down the beauty he saw in her. Looking into her eyes, he saw something familiar. The silk could now be seen to be red and blue. He sat up on his bed with his back to the headboard, crossing his legs in front of him. There was now room for Hsieh Sun to sit down, but she continued to stand. "How are you feeling?" he asked.

"Not good. But that will pass. I feel betrayed. Yuan Lin and I were becoming friends. But the Bao family…." She had been trying to hold her emotions back but felt her strength start to give when she thought about the Bao children. She changed the subject. "You heard Yuan Lin talking about New York. You asked him questions."

"Yes."

"You asked him if he was hit on the head. Why did you ask him that?"

"Long story."

"He was not hit on the head. It was this." She pulled a small, stone figurine of a Chinese guardian lion with emeralds for eyes—at least one eye was made from an emerald—from the cloth she was carrying. Hsieh Sun kept her finger draped over the other eye. It looked familiar.

"Where did you get that?"

"From Yuan Lin. He had been given this by an old man. It was after he stared into its eyes that he began dreaming as he did."

"He told you that?"

"Yes."

"You know he was telling the truth?"

"Yes. Kong Xiao told him to have me look into its eyes." Chang Huang straightened up and placed his hand on the bed for support. "You are dreaming as he was?"

"Yes. I am in New York as well…but a little before Yuan Lin. The towers still stand…the ones that Yuan Lin told me will fall before he is there." Chang Huang studied her. The familiarity in her eyes suddenly flourished.

(Friday – August 24, 2012)

No! Charlie tried to go back to sleep but couldn't. He knew he would not dream of Xin again even if he fell asleep but had to try. He looked over at Samantha. He wanted to wake her and ask her if she was Hsieh Sun. *No, I can't do that. If she isn't, that would be a terrible thing to ask.* He studied her skin, the lines at the corner of her eyes. *How old are you?* If Hsieh Sun was 19 in 2001, then she should be 30 now. But he couldn't gauge from her looks whether she was younger than that or not. He kissed her gently on the cheek and laid back down.

Thoughts of what to do next in his dream fought for control of his mind. *I could tell Hsieh Sun that Yuan Lin is a good guy and tell her to reach out to him in New York to explain my mistake. I can make sure she memorizes the description and find him. It could completely change everything, but it would save his life. Would I wake up to a whole different world where Yuan Lin is alive, and my relationship with Samantha is completely different? Would it be better or worse?* Charlie laid in bed conceptualizing different cause-and-effect models based on time travel—something he had not done since he was a teenager watching Star Trek. *I can't make this decision. I'm too close to it. I need help; but who? Not Dr. Thomason...maybe Francis? Not sure I trust him. The Egg? Kong Xiao...I need to talk to Kong Xiao. But that will have to wait. What time is it?* He looked at the clock: 3:47am. *Too early to wake Samantha, or Gina for that matter. They both need their sleep after last night. But there's something I can do.* Charlie jumped out of bed and went to the notepad he had brought down with his toiletries the previous day.

A stick figure of a crescent moon...waning. He slapped his forehead and shook his head back and forth. *It's a "C", idiot. It's also position 77. Ronald Reagan...81.* He looked at the partially filled in message on his notepad. He placed the "C" in the three positions and knew for certain what the middle word, and the word on the death mask, was.

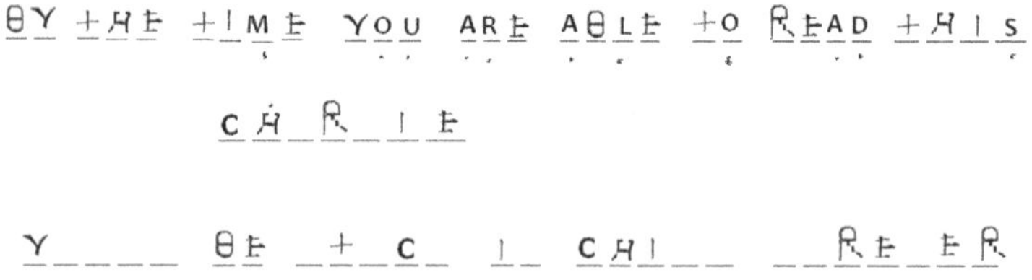

"Oh, my god!" he said much louder than he intended. *It's me...Charlie. But this was on the wall in China before I started dreaming.* He completed his name and took a guess at the second to the last word:

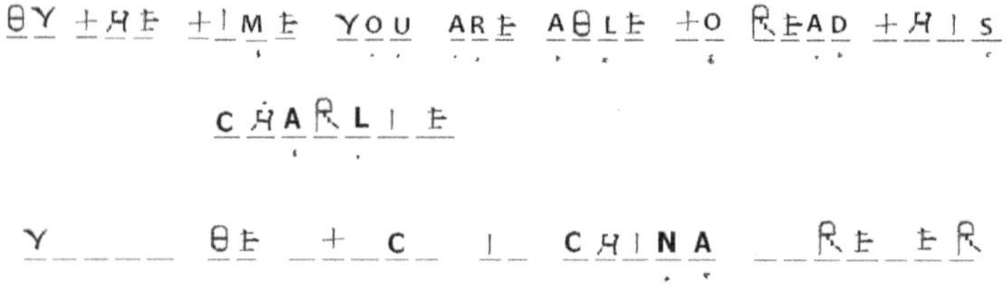

This message is for me. And since that's my name on the death mask, it's not a nice message. It had to be written by

someone who knows me here and there. Yuan Lin couldn't have written this, could he? I don't know when he started dreaming of New York, but he was here in New York long before I started dreaming. Someone would have to have told him my name. He didn't kill the Bao family, so it can't be him, anyway. Martin Killjoy doesn't seem...actually, I don't know him at all. He could be lying about everything. Francis said he has travelled in his dreams. But there has to be more. Hsieh Sun, me...there has to be more. Charlie pondered this as the darkness outside Samantha's apartment window started to glow with a hint of blue. He saw this and decided that Samantha had enough sleep. He spent the morning with her without mentioning any suspicion of her being Hsieh Sun.

Gina picked up Charlie at 2:00. Samantha seemed more at ease than when he left the previous day. More confident that he was coming home alive that night.

"Tonight's shift," he said to Gina when she started to pull away, "do we have any assignment, or do you think the boss will let us head off to Queens? Greg and Nora are gonna be sore with us for not telling them about our rendezvous with Yuan Lin ahead of time."

"I'm guessing we'll have desk duty after what happened last night."

"Then let's go in a little early. I need to sweet talk Sarge a little."

"Sweet talk? I don't think that works on Langmann."

"Maybe that's the wrong term. I'm gonna offer him a bargain." He rubbed the back of his fingers upwards against the side of his neck. "One he don't refuse."

"Forget it, Peltman. You and Baxter are benched tonight. End of story." He and Gina expected nothing less.

"It's not just a lead, there's something in there you will want to see."

"Do you even know me? When has my curiosity ever affected my judgment?"

"You've been to China, right?"

"Yes, Charlie. Several times."

"Have you been to sixteenth century China?"

"Dr. Thomason!" Langmann called out for show. All three knew Thomason was not in his office this afternoon.

"Come on, Sarge. You have to know I've made headway in understanding this recurring dream by now. Aren't you curious?"

"Again, my curiosity…."

"I can take you there." Langmann did not respond, but his eyes were showing strong annoyance. "Look, Sarge, I'm trying to solve something in this dream and I'm at my wit's end. I need your help. I think Martin Killjoy has what I need to take you there."

"Oh, my good God, Charlie, do you hear yourself? I'm at *my* wits end with *you*. This has gone on long enough. You go get whatever you need and bring it back to me. After I look at it, and I don't start dreaming, I want you to drop this shit…all of it. The stalker's dead and your old partner's back…it's time for you to get back to normal. You're lucky I don't send you home, talking this shit to me." He waited for Charlie to rebut, but Charlie held his words. "So, this Martin…he's just going to give you what you're after?"

"Yes." Charlie smiled. "I'm gonna make him an offer…."

Gina interrupted, "Really, the same reference?"

"Hey, my material is limited."

"Fine," Langmann replied. "Go see Martin Killjoy and get whatever it is you need, but then you are back at your desks the rest of the night. Capisce?"

Greg and Nora saw them come out of the sarge's office. "We should say something to them," Gina said.

"Yeah." They made their way to Deathrage and Peterson and were relieved to see that they looked more concerned than pissed off.

"You two all right?" Greg asked.

"Yeah. Looks like the case is settled," Charlie replied. "Sorry we didn't call you. I wanted to face him alone. Didn't really want Gina there, but she knew about it as soon as I did. Still don't know how Mark found out."

"I'd be lying if I said I was okay with it, but I understand. This was your guy, even if it was our case. You should be thankful Mark was there, though."

"Yeah, grateful." Charlie tried to sound as if he truly was but was afraid he aimed wide. "Hey, why don't we get together next week for dinner…or lunch…or drinks or something."

"Deal. Nora?"

"Count me in." She gave Charlie a quick hug. "Glad you're safe." She walked to her desk.

They arrived in uniform even though they were out of their jurisdiction. Charlie didn't think they would stay there long and thought the uniforms would keep the stress level up for Martin. They got Martin's attention as soon as Charlie and Gina walked through the office door. "Shit, what do you two want?"

"Easy, Mr. Killjoy. I might want to buy some cumin."

"Hardy-har."

"I have a strong feeling that you have been peeking into storage unit 4358."

"You can't prove that. Besides, I'm too chicken shit. What if he has a camera in there?"

"What if I have a camera outside the unit, right next to yours?" Martin did not respond. "Got your attention? Good. Now I'm not here to arrest you." Martin regained some of his confidence.

"'Course you ain't. You two're from Brooklyn. Got no jurisprudence here."

"Something like that. But hear me out. You asked Chang Huang how you could stop dreaming. I know how to stop it."

"You can stop it?"

"I can't, but Chang Huang can."

"How do I know you ain't lyin' to me?"

"You got me on video, right?" Charlie glanced up at the camera at the corner of the office. "I'm guessing you got me here on two other occasions with my uniform on. That's enough to get me in an awful lot of hot water." Martin scratched his chin. "I just need you to let me into 4358 for one piece."

"Forget it."

"It's a little stone figurine of a lion." Charlie suddenly wondered if there were more than one, and if they came in other animal shapes. "You know the one I'm talking about. You looked at it one day a couple weeks ago and have been dreaming about China since. Am I right?"

"How do you know…?"

"I just know it, Martin. You let me borrow the keys to that unit and I'll make sure Chang Huang ends these boring dreams you keep having." Martin looked around as if there were anyone else in the office who could see what he was doing. Then he disappeared into a tiny room behind the counter and came back with a key.

"Bring this right back."

"I promise."

Charlie turned to Gina. "You better stay here. I'm already dreaming about China, so I don't think this thing will work on me."

A small, lion figurine with two different colored eyes, one green and one red, was right where Charlie had seen it in the video: sitting on top of an unmarked crate facing outward so that it would be seen right away upon opening the vertical door to the storage unit. He wrapped it in a handkerchief he had brought specifically for this purpose and walked back to the office. After he gave the key back to Martin, he described to Gina how the lion figurine was placed in the storage unit.

"Why do you suppose he left it out?" Charlie asked.

"It's guarding. Whoever owns this understands more about how this lion works than we do. Somebody sees it, they start dreaming. I guess the owner is already a 'dream traveler', for lack of a better term, and can deal with any would-be thieves in old China."

"How would that…?"

"Don't know. I'm just guessing. Let's just get that thing back to the sarge."

"Good idea." Charlie thought about going back for the camera but then thought it might be a good idea to see the reaction of whoever opened the unit to find the figurine missing.

Gina drove, and Charlie studied the lion figurine all the way back to the station, being careful not to let Gina glance at its jeweled eyes.

"How're you going to stop Martin from dreaming?" Gina asked.

"I'm going to kill him."

"Ha-ha."

"No, seriously. I'm going to kill him in the dream."

"Charlie, no! You can't do that. What if he dies here, too?"

"Yuan Lin didn't die here when I killed him in Xin."

Gina thought for a second. "But Yuan Lin was from China originally. It might not work the other way around."

"One way to find out."

"You're gonna use him as a Guinea Pig?"

"Look, I'm nearly 100% sure this will work. I plan to have myself killed…and the sarge as well…once all this is cleared up. Not in that order, probably. Once the murder of the Bao family is solved, I won't want to go back there anymore."

"Charlie, I don't like this."

"G, if I had any doubt that this would work, I wouldn't do it. I wouldn't kill the man. You're taking a chance on killing me every time you drive me somewhere. This is nothing more."

"Come on, I'm not that bad of a driver." Charlie laughed.

"Of course you aren't. But even good drivers get in serious accidents. I really don't feel Martin is in any risk if I whack the Chinese version of him."

"We're almost here." Gina still didn't like it but did not think she could change Charlie's mind. "Better wrap that thing up before you get half the force showing up in your dream." Charlie put the lion in his pocket.

"Did you get it?" Sergeant Langmann didn't look up from his desk when he asked this.

"Are you ready to see it?"

"As ready as I'll ever be." He looked up and squinted as if he expected to see Charlie holding it out for him. "Where is it?"

"In my pocket. Before I show it to you, you have to be real sure you want to give up all your normal dreams. The only way to stop them isn't pretty."

"I'll take my chances. Just show me the damn thing, will you?" Charlie removed the lion from his pocket and placed it on his hand as if it were a live animal, sitting on his master's palm. Sarge looked at its eyes and then up to Charlie. "That it?" Charlie looked at the lion and then at Gina, very briefly.

"That's it, Sarge. I'll see you in China!"

"You'll see me off and on tonight. Now that your little mission is over, you and Ms. Baxter are back on desk duty."

"All right. Anything else?"

"No. Dismissed."

Chapter 19

Chang Huang looked at Hsieh Sun trying to see if the familiarity in her eyes was Samantha. Her eyes did not look like Samantha's, but the same caring and warmth was there. He felt that he knew without asking, but hearing it from Hsieh Sun would take away any doubt.

"Hsieh Sun. What is your name in New York?"

"My name? My name is Gina." *Chang Huang sat back. No…it can't be!* His first thought was to wake himself up and call Gina. But he could no longer sacrifice dream time in relation to his waking time. Gina had been his friend for several years. He mentored her and trusted her with this bizarre dream, and she did not say anything to him.

"Gina Baxter?"

"Yes! How do you know…?"

"I…" Chang Huang started. Hsieh Sun looked at him, waiting for him to continue. "This will be hard to believe. Did Xiao Kong explain anything about your dream?"

"He said it was more than just a dream, but I do not know what he meant by that."

"Well, he is right about that. I am…from this place where you dream. New York. It is a long time from now. The year is 2012, but you are in 2001, from your description. These numbers don't mean anything to you, though, as it is a whole different calendar." Hsieh Sun did not say anything. By her wrinkled brow, Chang Huang could tell she was trying to understand, which meant she did not just disregard his comment as crazy or deceitful. Chang Huang continued, "My name is Charlie there. Charlie Peltman. I am a policeman. One day, a couple of weeks ago in my time, I was hit over the head with a brick. Since then, every time I dream, I am here. As General Chang."

Some understanding lit Hsieh Sun's face. "That is why you asked Yuan Lin about being hit. And that is how you knew my family name in New York."

"Yes." *Thank God I said her last name before diving into this.*

"So, you know Gina?"

"I do. We are close friends." He thought about all the times that she was there for him. How she took care of him after he was hit on the head and set the coffee maker so it would start up as soon as his alarm went off. He realized that the only way she would believe his dream problem was if she had dreamed, too. "Very close friends," he added. *But Samantha accepted my dreams, too. Or did she? She never said she believed I was really dream travelling, or that others were sharing my dream. Just that she didn't believe I was lying. That's not the same, is it?* Chang Huang could remember Charlie's interactions with Samantha clearly, but all of it seemed distant, as if it were the dream. Samantha did not even feel real to him at that moment. Hsieh Sun was here, in front of him, and he loved her.

"I am glad," she said as she leaned against General Chang.

"Me, too." She looked into his eyes, and he could not stop himself from kissing her.

Hsieh Sun left shortly after the kiss, and Chang Huang was about to go to sleep when another knocking at his door woke him up. When he opened the door, an older man with cloud white hair and a thin beard that came to a sharp point in the middle of his belly was standing before him in a formal dress that touched the floor. "Mr. Mayor, to what do I owe this pleasure?"

"How do I look, Peltman?" The general blinked twice, then could see familiarity in the mayor's eyes. Just as with Hsieh Sun, this familiarity was not physical but something deeper.

"Sarge?" The mayor laughed out loud.

"Can you believe this shit? I am in old China, here with you!"

"I have to admit I was a little worried when nothing happened after you looked at the figurine," General Chang replied.

"So, what happens next?" Charlie thought for a moment, then grabbed his purse.

"There is something I want you to look at." He removed the message and showed it to the mayor. "You should be able to read that, right?" The mayor took the message and looked at the characters printed upon it.

"Nope. Looks like gobbledygook to me."

"Gobbledygook? I thought…do you not, as Sergeant Langmann, know how to read Chinese back in New York?"

"I do, but I took the time to learn it. I have some of the mayor's memories here, at least when I look about his house and recall where things came from. I do not think the good mayor ever had time to learn English. That is what you think this is, right?"

"Yes." Chang Huang looked back at his paper. "Well, it is pretty late, and the mayor's body is probably tired. We will need to be awake when we investigate tomorrow. You can go to sleep here in China and wake up in China, all within the same dream. I am going to study this a bit more and then go to sleep myself. Tomorrow, I am meeting Hsieh Sun for breakfast. I would ask you to join us, but we have something to discuss."

"Understood. Not sure it would be proper for the mayor to go to the tavern for breakfast anyway."

"Depends…is it an election year?"

The mayor chuckled. "All right, we should meet back here after you meet with Hsieh Sun. Late morning?"

"Okay. Night, Sarge."

"Night."

Chang Huang looked back at the message. *I was so sure he could tell me. Damn. Next letter…second letter in the third row. It's a circle. Hmm, same as the second letter in the last word. That's easy. Let's go for two. What's this here? These two letters at the end of the first word on the bottom row look like…hockey sticks. Hockey sticks…hockey sticks. "H – E – double hockey sticks." That spells "hell." These are L's!* Chang Huang put away the paper and went to sleep.

In the morning, he reviewed his message again to make sure he would not forget where the circles and the hockey sticks were placed in his message before heading off for breakfast with Hsieh Sun. Mr. Shen had placed the old Chinese equivalent to a "Closed" sign outside the door, obviously something that would not apply to a general in the emperor's army. Upon his entrance, Mr. Shen and a two woman wait staff retreated to the back where they could be summoned if needed but assured the general before they left that they would not hear a word that was said between him and Hsieh Sun—that they must raise their voices to call upon their servers. Hsieh Sun was sitting at a table with pickled vegetables, rice congee, and smelt laid out before her, along with a steaming pot of tea and two stoneware cups. An empty chair was placed across the table from her. The other chairs had been removed and were up against the wall.

"Good morning, Hsieh Sun."

"Good morning. Though, I did not sleep last night." He moved the empty chair around the table so that it was next to her, sat down, and took both of her hands in his.

"Hsieh Sun, I need to see Kong Xiao. I would like you to come with me, but I need to go today. If Mr. Shen needs you here, I still…."

"Mr. Shen has given me tonight off. I told him that I am being courted by the general. He knows that this must be discrete, and he does not want to interfere. When do we leave?"

"After meal at midday. I have been summoned by the mayor. He wants a full report concerning the Bao family after breakfast." Hsieh Sun looked down at the table upon hearing the Bao name. "I am sorry, I should not have said…."

"It is okay. I must learn to accept and deal with this."

"I think seeing Kong Xiao would be helpful to you as well, am I right?"

"Yes."

"Good."

"Can you tell me something?" Hsieh Sun asked. "How close are you and Gina…in New York?"

"It is complicated." Hsieh Sun looked disappointed in this answer. "You have to understand, this conversation you and I are having now took place a long time ago for the Gina that I know. But it is all new to Charlie. Gina had to let me get to know her on my own. Can you imagine how you would feel if someone came to you before you started dreaming about New York and said that you and he had met in a dream world?"

"Of course, I would not believe him. I could not imagine trying to tell Charlie something like that. But would Gina not just allow the two of you to fall in love on your own?"

"If she did that…crossed the line of friendship…then I came back here in my dream, I probably would not allow myself to fall in love with you. So, it is complicated." Her look back to Chang Huang was non-committal. "When I saw you for the first time looking at Yuan Lin and me talking on the street, I felt like I was back in high school catching a first glimpse of the new hot chick." Hsieh Sun laughed softly. "Interesting, I did not think you would get the reference to high school or hot chicks."

"I do not, though I assume a high school is some sort of military training. I am laughing because I was actually looking at Yuan Lin that day." Chang Huang struggled to respond to that. The gurgling of Chang Huang's stomach helped him push it aside for the moment.

"So, what have we here?" he asked, motioning to the food set out before them.

"This is the food I grew up with. The smelt is from a lake at the foot of the mountains, not far from Kong Xiao's temple.

They were caught yesterday. These vegetables are turnips, carrots, and cabbage. The tea is jasmine."

"I shall enjoy every bite."

After breakfast, Chang Huang walked back to his room, trying to put some sort of plan together for investigating the murder and theft. Chai Wen's men would be preparing to move on; replacements were on their way to guard against the Hei Shui gang in case they are still around. An accomplice to, if not the mastermind behind, the setup and murder was part of Chai Wen's company. Getting him to stay on the whim that the general was wrong and had killed an innocent man would be difficult to sell. They needed evidence that a second man was involved to delay Chai Wen's departure. The only evidence he had at this point was some dirt and a leaf of some kind. *Where would I get a leaf like that? Looked like spinach, sort of. We're in the freaking desert, though...there's nothing like that....* Charlie's feet rooted to the ground. *Someone who's traveled here from a more lush land. Someone who carries vegetation. Like a cook. Xu Ping was standing guard at the Bao's home when the mayor's men relieved him and Xian Li.*

Chang Huang shared his revelation with the mayor who looked to be still orienting himself to this new environment. "Let us talk about all that in just a minute, Charlie. Tell me, do you remember much about the Chang Huang who was here before you 'took over'?"

Chang Huang did not feel like taking such a non-sequitur, but he remembered what it was like when he first started dreaming and would have loved to have talked to someone else who had been through this. "Only when certain things are brought up, or when I see something of importance, like my scars."

"Fascinating! That is what is happening to me. It is like an empty canvass that gets painted a little at a time."

"Yeah, that works, Sarge."

"How is the food here?"

"I like it quite well. But Sarge…."

"Sorry, this is just all so…I know this was probably different for you, but I have been a China enthusiast ever since my first girlfriend. She was from China."

"Your girlfriend…?"

"That was a long time ago, but she got me so into the food, the history, the music, and the language. I just cannot believe I am here. You know what I did this morning?"

"No, Sarge."

"I went for a walk. I never do that shit back at home. Hey, do you find it odd that we cannot use contractions when we speak? I know the Chinese do not have contractions, but…."

"Sarge…."

"Yes, I know. Okay, let us talk case. You were saying that you think Xu Ping is involved, if not the lead assailant, right?"

"I do. But my evidence is circumstantial. I need something more."

"Like a pack of matching green leaves in Xu Ping's gear."

"Exactly. But I do not want to tip my hand. Besides, if he is smart, he probably buried the rest of that stuff. I can lean on him. It would help if I had one other piece of information."

"What do you have in mind?"

"If Xu Ping did set up Yuan Lin, he was likely the one who stole the idol from the Bao family's residence. He was watching their place with Xian Li when the mayor's men…your men…relieved them. Xian Li can tell us if Xu Ping had an opportunity to hide the idol when the guards changed. Maybe outside somewhere where he could pick it up later."

"So, we interview Xian Li first."

"Actually, I was hoping you could have your men ask him. I do not want to sound like I am second guessing myself in front of my men. I also want to go speak with the monk in the temple by the mountains."

"That sounds like fun. I cannot come along on this little expedition?"

"Another time, Sarge. I want to make this a quick trip."

"Okay. What do you not like about Xu Ping's guilt?"

"Xu Ping has no motive. The idol is back in your possession now. If Xu Ping's plan was successful, then what advantage did he gain? Even if he was paid to setup Yuan Lin, the idol did not change hands in the end. You had control of it before, and you have it now. So, I do not see who benefitted by the setup."

"Maybe the plan is not over yet. Maybe something is still coming. I mean, the idol is in my possession, not in the Bao home anymore. So, it was successfully moved, and the shadow of guilt is pinned to a dead man. Now all the killer has to do is let the investigation die down, and steal the idol from me. If it were still in the Bao house, it would be under the watchful eye of Yuan Lin's men until the relatives of the Bao family arrived." General Chang wondered again about the relationship between the Yuan and Bao families. It seemed too big of a coincidence that Yuan Lin came here around the same time the Bao family had been killed, considering they had known each other in the past. It felt as if something had drawn them both to this place and time.

"And now that Chai Wen's troops will soon be on their way to a new mission, the replacement troops would be less involved and less likely to question things. There are bound to be men in Chai Wen's unit that know Yuan Lin too well to accept that he is a murderer and a thief, whether some general says he is guilty or not."

"Exactly. Even more reason for you not to tip your hand," said the mayor. "So, what else do you not like?"

"I have not quite figured out why the mayor's men relieved Xu Ping and Xian Li in the first place. Do you have any of the mayor's memories of that?"

The mayor thought for a moment. "Yes, he was not too trusting of Yuan Lin's men in general. He was not what you would call the trusting sort. He wanted to make sure that all the Bao's stuff was still there when the next of kin came by to collect it."

"Interesting. The honor and reputation of the emperor's men did not…?"

"You do not really think that the Chinese army was completely chivalrous all of the time, do you? Just like any well-respected organization, many of these guys think their collective shit does not stink. Like the world owes them a knee or something. No, the mayor did not think much of the honor and reputation of the emperor's men."

"I see. So, you will have someone question Xian Li, and I will seek out Kong Xiao. I do not know when either of us will wake up, and I do not plan on waking up intentionally at this point. I have this strong feeling that my time is short and that I have a lot to do here in China…relative to the timeline back home, that is. Most likely, though, I will end up waking up at least once before I am back here in Xin, so the next time we talk should be in New York."

"Sounds good. We will trade notes back there."

Chang Huang met up with Hsieh Sun after midday meal as arranged. He wanted to eat with her but did not want Mr. Shen to close up shop again just so they could have the place to themselves. As before, Hsieh Sun's horse was ready and loaded with supplies by the time Chang Huang arrived. Hsieh Sun was mounted and ready for time alone with Chang Huang.

"Good afternoon, General."

"Milady." Chang Huang gave a short bow as he said this. The two did not speak again until they were sure that they were well away from unwanted ears.

"There is so much I want to ask you about the future," said Hsieh Sun.

"I would like to answer them, but I need to talk to Kong Xiao first. I do not know what problems might come if I tell you too much."

"Problems?"

"Yes, and I am not just talking the normal stuff, like paradoxes where you go back in time and kill your mom before she had any children. I am talking about more subtle actions with big consequences. Imagine if you had a conversation with someone because of information you had about the future. Then that person is an hour late getting home. As a result...," Chang Huang stopped, realizing this was probably way over her head. Her expression shifted from a poker face to one trying very hard not to laugh, shortly before losing it completely. Both laughed as they rode through the desert.

Nearly four hours later, they found Kong Xiao standing at the open gates to the temple with two of his pupils. Hsieh Sun and Chang Huang slowed as they approached the monk, who said nothing as they came close. "You are just a little on the spooky side, Kong Xiao," Chang Huang said.

"You both must come with me at once. These two will see to your horses." The two riders gave each other a quick glance before dismounting and following the monk, who had already turned and was walking away fast. He led them to his own sleeping quarters, which appeared much brighter than the last time they had been inside the room. In the corner was a small statue that Chang Huang had not noticed in his previous visit. It was the standing statue of a man, about two feet tall but completely featureless, like a mannequin that had not been painted. Kong Xiao kneeled down in front of it and reached out to caress its face. Then he turned back to his guests. "This spirit statue is your only hope. Tonight is not the night to use it, but now that Yuan Lin is gone, I know there is little time for me to give you all the information you need. Forgive me, I miscalculated how much time you had." He waited for either of them to ask questions, but they were both speechless. "Good, no questions. There is a cave; I will give you a map later tonight." He looked at Chang Huang. "After you solve the murder of the Bao family and kill the thief, and after Charlie is dead in his world, you must ride to this cave."

"After Charlie is dead?"

"Yes. He will die there. Soon."

"But how?"

"We do not have time for explanations. Just listen and follow my instructions. This next part will be difficult for you to believe."

"Even after all this?"

"Yes. When Charlie is dead in New York and you have defeated the thief in Xin you must go to the cave alone. The cave will be guarded by two standing statues that look just like this but taller. I will make sure this one," Kong Xiao gestured to the statue in his room, "is in the center of the cave. Before you enter the cave, you must recite this verse." He handed a piece of paper to Chang Huang. "Look at it, but do not read it aloud right now." Chang Huang looked at the words. "Once you are inside, kneel before this idol and read this." He handed another paper to Chang Huang. "When you do, you will cease to be Chang Huang. This statue will change as well. It will take on your facial features and your dress. It will not be you, but it will…contain you."

"I will be stuck in that thing?" Chang Huang showed visible signs of revulsion and horror.

"You will not experience being in the statue. It will be like you are asleep. Once you are freed from the statue, it will feel like no time has passed since you recited the verse on that paper. The statue will turn black and can never be used again."

"What about Hsieh Sun?"

"She will no longer be here." Chang Huang looked at Hsieh Sun, but she did not take her eyes off the statue. The monk looked at her. "Hsieh Sun, in New York, Gina must find a man named Francis Bremmer. He has the resources to come to the cave and retrieve this statue. Do not go through another company. The moment the statue is taken past the guardians outside the cave and touches new air, the sleeper inside will awaken somewhere nearby as a new person. The statue must be placed in an airtight container before it is removed from the cave." He turned back to Chang Huang. "Once the statue touches new air, it will feel like you are dreaming again, but it will be more accurate to say that you are waking up from a dream. You will have a new identity.

"When Francis is told about the spirit statue," he continued to both of them, "he will arrange to have it packed in a shipping container and insure that it is welded so that no air can escape. He will transport it to New York. When it is opened, Charlie, you will find yourself somewhere in the city. It should not be hard for you to find Gina."

"That is what Charlie is being hired to guard: myself." This was not a question. "What if Charlie in New York is still alive when the spirit statue touches air?"

"For you, all things are linear. Since I have asked you to wait until Charlie has died in his world before you recite these words, you will know the day, month, and year that Charlie dies. You will have experienced it already. When you are freed from the spirit statue and wake up in New York, I imagine you will look up the date and will know whether Charlie is alive or dead. You must wait until Charlie is dead to seek out Gina."

"You are giving me a headache." Chang Huang indicated Hsieh Sun with his eyes briefly and asked, "You will give her details?"

"There is not much to give, but yes, I will speak with her later tonight. You have questions for me that you want to discuss without Hsieh Sun, correct?"

Chang Huang looked into Hsieh Sun's eyes. He could see Gina in them more clearly now. He did not look away from them when he answered, "Yes. Hsieh Sun, this will only take a few minutes, but this is about…."

"My future," she finished. "I understand." She kissed Chang Huang, not knowing it would be the last time she would do so, and left Kong Xiao's room.

Chang Huang did not turn back to Kong Xiao until the door had closed. "There are things I want to tell her, and there are things I do not want to tell her. I am afraid if I do, she will change what Gina does in New York. And I am torn about that." Kong Xiao only looked back at Chang Huang with an air of omniscience that annoyed Chang Huang more and more. "I do not think it is right that I let her go on thinking Yuan Lin is a murderer. They were friends, you know?"

"You worry about the wrong things. What has been done in your past…in Charlie's past…cannot be changed. You can try, but you will not succeed."

"So, it is unchangeable. Like if I went back in time to prevent Kennedy from being shot, I would fail…or be the cause of him being shot?"

"Not exactly, but you are close."

"You know who Kennedy is?"

"I do. I have dreamed of your time. Though it is earlier there for me. I am only in 2008 when I dream."

"You are Francis?"

"No. Francis is a friend of mine here. He lives in Xin and travels here to see me frequently."

"But you know whether or not this plan works?"

"I am afraid not. Francis, in New York, will be killed before the ship carrying your spirit statue arrives."

General Chang pondered this but could not grasp what Kong Xiao was saying. "I do not get it. How do you know that Francis is killed before the ship arrives?"

"The man here in Xin stopped dreaming a few years ago when Francis was killed. He told me what happens up until his death. But beyond that, I do not know."

"Okay, so why is someone trying to destroy the cargo…my spirit statue?"

"Because you will be able to stop him from his plans."

"Which are?"

"You have a killer who is dreaming like you are. He is killing people here, and he has killed at least two police officers in 2012. If you were living in an old time, where simple, day-to-day objects are worthless, and you had the ability to live in a time and place where those same objects would be very valuable…."

"I could hoard them somewhere here in old China, hide them really well, then retrieve them in the future." Kong Xiao waited patiently for Chang Huang to think this through. "But that would not be illegal." More silence from Kong Xiao. "The Bao family idol. He got greedy. He wanted it bad enough to kill. But something got in his way."

"The idol is important. Greed is part of it, but there is more. There was a man who came to Xin…a very bad man, named Chu Heng. He would kill just for the enjoyment of it. I had known of Chu Heng's reputation. But when he came to Xin, I did not realize it was him until people started dying. The first to die was a young man who had drifted into Xin a few days prior to Chu Heng's arrival. Then a young girl was found in one of the clothes dying vats. Then the tavern owner and the mayor at the time. This was a long time ago. Once I realized this was Chu Heng, I went to face him. I thought I could fight him, but he was fast and strong. I was beaten nearly unconscious when I saw an idol in the window of one of the apartments. I started to dream as my body was dying. He kept kicking me, but I stopped feeling his boot. The idol dominated my dream. In my mind, I stood up and turned to look at my body. Chu Heng almost seemed to move in slow motion. I walked to him and grabbed him by the shoulders and turned him to look into my eyes. I saw his face change from hatred, to surprise, and then fear. He looked around confused. Suddenly, I was lying on the ground, back in my body, but Chu Heng was nowhere to be seen.

"I managed to pull myself up and stumble back to my apartment. I kept expecting him to burst through my door and finish what he started. But he did not."

"Did you ever see him again?"

"Yes, in my dream that night, and every night thereafter for a time. Every dream was the same. We would fight at the same place we previously fought. He haunted me as I slept for years, until I made this." He pulled a small figurine of a lion, identical to the one that Hsieh Sun had shown him and the one he had shown to the sarge. "You have seen this before?"

"Yes. At least one or two like it."

"I made several of these. You see how their eyes are made from different colored gems? The red one is for sleep, the green for awake. One must look at both gems to begin these dreams. I created them to escape Chu Heng. By controlling when and where I dream, I would no longer dream of the place and time where I fought him."

"You were right?"

"Yes."

"Why did you make more than one?"

"I did not know if these dreams would last, and was sure that each lion would only work so many times."

"You were that afraid of this man?"

"I still am."

"You never meant for others to dream this way?"

"No. But although I exist in New York, the body of Kong Xiao will not last forever. When I die here, I can no longer control what happens to these figurines."

"Why do you not destroy them? Since you know that someone has recovered them and caused all of this chaos?"

"There is no point. What has happened will happen. Besides, someone has already stolen one."

"The one that made Yuan Lin dream of the future. He told Hsieh Sun that an old man had shown him one of these."

"Yes."

"Was it the man who killed the Bao family?"

"That is my assumption."

"Was that Chu Heng?"

"As much as General Chang is Charlie. I believe that when I escaped my dream with Chu Heng, he also escaped, by dreaming as someone else."

The two men let those words hang in the air for a bit before General Chang spoke. "You said that you believe this. Does this mean you do not know?"

"I can never know for certain. However, the fact that whoever killed the Bao family is also dreaming of Charlie's New York makes me feel I am right."

"But there is something I do not understand. It was not one of these figurines that made Charlie dream of this place. He was hit over the head with a brick." Kong Xiao again looked at General Chang with curiosity but did not say anything. "Wait...when you fought Chu Heng, you said you were nearly unconscious when you saw an idol in an apartment. Was that...?"

"It was the Kwan Yin idol. This was before the Bao family came to possess it."

"You think this idol..."

"No, it was not the idol itself that allowed me to defeat Chu Heng. However, it gave me something to focus on outside of myself. Remember, an out-of-body experience is different than dreaming my way into a future time and place. However, stories of my battle with Chu Heng have spread. And Chu Heng believes that there is power in the Kwan Yin idol." *What if you're wrong, old man,* Charlie thought. *What if there's something to this idol you don't know, and Chu Heng does?*

"But he did not need to kill the family to steal the idol," said General Chang.

"Well, as I mentioned, Chu Heng enjoyed killing for the sake of it. But also, General Chang was known to be in the area, and Captain Yuan was assigned to protect Xin from the Hei Shui gang. These two were likely to discover what happened if he simply stole the idol. Killing both the Captain and the General would not be easy. So, he befriended Yuan Lin, and showed him the lion figurine that began his dreams. I suspect he was hoping to meet up with Yuan Lin in the future and convince him that he could be rich if Yuan Lin helped with his plans. But that is just speculation on my part."

General Chang shook his head. "In that case, we need to find out who Chu Heng is. Who he is living as in Xin. Yuan Lin describe him only as an old man. Would this mean he is an old man in New York?"

"Not necessarily. It has been many years since I fought Chu Heng and started dreaming of New York. If he started dreaming of New York at a time closer to when Charlie started dreaming of China, he would not be that old in Charlie's time."

"Then it could be anyone. Here, we are looking for an old man with the means to kill an entire family. He can write in English. He can also bring an idol, undetected, into a military bivouac and hide it in the captain's tent. That is a lot of talent for someone Yuan Lin described as old. Unless he had help." Chang Huang thought. "He has connections, both within and outside of Yuan Lin's unit. His talent is not strength or stealth. It is influence. He either buys or convinces people to do things for him. He deceives. Even me. I was convinced Yuan Lin stole the Kwan Yin idol because of how Yuan Lin reacted to my question. He knew how Yuan Lin would act, and how I would react."

"And he knows what Charlie knows," Kong Xiao pointed out.

"Then the events of New York are in the past for the China version of Chu Heng. He knows what happens there. He also knows what Charlie has seen here."

"Yes."

"Then I cannot trust any coincidence. Yuan Lin's connection to the Bao family. The Hei Shui gang's approach at the same time General Chang came to Xin. All of it could be manipulated by Chu Heng. If he is a young man in 2012 New York, he would have had decades in China to set this up. I need to warn Gina...and Samantha. They cannot tell anyone what I have told them." General Chang started breathing fast.

"I do not know who Samantha is, but if Chu Heng has set all of this up as you say, then it is too late. This setup has already happened. There is no way to stop that. Also, do not forget, Chu Heng may not have learned all this from Charlie. Someone who is dreaming forward or backwards may have knowledge even further in the future and may know things Charlie does not know."

General Chang shook his head. "I need to find out who Chu Heng is in New York. If I find out who he is here in China, maybe I can figure out the who he is in Charlie's time. If I find out who he is in New York, then it does not matter who he is here.

"And if I am going to die soon in New York, I have little time to make any difference there. I need to tell Hsieh Sun that Yuan Lin did not kill anyone."

"That is up to you. Now, as you said, you have little time to solve the puzzle. Go have some ale or wine and let me tell Hsieh Sun the details she needs to hear."

"Yes, I could use a beer right about now. One more thing: why did you have Yuan Lin show Hsieh Sun the lion figurine, rather than do it yourself."

"Ignoring logic and reason. I am still a human being. Though I continue to tell you how unchangeable things are, I cannot help but try sometimes. My thinking was that, if Yuan Lin and Hsieh Sun bonded over this dream adventure, maybe the two would partner in New York and that she could save him. I see that was a fallible notion. I shall not do that again."

It was near dark when Chang Huang left the monk's quarters. *I guess I was more than a few minutes. What time is it?* He saw Hsieh Sun praying at the altar. He waited for her to finish and then sent her to see Kong Xiao. *I know I should stay here, but before I decide what to tell Hsieh Sun about Yuan Lin or the future, I need to see Gina. Wake up.*

(Saturday – August 25, 2012)

The sun dripped through the mesh curtains in Samantha's bedroom, lightly rousing Charlie from his dream. Once he realized where he was, he quietly got up and called for a cab. He let Samantha sleep until the taxi arrived and gently shook Samantha until he could see her eyes. "Morning, Samantha."

"What time is it?"

"It's early, just after six, but I need to get going."

"So early?"

"Yes. I'll be back in a few hours." His kiss belayed any protest she may have offered. Her eyes threw concern at him as he stepped out of the apartment and left in the taxi.

Gina had not slept much the night before. In fact, she had only fallen asleep about ten minutes prior to Charlie knocking on her door. Before she opened the door, she called his name, "Charlie?"

"It's me." She opened the door. "You've been dreaming back and forth for what, 11 years? I guess that Hsieh Sun and Chang Huang are still together, considering you don't hate me or anything." She touched his cheek and kissed him.

"Come inside, Charlie. There's more you need to know."

"Yeah, I'll say. That message…."

"Forget about the message for a minute." She allowed his mood to slow down to her level before continuing. "You know that I am Hsieh Sun, eleven years older. Kong Xiao asked Yuan Lin to show me the lion figurine that made him dream of New York the night that the three of us rode to his temple in the mountains south of Xin. That was eleven years ago for me. I've loved you for that many years, and the pain that has been with me is almost like a friend to me."

"Pain?"

"Yes, Charlie. Pain. Your time with Hsieh Sun is short. I spent very little time getting to know Chang Huang, but in that time my passion was ignited…for the first time ever in my life. I can't say exactly what happened, but I stopped living in China. I was suddenly here in New York without first going to sleep and then never went back. Maybe Chang Huang and some empty puppet of Hsieh Sun played by another person took over. Maybe Hsieh Sun died. All I know is that I was looking at Chang Huang…at you…one second, and the next I was back here in New York." Charlie considered this. When he was in China, he could wake himself up and travel back to New York in the middle of the day. But when he was in New York, he had to go to sleep before he could be in China again. It should be the opposite for Hsieh Sun, because she came from China, originally. "I've missed you so much." She reached forward and held onto Charlie tightly. "Once I was stuck here, I knew you were somewhere in the city. But I remembered what you had told me about how weird it would be for you if I approached you, so I left. I stayed away from New York as long as I could. I was able to hold out seven years. But I couldn't stand it. I moved here in 2008. Becoming friends with you was comforting, but it also increased my pain. So yes, my waiting has gone on for a long time.

"But there's more." She hesitated. "I shouldn't tell you this, but it might not matter, now. Something must have changed." She looked into his eyes to make sure she still had his full attention. "In China, Chang Huang told me that Charlie was killed by a sword." Charlie stiffened up and leaned back. "I was fairly certain you were going to die last night, Charlie. That's why I was so afraid you would fight Yuan Lin. Francis told me that nothing could change that if it happened once. You still would have fought Yuan Lin, but you would have been more cautious, and I didn't want to be the one who caused you to die."

"Gina…."

"But something obviously happened differently. Mark changed it, somehow. Maybe you don't have to die?"

"I don't know. Kong Xiao says..."

"Screw Kong Xiao! He isn't a god, Charlie. He doesn't know everything." She paused, thinking. "Chang Huang has to visit Kong Xiao and explain the situation. Francis said that my hope is not in vain. Kong Xiao has a plan. You need to go see him again and tell him what I've told you…all of it."

"Chang Huang is actually at Kong Xiao's temple right now."

"He is?"

"Well, relative to my dream, that is."

"You have to tell him. You have to tell Kong Xiao that you faced Yuan Lin but were not killed."

"I will. In the meantime, there are a few things you need to know. Whether I live or not, you NEED to know these things. Sarge is dreaming of China. He's the mayor."

"The mayor?"

"Yeah, and he's…giddy."

"Giddy? Sarge?"

"Yeah. Anyway, he'll get a kick out of it if you address him as Mr. Mayor next time you see him. Oh, and I did not tell him you are Hsieh Sun yet. Not sure why…I just don't feel comfortable telling him. Probably because you haven't told him. Maybe that should come from you."

"Okay. It seems appropriate that he's dreaming he's a mayor."

"Why's that?"

"I was a waitress in Xin when I first dreamed about New York, and I was a waitress here, too. You are a cop here and dreamed you are a soldier in China. Sarge is in a position of authority here…so mayor isn't that big of a stretch."

"Okay. Can we use that information? Somehow?"

"Maybe. If we find the killer in one time and place, we might be able to figure out who he is in the other time and place."

"And if I'm dead here, the sarge will be our link." He pointed back and forth between Gina and himself.

"I haven't given up on the hope that you won't die here, at least anytime soon."

"We'll see. Sarge is questioning the cook from Yuan Lin's unit. He would likely be the one to have green plants and may have been the one to set up Yuan Lin. He's also one of the guards that was relieved by the mayor's men, so I'm thinking he may have chucked the idol out one of the windows of the Bao's place and into a bush or something when he and Xian Li were changing guards with the mayor's men."

"Did Sarge say why the mayor changed the guards?" Charlie told her about the mayor's distrust of soldiers. She nodded but was in deep thought. "How and why would a cook…?"

"I don't think he was the brains behind it. He was probably just paid well for his work. Kong Xiao thinks the man behind this is gathering up as much junk from old China as he can pull together and hiding it somewhere so that he can have it shipped back to today's New York where it will be worth a lot of money. Which reminds me, in the desk drawer at my apartment, there is a sheet of paper with three names and phone numbers. Those are the off-duties I told Francis about. I copied you on the email I sent to Francis with the details of my plan. If something does happen to me, you will need to fill in for me at the docks when that boat comes in. You'll need to call those three the day before to let them know the exact time and location of the boat's arrival. I've kept them in the dark on that just as a precaution." Gina looked uncomfortable at discussing this what-if scenario but nodded her head.

"Which leads me to what is in the container," he continued. "Do you remember a conversation with Kong Xiao and General Chang, where Kong Xiao explained about the spirit statue?"

Gina scrunched her eyebrows. "Yes, but I'm not sure I followed it, or believed it for that matter." Charlie summarized the conversation and explained and how General Chang was coming back to New York in the container after Charlie dies.

"That sounds familiar. So, what happens with the spirit statue if you don't die here in New York. I mean if your spirit is in that statue and is let loose on the city, but you're still here…"

"Then we never open that container. Hell, I don't know. But for now, let's protect it. Let's find the killer. Then we decide what to do next."

Gina reached up and touched Charlie's cheek. "Charlie, I know you love Samantha."

"Gina, I…."

"Shut up for a second. You fell for her, Charlie. I respect that."

"I didn't know you were Hsieh Sun."

"It doesn't matter. Here, in New York, you knew both of us, and chose her. I'm not going to be in your way."

He touched her cheek and kissed her softly. "Whatever happens, Gina, I care very deeply for you. Don't doubt that. I fell in love with you at the same time, back in China. Gina Baxter has always been off limits to me. You're a fellow officer. But I've always had an attraction for you. I just put up a barrier. Let's get through this situation first. I have a lot of thinking to do." Charlie looked away for a minute, then back at Gina. "You know, I was starting to think that Samantha was Hsieh Sun."

Gina nodded her head. "I thought you might."

Charlie looked down for a second in thought. "Something's bugging me," he said. "Everyone who is dreaming like me looked at that lion figurine. But my dreams started when I was hit on the head with a brick."

"It wasn't the brick, Charlie."

"Then how…?"

"I had a figurine just like the one we took from the Private Storage. Well, I still have it, but the jewel eyes burned out."

"Burned out?"

"Yeah. After I showed it to you, the eyes burned out."

"I don't remember that. I remember you showing me the bottle of aspirin."

"Aspirin?"

"Yeah, you showed it to me, and I passed out."

"That wasn't an aspirin bottle. That was the figurine. I showed it to you, and you fell asleep."

"So…you did this to me?"

"You could look at it that way. I mean, you were already dreaming when I met first met you...in China. And Chang Huang told me when I should show you the figurine."

"I did?"

"You told me that you started dreaming the night you got hit on the head in 2012. So, I figured that I should wait until you were hit before showing you the figurine." Charlie recalled the conversation with Hsieh Sun. "I was a little worried when the eyes didn't burn out after we showed the other lion figurine to Sarge, but I don't think they burned out when Yuan Lin showed the figurine to me, either. Maybe it works a certain number of times before the eyes go."

"So, the brick wasn't the cause, but it wasn't a coincidence, either." He looked at her sideways. "I feel like I'm supposed to be mad at you." Gina laughed.

"What are you going to do today?"

"I need to stop by the Private Storage in Queens. I just realized that I never stopped Martin's dreams like I promised. I don't need him reporting us to the Queens police. I'll buy some time with him."

"Wanna take my car? I can take a cab to your place later, then I can drive us both to work."

"Thanks, G. Stop by around one or two."

"Keys are on the hook by the door."

To Charlie's surprise, Martin greeted him with a wide smile. "General Chang!" he shouted. "Glad to see you!"

"Thanks," Charlie said with confusion. "Listen, I'm sorry I wasn't able to stop your dreams last night. I honestly didn't run into you at all."

"What are you talking about? You and the mayor took care of me early last night. I went back to sleep and had a wonderful dream that I was being chased by a rabid dog. It scared the hell out of me, but it was my own dream, and it wasn't in China!"

"When did the mayor…"

"You and the mayor. Don't you remember?" Charlie searched his memory. This didn't make sense. He didn't see Martin at all in his dream last night. *It was a long dream, but…wait a minute. It was long for* me.

"When did you start dreaming?"

"About two and a half weeks ago."

"That was about the same time I started dreaming. Did you start out with shorter dreams, and then they got longer as this went on?" Martin scratched his head.

"Mostly. I mean it wasn't like a steady increase or anything. Kind of back and forth, but yeah, overall they got longer." Charlie felt puzzled a moment longer but felt that an answer was swimming close by. As far as he could tell, their dreams seemed to be in sync. Then he remembered willing himself awake on several occasions, including last night. *Just because I woke up on purpose a few times doesn't mean he did. Martin would be further along on his timeline than me, wouldn't he? He very well could have been 'fixed' by me and the mayor, without me experiencing it yet.*

"Whatever the reason, I'm glad you're free of your China dream."

"Me too! Thanks, and thank the mayor the next time you see him. After all, he's the one who killed me."

"Will do, Martin."

When Charlie arrived back at his apartment building, he stopped in to check on Samantha before going up to his place. He wanted to shower and change clothes, as well as try to figure out the remaining letters on his notepad in the solitude of his own place. He focused on the message, filling in the circles and hockey sticks where he remembered seeing them in his last dream. *Circles go in the second position of the first and last word of the last line. Then the double hockey sticks go at the end of the first word.*

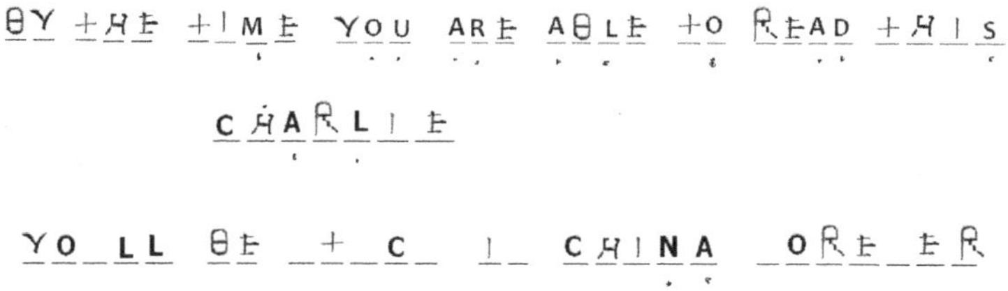

I take it that's a "U" in the first word. The last word..."forever"? Gotta be. He read the message out loud with the new words. "By the time you are able to read this, Charlie, you'll be something is…it…in…you'll be in China forever. Stuck! Stuck in China. I'll be stuck in China? But I'm still here in New York." Charlie saw the blade protruding from his chest a shaving of a second before he felt the pain. *It's my sword,* he thought, *from the Pawn Shop.* It was Charlie Peltman's last thought.

Chapter 20

Chang Huang felt as if he had just stood up too fast. His knees nearly gave out, but he managed to stay upright. "No! I am not done," he said aloud and then called for Hsieh Sun. Several of Kong Xiao's trainees stopped what they were doing and looked at Chang Huang. Hsieh Sun and Kong Xiao came outside and approached him.

"What happened?" Hsieh Sun asked. She stepped forward and looked deep into Chang Huang's eyes.

"Hsieh Sun," said Chang Huang, "it *was* a sword. I was killed by a sword. But it was not…."

Hsieh Sun did not feel anything. Chang Huang heard a "shlunk" sound with a slight ringing as Hsieh Sun's head went spinning in the air. Red streams pulsed up from her neck after it as if they were trying to shoot it back to the ground. Her shoulders remained in perfect posture as her knees buckled, allowing her core to drop straight down. Finally, her torso and arms appeared to coil like a rope into a pile that looked almost intentionally neat, except for the blood. This was accompanied by Charlie's screaming until his voice gave. He grabbed her and lifted up her shoulders. His eyes searched for her head. When they found it, they gave orders to his arms and legs to drop the body and run, or do something that vaguely resembled running, to look into her eyes one more time.

Before Gina headed over to Charlie's apartment, she took a walk to clear her mind. The sun was warm and comforting. She spied a Starbucks and decided her favorite Strawberry Frappuccino would put her back into a positive mood. While in line, she heard two teenagers laughing and jibing at each other as they walked in the door. "Why you wanna go here, anyway? We should be drinking tea or some shit!" The two laughed louder. The same voice added, "You're such a banana!"

"Am not. Just like my Frap, okay?" Gina felt compelled to turn around. The feeling was too strong to ignore, though she did not understand why. Her brow was furled as she turned towards them, trying to figure out what it was they said that grabbed her attention.

"What are you looking at, lady?" The two boys were Asian and had no accent. She stepped out of line and approached the speaker.

"What did you call him?" she asked.

The first boy laughed. "What…banana?" Both boys smiled big and continued giggling.

"Why did you call him that?"

"Cause he's a banana."

"Shut up, Craig," said the second boy.

"What does that mean?"

"Well look at him. Comin' in here for some Western drink. He's yellow on the outside but white as a ghost inside. A banana." The two boys must have seen the change in mood on Gina's face, because they both stopped laughing.

"Then an egg would be the opposite…," Gina continued. The first boy giggled a little, then sobered his face.

"Well, yeah. I mean it's white on the outside but yellow on the inside." Gina forgot all about her Strawberry Frappuccino.

"Thank you, boys." She left Starbucks and hopped a cab to Charlie's place.

Gina saw her car parked along the street outside Charlie's apartment building. The sun continued to shine in the bluest skies. Morning birds were calling out their playful songs. But in her heart, Gina felt this was all a ruse, set up to mask something darker. She ran up to the second floor pulling her pistol from her ankle holster. She left any sense of caution she had back at the Starbucks and ran in to Charlie's apartment, barely taking the trouble to reach down and twist the doorknob. Charlie had fallen forward, but the tip of the blade that went through his heart from the back had stuck into his desk, propping him up. Gina screamed a high-pitched, "No!" She ran to Charlie and almost moved his body, but her police discipline kicked in just in time to stop her. She barely noticed that the message on Charlie's desk was a little more complete and that something else was written on the notepad as well. She felt for a pulse but found none before calling the station. Sergeant Michael Stepford was on dispatch. "Stepford, this is Baxter. I need as many uniformed officers as you can spare, plus detectives, EMT, and CSU at Peltman's apartment, 2231 Avenue L, Apartment 211."

"Sure, Gina. What's going on?"

"It's Charlie…he's dead."

"Dead?"

"Just get the teams here!"

"Right away." He put her on hold and dispatched teams per her request. "Okay, Gina, we got Edmonds, Wratchette, Collins, Dunfee, and McGull all on their way, along with CSU."

"Thanks, Michael. Is Sergeant Langmann there?"

"No, ma'am."

"That's all right." She looked closer at the notepad. "What about Dr. Thomason?"

"Yeah, he's here. Or was…let me check. Yep, still here. Want me to get him on the phone?"

"Send him over here. He'll want to see this."

"Will do. You all right?"

"Of course not." She hung up and turned to the crime scene. She was careful not to touch or move anything, but she could look with her eyes. She looked again at the message in front of Charlie. "Almost had it," she said out loud. Then she looked more carefully and figured out what Charlie had figured out just before he had been stabbed. "So, you're back there now." Then, at the bottom of the notepad, she looked at the other thing she had seen: *888*. "Why would someone write…?" After trailing off, she ran to the door and looked out the peep hole. The numbers across the hall were the same as the numbers that were written on Charlie's notepad. Then her view of The Egg's door was blocked out by a shape. Gina was startled as someone knocked on the door. She quietly drew her pistol and opened the door an inch.

"Gina?" asked Samantha. Gina relaxed and opened the door a little more and stepped into the hall while holstering her weapon.

"Samantha. I can't let you go in there."

"Why not? Where's Charlie?"

"Can we talk in your apartment? I can't leave here for a few minutes until some of my colleagues arrive."

"What's happening? Is Charlie all right? I need to see him!" Samantha tried to push past Gina, but Gina didn't budge. Instead, she embraced Samantha as Samantha started to sob uncontrollably. "No! He has to be all right!"

Just then, two uniformed officers arrived. Gina told them to go on inside, and that she would walk Samantha back to her home.

Samantha started to calm a bit once she was in her apartment. Gina saw the tea containers and water kettle and got to work brewing. Samantha sat on the sofa staring at the coffee table. "I can't believe he's gone," she said.

"I'm sorry. Charlie talked about you a lot," Gina replied.

"He was going through something terrible. I'm not even sure how much I believe, but I know he wasn't lying to me." She looked up at Gina. "I know he wasn't."

Gina thought about what to say next. She decided upon the truth. "He wasn't lying, Samantha."

"What? How do you know?"

Gina sat down on a chair adjacent to the sofa and put her hand on Samantha's. "His dreams…he's not the only one having them. I know some of the stuff he told you seems impossible. But it's true. His dreams are shared dreams." She heard the other officers arrive. "There's a lot more I can tell you later, but I need to be with the other officers for now. Here," she said, "take my card. I will come back here, but I want you to be able to get a hold of me." Samantha stared at the card as Gina went back up to Charlie's apartment.

Dr. Thomason arrived a little while after the medics. The apartment was swarming with cops, some uniformed and some not. "Where's Officer Baxter?" he asked.

"She's in the bedroom being questioned," one of the uniforms said. When she came out, she was being escorted by a plain-clothed detective wearing a gray suit and a white shirt with no tie.

"Gina," he said as he approached her. He raised his arms as if to embrace her, but the detective held up an arm to keep him back.

"Sorry, Doc. Gotta take her back to the station," the detective said.

"What about the note on the desk?" Gina asked. The detective glanced in the direction of Charlie's desk and back to Dr. Thomason.

"Doc, Baxter wants to ask you something about Charlie's note." The three made their way to Charlie's desk.

"Oh, it's the message Charlie was puzzling over. From his dream," Thomason confirmed. Gina pointed to the additional numbers.

"Below the message, someone wrote this, '888'," she said.

"Are you sure it wasn't Charlie who wrote that?"

"It isn't his handwriting."

"Charlie had been living life as another person. Sometimes people with multiple personality disorders have different handwritings for each personality."

"Charlie didn't have multiple personalities. At least not while he was awake."

"Are you sure he wasn't asleep when he wrote this?" Gina thought before answering. Gina felt a sort of rage starting to boil but couldn't put her finger on what started this feeling.

"Quite sure." She left Charlie's apartment with the detective. She left Charlie's apartment with the detective and slammed the door. *Why did he piss me off so much?* Across the hall, she could see The Egg being questioned through his open door.

Chang Huang did not hear Kong Xiao order four of his trainees to subdue the student who had just killed Hsieh Sun. He did not see Hsieh Sun's killer force the blade of his sword into his own stomach before the others could reach him. He felt nothing but emotional pain until Kong Xiao laid his hand on Chang Huang's back. "Why?" Chang Huang cried. "Why did he do that?"

"Your enemy brainwashed him. Probably offered him riches in the future. I doubt if he will live long there, either."

"But why Hsieh Sun? Why would anyone hurt her?" For the first time since he was a child (for both Chang Huang and Charlie), Chang Huang felt lost and scared. "Why kill her?"

"He is severing anyone with links to more than one time and place, trapping them in either, so that he will have the advantage. He successfully split you and Hsieh Sun. Now you cannot work together. He is now stronger than either of you or both of you."

"There is one link. He will be going after the mayor next. He is my boss back in New York."

"You brought someone else back here?" Kong Xiao, who normally seemed to be the one in the know, looked genuinely surprised. "When did you do that?"

"Last night…or…yeah, last night. Either way you look at it."

"Okay, you must go back and warn him. Whichever world he wants to end up spending the rest of his life in, he should be particularly careful in that place and time."

"So, once I figure out who the killer and thief is here, I should, what…kill him?"

"Kill him, lock him up, or otherwise interfere with his plans. It is more important to kill the future version of him, since that is where the key to his success lies. Without prospering in the future, he loses." Chang Huang considered this.

"Then I ride to the cave, say the magic words, and I wake up in New York."

"Ideally."

"Ideally…what? Once I am in the spirit statue, I am safe, right? As long as the ship with the spirit statue in 2012 does not sink or something. Even then, if there are leaks in the container, once the statue is exposed, I can wake up somewhere in my own time, right?"

"There is one bane you do not know about yet." Kong Xiao pulled his arm up into his oversized sleeve. When it reappeared, it was clutching a handful of yellowish crystals. They appeared to glow, but Charlie thought they might be only capturing the light from the fire burning on top of the altar. "If one of these touches the idol in the first minutes after it meets air outside its cave, the stone will absorb whoever is being awakened."

"Absorb?"

"Kill."

Chang Huang wondered why someone would create such stones. "I have to see Gina again, so I must kill the bad guy and read your phrases at the cave." Kong Xiao closed his eyes and nodded once.

Gina went to the police station, not sure what she should do next. Waiting for Langmann was the only logical next step she could envision. To her pleasant surprise, she saw that Deathrage and Peterson were at the station. "Nora, Greg! I'm so glad to see you two." It wasn't until she saw them that she realized how badly she wanted to cling onto something familiar. "I thought you two were off today?"

"Good to see you, too. Got the word about Charlie, so we came in." Greg said. "You with the detectives this morning?"

"Yeah," she said in a soft voice. "But it's Dunfee and McGull. They don't like working with the uniforms, so they kind of blew me off after our initial discussion."

"Great, the two biggest assholes are on Charlie's case," Nora commented. "He deserves better than that." She wasn't tearing, but Gina could tell she was fighting it.

"I need to talk to Langmann, but I don't know when he'll be back." Her stomach sent up a gurgle of complaint. She had not eaten anything yet today, having left the Starbucks before reaching the counter. "I'm suddenly feeling very hungry. You two eat yet?"

"Yeah, we ate," Greg replied. "Besides, the boss will be back any minute. If you want, I got a plate full of cookies back at my desk. Just made 'em this morning. Help yourself." Gina's appetite disappeared. *"I'll have to have all of you over to my place for dinner. I'm an amateur chef of sorts,"* Deathrage had said when he first started working with Charlie and her on the stalker case. Charlie said that it was a cook in Yuan Lin's company who set him up. *Oh my god. I'm standing next to the man who....*

"No. Thank you. I'll wait for Sarge." She wanted to pull Greg's eyes out of his head.

Sergeant Langmann walked in as if on cue. "Great, the three I wanted to see. Let's go into my office, shall we?" The pain in Gina's heart competed with the anger in her head. She desperately wanted to tell Sergeant Langmann that she needed to talk to him alone first but held her tongue as Deathrage stepped into Langmann's office. Once the four of them were inside, he closed the door and turned first to Gina. "I'm sorry, Gina. Really, I am. How are you feeling?"

"Been better."

"Will you be all right to wait for about ten minutes? I need to debrief Deathrage and Peterson here." She nodded. "Good. If you can wait outside, I'll take you to lunch as soon as we are through." Her eyes fired a snipe at Deathrage, who missed the look completely, then she nodded again. If Langmann saw this, he didn't let on. He opened the door for her and turned back to Nora and Greg.

Gina sat at her desk while the sergeant talked with her two cohorts behind a closed door. *Greg is working the boss. I know it, but I don't know what he's up to.* She sat there for a little over fifteen minutes before Deathrage and Peterson walked out. Langmann followed a couple minutes behind them and indicated with a quick tilt of the head towards the front door that she should follow him outside.

Chang Huang's trip back to Xin from the temple was long and lonely. There was plenty of time for him to memorize the map Kong Xiao had given him and ponder the cave. He wanted to tell Mr. Shen that Hsieh Sun was dead, but his sense of urgency overpowered that desire. Xin felt dead to him. At least with Yuan Lin and Hsieh Sun, he had friends there. The sarge was there now, but that was not the same. The sarge was his boss, not his friend. All he wanted to do was solve this case and leave Xin forever. Even if there had been no hope for ever going home, he would want to ride Horse to Beijing or anywhere that would let him forget this desert town. But there was hope. There was a 'spirit statue' that the monk was taking to a cave even now. He knew that statue would be there in his time, because Francis was having it shipped to New York. Whether or not his soul was really in that statue was another thing altogether. And the sergeant would help find out who is responsible for all of this in both Xin and New York. Then he could leave. He would try the cave first, and if nothing happened, as he suspected, he would ride east.

There was no reception waiting for him this time. By the time Chang Huang was close enough to the bivouac site, he could see that Chai Wen's men were loading up their horses, preparing for a long journey. "Lieutenant Chai!" he called out as he approached.

"General, I am glad you returned before we left. Our replacements will be here within the hour. I do not plan to dawdle." His voice was trodden; his expression downcast.

"What has happened?"

"We lost two men outside of battle in this town. It is cursed. They were both good men. And I do not believe either to be guilty."

"Two? Who else?"

"The mayor felt compelled to relieve us of our cook."

"Xu Ping is dead?"

"Decapitated." Chang Huang's guilt was compounded. He expected Xu Ping to be questioned, but Langmann had not been here long enough to start executing people.

"You are a good man and a good leader, Chai Wen. If I make it back to Beijing before you, I will make sure you receive recognition." Chai Wen bowed his head.

"Thank you, General. Though I do not seek…recognition."

"Of course not." *I underestimated Chai Wen.* He put his hand on Chai Wen's shoulder, then led Horse back to the stables on foot.

The sarge took Gina to a soup and sandwich place across town from the police station. The owner had a passion for red, as the floor, walls, tables, and chairs were all nearly the same ruby color. Potted plants hung down at seemingly random intervals. A refrigerator with a glass door full of products strictly from the

Coca-Cola Bottling Company offered stronger lighting than the muted fluorescents striping the ceiling. They found a corner table that was far enough away from prying ears. "How is General Chang?" Gina asked.

"I wouldn't know."

"Didn't the lion figurine work?"

"Oh, it worked all right. It's just that I missed the boat. General Chang has left." *He's lying,* Gina thought. *But why?*

"So, what are you in China?"

"I've just led a platoon into Xin. Replacement for a group that's left. I'm to protect the town from some gang that might not even be there. Might need to see Thomason and find out more about what Charlie's latest dreams are all about. Figure out what I'm supposed to do."

"Do they know who killed the Bao family?"

"Not sure. Looks like I was about to be briefed by one of the mayor's men when I woke up back here in New York." *Charlie said you were the mayor. You're protecting me...aren't you? Something bad happens to General Chang, doesn't it?*

Gina shook her head. "The Egg killed Charlie."

"The Egg?"

"Charlie's neighbor."

"I know who he is."

"He'd been teaching Charlie how to fight with a sword. He has a ton of old Chinese crap worth a fortune today. Charlie thinks…thought…that the killer back in Xin is hoarding stuff that would be worth a lot now. He also lives in apartment 888, which is the number Charlie wrote on his notepad. Or Chang Huang wrote it…it's in a different script than Charlie."

"Do we got any evidence?"

"Nothing leading to The Egg other than the apartment number. But that's weak."

"No, we don't want to arrest him based on that. We could ask him some more questions, but…."

"But what could we ask him that wouldn't make us sound crazy? Even if he doesn't think we're crazy, a judge sure would. But there's more. I think Greg Deathrage is involved?"

"You're joking!"

"He's called himself an amateur chef. Charlie said there's a cook in Chai Wen's unit that might be involved in framing Yuan Lin."

"Be careful, Gina. There's lots of cooks, chefs, or other similar trades here in New York. And we don't even know if Chai Wen's cook is dreaming here. Greg's a good man, and you really can't jump to conclusions. Take the rest of the evening off. Go home. No more investigation, or even thinking about this. Get some rest, or call a friend." Gina's instinct was to argue against this but realized she would just be benched if she stayed at the department. But it was true what he said about Greg. There really was nothing linking him to Xu Ping other than the fact that he likes to cook.

The mayor was waiting in Chang Huang's apartment. "Sarge, how long you been here?"

"Just a little bit. I saw you riding in, so I headed here. Figured you would want to talk about Xu Ping."

"Damned right! Why did you kill him?"

"Easy, Peltman. He was getting unruly. Started to answer my questions at first but then came all undone. Then he tried to fight my men. One of my guards looked at me, and I nodded. Apparently, that is a signal to kill. It took me by surprise, too." Chang Huang sat on the edge of his bed and wiped his eyes with the sleeve of his shirt.

"We have to kill someone else, too," Chang Huang said.

"Who?"

"The spice store owner."

"What the hell did he do?"

"Nothing. He is Martin from Queens. The Private Storage guy."

"Oh, I see. You think killing him will fix him?"

"Yes, I do. Can we get him to a place where we can take care of him quietly?"

"I am the mayor; I think I can arrange that."

The two left for the mayor's residence. Once they arrived, the mayor sent one of his guards to summon the spice merchant. The mansion was located on the northeast corner of Xin. Enough buildings had been constructed to block its view from the town center. Lavish would be an understatement when describing the house where the mayor lived. Charlie's New York apartment could have fit into the entryway, which seemed to serve little purpose other than to allow people to remove their shoes. To the right of the entryway, a wide, carpeted stairway led up to rooms Chang Huang could only imagine. "Seventeen bedrooms up there, Peltman. Can you believe that?" A door to the left, Chang Huang was told, led to a dining area and a kitchen that would have catered more people than the tavern could serve. Beyond the entryway was a large room with a fireplace on one side and countless Chinese paintings filling up the rest of the walls. A wooden table, low from the ground, filled a six-foot by six-foot section of the room. Sofas and chairs with matching, teal-colored cushions surrounded the table. The wood from all of this furniture was so dark that it was almost black.

An archway on the other side of this conversation room led to a rectangular room with a round table and six, less comfortable looking, wooden chairs. This room may have had more square footage than the entryway, but the shape made it seem smaller. Against the wall that was shared by the conversation room was a Chinese herbal medicine chest. It seemed to be made of the same, dark wood as the rest of the furniture. Five rows, each containing seven, four-inch by three-inch drawers, lined the chest. It reminded Charlie of a card catalogue from an older library back home. Upon each drawer was carved a description of the Chinese medicine that was stored within. A series of figurines was arranged in a diorama of sorts on top of the cabinet, but the story to which they referenced was not one with which Chang Huang was familiar. More paintings dressed the walls in this room as well. One of which looked out of place. A man, almost Western looking, sat at a table drinking what looked like a coffee. A sign hung in the background of the painting that Chang Huang could not read.

On the far end of this room was a wide door that slid apart at the center, revealing a well-manicured garden, large enough for a barbeque that would serve the second shift from Charlie's police department. There Chang Huang and the mayor waited until Du Hung was escorted to them. He looked a little confused but was far from scared.

"How can I please you, Lord Mayor? Do you require an herb that might be considered eccentric in these parts? Or is there a spice from the northern region of which you find yourself yearning…maybe a nostalgic taste that reminds you of your youth? Certainly, you do not require my fighting abilities in your guard." He underscored his last sentence with a roll of his eyes.

"Knock off the jest, Martin," the mayor said. At this, Martin stiffened his posture. "Do you want to stop dreaming of this place, or should I send you back to your shop?"

"You are with him?" He pointed to Chang Huang. "I am sorry for my tone, Mayor. I would definitely like to stop dreaming of this God forsaken patch of sand."

"This is my home you are talking about."

"And what a lovely home it is, Lord Mayor. But I fear I have worn out my welcome here. You believe you can help me?"

"I am sure of it." Chang Huang stepped behind Martin and drew his sword without so much as a whisper from his scabbard.

"Thank you, Mayor. I have been tempted to take this in my own hands, but I am afraid I do not have the guts. Is it death? Is that the way out?" He noticed the mayor looking behind him and turned around to see Chang Huang's sword held above his head and over his right shoulder as if it were a baseball bat. "Thank you, Officer Peltman." Chang Huang cocked his arms back and prepared to strike at Martin's neck.

"I cannot do it."

"What?" both Du Hung and the mayor said together.

"This does not feel right. I know this was my plan, but I am not sure about this any longer."

"Peltman, you pansy," the mayor said.

"I cannot help it, sir. Just taking someone's head off who does not deserve it is not in my heart or my hands."

"But I do deserve it!" Martin cried out. "I am a terrible man. Just this morning, I cheated and old woman out of her retirement. Sold her toadstools and told her they were wild mushrooms from a magical land."

"You do not lie very well, Martin," Chang Huang began, but Martin never heard his name. The mayor pulled a dagger from a pocket sewn into his sleeve and flung it into Martin's throat. Martin gurgled a protest, apparently hoping that his heroes would have chosen a less painful method of ending his dreams.

"Peltman, that is the best I can do with what I got. It will take him a little while to die like this unless you," the mayor said as he indicated Chang Huang's sword. Chang Huang knelt down, pulling the silk from his purse which recently served to cushion the mask with his name on it. He put the whole silk on Du Hung's neck, but the blood was coming too fast. By the time Chang Huang made up his mind to finish him, Du Hung had stopped moving. He wanted to wake himself up as he had done many times before, but there was nothing to wake up to. Charlie was gone.

Gina knocked on apartment 888 wearing her dark blue uniform, although she was off duty. She rarely went against direct orders from Sergeant Langmann, but her instincts told her that she needed to interview The Egg, and that the time to do this was short. "Just a minute," came an old voice from behind the door. *All right, Gina, your gut brought you here, but is it going to tell you what to ask?* Nearly a half-minute later, the door opened. "Yes? Can I help you?"

"I hope so. I need to ask you a few questions about your neighbor across the hall."

"Sure, come in." He showed her in and offered her a seat. She remained standing. His face looked tired. "Can I get you some tea or anything?"

"No thank you." She looked around as if in a trance. Charlie had told her about his Chinese décor, but she had not been prepared for the extravagance of his ornamentation. "You knew Charlie well?"

He sat down on a small, wooden chair next to a matching, round table in his dining nook. "Not well, but he has been a neighbor for a long time." Gina studied him carefully. She had seen guilty men fake pain. The Egg did not show any of the signs of false grief. *I can't be wrong. It fits too well.*

His voice was almost a whisper. He looked up at Gina. "How did it happen? They won't tell me."

"That's not been released yet. Did you see anyone suspicious here this morning, or possibly last night?"

"No, not see. I heard Charlie come home last night, maybe around 2:30. His door open and closed. I was Skyping with some friends of mine in Shanghai."

Gina walked over to some of the decorations to see them up close. "Where did you pick up your interest in China?" The Egg took a sip of his tea and went back to looking at the floor.

"It started in high school." He looked up to Gina again. "Our Italian teacher was a master in many languages. Chinese was one of them. She knew quite a few dialects: Mandarin, Cantonese, Shanghaiese, Toisanese, Hakka…I'm not sure how many to be honest. Our school didn't offer courses in those languages, but she taught a few of us Mandarin on the side. I picked up Cantonese a little later in college. I also studied the history and culture in my undergraduate school. Then I began my trips. Just felt more at home with Chinese people than I did with Americans. I'm sorry, I'm a little distraught to go on about this now." He brought the tea up to his lips and then set it back onto his table.

"Charlie said you expressed interest in his sword."

"Yes, I did. I would have gladly paid him. Seems so insignificant now." His eyes widened as if he just realized an obvious fact. "Is it missing? Is that why you asked me that?" Again, his inquiry felt real to her.

"No." *If he is that good of an actor, I won't get anything out of him. Evidence. I need evidence.* "No, just verifying my notes. You're not going on vacation or anything in the near future, are you Mr. Egg?"

"No. No, officer, I'll be right here. I won't go anywhere until we know what happened over there. I want to help, in whatever way I can."

"Thanks. I'll be in touch." She started to leave The Egg's apartment.

"Hsieh Sun," said The Egg. Gina drew her pistol and turned to face The Egg.

"What did you say?"

"Hsieh Sun. I know it's you."

"I can't think of anyone still alive who knows that name and doesn't want to hurt me."

"There's no need to be afraid. I am the one who sent you here. Though it's been a long time." Gina looked into his eyes. There was something there. "I wasn't sure whether or not I should tell you, but what the hell?"

"How can I know you are Kong Xiao?"

"Moments before Hsieh Sun died, I spoke to her. Do you remember?" Gina nodded. "I told her about the spirit statue in the cave and the story of Chu Heng." Gina stared at him, betraying no feelings. "There's still hope for Charlie. But there's something I wish I could have said to you. Had I known you were going to be killed, I would have told you that the next day I would travel back to Xin and visit Mr. Shen's tavern. That I would explain to him that you would not be back to the tavern. That you had gone away. And that I would show him one of my little figurines."

"Mr. Shen? He's here?"

"He will be. His dreams start in 2013."

"Then he knows how this all turns out. He can tell you in China and..."

"If it were that simple. I told him how to look you up, but before he could find you, Kong Xiao was killed. It seemed that Chu Heng had more than one man infiltrating my temple." Gina looked into The Egg's eyes. She supposed he could make all of that up, but Chu Heng would not likely have been able to know of what she and Kong Xiao spoke the night she was killed. Even if one of Chu Heng's spies had heard, there was little chance he would know what Mr. Sheng meant to Hsieh Sun.

"Whether you believe me or not, you need to act fast. I don't know how this story ends, but I have wanted to find out for a long, long time. Just know that once that ship comes in, you may need my help. I will be here."

She holstered the pistol and backed towards the door. Reaching behind her, she opened the door. She opened her mouth to say something but changed her mind, nodded to The Egg, continued into the hall, and closed the door.

Across the hall, the door she had been through many times had yellow tape across it warning her that inside was a crime scene, and that she would be breaking the law if she entered without authorization.

After leaving The Egg, Gina stopped by Samantha's apartment. Her eyes were red and puffy, but she seemed composed. "Hey, come in," she said. "Thank you for coming back."

"Of course. How are you doing?"

"Okay, I guess." Samantha had more hot water ready and poured a cup for Gina. The two sat in the same places they had earlier. "A detective stopped by a little while after you left. It must have been horrible finding him the way you did."

"I've never seen anything like it. And for this to happen to a close friend…."

"You've known Charlie for a while?"

Gina took a sip of her tea. "About four years." The two exchanged Charlie stories and were actually able to laugh a little, though the laughing sometimes transitioned back into tears. "Samantha, how much has Charlie told you?"

"He told me some of his dreams. He said that other people are sharing his dream. Mentioned a guy from Queens…runs one of those self-storage places. Said he was having the same dream. I mean literally the same dream, like they could talk to each other."

"It's worse than that. What I'm about to say will be a lot to take in all at once, but we don't have much time. I'm also having those dreams."

"What?" Samantha sat up on the sofa and leaned away from Gina. "Charlie didn't mention…."

"He didn't know. At least not until this morning."

"He did seem different this morning. He left early." She looked at Gina as if realizing something for the first time. "He went to see you, didn't he?"

"Yes, but please don't get the wrong idea."

"What idea am I supposed to have?"

Gina felt she had to be careful. She looked at the window for help, but there was none there. "My dream is the reverse of his. For me, this city, this time is the dream."

"No…no, no, no, no, no! You can't expect me to believe that you are really some girl in old China traveling…and that Charlie's traveling…." Samantha stopped herself. Her grief overpowered her ability to think for a moment. As far-fetched as all this was, part of her wanted it to be true, because that would mean that maybe Charlie was alive. And that Gina could talk to him for her.

"Look," Samantha continued, "This is whacky…so don't think for a minute that I believe this. I don't think Charlie was really sharing dreams with other people, let alone traveling back in time. But I don't think the Charlie was lying to me, either. I just think he was having issues, and somehow people like that stalker and that guy in Queens, even you, might be messing with him." She paused to see if Gina would try to persuade her. When she didn't, Samantha continued. "Are you in love with him?"

"Yes."

"Is he in love with you?"

"I don't know. General Chang and Hsieh Sun were starting to get close. But they weren't quite there. Charlie was starting to think that you were Hsieh Sun."

"Me?" Samantha asked as her eyes opened wide. Samantha saw that there was some pain in Gina's eyes. She also started to wonder, if all these people were conspiring to mess with Charlie, what good would it do to try to convince her that Charlie's dreams were real. "I'm not saying I believe any of this, but if there's any chance that it is true, can you talk to Charlie for me? Pass messages back and forth? I know that would be asking a lot."

Gina reached out and touched Samantha's hand. "It's not asking a lot. And I would gladly do it. But just as Charlie was killed here in New York, Hsieh Sun was also killed in China."

"What? So, you can't…?"

"No. But there's more. This next part is hard for even me to believe, but it comes with some hope, so I'm trying real hard to believe it."

"Hope?"

"Yes, hope. There is a way for Charlie to come back. Back here to New York. There's a ship coming in on Tuesday. It is carrying a…a small statue that supposedly has Charlie's spirit…his soul if that makes more sense. Once the container is opened, Charlie will be here. He will feel like he is dreaming, at first, that he is someone else. But that will be Charlie. He will seek us out."

"Are you kidding me?"

"No."

Samantha felt as if her entire world flipped. Part of her wanted to kick Gina out. But the other part…. "Can I be there? When the ship comes?"

"That would be dangerous. There's someone here trying to stop that from happening. Whoever that is will kill to stop it."

"The same guy who killed Charlie," Samantha realized. "I don't know about all this. And honestly, I don't know about you."

"I don't expect you to. There's a guy here in the building. I think he is also from China, dreaming of New York like me."

"In this building?"

"Yes. Charlie calls him The Egg."

"I know him. He knows more about China than I do." She looked puzzled. "He's a nice guy. You don't think he killed Charlie, do you?"

"At first I did, but I think that less and less." Gina searched her feelings and realized that this was a true statement. "He is a man named Kong Xiao. There are things about me…Hsieh Sun, that is…that only he would know. If he is Kong Xiao, then he definitely did not kill Charlie. He can help. Once I know for sure, I will let you know. He can explain more about these dreams, and you can make up your mind about them. Until then, please keep an open mind. Charlie loves you. If he does come back, he will look for you. Maybe even before he looks for me. Be thinking about things only he would know."

"I will keep my mind open but just a little. It's more out of an unreasonable need for hope, and that door will close soon."

"I understand. It won't be long before you know the truth."

Chang Huang buried Martin's body in the mayor's courtyard. He put the last shovel of dirt onto Martin's grave just as two of the mayor's special guards arrived with news of the replacement troops. "Mayor Chan Xiang," one of them spoke, "the replacement troops will arrive within the day. Lieutenant Chai Wen's men have packed their belongings and are ready to move out."

"Thank you, Jiao Min. Please make sure the new troops are welcomed and that the current troops are sent away with provisions and our gratitude."

"Yes, Lord Mayor." The two were off before Chang Huang could say a word. He followed the mayor back into the house.

"Sarge, are your men on the lookout for any signs of the Hei Shui gang?"

"They are. They have not seen any sign of the gang. They would have said something if they had."

"What happens if the gang pays them to keep quiet?"

"Their loyalty is beyond question. The mayor had been very generous to those men and their family. Their extended family, even. Before you showed me that lion figurine with the two different colored eyes yesterday, the mayor had been like a father to them. I wonder if they will see a difference in me."

A tingling of suspicion rose in Chang Huang, but he did not fully understand why. "In my experience, there really is not a difference between the old Chang Huang and me. As I remember things Chang Huang has done in the past, I do not think I would have chosen different courses of action that he chose." *Something about what the mayor just said...about the lion figurine.* "I do not think we really replace or supplant other people when we dream like this. It's kind of like the history of these 'characters' are dreamed up by us. Other people have memories of interacting with them, but it is really just us."

"Whatever you say, Peltman. I really do not care." *He said I showed him the idol yesterday. Did he really say that?*

"Sarge, I was wondering something. When I started dreaming, they were shorter. At least most of them were shorter. They got longer as I kept dreaming."

"Yes, they're pretty short now. I have been awake about three times since I showed up here. Why, have you been asleep this whole time?"

"No, I woke up once."

"Just once?"

"Yeah, just once, Sarge. But you just mentioned that I showed you the idol yesterday."

"Yesterday…few days ago…what does it matter? Dreaming like this kind of messes with you."

"You are not kidding about that." Chang Huang felt he had him now. "When you go back to New York, you got to be several days ahead of me by now. What is happening there?"

"I…I am not sure I should be telling you about what is happening there." The mayor could see that the suspicious fire in Chang Huang's eyes was not yet doused. If anything, it had been fanned. "All right, look, I have been here a while longer than you know."

"What? How long?"

"Really long. About eight years."

"Eight years? But I just showed you the idol a few days ago!"

"Just because the lion figurine sent you back to this time, it does not mean it sent me to this same time. After you showed me the figurine, I found myself here in this town, but you were not here. Yuan Lin was not here. I could not even figure out how far back I had gone until Hsieh Sun showed up and started working in that tavern. Once I saw how old she was, I figured out about when you would arrive. When you killed Yuan Lin, I knew that would coincide with the time you showed me that damned figurine. Look, how would it look if I came up to you after you started dreaming about Chang Huang and I told you that I am your boss back in New York and that I have been here forever? Everything that is happening or was happening to you back in New York was eight years ago for me. I know how that whole situation back there turns out for you, and buddy, it is not all pretty. If my memory serves me, you should be dead by now, right? You figured out that damned message, for all the good it did you, and then someone stuck you from behind. Gina and I think it was The Egg, but we could never prove it."

Chang Huang felts shock at the mention of The Egg having killed Charlie, but he could not let go of his train of thought. "You have been the mayor for eight years, right? Tell me why you replaced Chai Wen's guards at the Bao home."

"When I told you that the mayor did not trust the Emperor's army, I meant that I did not trust them."

Chang Huang stopped listening. The out-of-place painting caught his attention once again. "Did you paint that?"

"Yes, I did! Do you like it? A little bit of home."

"It's nice. That sign in the background…is that English?"

"Yes, it advertises the house special, 'Cherry Pie $1.50 per slice.'" Chang Huang drew his sword from the scabbard.

"You said you could not read the message. The one I have been trying to figure out. I showed it to you last night, and you said you could not read it."

While Chang Huang had been reviewing his chain of logic, the mayor had been moving slowly closer to the medicine chest. He rested his hand on the top near one of the figurines at the edge closest to him. "I lied, Charlie." The mayor grabbed the nearest figurine and flung it at General Chang.

Chang Huang dodged the figurine and raised his sword, walking quickly towards the mayor. At the same time, the mayor grabbed the top of the medicine chest with his left hand and lifted it, separating it from the rest of the cabinet and knocking the remaining figurines across the room. With his right hand, he grabbed a sword that was just underneath the false top of the cabinet and swung it at Chang Huang's charging blade, knocking it aside.

Chang Huang was surprised but recomposed himself enough to spin with his blade and bring it all the way around to block the mayor's retaliation strike. He also allowed his momentum to take him past the mayor and further into his house. When Chang Huang turned around, he could see that the mayor was facing the other way. The mayor moved into the courtyard. In one movement, Chang Huang pulled his dagger from a sheath at his belt and flung it at the mayor, sticking it into his left shoulder.

The mayor muffled a scream and turned back to face Chang Huang. "That was not very sportsman like, Charlie." He pulled the dagger from his shoulder and tossed it back at Chang Huang, who deflected it with his sword. "I thought you were better than that." The two ran towards each other, meeting at the doorway between the house and the courtyard, swords crossed pointing upwards. Chang Huang was stronger, and his blade pushed the mayor's blade downward. When the mayor took a step back to free his sword from Chang Huang's hold, Charlie brought his sword back up and slashed right, aiming for the mayor's midsection. The mayor backed up and shifted his weight to his right, barely avoiding the swipe. Not wanting to let the mayor get by without a touch, he lunged forward, bringing his blade back to the left and drawing a thin line of blood on the mayor's abdomen through a new hole in his dress. The mayor hopped back twice and held his sword across his body in defense.

"You are no swordfighter, are you, Sarge?" The mayor did not respond. "Why did you not kill me earlier? Slide a knife in my back or something?" The mayor remained quiet. His eyes would not leave Chang Huang's sword. "In 2012, you are trying to destroy Francis' boat. The whole point is to kill me. Why did you not just kill me by now here in China? It would accomplish the same thing." The mayor's eyes continued to focus on Chang Huang's blade. Chang Huang jerked his arm, but the mayor still did not react. *He needs something from me.* Chang Huang charged at the mayor, dropping his blade low and to the right, and then feinting a swing at the mayor's left leg. The mayor lowered his sword to block, but Chang Huang arced his blade upward instead and then dropped it back down on the mayor's left arm, nearly severing it.

The mayor screamed as he dropped his sword and collapsed. Chang Huang lifted his sword to bring it down into the mayor's heart when he heard, "Drop it, General!" from a man holding a drawn bow in the doorway to the house. Chang Huang took a step toward the bowman. "I said drop it, General!" Chang Huang could tell that this man had never shot a bow at someone in his life. The tip of the arrow bobbed and shook. He took another step towards the bowman. "Last chance, General!" Sweat appeared on the bowman's brow. His eyebrows were already drenched, and a bead of saline appeared ready to drip into his right eye. Chang Huang waited. As soon as the drop of sweat touched the bowman's eyelash, causing him to start blinking rapidly, Chang Huang yelled as loud as he could and jumped to his right. The bowman let go of the string, letting the arrow fly wild into a fencepost. Before the guard could rethread a new arrow, Chang Huang was upon him, piercing his heart. Both arrow and bow dropped to the floor. Chang Huang used his boot to push the guard's body off of his sword. By then, two more guards were rushing through the mayor's front door with swords of their own. *I can't take them both at once.* Chang Huang dropped his sword and picked up the arrow and bow at his feet and aimed at the mayor's still breathing body. Both guards halted their advance just out of sword reach from the general.

Chang Huang waited to see which one looked at the mayor first. For nearly a minute, both guards kept their eyes trained on Chang Huang. Then the guard on the right glanced in the direction of the courtyard. Chang Huang let go of the string and let the arrow fly into the stomach of their boss. Chang Huang stepped to his left as the guard on the right dashed by to assist the mayor. At the same time, he swung the bottom end of the bow up to the other guard's midsection and leaned into it, hoping it would knock the wind out of him and throw off his attack. This mostly worked, but the guard's sword did manage to steal a slice into Chang Huang's thigh. Chang Huang ignored the pain as best as he could and ran past the guard, knocking him down with his left shoulder on the way to the mayor's front door.

Outside, three other guards were running from the bivouac site towards the mayor's house. He hobbled as fast as he could back to the inn. Horse was still tethered to the rail there. Chang Huang unwound the rein and mounted Horse before the first guard could reach him. He kicked at Horse harder than he ever had and left the town of Xin for the cave behind Kong Xiao's temple. As he rode, he started to puzzle over a circular chain of events that followed from what he just learned. *The mayor showed Yuan Lin the lion figurine, who then showed the figurine to Hsieh Sun. Hsieh Sun, as Gina, showed it to me, and I showed it to the sarge, who is also the mayor. But that can't be. There is no beginning.* General Chang slowed his horse and looked over his shoulder back towards the town of Xin. *Either there is someone else in this link...or the mayor is not Sarge.* He kicked Horse and raced in the direction of the cave.

Chapter 21

(Sunday – August 26, 2012)

Gina arrived at the station shortly before her shift. The entire day felt unreal—dreamlike. Though New York was merely Hsieh Sun's dream, it had been her real world for eleven years. The last four of which she spent befriending the man she fell in love with in her "past life." Now that he knew who she was, he was gone. Francis' boat and its cargo was her only chance to see him again. Even though the boat had not yet docked, and someone was hell bent on destroying it.

Langmann was in his office when she arrived, and a note on her desk told her that he wanted to see her right away. His door was closed. She opened it without knocking and saw the sarge was on the phone. "Hang on," he said to the handset. Then to Gina, "Give me five minutes, then get your ass back in here, pronto." She left his office and poured herself a coffee she knew she wouldn't drink. She wasn't afraid of the sergeant. She expected him to be pissed off. Knew this would happen the minute she interviewed The Egg. After rearranging papers on her desk for a bit, she went back to Langmann's office and opened the door.

She intended to start in with, "I know what you're going to say, so you can just save it." Instead, she entered the room, closed the door, and sat down in front of the sarge's desk waiting for the explosion of expletives she'd heard several times in the past few years.

"Are you satisfied with yourself, Officer Baxter?"

"Not in the least," she said quietly.

"Imagine how Peterson felt when I sent her to question The Egg, only to find out she was the third cop to talk to him today. What's gotten into you?"

"What do you think? Haven't we lost enough cops to this guy?"

"If you screw this up, he'll get away with it and kill more cops."

"Anyway, I don't think he's our man."

"Whoever our man is, these missteps will cost us. Can you understand that?"

"Yes, Sarge."

"At least have the intestinal fortitude to tell me right away after you do something against orders like that so I don't embarrass myself and my officers."

"Yes, Sarge. I wasn't thinking."

"You better *start* thinking, Baxter." He paused and screwed up a more sympathetic tone. "Look, I'm sorry. I know you are dealing with this the best way you know how. I'm probably dealing with it in the worst way I know how." He looked down at his desk and back up to Gina. "That off-duty security detail Charlie was on…are you filling in for him?"

"I'm going to have to. You don't mind me taking leave, do you?" Gina asked.

"Mind? I prefer it. Starting today. When does the ship dock?"

"Tuesday."

"Did Charlie have a plan that he shared with you?"

"Yes."

"Could you use my help?"

"I might. I'll see if Francis was able to take care of some arrangements that Charlie requested. I'll figure out from there if I need help. Thanks for offering." Despite the initial chewing out, Gina held a lot of respect for the sarge, and was glad he was on her side.

Francis knew something bad had happened when Gina showed up alone. “Charlie?” he asked. Her emotions, barely contained to begin with, overtook her. “You knew this was coming.”

“I know,” she said, gaining composure. “It just happened so fast after Charlie learned who I was.”

“He’ll be back in your presence before long. Now is not the time to lose control of yourself. Harold was able to acquire a decoy boat and has identified a location where it can be switched with the real one well offshore. In fact, the switch should have occurred by now. The real boat should be idle while the decoy is being guided remotely toward New York. In another twelve hours or so the decoy will be destroyed, and Charlie will be on his way in. Harold will be here in a little bit to review the details.” He studied Gina for a moment. “Do you know who killed Charlie?”

“I’m not certain. I thought it was The Egg; he’s this guy who lives across the hall from Charlie. I was certain of it in fact, but now I’m not so sure. He may be one hell of an actor, but my gut tells me otherwise.”

“Your gut? What does your heart tell you?” She thought this through carefully.

“Do you now know The Egg?”

“Should I?”

“He says he is Kong Xiao.”

“That wouldn’t surprise me.” Gina looked surprised. “I know that Kong Xiao is here in New York. It makes sense that he would want to be close to Charlie.”

“But why wouldn’t he reveal himself to you?”

“Kong Xiao has his reasons. He was dreaming several years back. Similar to you and Yuan Lin. Maybe even earlier. So, I will ask you again, what does your heart tell you?”

“The Egg did not kill Charlie.”

“Then after you review the details with Harold, go find out who did.”

Gina returned to her apartment and booted up her laptop. She knew her feelings about The Egg's innocence were not based on personal bias. She didn't know The Egg well enough to like or dislike him. Or to truly know whether or not he was Kong Xiao. In her experience, such feelings were based on underlying facts that she hadn't consciously pieced together properly. As her startup programs loaded, Gina started to realize how sleepy she was. She began to wonder what she hoped to accomplish on her computer. Originally, she thought she could list every seemingly unrelated fact into a spreadsheet and try to connect dots. Her fingers were sluggish on the keyboard. The various programs that were open on her screen started melting together. Her neck bent forward and her eyes submitted to a long blink. When she looked back up, she was no longer in her apartment. She was standing in Francis' office, but Francis was not there. Instead, a young Hsieh Sun sat frozen, as if she were a mannequin, behind Francis' desk looking at Gina as if she were waiting for her to speak. Not knowing what she was expected to say, she blurted out what she had said to Francis in this office a little more than an hour ago, "The Egg did not kill Charlie."

"Who did?" Hsieh Sun replied. She looked slightly more lifelike now.

"I really don't know," said Gina.

"Find out."

"How?"

"What made you originally think The Egg killed Charlie?"

"He's been collecting Chinese artifacts."

"That is not much. Earlier, you were quite certain The Egg killed Charlie. What made you so certain? There must be something more concrete. That is where you took a wrong turn. The fork in the road."

Gina thought for a moment. "I guess it was Charlie's notepad. Charlie wrote 888 below the message he was trying to figure out."

"Why would he not have written 'Egg'?"

"Yeah, he would have written that, wouldn't he? It was also different handwriting. But Dr. Thomason said that Charlie's other personality had a different handwriting." Hsieh Sun smiled.

"How would Chang Huang have written '888'?"

"What do you mean?"

"Back in Xin, would Chang Huang have written 888 in English?" Gina suddenly realized why she had been upset with Dr. Thomason in Charlie's apartment. He pushed Gina to accept that it had been Charlie who wrote '888' instead of the killer. It sounded innocent enough on the surface, but it was not his place to persuade her. And if he truly believed that Charlie's last words were written by his other personality, he at least should have mentioned the oddity of Chang Huang writing those numbers in English. He might not have expected Charlie to write in Chinese—considering Charlie didn't know Chinese—but maybe some gibberish that vaguely resembled Chinese characters.

"I think Dr. Thomason is involved."

"Dr. Thomason?"

"Yes. But I need evidence."

"What else have you got?"

"Nothing. I got nothing."

"That is not true. Did Yuan Lin not write several notes to Charlie? Those notes must be in the evidence lockers. Why not compare the handwriting?"

"Those are from Yuan Lin, and we know Yuan Lin didn't kill Charlie."

"Are all the notes from Yuan Lin?"

"Yes."

"Are they?" Gina squinted as Hsieh Sun seemed to go out of focus for a second. "You no longer believe Yuan Lin killed McAllister and Jameson. But there was a note left in Fred's mouth."

"But that note was originally written by Yuan Lin. We know that because he gave it to the actor from the theater."

"Not all of it. Was there not something new added to the letter?" Gina thought back to that note. The first part of the message only had instructions when and where to meet. That was in black ink. The second part was in blue ink, and was obviously written later, "Next time come yourself, coward."

"Yuan Lin couldn't have written the last line. Yuan Lin didn't know about Fred and Peter when Charlie asked him about them." She thought about this before adding, "But it was in the same handwriting as the original note, which *was* written by Yuan Lin. What am I missing?"

"Thank about the letter. Who touched it? What was the chain of custody?"

"Yuan Lin gave it to the actor from the theater. The actor gave it to Charlie. Charlie gave it to Fred. No…Charlie gave it to the sarge, who then gave it to Fred." Gina looked at the floor and chewed lightly on her thumb. "Could the sarge have switched the letter? Why would he do that?" She looked up at Hsieh Sun. Her expression was frozen, as if she were a store mannequin again.

"Wait a minute. The shooter could have rewritten the note and then added the second part. Then he could place it in Fred's mouth and take the real one." Gina sat down in a chair on the other side of the desk from Hsieh Sun. "I need to match that note with the '888' on Charlie's notepad. Both will be in evidence lockup. That will be hard, comparing numbers to letters. But it's the best I have. Then I can compare the note with Sarge's and Thomason's handwriting."

Then she woke up.

Before visiting Dr. Thomason, she had another thought she wanted to check out. Charlie had told her that he bought his sword at a pawn shop near his apartment. The only one close was on 28th near Avenue M. The clerk's senses were on alert, as Gina made straight for him without browsing any of his fare. "You sell a sword to someone with one of these?" she asked, pointing to her badge.

"Yes ma'am."

"How long ago?"

"I don't know…week or two. He kill someone with it?"

"I'm looking for the man who originally sold it to you. Can you tell me anything about him?"

"Yeah, I remember him 'cause I think he was a cop, too. Tall but not as tall as me. Skinny." *Skinny,* Gina thought. *The sarge is not skinny.* "His hair was lighter than mine. Not blonde but lighter." *Hair color might be Sarge's, but I can't imagine anyone calling him skinny.* "I thought I got a bargain off him. He said the sword was a replica, but I didn't think it was. Then the cop who bought it confirmed it was junk. Funny thing, though: when I bought the sword, I started to write up a ticket so he could claim it back, but he said he wouldn't be back for it and I could sell it whenever I wanted."

"Was his hair long?"

"No. Buzz cut, actually. Also, he had glasses. Thick frames."

Bingo. "Thank you."

Dr. Thomason's newspaper was spread out in front of him when Gina walked through his door. She closed the door and locked it without taking her eyes off of him. His eyes and body language let her know he was uncomfortable seeing her. She placed a small figurine with a jewelry bag over its head on his desk. He didn't seem to understand its significance at first. Then his expression changed from unease to fear as he realized what this figurine meant. He turned his head away from his desk and said, rather loudly, "Get that away from me! I'll yell for help!"

"Then what? Some of my fellow cops will bust in here. They'll ask you what is wrong, and you'll tell them I'm trying to scare you with a small, stone lion?"

"What do you want?"

"You already gave me half of what I want. You know about this, and you know what it can do. You've been screwing with Charlie all this time."

"He wouldn't believe me if I told him his dreams were real. I couldn't just tell him that."

"How did you know about this figurine?" Dr. Thomason remained silent. Gina picked up the figurine and brought it around to Dr. Thomason's face. He jerked his head the other direction. "You want to play? I can make sure you gaze upon this thing…today…tomorrow…next week. Most likely today." Thomason remained quiet. "Okay, have it your way." She turned to leave.

"Okay! Okay! Just put it away." He glanced toward her and could see the lion figurine was no longer visible. Her pocket, he guessed. He picked up the glass globe from his desk and nervously rotated it in his hands. Gina instinctually saw this as a potential missile.

"Please put that back down on the desk, Doctor."

"Fine." He set it back on the far corner of the desk from where he sat. Then he took a deep breath and answered, "It started out as just a favor to the sarge. 'Just humor him,' he told me. After the first session, I wanted to take him off the roster and have him examined by someone higher up. That's when the sarge started 'helping me.' He knew I was over my head in debt, and he paid off my car…just like that." He snapped his fingers. "Then he started paying me for each session."

"How much?"

"A lot. The first time it was ten grand. I had no idea how loaded he was. I got suspicious. Started thinking he was dealing or something. Then he told me about the figurine and his dreams. He took me out to a storage place where he has a whole garage full of Chinese tools, weapons, statues, and even furniture."

"Wait, when was this?"

"After the fourth session."

"When was that?"

"A couple weeks ago." *That was well before Charlie showed Sarge the lion figurine. He's been dream traveling a lot longer than we knew.*

"Do you know anything about how he killed McAllister, Peterson, and Charlie?" Dr. Thomason winced when she said McAllister's name. "You do, don't you?"

"The sarge has gone mad. By that time, I knew he was capable of killing me. So, I continued to help him."

"You showed him Charlie's journal, didn't you?"

"Yes."

That's how Mark knew about the Statue of Liberty. Langmann or Thomason emailed Mark. "If I can bring the sarge down, will you testify?"

"If you can assure me I would be safe."

"Just so you know, I have you on tape. All of what you just said. I doubt it can be used against you in court, but it could ruin your reputation and your career."

"My career's over either way." He drew in a deep breath. "I just want to get out of this situation. I really don't care about my job. The sarge's gonna kill me sooner or later. I know too much. I do want immunity from prison, though. As it stands, I don't go to prison if I don't testify."

"That'll be up to the D.A." Gina said as she turned and reached for the doorknob. Then she stopped. Something had caught her eye. She turned back to look at a photograph laying on a table next to a file cabinet. It looked like a medallion of an eagle with its wings spread, grasping a swastika in its talons. The head was turned to the right, and a red gemstone served for its eye. "Where did you get that?" she asked.

"Fred gave it to me. I was helping him…I shouldn't really talk about it, but he's gone now, and my career is soon to be shot, so what the hell. His brother is in a German prison. This item was stolen from a museum. Fred says his brother has nothing to do with it." Gina looked at it for a few seconds before slowly walking out of the office.

Gina knew Fred very well. It took Fred a while to warm to her, but when he did, they were like old friends. Fred had two brothers. She knew that she should focus on the matter at hand, but she had to know if the eagle medallion was related to this. The red gemmed eyeball was too similar to the lion figurine.

Jerry McAllister was a hard-working machinist who lived in Brooklyn. He was usually home on Sundays with his wife and three kids. When she arrived, she was still struggling with what she would say. Jerry would no doubt still be grieving the loss of his brother. She was still wearing her uniform and was aware that this might look like official business. As she reached up to knock on the door, it opened to reveal Jerry with a worried look on his face. "Gina?" he asked.

"Hi Jerry," Gina replied. "Sorry to bother you."

"Not at all. Come in, come in."

"Thanks." She noticed the home was sparsely decorated but impeccably clean.

"Want some coffee? Jane and the kids are at the store."

"I'd love some, but I don't think I have time to drink it. I feel like I'm fighting the clock, and I'm not sure if I'm on a wild goose chase. Your brother…Jim, not Fred…when's the last time you heard from him?"

"Jim? It's been a few weeks. Why?"

"Did he send you anything? Pictures of the medallion he supposedly stole?"

"Well, his lawyer did. Wanted to know if I had seen it before. You need to see it?"

"I might…do you know if the head is facing right or left?"

"I got one of each. One second." He walked into one of the rooms on the right side of his hallway. When he returned, he handed two pictures to Gina. The first one she had already seen. It was the one where the eagle's head looked to the right. The eye was red. In the other picture, the head was looking to the left, and the gemstone for the eye was green.

"My God," Gina said.

"What?" Jerry asked. "Does this mean something to you?"

"Yes. I think that I may need to get involved with Jim's case."

"Well, I don't know what that means, but any change in the situation has got to be better than where we are at the moment. Do you think he stole it?"

"I don't know, but there's more to this figurine than just the financial value. I don't have time to explain, but I will come back in a few days." *If I'm still alive,* she almost added.

"Thank you, Gina. Thank you, and I look forward to you coming back here." There were tears in his eyes. She never thought she would see this big man cry.

Gina was tempted to pay Martin a visit but wasn't sure that would be safe. Sergeant Langmann knew she and Charlie had been out there. A phone call to Martin might be safer, but she decided she could do that from home. Since she wasn't going back to work, she changed into civilian clothes but strapped on her ankle holster. Gina hated wearing it but did not want to be left without any defense if she ran into the sarge. She looked up the phone number for Private Storage franchise 32405 on the Internet and dialed Martin's office. A downcast voice answered. "Hello," it said in a baritone.

"Hello, can I speak to Martin Killjoy, please?"

"He ain't here. He's not…well, he's dead."

"Dead? Are you sure?" Gina yelled to the young man on the other end of the connection.

"Yeah, someone shot him. In the face." The voice on the other end was audibly upset.

"I'm so sorry," she said.

"It's okay. I'm sure the new owner will keep me on. Even if not, I'll find another job." Gina pulled the phone away from her ear and looked at it before she asked her next question.

"Was it a robbery?"

"Not that we can tell. Nothing's missing."

"Thanks," she said and hung up the phone.

"Hsieh Sun," said a more familiar voice from behind her. Her body jolted a little, but she did not scream before turning around to face Dr. Thomason. His eyes commanded her attention. She did not think about Charlie as she looked into those eyes, or Yuan Lin, or even McAllister and Jameson. Instead, images of the Bao family flashed into her mind—the children whom she taught to read. They died eleven years ago for her. In real time, it was over four centuries ago. Now it felt like she had just heard the news of their murders.

"How long have you been here waiting for me?"

"I came here right after you left my office. Figured you'd head over to see Jerry after you asked me about that picture in my office. So, I had time."

"Did Sarge send…no…." Thomason smiled. "He had nothing to do with this, did he?"

"Sergeant Langmann couldn't plan a dinner party, let alone what I cooked up." In a gloved hand, he produced another small, lion figurine, almost identical to the lion she had seen first as Hsieh Sun before her New York dreams started, except both of the eyes were red crystals. She tried to look away from it but could not. She felt weak and sat down on her recliner without breaking her gaze from the lion's ruby eyes.

"Fred showed you the note." Sleepiness caused her speech to slur. She sounded drunk to Thomason. "You switched it with one that you wrote in your handwriting so that you could write the last part and make it match. The part calling Charlie a coward. Then you killed Fred and stuck it in his mouth!" Thomason said nothing. Drowsiness started to overcome her. "What is that lion fig…?" she started but found herself feeling too drowsy to talk any more.

"You will sleep now," Thomason said. "No one will miss you since you are on leave. By the time anyone finds you, your body will have succumbed to dehydration." That was all she heard before her world went dark.

Chapter 22

(Tuesday – August 28, 2012)

Officer Robinson looked upon an old Jewish man as he made his way up the steps to Gina's apartment building. The man seemed to be smiling back at him, but he couldn't be sure. No sound came from Gina's apartment door as he approached it. He put his ear against it. *Probably taking care of Charlie's security detail for him.* He knocked. No response. He knocked again. No response. "Gina! It's me…Mark!" He waited. No response. *Yeah, probably doing the job.* He turned around and descended the steps to the ground level of her building.

Outside, the old Jewish man scrutinized him but still seemed to retain his smile. Robinson almost passed him by but decided it wouldn't hurt anything to ask about his coworker. "Hi, there."

"Hi, young man," the older man responded.

"Do you know Gina Baxter up in…."

"Apartment 2B? Yep, know her fairly well."

"Great. You seen her around today or yesterday?"

"Not since Sunday. She came back around 11:00 in the morning. I must have missed her when she went off to work."

"She didn't work on Sunday. Boss said she was on leave."

"Leave? Doesn't sound like her. She usually tells me these kinds of things. But no, I haven't seen her come or go since then. Though she might be at that other officer's place: Charlie's apartment." Mark felt a physical pain at the mention of Charlie.

"No, she hasn't been there."

"Really?" The old man looked concerned.

"Tell you what: I'm a cop, too." He showed the old man his badge. "So, I'm gonna bust in there to see if she's all right. Unless you can give me a reason why I shouldn't."

"No, I can't think of a reason. Let's go check on her." The two went back up to apartment 2B. Robinson tried knocking and calling out to Gina one more time before kicking the door in. It gave way on the second kick.

"Gina!" Mark called out before seeing her sound asleep on her recliner. He ran over to her and slapped her face, gently at first, then a bit harder. "She's not responding." He felt her wrist and listened to her nose. "She's breathing and has a pulse. Get me a glass of water." The old man started opening cabinets until he found one with glasses. He filled one with water from the sink and handed it to Robinson. Mark grabbed the glass and doused her face. With a start, Gina's eyes came open. "Gina? Can you hear me?" She looked back at Robinson, obviously confused.

"Mark?"

"Yes, Gina, it's me!" Gina looked over at Paul.

"Paul?"

"Yes, honey; I'm here, too." The confusion started to lift, then her eyes opened wide.

"Don't move, either of you!" The two men continued to look at Gina. "I'm gonna stand up, but keep looking at this recliner." She nearly fell down upon her attempt to stand but caught herself and slid back into the chair.

"Easy, Gina. Why don't you…?" He started to turn around and rise.

"No! Do NOT turn around!"

"Okay…okay, Gina." She struggled to her feet and walked around Mark towards the figurine with two red eyes that was still positioned in front of her. She grabbed it and put it into her pocket. "Apparently, that doesn't work more than once on the same person, either."

"What?" Mark asked.

"Oh, you both can turn around now." They did.

"What was that all about?" Mark asked. Gina ignored his question.

"What time is it?"

"About ten o'clock." Gina looked out her window and saw the sunshine reflected brightly off the greenery outside.

"You must be joking. It's still daylight."

"Ten in the morning, sweetheart," replied Paul.

"I slept a whole day?"

"At least. This man says he hasn't seen you since Sunday," said Mark.

"What day is today?"

"Tuesday," said both Paul and Mark.

"Tuesday?" she asked. "Oh, shit! Francis' cargo's coming in today."

"Take it easy, Gina. You aren't in any shape...."

"I need to get downtown, fast. The decoy would have blown long ago." *And Charlie's team never got a phone call yesterday.*

"Decoy? Look, you need food and water if you've been out two days," replied Mark. But Gina was already grabbing a six pack of bottled water and a box of Little Debbie Zebra Cakes. "I was thinking something a little more nutritious."

"No time. Can you get me down to 57th and Park Avenue? I don't think I'm in any shape to drive."

"Sure." Robinson realized that there was no stopping Gina. "Let's go."

"I'll lock up for ya, honey child," Paul said.

"Thanks, Pauley." She kissed him on the forehead and staggered into the hall. Once she was in Mark's car, she downed a 12-ounce bottle of water and opened another one. "I may have to pee along the way." She meant that to sound funny, but Mark just replied that that would be fine. She tore open one of the double Zebra Cake packets and ate each in two bites. It wasn't until she felt her blood sugar coming back up that she started to wonder why Mark had shown up at her apartment. She looked at him with suspicion, but his eyes were focused on the road ahead of him. "Why did you come?"

"Say what?"

"Why did you come to my place?" He took in a deep breath and let it out slow.

"You're not the only one hurting. When the sarge said that you were on leave, I figured you were upset about Charlie. He was partner to both of us. I figured he was a little more than a partner to you. Just wanted to see you." He glanced at her, then back at the road. She smiled at him.

"Thank you, Mark."

Francis' secretary told Gina and Mark that Francis had not come into the office this morning. He had been expected to be in, but he did not show or call. She had tried to reach him at his home and cell numbers but got voicemail on both tries. She left messages, a text, and an email. She promised she would let Gina know as soon as she heard from him.

"Gina, what the hell is going on?" Mark asked once the two of them were alone on the elevator.

"It's Dr. Thomason. I can't explain all of it, but he killed Charlie."

"What?"

"He killed all of them. McAllister, Jameson, even the guy who owned the Private Storage in Queens."

"Why would he do that?" She looked at him through the corner of her eye.

"I don't know where to begin. I can tell you it was Thomason in my apartment who knocked me out."

"Did he hit you?!" He looked closely at her cheek to see if there were any marks.

"No, it's more like a drug."

"A drug?" Gina hit the emergency stop on the elevator. She turned towards Mark and placed both of her hands on the sides of his face and looked into his eyes.

"Mark, listen to me. Even if I had time to tell you what is happening, you would not believe it. Thomason is our colleague, but I'm your friend. You found me after I've been asleep for two days, and I'm telling you that Thomason was the one who put me to sleep. If we get through this, I will be able to tell you what is going on and I'll have support to back me up. Right now, however, I need you to trust me. I need that like I've never needed anything before. The cargo that is coming on that ship in…," she looked at her watch, "…one and a half hours has something very, very important on it. Thomason wants to destroy it. He will kill anyone who gets in his way. He already has." Tears of frustration escaped her eyes.

"I trust you, Gina." She closed her eyes and wrapped her arms around him, squeezing him tightly.

"Thank you." She pulled herself away and wiped the water from her eyes with the heel of her palm. "Now let's get to Yonkers." She slapped the emergency stop again and the car started moving downward.

Gina was looking straight ahead and did not see the police cruiser that pulled up beside Mark's car at first. She first thought Mark hit a pothole when Thomason swerved his car hard into Mark's. "What the hell is he doing?" Mark shouted. Gina looked and saw Thomason grinning back at her, wearing a police uniform. His sunglasses disguised his eyes, though she imagined they were swirling pinwheels of white and black underneath the shaded glass.

"Oh my God! Lose him, Mark!"

"I can't lose a cruiser. Those things are turbo and handle far better than this twelve-year-old piece of shit." He tried swerving back into Thomason's car but only succeeded moving him inches. Mark looked around and saw that no other cars were currently sharing the small access road that led to Pier 27. He stepped hard on the break, trying to force Thomason in front. If he could not outmaneuver or outrace the doc, he needed to face him outside of the vehicles. Providing Gina also had a piece on her, they would have an advantage. But before the Thomason's car passed his front bumper, a final bump pushed his center of gravity over the edge of the road and into a four-foot drainage ditch. Mark and Gina yelled as the momentum of the fall rolled the car onto its roof.

Gina was the first to wake up. Her head felt like it was being eaten from the inside. She felt blood on her forehead but it was not running down into her eyes, which confused her until she realized she was upside-down. The expended airbags hung from the console. She thought her arm was broken at first but was encouraged when moving her fingers brought her no additional pain. Mentally running her own diagnostics, she started to think she might not be too bad off. She clicked her seatbelt button and fell to the roof of Mark's car. Mark was still unconscious. She didn't want to unbuckle him, as she was afraid she could not handle his weight in her condition and could damage his neck by letting him fall. She slid her cell phone out of her pocket and dialed 911, looking around to make sure Thomason or his car were nowhere in sight.

"Officer down...vehicle collision. We're on an access road to the Hudson shore off of Warburton…north of…Arthur St. Yonkers." Mark opened his eyes and turned to look at Gina.

"Where is he?" he managed.

"I think he went on to the dock."

"Go get him."

"I'm not going to leave you."

"Medics are on their way. I'm fine. Go get that shit-eating bastard." She kissed his cheek and started to open the car door. "I have a piece…." He started to say. Gina felt at the bulge at the ankle of her pantleg.

"Don't need it. Got mine right here." She left the car. She had been out for a half an hour according to her watch. The shipyard looked to be a quarter-mile away. *We must have gotten closer than I realized.* Her leg was hurting, but it wasn't broken, so her pace was not considerably slowed. She reached the main gate only to see that it was chained and locked. No guard was stationed in the guard shack, and there was no sign of the patrol car Thomason was driving. She could see the *Skipping Stone* docked behind the building, and an empty crane stood guard over the ship with its hook hanging motionlessly over an empty spot where a truck was likely parked not too long ago. *I'm too late. Charlie came early.* The gate was wide enough for a car, but unless Thomason had a key for this chain, she could not see how he had gotten to the shipyard. Unless someone let him in and locked it behind him. She started to walk the perimeter of the fence when movement from the corner of warehouse caught her attention. Two security officers were making their way to the front of the building in a casual manner, looking as if they might be on rounds. The thought that these men might be working for Thomason crossed her mind. *Well, if I'm too late, I got nothing to lose.* "Hey!" she called to the guards. She took out her wallet with her badge and waived it in the air. "I'm a cop! My suspect is on your grounds!" The two men started to sprint in her direction.

Inside the warehouse, Dr. Thomason subconsciously moved his hand to the butt of his holstered pistol. *Stop it. We are well beyond pistols.* He then reached into his pants pocket and withdrew the black, glass globe from his office and smashed it onto the concrete floor. The yellow crystal from inside began to glow. Thomason retrieved the crystal and moved to the front of the shipping container. It was still welded shut. "Let's do this," he said to the federal agents who were standing nearby. They put on welding masks that they had been carrying and started to dolly pressurized tanks with hoses and torches towards the cargo container. The men went to work melting the edges of the door to the shipping container without saying a word. The task took less time than he expected. When they finished their work,

Thomason smiled as he watched the end of the container fall. The idol inside began glowing as fresh air connected with its surface. "Get back! Everyone, get back!" Thomason shouted to the men, who wasted no time in putting as much distance as possible between themselves and the container. Thomason's smile turned flat, however, as he stared at the image on the idol. "That doesn't make any sense at all." It was the last thing he said before a bullet sliced through his throat, severing both the jugular vein and carotid artery.

The security team wasted no time in training their weapons on the window from where the shot came as the glow from inside the container grew brighter. Gina dropped below the window sill and turned back to the two guards who let her onto the grounds. "Did you hit your target, officer?" one of them asked.

"Yes." She could hardly believe it. "Let's go tell your buddies what's going on. I need to get to that container…now!" The guards helped her up, being careful not to expose themselves to the window.

"I'll try my radio again," the second guard said. He attempted to reach his supervisor, but only static replied. "No good."

"There's an intercom in the office," said the first guard. The three walked twenty yards to an external door. The first guard opened it no more than an inch before calling out to his fellow, "Hey Bert…it's Benson and Lewis."

"Got anyone with you?"

"Yeah…a badge from Brooklyn. She's clean."

"Come in," Bert said. The external door led to a small office, which had little more than a desk, some lockers, and a corded black phone with a lot of buttons on it. A man sitting at the desk looked nervous and gripped a pistol so hard his knuckles looked as though they were about to break out of his skin.

"For God's sake, Bert, will you put that thing away?" Bert looked down and realized he was still holding his weapon, loosened his grip, and holstered it.

"Shit, sorry guys. I heard the gun shot, and my radio doesn't seem to work. Thought we were under attack."

"Nearly were. Radio's still out. I need to use the intercom."

"Knock yourself out," Bert replied and pushed his chair back from the desk. Benson picked up the receiver to the black phone and pressed an orange button, followed by a yellow one.

"Attention all agents, the warehouse is secure. The radios are not working. You'll find a signal scrambler on the body of that cop in front of the container. I need someone to search him and shut the scrambler off." He waited a few seconds before he heard a double squelch from his own radio.

"Benson, this is Wilkinson. Over."

"Benson here. Over."

"That you on the intercom? Over."

"Affirmative. Over."

"Come on back. Out." Benson, Lewis, and Bert escorted Gina out to the warehouse main floor. Another guard, who Gina took to be Wilkinson, approached them as they made their way to the container and Dr. Thomason's body. Light was no longer emanating from the container. "Who's she?" Wilkinson asked.

"She's another cop. She says this one here," Benson pointed to Thomason's body, "was going to set off a dirty bomb."

"Funny, he said he was going to disarm a bomb." All three men turned towards Gina as she made her way to Thomason's body.

It was over; Charlie was free and was out in the city somewhere. He would find her. She clicked on her LED flashlight to see the face on the idol, and nearly dropped her light as her legs began to give. She screamed out loud, "No! No!" and dropped to her knees. Benson and Wilkinson ran to her, absent mindedly dropping their hands to their pistols. She managed to regain control of her flashlight and shine it back on the idol to make sure she saw it correctly. Her eyes flooded and her breathing morphed to wailing cries. "Oh, Charlie," she said out loud between sobs. "Charlie…what happened?" Instead of seeing the darkened image of a familiar Chinese general, her light reflected back the image of a one-armed man dressed like an ancient Chinese mayor, smiling down on her.

Epilogue

Paul was waiting on the steps of Gina's apartment building when she returned. He was smiling, even though Gina was decidedly not. She mumbled something that sounded like a greeting, but she just wanted to get back to her apartment. He responded with a question, "Did you get to the dock on time?" in his German accent.

"I wasn't fast enough." Gina responded.

"But you saw the statue?" Paul asked. Gina looked back at the old man.

"How did you know about the statue? Or the dock for that matter?"

"It didn't look like what you expected, did it?" She sat down on the step next to Paul.

"No, it didn't." She continued to look into Paul's eyes.

"I wish I could have told you earlier, but I knew you would not see General Chang's image."

"How do you know about all this?"

"It will be easier to show you than to tell you. Please, help me up. What I have to show you is back in my apartment." Gina helped her friend to his feet and held onto his arm as they walked to apartment 1A. "When I was a boy, I spent what seemed like an eternity in a concentration camp. Auschwitz." He paused to pull a key from a bandolier around his neck and unlocked his door. The inside smelled like an old man's home. There was a mustiness to it, combined with the smell of coffee and cigarettes. "In January of 1945, I was five years old. I don't remember much before the camp, but I can remember every single day I was inside. I'll spare you my experience for now. Actually, I'm sparing myself by not telling you about it. All these years later I still feel the death of that place. You know, I was one of the last ones to receive one of these?" He pointed to the tattoo on his arm.

"Anyway, it's my last day at the camp I want to tell you about." He kept walking as he talked, loosening his arm from Gina's hold. "As a five-year-old, my usefulness to the Nazis was minimal at best. They killed most of us children the day we were brought through the iron gates. I was a good runner, so they kept me around to fetch things that the guards needed. Mostly towels, water, first aid kits, stuff like that. How I dreamed of poisoning the water or hiding a knife underneath one of the towels so that I could take out at least one of those devils." He pulled a wooden box from between two books on his shelf and started to spin the dials on the side next to a latch. "Imagine a five-year-old having such thoughts. But the last day…the last day something unusual happened. I was digging a hole, under orders of course, I have no idea why, when a colonel came up behind me and kicked me in the trousers. I turned and looked at him. He looked back at me. I was angry at the way he looked at me. It was as if he was judging me the way someone would judge a horse before a race. He asked me if I could read. I said, yes, I could read. He asked me if I could keep a secret. I said yes.

"He bent down on his knees and said to me, 'I'm not really a Nazi. I hate the Nazis.' I didn't believe him, of course. I figured he was trying to trick me. I almost shouted for the guards, but I didn't. He put his hand inside his trench coat. I thought I was going to die. But instead of a gun, he pulls out this." He pressed a button below the dials on his box and the latch popped open. Inside the box was a stack of papers tied together with string, both vertically and horizontally. "He also gave me a map. It was all of Europe, but it had little swastikas on it in various places. It also had the Star of David in several locations, too. Then he pointed to the woods outside the fence and asked me, 'If I can get you through the fence and to that tree line, can you run as fast as you can for about two thousand meters?' I said that I could, and I started to cautiously allow myself to get excited. I was either going to get out of there or shot in the back. Either way, my time in that camp was going to be over." He chuckled. "He said, 'Here's what's going to happen. I will take you out of here and will get you to the tree line. You will run like I told you. When you get to the other side of these woods, you will see an American fortification. Ask for someone who can speak German. Then you will give them all of these papers. You tell them they can have the map, but these letters are part of a story you are writing. They will want to see them. Give them to the Americans as well but tell them you want the letters back. Beg them not to mess up the order. But if they do, they are numbered.' He had written little numbers at the top right corner of these letters. I did have to put them back in the right order later. 'They will give them back to you, though it might take them a while. Eventually, you will be taken to America and granted citizenship. How old are you?' I told him. 'When you are…,' he looked like he was calculating, '72, you will give these letters to a woman named Gina Baxter. Her address is at the top of the first letter. At the time, she will be friends with a man named Charlie. He will die when you are 72. Can you remember that?' he asked. I nodded my head. 'Repeat it to me." I did. Then he casually walked me to the edge of the camp. A hole had been dug underneath the fence. He handed me a large envelope. I couldn't see how I could survive just running away, but the colonel did not look worried. 'Go through and run like hell. But do not be afraid. Have faith. You will get through these woods. I can't tell you how I know, but trust me that I do know you will get through.'

"As the colonel said, after I gave the envelop to the Americans, they took care of me and gave the letters back to me. I guess they had to make sure they didn't contain code or anything like that, because they kept them for over a year. Then the war was over, and they were returned to me. I was living in a foster family at the time, and they were good to me. I wasn't sure at the time whether or not I was supposed to read these letters, but I was a kid, so of course I read them anyway. After reading them, I knew he meant me to. They tell a story of a man who dreams of other times. I knew from these letters that I wasn't supposed to give them to you until after Charlie died, and after you came back from trying to save him. That's also how I knew that the statue wouldn't look like General Chang." He held out the letters to Gina, and she took them. She looked at the cover and saw that the first letter started with, "Liebe Gina." She glanced at the bottom and saw that it was signed, "Dein Charlie." Her tears returned to her and she began to shake. She looked back at Paul and kissed him on the cheek.

"Thank you, Pauley. Thank you, thank you, thank you."

"You should take those back up to your room and read them," he replied. Gina glanced through the first letter and then flipped through the others.

"That will be difficult," she replied. "I think I'll need your help. They are all in German."

Acknowledgements

This book has been a long time in the making. Although I love getting into my own headspace and creating a world with my own rules, there are certain parameters of reality I want to respect. I would not be able to do so without reaching out to others.

First, I want to thank John Grimpel of the New York Police Department. Without knowing me or anything about me, he took time to discuss police procedures with me, leading to several changes in my story. I also want to thank Patrick Kanouse, Michele Carroll Robb, and Wes Herron for taking a look at an early draft and providing excellent feedback. A big thank you to my son, Matthew, for his work on the design and illustrations. Last but not least, I want to thank my wife, Stephanie for encouraging my writing while keeping me grounded.

And thank you all for taking the time to read my story.

About the Author

Douglas W. Bowers was born near Pittsburgh and raised in a small town in south central Indiana. After earning an MBA, he moved to the Seattle area to work as a project manager where he lives with his wife and son. *My China Dream* is his first book. For more about Doug and upcoming writing projects, visit douglaswbowers.com.

Made in United States
Orlando, FL
23 April 2022

17117964R10173